NUN OF THIS AND NUN OF THAT

Convent Life in the 1960's

NUN OF THIS AND NUN OF THAT

Book One

Mary Hilaire Tavenner, Ph. D.

To order additional copies of this book, contact:
Xlibris Corporation
1-888-795-4274
www.Xlibris.com
Orders@Xlibris.com
5556

CONTENTS

To the memory of my Mother and Father, Mary Catherine
Montgomery and Robert Henderson Tavenner:

For my brothers and sisters:

Kathleen Ena Miller, Ph.D.
Robert Henderson Tavenner, Jr.
Garth Montgomery Tavenner, deceased.
Patrick Francis Tavenner
Michele Elise Tavenner
Christopher Ned Tavenner
and their families.

TO GOD BE THE GLORY!

ACKNOWLEDGEMENTS

The nuns and priests who made these stories possible.

FORWARD

I lived in the convent for almost twenty years. Above all else, I wanted to be a saint, and at the age of 17, entered into religious life. I was led to believe that being a nun was the highest calling a soul could receive—and the surest road to holiness. It took me many years and many lessons to learn that is not, at all, true.

The names and places in this book are purely fictitious, but the characters and circumstances are based upon personal experience, observation, speculation, or testimony. Still, I prefer to call these convent stories "realistic fiction."

SPECIAL THANKS TO:

Margaret Goodson
Ruby Crockett Tatum
Elnora Alferio
Barbara Molnar
Christine Miranda
Jack and Nancy Woolard
Michele Elise Tavenner Skinn
who helped to make this book a reality.

This is the first of two books entitled:

NUN OF THIS AND NUN OF THAT.

NUN OF THIS AND NUN OF THAT

"Article 13. Aspirants who are already over the age of thirty, illegitimate, or widows who have formally belonged to another religious institute are not to be admitted to the community unless the Mother General, for grave reasons and with the approval of her Council, has granted them a dispensation."

CHAPTER ONE . . .
PRE-ENTRANCE

CHAPTER ONE . . .
PRE-ENTRANCE

The reasons young women enter religious life are as diverse and complex as the women themselves. There are both conscious and unconscious motives. These are three teenagers preparing for entrance: the stories of Angie, Ginny, and Linda.

ANGIE

1

It was late one Saturday evening in August, 1962. Angie climbed up on the bar stool next to her dad. She was only 16, but she was "at home" in any bar within a 10 mile radius of her home in Sandusky, Ohio. As long as she could remember, her father, Roberto Masucci, had taken her along as sidekick and companion, especially since her mom, Theresa, had long tired of her father's routine. Now Angie was old enough to drive him home when he had too many to drink. After the ritual greetings and "the usual" was ordered, Angie decided it was a good time to tell her father.

"Dad, I know I don't talk about it much, but, well, you know how you and mom have saved some money for me to go to college after I graduate?"

"Yeah, you've always said you wanted to be a teacher. We can't help a hell of a lot, but we can get you started for a year or two."

"Dad, this may sound weird, but really what I want to do is enter the convent and be a nun."

"A nun?" He sounded as irritated as he was surprised. "I'll be god-damned if my daughter is going into some nunnery. I told your mother that you were hanging around that convent too much. I didn't mind you visiting once in a while, but they've brain-washed you, Angie!"

"No, Dad. It isn't like that at all!"

"Angie, I'm not going to let them make church property out of you." His voice became stern and frightening. "If you ever so much as try to join that outfit, I'm going over and knock those god-damned walls down. You're going to college. You're going to get married. You're going to have kids and be happy." Down went his second shot, and his beer for a chaser. A third was ordered with a wave of the hand.

"But, Dad . . ."

"But Dad nothing. I'm just *not* going to let the god-damn church own my little girl."

The case was closed. Besides, Angie knew it was better not to pursue a topic that made her father angry. He was a Methodist, not much of a church-goer, and not fond of church institutions.

Years ago, Roberto's mother had been a devout Catholic. When Bob was just a toddler, his father had suffered from depressions and poor health. He eventually took his own life. When his mother sought understanding and solace in the Catholic parish, the priest informed her there would be no funeral Mass, only a graveside service. He explained, "Suicide is murder, and your husband's soul has been taken to hell." Neither could Bob's father be buried in consecrated ground belonging to the parish cemetery. It was all too harsh for Bob's mother to bear.

Devastated by the priest's response, Roberto's mother found compassion and understanding in a young, single Methodist minister newly assigned to a congregation located only several houses from her home. Under the minister's influence, Roberto's mother became a Methodist.

Roberto became very fond of an Italian Catholic girl at Sandusky High School. Several years after they both had graduated,

Roberto and Theresa eloped to Kentucky to secretly marry before a Justice of the Peace. Theresa returned home for a week before she finally told her parents of her marriage. They, in turn, swiftly led the "newlyweds" directly to the Catholic priest for the Church's blessing and the priest performed a short marriage ritual in the parish rectory.

Marrying the minister left the entire city, her family, and the Sandusky Catholics talking for years. This scandal was rivalled only by the talk in his father's Methodist congregation when Roberto married the Italian Catholic girl he sat near in the Sandusky High School history class!

Bob Masucci was a well-known athlete. His athletic career blossomed in high school and he had received a large scholarship to play basketball at Ohio Wesleyan in central Ohio. His Sandusky High School basketball team had won All-Ohio-State Championship. Bob had also won the city championship for tennis and was recognized as an outstanding swimmer. During the summer of 1940, he and several of his friends swam almost two miles from Century Park to the old lighthouse port landmark. City folk said it was a foolish thing to try, with no boat, but Bob and his crowd were usually trying to prove something.

Roberto Masucci studied theology at Ohio Wesleyan, and may have been the only Italian-American in class. After getting kicked out in his third year for poor grades and misconduct (he and some classmates stole a portrait of the Ohio Wesleyan founder from the President's office and were caught enthroning it just above the altar in chapel), he thought less of organized religion and more about drinking.

Angie was well acquainted with the inconsistencies of an alcoholic father. His reaction to her sharing was so intense she never even mentioned the topic of convents during her junior year at Sandusky High. In the fall of her senior year, she knew the idea would not go away. She had wanted to be a nun almost as long as she could remember. Her father was the first person to learn how serious she really was, but his response kept her from saying much more about it. Angie was a girl with many dreams but believed there was only one choice—one life to live. She wanted the life of a nun.

Angie attended Confraternity of Christian Classes—sometimes referred to as CCD or "Sunday School"—though it wasn't only held on Sundays. Angie did not go to St. Rita's Catholic School, only a block away. The public school felt safer and more secure. Angie was afraid of the nuns and they seemed so critical.

"Angela Marie, stand up, straight and tall. Don't bite your nails, it isn't ladylike." "Angela," the twelve-year-old was asked, "is that you whistling? Would you have the Blessed Mother cry to hear such a thing?"

They were a mysterious lot, those nuns. Sometimes she would see them come back from communion and lower an opaque, black veil in front of their faces to shut out the world, so they could be totally alone with their Beloved, in Eucharist. Parishioners did likewise by cupping their two hands, placing their head into them to bury their faces into darkness and solitude for a few private moments of prayer after they swallowed the wafer whole. Chewing or detaining consumption of Eucharist was considered impolite and even immoral.

Distant and critical as the nuns seemed, there was the memory of her fourth grade Sunday School teacher, Sister Mary Paul, who seemed to bubble with an inner joy. Sister Paul was a talented artist who had designed the magnificent wooded stations decorating the newly built St. Rita's Church. Sister Paul was different. She seemed happy. She liked children. Even the kids could tell.

Angie believed the ideals of sisterhood were the most noble she had ever known: to be everything for others; to give your life for the love of Holy Mother Church; and to win heaven and lead souls into paradise. But, in her heart, Angie did not believe nuns did that very well. They just didn't seem to reach the ideals of sisterhood. Perhaps it was pride or sheer arrogance that made Angie believe she could do it better than these women. Angie wanted to show them that people needed nuns to be kind, sympathetic, compassionate, and caring. Angie didn't want to be like most nuns she had known. She wanted to be different . . . maybe a bit like Sr. Mary Paul.

Nevertheless, Angie wanted to be a nun, a teacher, and, above all, someday—a saint. Yes, her dad was proving to be an obstacle, but Angie was his daughter, and she shared his almost reckless sense of determination.

During the fall of her senior year, Angie brought up the forbidden subject again, this time to her mother. One rather cold November evening, Theresa was sitting on the couch immersed in her daily crossword challenge. Angie had school books sprawled about while watching Peyton Place and working on her world history outline. A commercial interrupted the program and Angie chose this moment to tell her mother.

"Mom."

"Yes, Angie?" Theresa's eyes lifted only momentarily from the crossword to assure Angie she was listening.

"Mom, I've been thinking about next year, when I graduate." Angie paused. "I think I'd like to apply to the community of sisters, here at St. Rita's, but I'm told I'll have to go to Albany, New York for my training."

Again Theresa looked up from her crossword. But this time she made eye contact.

"Is this what you *really* want to do?" She sounded matter-of-fact.

"I think so. Dad doesn't like the idea at all. I know you both wanted me to go to Toledo State and study education. But I want to be more than just a teacher. I think I'd make a good nun."

There was a short pause, but her mother's words sounded supportive, unlike her father's. "If that is what you want, we'll find a way to convince your father." Theresa was from a long line of Italian Catholics. She secretly considered the idea of her daughter becoming a nun a blessing beyond words. Yet, she never overtly attempted to plant such seeds of desire, fearing the idea would not be Angie's, but her own innermost wish.

By late spring, her mother had purchased a second-hand trunk from a woman who had failed at living with a local community of sisters. After three years of trying, she was now back home. Angie and her mother were glad for the reasonable price the woman was asking, yet Angie felt the curious glances the woman gave her as her mother paid for the trunk. Was she wondering how Angie would measure up? Could she live what this woman could not? Would Angie persevere or succumb as so many did?

The list of items to bring included eight linen napkins and tablecloth, an assortment of towels, a black bathrobe, two white floor-length nightgowns, two sets of white linen sheets, a Baby Ben clock, six pairs of opaque black stockings, six cotton tee shirts, six pairs of mid-thigh cotton underwear, a well-equipped sewing basket, two pairs of black heeled oxfords, and a copy of *Imitation of Christ*. All was neatly packed away in Angie's regulation steamer trunk which stood in plain view for six months on the enclosed front porch of the Masucci home. No one spoke of its presence. It was just there, imperceptibly prepared for a trip to New York in September.

The pastor had to write a letter of recommendation. Baptismal and birth certificates were requested along with a high school transcript. As long as Angie was in the upper third of her graduating class, she was academically acceptable to the Albany Franciscan Community. Money was also required. The dowry was $100.00, far less than several other communities she had inquired about. Angie considered joining the Daughters of Vincent, but to qualify she had to be in the top 10% of her Sandusky High School class. Different religious communities had different standards and different dowry requirements. Exceptions could be made in most communities with the consent of Councils or Mother Generals. Angie wanted to belong to the Albany Franciscans, Sr. Mary Paul's community. She felt she knew them more personally. Even though her mother preferred she join a local motherhouse in Sandusky, Toledo, or Cleveland, Angie remained firm in her decision.

Everything was set. She had been admitted for entrance and would fly from Toledo to Albany on Mohawk Airlines in the early afternoon of September 8th, 1963. This was a traditional "entrance date" for many religious communities. It was celebrated as the, the Nativity, or birthday, of Mary. All was arranged with the help of her mother. Still, the topic had not been openly discussed with her father for over a year—since their talk at the Greenwood Inn.

Angie had an exceptionally good summer. She had grown more excited with the passing of each day and now it was September 7th. Tomorrow, Albany. But what of Angie's dad? Would he refuse the 17-year-old permission to leave for New York?

In the early evening Angie returned home from a few final farewells to her dearest neighborhood friends. Diane and Sue had arranged a "convent shower" during July. It was a big help financially to receive many of the required items from the list as gifts, and it was great fun to be teased and fussed over. These two girls had been Angie's best friends since she was old enough to cross the street. Coming back from her final visit with them, Angie opened the front door and passed through the sunporch. She greeted her mother in a familiar surrounding of ironing board and basket of clothes.

"Angie, you aren't thinking of leaving without talking with your father, are you?" Theresa was all too aware of how unpredictable her husband could be if he were drinking.

"Mom, it isn't any secret that I'm going." Angie sounded defensive. "My trunk has been on the porch for months. He watched me fill it." Angie paused. "What time do you expect him home?"

"Very soon. In fact, I think he's pulling up in front now."

Angie whisked her mother a "Wish me luck" and turned to go outside. Bob Masucci was walking up the front sidewalk with just enough sway in his stride to indicate he had been drinking.

Still, this had to be done and Angie knew it.

"Dad, could we talk for a few minutes in the sideyard?"

He looked at her and paused. As they caught each other's glance with the help of lights from the house, they both knew what the talk was about.

"Yeah. Sure. Why not," he replied.

In the sideyard they would have some privacy. Angie was eager to get the scene over. She was sure if he was going to fight her decision, he would have done something before now. But, when it came to her father, she was never *completely* sure of anything.

"Dad, you *know* I want to be a nun. I told you before I told anyone, but you were so angry I couldn't talk with you about it anymore. I was too scared to bring it up again. Tomorrow is our entrance date. I'm flying to Albany, New York. They will have a sister there to meet me at the airport. Everything is arranged."

Bob was silent for what seemed to be a long time. Angie was unsure of herself in that moment of awkward quietude. She was his little girl, his only child. She knew only too well his power to change all of her plans.

"God-damn, you have one hell of a lot of nerve. I know what you want. And hell, I also see the courage it's taking you to tell me. You want this very much. I knew that. Your mother and I have talked about this often. It's just very hard for me to accept, but I have decided to let you go under one condition."

Angie's heart leapt with hope and excitement. Any promise, any condition was acceptable, if she could pursue her lifelong dream.

"What condition, Dad?"

"Promise me you'll come home in a year. I'll let you go to Albany and be a sister, or whatever it is you want, for one year. But that's all. One year."

"Dad, nuns don't do it that way. They do it for years and years, and often their whole lives. I just can't quit and come home in a year. But I can and will promise you this: If I come to believe I don't belong there and I find the life miserable, I'll leave. I won't stay if I don't belong, I promise you."

"I guess that will have to be good enough. You're damned set on doing this. Well, hell, I guess you can plan on both your mom and me taking you to the airport tomorrow." He put his arm around her shoulder, and they walked into the house together.

. . . .

GINNY

2

Virginia was born in Pau Pau, West (by God) Virginia, along with her four older siblings. The four youngest had been born in Silver Spring, Maryland, near Washington D.C., where the Crow family "had nested." The suburb had many well-to-do families. Ginny's father was a plumber. The family was well-fed and well-clothed, but much because Mrs. Crow was such a wise manager of money.

Yes, the Crows were relatively poor, but most of the children didn't fully realize it because they had what they needed. They were well cared for and deeply loved by both attentive parents. All of the Crow children were to have a Catholic education from kindergarten to at least eighth grade. After eighth, they were free to choose high school at either Cardinal McNamara or Central. Dick and Ethel Crow believed the best investment they could make for their large "flock" of nine was a good Catholic education. Most opted for the public high school, but Virginia chose Cardinal McNamara. She had not kept it any secret that one day she would be a nun as well as a doctor. Her brothers and sisters made light of both definitive statements because they all knew how much she enjoyed boys and a good time. Her B average in high school hardly seemed medical material for any university. What they didn't consider was that Ginny was not in the custom of saying something without acting upon it.

There wasn't a lot of money available for the care of the Crow's nest, a three-bedroom home with one room for four boys and another for five girls. Ma and Pa Crow enjoyed the privacy of a small addition to the first floor. Ginny, as did other members of her family, felt a shared responsibility for the care of their home. She often made extra money mowing lawns and doing garden work.

Ginny's older brother, Patrick, and her father had managed to cut down two blighted elm trees which had shaded the front of their house, leaving eyesore stumps.

When Ginny announced that she would get rid of the stumps, her family was skeptical. But Ginny worked two long days weeding at the Robinson home. She earned enough to hire men with a shredding machine to grind the stumps into piles of woodchips— one of her many examples of "saying it, then doing it."

That same summer Ginny planted two small trees she had uprooted from behind the garage next to the back porch where they were growing as weeds. These two trees replaced the elms. They marked a milestone summer and the year of entrance into the convent for Virginia Elizabeth Crow.

Ginny graduated from Cardinal McNamara High and was looking forward to her September entrance into the Albany Franciscan Community. She worked that summer at a nearby pharmacy delivering prescriptions. On weekends, she mowed neighborhood lawns and earned her dowry for the convent. Ginny had, for the past several years, paid for her own clothes, high school expenses, and active social life. The Crow family was dependent upon the older children paying as much of "their way" as possible.

Ginny was a favorite with the neighborhood men. Remarkably, she found as much pleasure talking with and passing time with them as she did with friends her own age.

Jim Crockett, across the street, had three sons. Maybe that's why he enjoyed teasing the daylights out of her. When Ginny was eleven, he promised to take her to the county fair, if only she would have his breakfast ready for him at 6:30 on Saturday morning. Mr. Crockett knew all too well that on Saturdays, Ginny seldom rose before noon, except perhaps to take in Saturday morning cartoon shows with the youngerlings.

"Mr. Crockett, do you *really* promise to take me to the county fair if I fix you that breakfast on Saturday?" Knowing what a tease Mr. Crockett could be, Ginny reserved some serious doubt.

"You bet, Mop-Top." (That was his favorite name for her.) Ginny had the most unmanageable set of curls a girl could have. Her sixth grade teacher said that it looked as if she had combed her hair with an egg beater.

"Well, if you guarantee you're not teasing, I'll guarantee I'll be over here with breakfast on Saturday—coffee, eggs, toast, and juice, at 6:30 *A.M.*!"

"But only if you're sitting on that stump just outside my bedroom window." His head indicated another elm tree fatality in his side yard.

"I'll do it," was her reply. And she did.

"Mr. Crockett, Mr. Crockett." The birds were welcoming a new summer day as the rising sun began to chase away the dew of the early hours.

"Mr. Crockett. Mr. Crockett!" Ginny called again, only louder now. Finally a figure appeared at the window.

"Ginny." It was Mrs. Crockett. "Mr. Crockett is asleep. He doesn't want any breakfast. Honey, he was only joking. Go home and get some rest."

Ginny sat on the stump with her tray of breakfast upon her lap. She looked up to the screened-in face and replied, "Okay. I'll see you later." But she sat there without moving. She decided to breakfast in the Crockett yard. She wasn't angry. She did muse, "That rascal! Wait till I see him!" She ate everything, except the coffee, before the street awakened.

Several weeks before Ginny's trip to New York, her brother bought his first car. Patrick had been two years in Chicago and then two years in Ireland after joining the U.S. Navy. Now he was home and fortunate to get a good paying factory job. He offered to drive Ginny to New York because he knew she did not have the money to travel any other way. Patrick offered to pay the cost of gas as well. There had always been a special understanding between Pat and Ginny. Patrick knew how important this becoming a nun was to her, though other family members remained more than dubious. He was only five years older, but they seemed particularly in sync with each other. Perhaps it was because Pat had mentioned thoughts of priesthood and enjoyed his obligation to attend Mass.

It was Pat who took Ginny to Mass for her first "official" time. Mrs. Crow would sometimes take the younger children to Mass, which was still in Latin in those days. Mr. Crow was known to be far less frequent in his attendance but still totally supportive of Catholic traditions. Mrs. Crow was a beautiful woman with auburn hair flowing over her shoulders. Her blue eyes and freckles revealed her Irish descent.

When Ginny was only five, she walked into her parents bedroom and told her mother she wanted to begin going to Mass. "Patrick is willing to take me tomorrow, if you say we can go," she told her mother.

"Virginia, you know what it means if you start going to Mass now, don't you?"

"Yes, Mom. You told us that if we start going to Mass on Sundays, then we can never stop going, and we'll *have* to go every Sunday. I'm ready, Mom. Can Pat take me?"

"All right. As long as you understand what you have to do if you begin."

It wasn't a long walk to church. She enjoyed Patrick's companionship and felt proud to sit next to him in church. He had been the one to lead her into her church life; now he was the one to take her to the convent.

Ginny felt a little unsure of herself as the date for entrance approached. She worried that perhaps she would be lonely or that she wasn't doing the right thing. But, even more deeply, she knew she had to try it. There was only one way to see if she had "a vocation" and that was to go to Albany. She had to "Come and see."

Everything was prepared. Neighbors openly voiced their disappointment and cynicism. Mrs. Maxwell quipped, "Ginny, I'll give you three months at the most. You like fun too much to live in any convent."

Her large family would go on with life as usual, and there was a little more room to be parcelled out when she left.

Only two days before her departure, Ginny asked her parents for a "sleep out" in the back yard. She wanted to put up the family tent and invite some of her best girl friends. They would plan to sit up most of the night and talk. Ginny's youngest sister, Michele, only nine, begged to sleep out with them. Ginny didn't object because she knew she would be more likely to get permission with Michele there. Mrs. Crow granted the request. The tent was put up, and the guests arrived.

As planned, that same night, only eight blocks away, the Hallahans had a "sleep-out" for the boys. They were brothers and friends to the group of girls tenting in the Crow's backyard.

About 1:00 A.M., when conversation had become a whisper, the boys arrived, quite on schedule. The mixed gang had planned to go for an evening walk in the neighborhood. This was, by no means, the first time Ginny and her friends patrolled the streets during the wee hours of the morning, during an overnight sleepout.

In times past, they were guilty of adolescent pranks, not always prudent, but never truly destructive. Occasionally, the night patrol would place garbage cans as a street blockade, put toothpaste under a few car door handles, or toilet paper a few trees. Mostly, the fourteen-to-eighteen-year-olds and one nine-year-old simply enjoyed owning the night, being together, and sharing their spirit of adventure.

But tomorrow Ginny had to leave for New York. Early in the evening, she decided to leave the wandering mix of girls and boys for her tent in the backyard. Besides, her little sister was ready for sleep.

About an hour later, Bev was waking Ginny. "Ginny, Ginny! The cops are after us!" Her friend was out of breath and shaken.

"They put on the siren and we all scattered! I know some of the kids had to be caught." Bev was soon joined by Ruth, Eddie, and Frank, all just as breathless from running back to the Crow's yard.

"What were you guys doing? What happened?" Ginny asked.

"We were walking through an alley and I think the stones under our shoes woke up some people. Someone must have called the police," Bev explained.

"Where did everyone go?" Ginny was awake now, but Michele continued sleeping.

"I don't know. I think they went to the Hallahans, but we decided to double back over here."

"Well, there's not much we can do now. Do you think the other girls will find their way back here?"

"It's hard to tell," Ruth added. "They don't know these streets as well as we do."

"Eddie, Frank. Can you guys get back into your house?"

Ginny asked. They were brothers, and Ginny felt it might be safer for them to go home.

"Sure. Frank and I know where we hide the key. My parents wouldn't care if we sneak in. But what about Bev and Ruth?" Eddie questioned.

"They can stay here. There's really nothing we can do about the cops now. Why don't you two just try to get some sleep? If you guys weren't really ripping up, we can't be in too much trouble," Ginny offered.

The boys left for home and soon thereafter, the Hallahan family station wagon pulled into the driveway. Mr. Hallahan called for his daughter, Ruth. Surprised by the arrival of her father, Ruth left for home, leaving both Beverly and Ginny to wonder what must have happened. They would have to wait until morning to find out.

Apparently Tim Hallahan had been caught by the seat of his pants by one of the officers who left his car to pursue the kids on foot. They had scattered in every direction. Tim was escorted to his parent's front porch in a police car at approximately 3:30 A.M. Several of the boys and girls had arrived just moments earlier, burying themselves under sleeping bags scattered at the far end of the Hallahan front porch. They saw and heard the police approach but remained motionless undercover.

One police officer rang the front doorbell. The other kept his hand upon Tim's shoulder. Several minutes later the lights turned on. Mr. Hallahan approached the door and opened it.

"Mr. Hallahan," the policeman explained, "your son, Timothy, was picked up while disturbing the peace in an alley near Illinois Avenue. He was with a gang of friends, but we only managed to catch your son. We aren't sure where the rest of them are. We thought you might be able to help us."

"Timothy!" His father played the role of a much perturbed parent, partly because he felt he needed to be firm and partly because he was genuinely perturbed. He stepped outside to speak directly with his son.

"Where are your brother and the other four boys who were supposed to be sleeping out with you tonight?" Mr. Hallahan sounded impatient.

Tim responded sheepishly, "I really don't know, Dad. They just ran everywhere."

One of the officers glanced to the right and, with the help of the porch light, noticed the conspicuously large lumps at the far end of the porch. He stepped over and lifted a blanket to find two of Ginny's girlfriends and the four boys who should have been asleep for hours.

Names and addresses were recorded by the patrolmen. After the necessary phone calls were made, Mr. Hallahan offered to drive the kids home, but he also decided to retrieve his daughter, supposedly sleeping at the Crow's. Each of the captured youngsters was obliged to appear in court in three weeks. The charge was "disturbing the peace", but the newspaper and radio reports made it sound as if the Hallahans had entertained a teenage orgy. For weeks, students at McNamara High and Central probed their friends about the "party" as if it were lurid and lascivious behavior. In fact, this harmless episode led the community to believe a different gang of nightwalkers, responsible for rather destructive conduct, was finally captured. Ginny's best friends were unfairly taking "the rap". There wasn't anything Ginny could do. Only she, her friend Bev, and little Michele were not summoned to juvenile court.

For years afterward, Ginny often reflected, "What would have happened if, on that one night, I had not excused myself early?

What if I had been on the Hallahan porch? What would have happened if I had to report to court on the first of October? "I'm sorry, Sisters, I'd love to come as expected on September 8th, but I'll be arriving late because I've been arrested for disturbing someone's peace," she mused. "Would the nuns even take someone with a police record?"

As planned, Ginny left for Albany the next day with her brother Patrick. He wanted to leave late, drive all night, and arrive in the early morning. Just as they attempted to load the trunk into Pat's car, they discovered it wouldn't fit in the trunk of the car or on the back seat. Everything had to be emptied out and put into piles. Mr. Crow would send the trunk by train later in the week.

The car was filled with bags and boxes. The send-off began. There was a flurry of hugs. It seemed especially hard to leave the youngest of her siblings; Ginny had helped a good deal in their raising. She felt sad to say good-bye to her family, but she felt a great excitement and was looking forward to the adventures ahead.

The girls were to enter officially at 2:00 P.M. Pat and Ginny drove all night long and arrived in Albany about 7:00 in the morning. The sun was up. Pat suggested Ginny call the Motherhouse and see if he could bring her in early, so he could head back to Maryland. He didn't have money for a hotel room and planned to sleep at a rest stop on the way home.

Ginny called from a gas station and interrupted the postulant mistress at Mass. She was gracious and receptive to Ginny's inquiry. After getting helpful directions, Ginny reported the news to Pat and proceeded to change into a skirt and blouse in the gas station's restroom.

Ten minutes later, they drove past a large stone wall just off Central Avenue. "This must be the place," she suggested to her brother. Ginny never thought in terms of large convent walls, but it made sense. Pulling up to what seemed to be the front gate, Pat waited in the car while Ginny walked into the courtyard past a large central statue of St. Francis. The wolf of Gubbio at the feet of Francis and the birds upon his shoulder helped Ginny identify the sainted founder of the Franciscan Orders.

Ginny knew the story of the wolf of Gubbio. Gubbio was a village in Italy where a hungry wolf had been attacking children. When Saint Francis heard about this, he approached the wolf and asked why the wolf would do such terrible things. The wolf explained that a famine had caused a scarcity of food in the woods, and the wolf had to attack the villagers to stay alive. St. Francis made a pact with the wolf that if the people left scraps of food for him every day, the wolf would no longer do such evil deeds. The wolf agreed and became a pet in Gubbio for the rest of his life.

Ginny had been taught in grade school by the Albany Franciscan Sisters and had heard so many St. Francis stories, she almost felt as if she knew the man personally. Ginny was now impressed by the largeness of the Motherhouse structure, the old brick, and the beauty of her surroundings.

There was a knock on the door and the ring of a bell. Ginny waited. Finally, a little nun, surrounded by a black habit and veil and wearing a white, bib-like collar, answered.

"Hi! I'm Virginia Crow from Silver Spring, Maryland. I called Sister Humiliana to see if I could arrive early today because my brother needs to get back to Maryland. Today is entrance day."

"Welcome, dear, but this isn't the door that you want. This is the motherhouse entrance; you want the novitiate. Do you have a car?"

"Yes, Sister. My brother is just outside the front gate. We drove all night to get here."

"Well, you tell him to drive around the block to the other side and he'll see a sign that says 'ENTER'. Follow the road, bear left, and you will see a breezeway with a sign reading, 'NOVITIATE'. Sister Humiliana is there waiting for you, I think. If she isn't, I'll send word to have her come, all right?"

"Sure thing! Thanks so much, Sister." Ginny turned with her usual zip and energetically returned to the car.

"You found the right place, Pat. I'll show you how to get in." Arriving at the breezeway, they both got out of the car. Patrick was especially glad to stretch.

A nun, dressed like the other at the front door of the motherhouse, welcomed them. She may have been in her mid-fifties or early sixties. Ginny was not good at guessing the age of nuns. Ginny and her brother began to unload the things from the back seat after introductions were made.

In the postulate, after giving Sr. Humiliana an envelope with her hundred dollar dowry, Ginny accidently dropped almost twenty dollars in change. She had not gotten around to putting it all into bills. It was amusing to see them all scatter for the coins rolling about. Sr. Humiliana seemed a good sport about it. Sister then invited both to a hot breakfast to be served in a downstairs parlor. She left them to eat privately.

"Gee, Pat. We've never had applesauce with breakfast before, have we? Mom usually serves it for dinner."

"It's delicious. Everything is. It was nice of them to feed us. Look, you don't mind if I head home when we're finished, do you? I can get back by tonight if I leave now and sleep a few hours in some roadside park."

"Sure, that's a good idea. I guess they'll find something for me to do while I wait for entrance at 2:00. I don't feel tired, but you drove all night and I did get a few good naps in."

Sister Humiliana returned shortly. She and Ginny walked Patrick back to his car. Again there was a tug at Ginny's heart. It wasn't like she'd never see Pat again, or ever go home again. She had made sure this was a community that believed in home visits. So many of the other religious communities didn't.   Waving her brother off, grateful and a little weary, she and Sr. Humiliana turned back to enter the novitiate doors once more. Sister suggested that Ginny get a few hours rest before the entrance reception that afternoon. She escorted her upstairs on the elevator to the fourth floor, then showed Ginny the bathroom, shower room, and what was to become Ginny's "cell." It held a bed, a desk, and a built-in closet. It had one window. It was a good deal more space and privacy than Ginny had at home with four sisters and two sets of bunk beds.

"I'll wake you before lunch. You can eat with the novices."

Ginny decided that maybe a little sleep was a good idea, and within only moments of placing herself in bed, she quickly succumbed to sleep.

. . . .

LINDA

3

Linda was an attractive girl who enjoyed the company of boys. They were good friends and companions, but somehow, the older she grew, the less fond she became of them.

Growing up in Albany, New York was as good a place as any during the fifties and sixties, but having a mother *and* a father who were teachers was not easy for children expected to live by perhaps, a greater social standard. Linda enjoyed taking chances, wanted the most from life, and wanted to make a difference.

Linda's sister Margaret was eight years older and had graduated from Sierra College with a degree in English. Her life was immersed in social work. Margaret no longer lived with the rest of the Pettigrew family in the two-story duplex which bordered Washington Park. She had finally married at the age of twenty-three, after three wedding engagements. Linda's brother-in-law, Jack, had taught high school biology for two years but soon preferred the salary of a business manager at a branch office of General Motors.

Linda's brother, Larry Jr., was a year younger than she was. In fact, their birthdays were only two days apart. They usually celebrated together. Linda and Larry were "a second family" for Elizabeth and Lawrence Pettigrew who did not expect to have any more children after the birth of Margaret. The disappointed couple had inquired into adoption, but then had two children only a year apart. "When it did begin to rain, (so goes the saying), it poured".

Other than a spirit of competitiveness between the two younger Pettigrews, they were very compatible and grew up as playmates and pals.

In the upstairs of the brick duplex, Richard (who was Linda's age) lived with three younger Vercillos. Richard, Linda, and the others explored their childhood sexuality, playing "house" behind a neighbor's garage. Linda played "Mother", Richard was the "Father" and the Vercillo siblings were their children. The "children" used a pile of stones as the "family" toilet.

Some of their early exploration games such as "Doctor" were played indoors. During junior high years, these same friends enjoyed the amusement of "strip poker", though by now, no one ever ventured to cash in their undergarments. It was their version of wild fun. The fivesome engaged in many childhood games such as baseball in the park, football, or p-i-g basketball in the driveway, complete with backboard and rim.

When Linda was ten, while swinging at nearby park, a strange man approached and began to talk. He asked if she would like to sit on his lap and swing. She was too naive. After all, this was a public park, and she felt safe enough. After a few minutes, he slid his hand under her shirt and rubbed her undeveloped chest.

Linda did not know what to do. She was afraid of the man now and felt too vulnerable to confront him. Eventually, he let her free when Linda asked to climb the monkey bars. Once a safe distance from the scary intruder, she waved good-bye and ran to the safety of her home.

She looked for Richard immediately. This was something she couldn't tell her parents, but she shared all her thoughts with Richard. She felt guilty about the episode, but Richard was reassuring and told her to run away if she ever even saw this guy from a distance. He was serious trouble. Richard was always a sensible advisor, wise beyond his years, and Linda felt closer to him than to her brother Larry.

High school was an impressionable time for Linda. She enjoyed many free flowing relationships with her Convent School friends.

Often there were dances and other social events shared with Boys Academy and Convent School. Both were privately owned by religious communities. The Albany Franciscan Sisters staffed the all girls Convent School. Richard was an honor student at the all boys "brother" school, Boys Academy.

One evening, while at one of these co-ed dances with several of her girlfriends, Linda had a (probably normal) fleeting feeling of being ugly and unpopular. She decided to go home before the dance was over. Usually she loved the high school parties and socials, but tonight was different. She informed her friends she was walking home. The walk was more than a mile and she would be alone. The girls were concerned and suggested she ask Richard to go with her. Linda could see he was having a good time and didn't want to impose.

"I'll be fine," she assured them. "It's a beautiful evening; I'll be home in twenty minutes." With that, she left.

While passing a taxi cab outlet, she considered using some of the money she had in her purse to secure a ride home. But the evening was perfect for a walk, and she assured herself once more it would be safe.

While crossing a short bascule bridge, two boys, perhaps a year or two younger than herself, were walking in the opposite direction. This was no cause for alarm. What possibly could happen? Suddenly, one of the youngsters grabbed for her breast, while the other quipped, "What a good piece of ass," all within a moment of their passing. She wanted to defend herself and probably could have but believed herself no match for the two smaller boys.

After sharing the story later with Richard, he became angered. "Why didn't you kick them in the groin? That kills a guy. Women can't imagine the damage of just one "balls-eye". And why didn't you ask me to come home with you? It wasn't that great a dance for me either!"

"You looked like you were having fun. Besides, if you can walk home and be safe, why shouldn't I be able to? Those boys were punks. I'd love to know who they are. How can boys be so ugly to a stranger? I never did a thing to them."

"Listen, Linda. Some guys have something to prove. What they really prove is their ignorance. They wouldn't like someone treating *their* sisters that way, but they don't think that "this might be someone's sister". But then, some wouldn't care even if they could reason that far. Some guys just hate girls. They're sick, and consequently you just can't feel safe alone. Even when I'm alone, I'm on guard. Some guys would just as easily assault me. I think it's just some animal thing; they never became a person. No evolution or something like that."

Linda was constantly trying to find reasons to support her respect for the opposite sex. Her father, brother Larry, and Richard were all such good examples, but there were other experiences. On some of her dates the guy wanted to see how much he could "get" for a movie, coke, fries, and a hamburger. Richard's friendship was a delightful refuge from such unpleasant experiences. He was her best friend.

Walking home after the dance that night changed Linda. She wasn't as trusting or secure. The worldly values that the kids had such as, "be sexy, be pretty, be in love, acquire material wealth, and you will be accepted," were not setting well with Linda's idea of how life should be. Linda liked looking nice and took great pride in her pleasing appearance, but pressures to buy the latest record, wear the newest fashion, and be steady with some boy did not satisfy her deeper self.

Linda's comfortable middle-class standing was not taken for granted. She wondered what other values she might embrace. Sometimes her high school routine seemed very unsatisfying and, even then, she didn't believe having money and going steady was everything it was cracked up to be. It seemed paramount to so many of her female friends.

Linda wanted a job. She wanted to "earn her way." She wanted something less frivolous than make-up, a sexy walk, or the empty talk so many of her friends enjoyed. Her mother and father were firm about her request to find a job.

"You shouldn't have to work in high school. You should enjoy these few years with little responsibility. After all, once you begin to work, there won't be an end to it! Make friends; we can give you what you need these few years," they would tell her.

One day, a month after the bridge episode, Linda was passing her parish church, Our Lady of Angels on Central Avenue. She decided to stop in and light a candle. She discovered a leaflet in the back of church. It read, "If you are between the ages of 16 and 30, want to live a vocation of love, feel drawn to a state of virginity, and cannot accept the values of a secular life, perhaps God is calling you to be a religious sister. Contact the Franciscan Sisters of Albany."

Linda had been in Catholic Schools all her life and attended Convent High for the past two years. Even with the frequent suggestion of the "good" sisters to enter a convent, Linda never entertained such a thought before now. She mused over the contents of that little pamphlet privately for months before deciding to approach her high school teacher, Sr. Matilda, to discuss some of her new and different thoughts.

Sister listened attentively and responded, "You still have almost two years of high school, Linda. Why don't you give your feelings a little more time. If you still feel this way after graduation, maybe God *is* calling you."

Linda was surprised to have this new interest in the nuns. Before, she saw them as running interference of good times. In her theology class, Sr. Bertilla told the girls that French kissing was a mortal sin. Linda resisted.

"Sister, how can you say that?"

"Linda, you are young and naive. Such a kiss often leads one to fornication."

"I can't believe that, Sister." Linda was shocked to think how many times she must have committed his deadly sin and never considered it anything but playful. "*Everyone* French kisses!" she insisted defensively. The others could not keep from bursting out with laughter.

"Linda," said Sr. Bertilla, sounding and looking more stern than ever, "such a teaching is not for you to question or to accept. It is for you to *refrain* from doing at all costs. Would you choose hell?"

Linda's posture and facial expression indicated her resistance to the nun's position, but she had been in Catholic schools long enough not to take her crusade any further for fear of later reprimands.

"No, Sister. Thank you, Sister," she conceded in public, but privately she believed French kissing to be, at worst, venial, and refused to confess it as mortal. The nuns seemed to make her feel guilty about almost everything, but still the idea to become one of them would not go away.

Linda escaped from the judgments of Sr. Bertilla to thoughts of her recently deceased grandmother. "Maa", as her mother's mother had been so affectionately called, had taught Linda her first prayer, the Hail Mary. At the age of five, Linda took pride and satisfaction in being able to recite an Ave.

Maa was the only grandparent Linda ever knew. Linda loved her dearly. The nickname stuck when her older sister, Margaret, couldn't say "Grandma or Grandpa." Efforts from the firstborn grandchild, at the age of three, sounded more like "Maa" for grandma and "Baa" for grandpa. Thus, Linda only knew her as Maa. Baa had died before Linda was born.

Linda's other grandmother lived in Maine. She died of cancer when Linda was nine, and probably, because of their few visits, Linda was not been as affected as she was with the recent loss of Maa. Her other grandfather had also died before Linda was born.

Maa was a classic. As Linda matured, she discovered that Maa was "old stock", like a vintage wine, sweetened to perfection but never to be tasted again—and never fully appreciated until its passing.

Maa had been a dynamic example of Christian charity. She walked a mile to Mass each and every morning. Often, during the coldest of winter days, Maa insisted, "The brisk walk keeps my blood circulating. The worst thing I could do is stop my walking."

Maa never learned to drive a car. Her generation had not encouraged women to learn. Driving the car was a male thing. Maa referred to the automobile as the "machine". Her suspicious tone made the word sound more like "contraption".

Every night Maa knelt at her bedside to pray a rosary before retiring. Linda loved sleeping over at Maa's house. There she was spoiled and pampered. She did not have to vie with her brother for control over the television and could bask in the doting attention of her grandmother.

Linda loved sleeping with Maa in the double bed, once shared by her grandparents. She enjoyed listening to her grandmother's stories before they both fell off to sleep. Maa would have loved to see Linda become a nun. It was sad to think Maa didn't know what she was now considering, but maybe, just maybe, Maa did.

Before graduation Linda received her acceptance papers from the Franciscan community. Her mother and father were supportive of her decision to enter in early September, only three months after high school graduation, though they both would have preferred she wait until after college.

That summer, her parents finally allowed Linda to get a job. She worked in a law firm as a secretary to a legal secretary. She earned her own dowry fee for the convent, the things she needed for her trunk, and even had a little left over. In mid-August, Linda asked her parents for permission to rent a car for a weekend.

Her father asked, "Why do you need to rent a car? We have one here for you to use."

"I'd just like to drive it around, go out with my friends, and have some fun. You know, pretend like it's mine. I'll use it all weekend."

"Linda," her father cautioned, "a car is not a plaything, even for a weekend. I'd rather you ask for the family car."

Her father thought it a foolish waste of money, but Linda knew her mother might buy the idea, even if her father wouldn't.

"Mom, I'm entering the convent in three weeks! Why can't I have a car for just a weekend? I'll pay for everything—even the gas! We won't have to tell Dad, but I need you to sign for me."

Her mother was more easily persuaded. Dad often worked weekends at a local funeral parlor. It was good pay and required little effort other than answering the phone or door. He would not likely notice the rented car parked around the corner.

That weekend proved to be most eventful. Linda went horseback riding in the country on Saturday morning, swam at a private club in the afternoon, and, that same evening, attended a dance at the CYO. Linda and her friends decided to leave early. Some of the guys they had been with at the dance got into another car to follow.

What seemed to be a harmless game of "chase the girls" became faster and more reckless as the two cars proceeded through Albany's streets. Linda accelerated and turned into an A & P parking lot. As she turned past the building, she barely missed a lamp pole. She had turned the car so sharply, it literally continued forward on two wheels, avoiding the obstacle. This was all it took for Linda to realize what might just have happened.

Suddenly she remembered the boys speeding just behind her. Would they turn in time? Thank God they had. Linda slowed her rental car and explained to her friends, "I'm telling them we have to go home. That was too close a call for me."

Linda approached the boy's car. "Look, you guys, that was stupid and dangerous. If we had been going even a little faster, we might all have been killed. We want to quit for tonight."

The boys agreed and the two groups parted company. Without realizing it, Linda was still driving too fast for side streets. Adrenaline from the near miss caused her to turn at too wide an angle right into the back panel of a brand new convertible approaching the intersection.

"Damn! I don't believe I did that!" The girls were all quite safe and the impact was hardly more than a jarring. Linda's rental car was unscathed, but the red convertible was seriously dented. Linda got out of her car to assess the damage.

"Hey, don't go anyplace!" the young male driver demanded. "I need your name, address, and license number." Linda complied. She knew it was her fault entirely.

"This is my sister's new car. You did this and you have to pay for it."

Linda confessed the accident to her mother that very evening, leaving out the part about the "chase". Father was not to be told, but Linda would have to pay all the damages to keep her father from knowing. The cost of repair included *all* of her savings as well as $30.00 of her dowry.

Linda called the postulant mistress to ask if she would have to wait for entrance, perhaps until she earned the extra $30.00. Sister Humiliana told her to come as planned on September 8th, and that the shortage of dowry was no reason to detain her entering.

By this time, Linda knew of five other girls entering the Franciscan Sisters of Albany, all graduates of Convent High School. They weren't her best friends, but she knew them by name and face, and had even had a few classes with several of the girls. In June, during the awards assembly, the six candidates from Convent High were asked to come up on stage and be recognized. Some of the girls entering surprised her. She didn't imagine them to be "the type". Then she caught herself thinking, "What is "the type"? Am I "the type"? Actually, finding herself asking entrance into a convent with religious women was a greater surprise to herself than anyone else.

. . . .

CHAPTER TWO . . .
POSTULANCY

4

"Virginia, Virginia." It was the soft spoken voice of Sr. Humiliana waking her. "Lunch will be ready in fifteen minutes if you would like to dress and come down to the first floor." She spoke from the half-drawn curtain in the doorway.

"Yes, Sister. I'll be right there." Ginny sat up and tried to remember where she was. She looked around the small but adequate room. It was so clean, perhaps bordering on antiseptic. This was the convent. Eagerly she dressed and rode the elevator to the first floor. Sr. Humiliana was there to greet her as she stepped off and then guided her into an office directly to the right.

"Virginia, after lunch, we'll find a postulant dress for you. For now, these clothes are fine. Let me show you where we eat." Virginia was led into a dining hall just around the corridor. She followed the nun dutifully, but couldn't help feeling ill at ease. She must learn to trust the kind and protective manner of this woman.

Outside the dining room door was a sign reading "refectory".

Inside there were sisters dressed in habits with white veils. The dining tables were in three rows. The sisters were still entering from several doorways, filing into some order at table.

When the activity stopped, a short nun with a black veil began to lead the prayer before the meal, after which everyone sat down. One sister took up a book, centered herself somewhere at the end of the dining hall and began reading. Ginny's back was to the reader; she preferred not to search out the voice. Dishes were passed in circular fashion, counter clockwise. She felt comforted sitting to the right of Sr. Humiliana; the setting seemed almost foreign, and Ginny, the foreigner.

When the bread was passed, Ginny took a piece. She remembered that table etiquette required her to break the bread in half before buttering it. She felt some relief in knowing some proper conduct at a table where she sensed good table manners were observed. In fact, that's exactly how she felt—observed.

The passing of dishes and the sister reading were the only sounds to break the silence of the refectory. Ten minutes had passed. A bell pinged.

"Do thou, O Lord, have mercy on us," interrupted the same sister who had led the grace before meals. The sisters responded in unison, "Thanks be to God." The reader ceased, closed her book, and joined the others for lunch.

"Pax et Bonum, Sisters," the little nun spoke again.

"Pax et Bonum, Sister," the others echoed. Soft-toned conversations emerged as Sr. Humiliana explained to the young sisters at Ginny's table, "Virginia Crow arrived early this morning. She and her brother drove during the night from Washington, D.C." Ginny explained that she actually lived *near* Washington, in Silver Spring, Maryland. She spoke of her family and parents. The conversation was pleasant, and her first meal with the sisters passed without incident. Ginny was relieved; she had almost half expected to spill her food, or say something stupid.

When most everyone appeared to be finished, Ginny heard the single "ping" of a bell that, once more, silenced the room. In a regulated fashion, dishes were stacked, and a cart whisked everything into the kitchen. When the carts left, all stood to face the crucifix upon the wall.

"In the name of the Father and of the Son and of the Holy Spirit, Amen. We give thee thanks, Almighty God, for all Thy benefits, Who livest and reignest forever, and may the souls of the faithful departed, through the mercy of God, rest in peace. Amen.

In the name of the Father and of the Son and of the Holy Spirit, Amen," they prayed together. Then the sisters all seemed to disappear into many directions, attending to tasks before them.

Sister Humiliana turned to a short stocky novice with large glasses, "Sister Alicia, please take Virginia to the classroom and find her a postulant dress that fits. Then take her to the parlor. The other girls will be entering soon. Have her sign the registration book before the others come. Virginia can greet the girls as they arrive."

"Yes, Sister. I'll be happy to," Sister Alicia responded cheerfully. "This way, Virginia," she said as she led the first postulant to the nearby classroom. Opening large built-in closets, Sr. Alicia revealed a large selection of black dresses. Eventually, she discovered one with a hem that fell about mid-calf. "This will do." Virginia noticed a name tag, "Clare Ryan."

"Who is Clare Ryan, Sister?" Ginny inquired.

"One of the novices, but that was her name when she entered. She doesn't use her secular name anymore."

"Oh, I see."

"This one should fit you well, but they'll give you a second dress later. That will be for cleaning, so you don't mess up this good one."

"Oh. Good idea."

"And, Virginia, if you'd like some first day advice, let me tell you that we don't talk about our families here. I don't know why. Maybe we're afraid it will make us homesick. I've been here for a year now, and take it from me, talking about your family is something you *don't* do. It's like an unwritten law."

"Unwritten law?"

"Yeah, and there's lots of them around here. Written and unwritten. But you'll like the place. It grows on you. You gotta put on black stockings and your oxfords with this dress. Did you bring them?"

"Yes, Sister. I left most of my things in the room next door."

"Okay. Well, we call that room the postulate. Everything around here seems to have a name. I'll help you get your things up to your cell."

"Thank you, Sister." Ginny found every impression a memorable one. She took the admonition not to speak of her family to heart. Now, it seemed unfortunate that she had filled the convent table conversation with so many stories of home.

. . . .

5

The new girls were arriving now and nuns were everywhere, it seemed. Parents, daughters, family, and visitors were bustling about. Each new arrival signed the registration book as she entered the door. Ginny had been the first to sign. She had no idea that signing in first would rank her as "the oldest" in her group (not age-wise, but in rank).

The new girls were being taken, one by one, to that upstairs classroom and fitted with a black postulant dress and small white collar. While milling about, Ginny decided to introduce herself to one of the girls who, like herself, also seemed to be alone.

"Hi, I'm Virginia Crow from Silver Spring, Maryland. I got here early this morning." Ginny offered her hand in a welcoming gesture.

"Nice to meet you, Virginia. My name is Angela Marie Masucci, but everyone calls me Angie. I'm from Sandusky, Ohio. One of the nuns brought me from the airport about twenty minutes ago."

"Well, actually, I'm Ginny. Virginia is so formal. I was named for the state I was born in, but my mom and dad didn't want to call me West Virginia. They used to tease that I was supposed to marry someone with the last name of West. Where's your family? Isn't anyone with you?"

"No. Mom and Dad really couldn't afford to come with me just for my entrance day."

"Same here. No family, I mean. My brother drove me from Maryland. It took us most of the night. We arrived in Albany around 6:30 this morning, I think."

Behind Angie came a familiar voice, "And so, this is the gift you have for Our Lady upon the feast of her birth!" Angie turned.

"Sister Mary Paul! I never expected to see you here! I'm so glad you came!" Angie lunged into an affectionate embrace that almost cracked Sister's celluloid collar.

"Angie, I just couldn't miss such a happy occasion. I have asked permission to join you in chapel for the ceremony."

"What ceremony? What's happening in chapel?" Angie asked. Ginny was just as interested in knowing what Sister Mary Paul was talking about.

Just then, Sister Humiliana called for the group's attention. Her soft mannered voice managed the crowd remarkably well. "Will all of the girls who have signed in and received their postulant dress please now return to the classroom, and will parents and family members please go to the chapel at this time."

Hugs and kisses were everywhere and sometimes a tearful farewell as one group headed for the classroom, another to the chapel.

"Angie, I just want you to know I'm there for you. You'll be fine. There's nothing to fear. I brought you a little gift."

Angie opened the white box to find a black leather pen and pencil holder. She recognized it as the type nuns wore snapped onto their waist cords. She would save it for the day when she would receive a habit.

"Thank you, Sister. I love it. I'll wear it proudly someday—when I get my habit." The crowds were thinning now, and Angie knew she had only a few minutes more. "Sister, this is Ginny from Maryland."

"It's so nice to meet you, dear. Welcome to the community. Both of you must hurry now. I'll be there in chapel for both of you."

Up in the classroom, the girls were seated in desks neatly filed in rows. The large group seemed to fill the room. As Sister Humiliana spoke the young women listened attentively.

"Girls, you all have met me at least once before. I am Sister Humiliana, your postulant mistress. I know Our Blessed Mother is happy to see so many fine young women follow her example of holiness."

"There are twenty-five in your group! One girl is arriving later this evening from Hawaii. Her name is Sandra Mahala, and I hope at least a few of you will choose to stay up and welcome her. We expect her sometime around 8:30."

"Twenty-five postulants is a wonderful number. This year the Albany Franciscan Sisters celebrate one hundred and twenty-five years since our founding! We were started by Blessed Paul Holdfelder in 1838. Twenty-five postulants is a perfect way to mark our anniversary year! I know it will be a year of grace and blessing for each of you and for each of us."

Some of the girls were struggling to focus on Sr. Humiliana's discourse. Their thoughts had drifted to chapel, their families, and curiosity about what would happen next.

"At this time, we will all go to chapel where your families await you. Please file in two lines and sit only four in a bench on either side at the front of chapel. Your families are seated in the back pews."

"When I call your name, come to the altar rail, and I will place a veil on your head. It will be a symbol of your entering. There will be a brief prayer service, and then our guests will be asked to leave. Try to be brave and not show them tears. It is difficult for parents to give their daughters to God. I have always believed the one they give to God is the one they keep. Today, they will not feel that way. You must be brave for them.

Does anyone have a question?"

There was silence. "All right then. Please form two lines and come to chapel."

The prayer service was brief as Sister had indicated. No one missed her cue to be veiled. Ginny heard a lot of nose-blowing and sniffles in the back, but no one turned around to look. After the closing hymn, the families must have been asked to leave chapel. The only sound was of their departure.

For a spell, Ginny wished Patrick, her brother, might have stayed for the official entrance ceremony. She thought, "There are probably others like myself, far from home. And what about that Hawaiian girl coming tonight? What a trip *she* is taking! All the girls needed to be courageous today. It was a very memorable moment."

That afternoon trunks were inspected and emptied. Girls went up and down the stairs, and the elevator was constantly in use. Linen table cloths and napkins were sent to the motherhouse dining room for the dining tables.

Sister Humiliana explained that only three sets of underwear were to be kept in the cell. The rest remained in the trunks. Only two sets of towels were needed. The girls who had brought extra had to give them to a novice who placed them in community storage.

"Only one religious item and your Baby Ben clock may be on display in your rooms. Everything else must be out of sight. Rooms are to be dusted every day; you'll find a mop in your closet. Even books are to be cleared from your desk when not in use."

Sister went from girl to girl, checking items and giving suggestions. Taking the box of tampons from Linda's trunk, and from some of the others, she explained, "You won't be needing these. We don't use them in the convent. Only sanitary pads are acceptable."

Candies and other treats were collected and put in Sr. Humiliana's office to be used for the group later on. It was a busy and exciting afternoon. Most of the girls had little time for remembering what happened in chapel and how their parents had slipped out the back door, leaving their children to the care of Jesus and Holy Mother Church.

Supper also proved to be a positive and pleasant experience for the girls. Sandwiches and salads were served, with fruit for desert. After dinner the postulants were led to the postulate for recreation and then to chapel for a short night prayer.

At 7:30, Sister Humiliana reminded the girls they were welcome to stay up and greet the twenty-fifth member of their band coming from Hawaii. For those who chose to go upstairs to bed, there was to be no talking or socializing once they left the first floor. Upstairs was considered part of the cloister, and night prayer marked the beginning of grand silence.

Most of the girls did retire, but six decided to welcome Sandra. Linda, Angie, and Ginny wanted to wait. They were joined by Janie, from Syracuse, and Helen and Brigit, who seemed to be friends.

"The last of your postulants is here, Sister," a tall, thin white-veiled novice reported to Sr. Humiliana, after knocking on the postulate door. The small welcoming committee, led by Sister, walked down the hall to the front entrance where a brown skinned, black haired, very attractive eighteen-year-old was coming through the front doors. She was greeted warmly by Sr. Humiliana's embrace, while the rest of the party shook hands. The welcoming was fun, and the girls were glad they had waited for their last group member to arrive.

Sandra was taken into the postulate for refreshments and a visit with her welcoming delegation. Conversation was easy and light-hearted.

"Oh dear, I could not believe what I almost did in Hawaii," Sandra shared.

"What happened?" Ginny asked for the group.

"Well, I had my plane tickets all arranged for my trip to the mainland. I was to fly into New York City earlier this afternoon. When I went to say good-bye to the sisters in Pearl City several days ago, I also stopped at the airport to get my ticket. One of the sisters just happened to notice." The girls were curious and attentive to Sandra's tale.

"Well, I'm just so glad Sister noticed I had a New York City destination. I had planned to take a taxi from New York City to Albany because I thought it was nearby."

The girls laughed heartily with Sandra. They liked her immediately; she was open and direct, with a wonderful sense of humor.

"Can you imagine what my cab fare would have been? When I found out Albany was over 150 miles from New York City, I thought it might be cheaper to buy a cab and drive it myself!" They laughed again. "I was really lucky to get this flight to Albany, even if I did have to arrive so late."

Everyone was having a good time, but Sr. Humiliana knew it was time to take Sandra upstairs and help her get situated in her new surroundings. Sandra's cell was next to Ginny's, and Ginny was proud of that.

The next few days were busy ones. There was so much to learn and do. Sr. Humiliana had several special classes with the young women to explain the schedules and expectations of the community.

"Next week you will all begin classes at our junior college next door, Regina College. You will need to register, but your class schedule has been completed for you. Each of you will be expected to earn an Associate in Arts degree in Liberal Arts. Textbooks will be provided, and I believe you all have notebooks from home." Several heads nodded in agreement.

"On Tuesday you will take a psychological test which you need not be anxious about. If you have been allowed to enter, you will not be sent home based upon the test results. The test is only meant to help us better understand you as individuals. Even though most of you are recent high school graduates, several girls have worked a few years.

"You have come from many different places. We have one postulant from Ohio, one from Maryland, one from Pennsylvania, one from Hawaii, two from Vermont, and four from New Jersey. The other fifteen are from New York State. Six of our New Yorkers come from our very own Convent High School right here in Albany! You are the largest group of candidates to enter from Convent High in over ten years!"

Sr. Humiliana sounded so impressed that it almost seemed appropriate to clap, but instead the girls merely nodded approval toward each. Sister continued.

"Now, I ask that in the future you use the stairways at either end of the hall unless you are sick or have a large package. The exercise is good for you. As you know, your rooms are on the fourth and fifth floors, but you need to know that canonical novices live on the second floor and constitutional novices live on the third.

"You are never to visit these floors or talk with these women without my permission or the approval of Sr. Geraldine, the novice mistress. The novices mean well, but like their name implies, they are only beginners in religious life and, like yourselves, have been known to give misinformation or poor advice concerning the convent lifestyle. They may, unintentionally of course, lead you astray."

The canonical novices wear a white veil to indicate they are new to our community and are experiencing a year of prayer and solitude. They entered the community only a year ago, as you did, on September 8th.

"Sister?" Kathleen raised her hand.

"Yes, Kathleen?" She was quickly recognized.

"Sister, what do you mean by 'constitutional novice'?"

There were so many questions to ask, and so much to learn during postulancy. Most of the girls came from Catholic schools, but almost a fourth were from public schools, and their Confraternity of Christian Doctrine (CCD) education was minimal Catholic instruction, especially in regard to convents and the sisterhood. Angie's CCD experience was that it was an evening to be with her friends; a chance to drive volunteer parents crazy. Angie thought of CCD class as time for fun, not so much as time for learning.

"Constitutional novices are those learning the rules and constitution of our community. They are preparing to take vows.

At the end of their constitutional year, they will be allowed to make their vows for a period of three years. If all is in good accord, they will be permitted to renew vows for another two years. After that, if all is acceptable, the sisters will make their final vows."

"Does that mean," Sandra was counting on her fingers, "it will take us eight years to become fully pledged, or whatever it is that you call it . . . nuns?"

"Technically, you have come here to become "sisters". Traditionally, the word "nun" is used to refer to women who live in cloisters. Sisters are actively engaged in social needs of the church. People interchange the terms so often that most assume it means the same thing. And yes, Sandra, to answer your question: The process does take nearly eight years. First you must complete your postulancy. It used to be that our candidates were required a six month postulancy, but we've changed that policy to nine. Some communities require even more than nine months. This forthcoming June, you will receive your habit and your religious name. That will begin your official novitiate training. Sr. Geraldine will be your instructor then."

"How will we get our habits, Sister?" Kathleen interrupted again.

"You will make them."

That caused something of a stir. The girls could not even imagine how one put the habit on, let alone put it together.

"I'll teach you how to sew your habits. I've made them for forty years, and after a while, you will learn. Don't worry about that now. Another thing I need to remind you of, after evening prayer and recreation and you have gone upstairs, no one is to speak until after breakfast in the morning."

"We call this grand silence. We do this because so many sins are committed during the night. We ask you to make this little sacrifice to atone for the imprudence and evil deeds of others. For some of you this may seem difficult. Do you understand there will be many new customs for you to learn if you are to live among us?"

"Yes, Sister," they responded in unison. Even if they didn't understand, they wanted Sr. Humiliana to think they did. No one really wanted to question her; they wanted to please her. They wanted to belong; to fit in. Besides, these young and eager postulants knew Sister to be all-wise. She was a good choice for this role of preparing girls for convent life. She practiced what she preached and her sincerity was surpassed only by her humility. In later years, probably the *only* thing the group could ever agree to was that Sister Humiliana was a saintly and unusually credible religious woman.

"Tomorrow, when you have your 10:00 o'clock snack, I'll meet you in the lunchroom to demonstrate how we peel oranges, bananas, and eat soft boiled eggs out of a shell," Sister Humiliana continued. "But for now, I thought perhaps you would like to put on your tennis shoes and recreate outside in the courtyard before prayer." The girls were delighted.

This was the first day the postulants were given permission to wear gym shoes. What a good familiar feeling it was after three days in granny oxfords.

Ginny was particularly affected and darted into the courtyard with a winning sprint. The green park bench was directly in her path, but Ginny didn't hesitate or alter course. Unexpectedly, she leapt over the bench like a gazelle, swift and deliberate. Safely past the obstacle, she amazed herself with her skill and dexterity.

Ginny returned to the others and asked, "Did you see that?" Most of the group were conversing, some even singing by now.

"See what?" Linda spoke for them.

"See what I just did!"

"What did you do?"

"Do you see that green bench over there?" Ginny asked and nodded toward the distance.

This time Sandra answered, "Well, of course we see it, Cunchie."

"Well, I just jumped clear over it!"

"Impossible," they murmured.

"You didn't."

"How could you?"

"Do it again," Linda directed. The girls could not imagine Ginny leaping over something so large as a park bench.

"Okay. I think I can," Ginny responded to Linda's challenge. Only this time things were different. It was not spontaneous; Ginny felt the watchful eye of her disbelievers.

She raced and leapt gracefully into the air but came down before she should have, breaking the top slat in half.

"Ooouch!" she howled aloud, hobbling in circles. The postulants howled equally aloud, with laughter.

"Are you all right?" Kathleen inquired, once the laughter subsided.

"Oh sure. Nothing a new leg couldn't fix. God, that smarts," Ginny confessed.

"Speaking of new legs, you might want to get a new bench too. Look, it's broken," Sandra observed.

"So am I," Ginny winced. They stood around and examined the broken bench.

"How could your leg possibly break such *thick* wood?" Linda asked.

"Linda, I haven't a clue. I just hope I don't get my other leg broken when I tell Humiliana what I've done. Don't anyone breathe a word; I'll tell her after supper." Ginny was not looking forward to that, but she had managed to make recreation memorable and entertaining that afternoon.

Meals were often eventful. The same evening as the park bench episode, Georgette caused a scene with her dessert. It was only half a canned peach. Georgette conspicuously tried to break the peach with her spoon and her fork. It would only splash reluctantly about in peach juice. Finally, Georgette used her knife and fork. This worked, but unfortunately not without tipping the dish and putting half of her dessert in the lap of her black postulant dress. By now, the entire table was aware of Georgette's battle with the troublesome dessert. The end result brought laughter to Sr. Humiliana and all those watching. Ginny was glad to see Sr. Humiliana in such good spirits. She was not eager to bring up the broken bench, but knew she'd better.

A bell signalled the stacking of dishes. The novices and postulants stopped their conversations and prayer was said by all. Novices went off to the kitchen. Soon postulants would be expected to help, but the first week, they would step directly into the postulate for evening recreation. Reluctantly, Ginny approached Sr. Humiliana.

"Sister, may I speak with you about something?"   "Of course, Virginia. What is it?"

"Well, Sister, today during recreation in the courtyard, do you remember how we had permission to put on our sneakers?"

"Yes."

"Well, Sister," she hesitated. "I guess I just got carried away because I started to run. I, uh, well, could I just take you outside and show you what happened?"

"Of course, dear."

"We have to go to the courtyard, Sister."

Humiliana had a puzzled look on her face, but she was most compliant. Finally, they both gazed upon the broken slat.

"Sister, I was running so fast. I just ran into the bench."

"You *ran* into the bench???"

"I guess I just didn't watch where I was going," Ginny lied, preferring not to admit she was attempting to hurdle the park bench. She was afraid of Sister's disapproval more than her wrath.

"Are you hurt, Virginia?" she asked with genuine concern.

"No, Sister." Lie number two. Earlier Ginny had inspected the damage to discover that the back side of her right thigh was black and blue. She hoped the pain and discoloration were merely bruising and nothing more. She would not confess the truth for fear of continuing her embarrassment any further.

"Well, don't worry, Virginia. We can have the bench repaired, but the wood is so thick and sturdy, I can't imagine how you could break it without hurting yourself."

"Just lucky, I guess," Ginny shrugged.

· · · · · · · ·

6

That night, upstairs on the fourth floor, Angie heard the "soiled linen" closet open and something fall down the chute.

"Who's up there?" Angie whispered into the passageway.

"It's me, Brigit."

"It's me, Angie. I'm on the fourth floor in the hall. What are you doing up there?"

"Sending my underwear down to the laundry." The girls had been instructed to wash out underclothing every night by hand in the bathroom sink and then send it down the laundry chute.

Angie was a friendly type and had taken a liking to Brigit. She continued their visit, "How's life on the fifth floor?"

"Fine, but I think we broke it."

"Broke what?"

"The grand silence."

"Yeah, I think we did. Let's talk tomorrow."

By now, most of the girls were making a serious attempt to keep the silence as Sr. Humiliana had directed. It was difficult and unusual for the young women to remain silent from 7:30 P.M. until after breakfast the next day. There was a noble effort, especially noticeable in Janie. She never spoke upstairs; not even in a whisper.

Angie thought about Brigit's concern over breaking the silence and decided to turn over a new leaf. Angie was definitely a free-thinking postulant and quite popular with the girls, but Brigit's reaction gave her an idea. She went to her cell, drew a sign, and pinned it to the back of her regulation black bathrobe. It read: "Please do not talk to me. I am trying to keep grand silence."

After brushing her teeth, Angie opened the door to leave the community washroom. Sandra noticed and read Angie's sign aloud. Then she commented, "Get her. She's in the sign making business." Even Angie laughed, but in truth, the girls did begin to lessen and almost cease conversation once they left the first floor.

. . . .

7

The postulants reported to Regina College to be tested by the community psychologist, Sr. Imelda, one of the few sisters to have earned a Ph.D. The girls listened attentively as Sister gave the instructions. Sr. Imelda was a heavy set women, with kindly eyes and voice, matronly and similar in some respects to their directress.

The neophyte religious soon found themselves immersed in circling their respective answers. The testing was quite underway when Sr. Imelda left the room for a few moments.

Noticing her absence, Sandra commented aloud, "Check out number 14." The girls chuckled in response.

"Wait until you get to question 19 if you really want weird," Helen said from the back of the room. "Why do they keep on asking us if we urinate frequently?"

"Maybe there's some kind of regulation on how often we can go," was Sandra's quick comeback. Again there was laughter.

"If they ask me one more time if I feel like I'm being followed, I think I'll tell them about my shadow," Angie added. Just then, Sr. Imelda entered the room. Noticing that silence had not been observed in her absence, she sounded exasperated as she spoke, "You don't mean to tell me you were talking during this test?" There was no response. "I heard laughter from the hall and conversation as I entered. Have you been discussing this test? If you have, it is totally invalid! All of it! How could you have discussed these questions?"

"Sister," Helen was the first to speak. "We didn't say much. We just sort of laughed at some of the questions. They were pretty silly, don't you think?"

Imelda looked defeated. "The test is useless. The time and expense are wasted. I can't use it. Pass your papers up. You may return to Sr. Humiliana and tell her what has happened." Sister was as politely annoyed as possible.

Once outside the classroom, Susan turned to the others. "We can't go back. Sister Humiliana will have a cow. I just know she won't be happy about this. We have to apologize now."

"Good idea," Helen seconded. Angie, Linda, and the others nodded their agreement. Helen then suggested, "Susan, you be our spokesman. It's your idea to try this, you lead the way."

"Okay," she agreed, and the band turned about and returned to the classroom where Sr. Imelda remained sitting at her desk, her chin resting upon her open palms before the unfinished tests.

"Sister, we're really sorry that we were inconsiderate of those being tested, but honestly, we didn't say very much when you were gone. We only referred to a few of the questions. Please let us finish the test. We couldn't have messed up very much." Susan's plea was sincere and she sounded convincing.

"Well, I guess we could finish the tests. But not a single word more!" Sr. Imelda seemed gratified for some resolution to the problem, and so were the girls. They did not want to be sent home only a week after entrance for "cheating" on some test. The exam was completed without further incident. No one was ever discovered if Sr. Humiliana heard about what had happened that day. Sr. Imelda probably didn't want her to know any more than the postulants wanted to tell.

One warm day late in September, the postulants and canonical novices were given permission to have recreation together outside on a hill banking the convent wall. Several novices and three of the postulants put their guitars together to lead the group in song. The guitarists stood before their music stands, Sr. Humiliana and Sr. Geraldine sat on chairs, and the rest of their clan rested upon the freshly cut, cool green grass. A ladybug climbed upon Humiliana's habit and Susan commented to Georgette that it was a sign of good luck to have a ladybug light upon you.

The group of novices and postulants sang one song after another. The forty or so voices created an instant choir that could sing three and four part harmony. They sounded, shall we say, heavenly.

"Let's cut a record," Angie suggested.

"Yeah, and make a million dollars for the community," Sandra directed her comment to Sr. Humiliana, who was fun to tease when the coast seemed clear.

Humiliana went along with the idea, adding, "Yes, Sandra, then we can all go on pilgrimage to Europe and pray throughout the Holy Land."

"That wasn't exactly what I thought we'd do with a million, Sister, but if you think we should use it to pray in the Holy Land, we'll pray in the Holy Land." The whole group laughed, especially the postulants, who knew by now Sandra's fun loving nature didn't make her most likely to be found in chapel.

Praying didn't come naturally to many of these young women. They lived worldly and active lives.

As the girls sang, Humiliana suggested they spiritualize their music. "Sing from your soul, girls. Think that you are speaking to our Beloved. When you sing the words to "More", ask Jesus to remind you He alone has loved with more than the greatest love the world has known. This is the love He has for you alone." Sr. Humiliana had simple but helpful suggestions to help these very normal young women adjust to a very different way of life. Love songs could never be exactly the same now that these girls were being encouraged to make them a prayer.

"You know it was St. Augustine who taught us, 'He who sings, prays twice.' Once, for the prayerful words sung and once again for the prayerfulness that becomes the prayer within the singing."

The evening concert was a truly memorable experience. Many songs were sung that night, familiar and popular songs as well as religious ones.

Linda was thinking of home. She felt homesick perhaps, but she also reflected upon the beauty of these talented voices, these good people, this picturesque setting. Linda was becoming more content, more comfortable with each passing day. She thought of how the others must feel, hundreds of miles from home, while she lived only a five-minute drive away. The girls seemed to take turns being homesick. Like Angie, for instance.

Missing her mother and father, especially just before the arrival of her 18th birthday, Angie decided to go into the dark of chapel where only flickering candles and the skylight above the altar offered any light.

Angie sat in the last bench and felt hopelessly alone. She wanted to cry. If only there was someone to comfort these pangs of loneliness and abandonment. She wanted someone to hold her, assure her, convince her of friendship. She told God how she felt. Soon thereafter came the sounds of footsteps from behind. Could this be the answer to her prayers—someone to comfort her? The footsteps came directly to Angela, and a canonical novice, Sr. Dorothy, bent down to speak with her as she knelt in prayer.

Angie stretched her ears and heart to listen.

"Angela, this bench is Sr. Geraldine's. If she sees you in it, you might be killed. If you want to pray, turn on a light and go up closer to the altar. People are pretty serious about their assigned places in chapel."

"Thank you, Sister." Angie gratefully acknowledged Sr. Dorothy's admonition, then moved closer to the flickering candles. Tears began to flow and she decided to leave chapel for the privacy of a closet-sized bathroom just outside of chapel. She passed Brigit in the hall. Brigit instinctively knew something was wrong.

"What's wrong, Angie?" she asked. Angie was reluctant to speak. She was afraid that if she tried to explain, she might dramatically burst into tears. She swiftly entered the lavatory and tried to close the door behind her.

Brigit was persistent. "Angie, maybe I can help."

At that precise moment, Sr. Humiliana entered the hall. She asked Brigit to explain. By now the bathroom door was closed and Sister Humiliana had an idea what was happening.

"I'll take care of it now. I want you to return to the postulancy. Don't worry, I can help her," Sister assured Brigit. Brigit obeyed, her face still showing a concern for Angie's well-being.

Humiliana knocked gently upon the door and easily gained entrance. She suggested they both go to her office. There Angie spoke of her homesickness and Humiliana listened with the patience and compassion of a saint.

"Sister, I just miss my parents and friends. Ohio seems so far away. Tomorrow is my birthday, and I just wish Diane or Sue could be here with me. I had *so many* friends at home. Don't get me wrong, I like these girls, but I don't really know them."

"I understand, Angie. I'm sure you were very popular in school." This was true; Angie was very popular with most anyone who knew her.

"I had a lot of friends in Sandusky. Probably a couple hundred." Angie was sincere in her estimate, but Sr. Humiliana could not keep from chuckling, though politely.

"Dear, this may sound strange to you, but I believe it has been said, and I wholeheartedly agree, that if you are fortunate to have even *two* or *three* true friends in life, you have been richly blessed. It appears some of us never even have one."

Angie was surprised to witness what seemed to be Sr. Humiliana's confession. It sounded as if she were admitting to a serious lack of friends. Could someone so kind as her postulant mistress be so deprived of friendship? Angie felt sorry for the woman and thought less of her own momentary circumstance. They continued their talk, and Angie soon felt restored by the understanding and gentle nature of the older woman.

Sr. Humiliana suggested Angie join the others for recreation. Angie found Brigit sewing her habit. Angie explained the whole incident and they now laughed at the part when Angie expected an answer to her prayer for deliverance from loneliness but instead the "messenger from God" told her to get the heck out of Sr. Geraldine's bench.

Most of the girls sewed their habits during recreation before retiring. Sr. Humiliana told the girls to make every stitch a prayer for perseverance. Perseverance seemed a key issue. The girls were always encouraged to pray for it.

In the next few weeks Sr. Humiliana finally did get around to showing the postulants how to eat a soft boiled egg directly from its shell, how to peel a banana with a fork, and how to remove an orange peel by cutting the peel into fourths and then lifting off one section of peel at a time with a spoon.

Apples were always to be cut into fourths before biting into them. "Goodness! A lady never chomps into an apple with bare teeth!" Sandra teasingly would mimic when the girls were alone.

Soup was to be spooned away from you. It was served every day at the noon meal from the first of October until the first of May. (Remember how delighted Ginny had been with herself that first meal when she knew to break the bread in *half*? She soon learned that bread was buttered on only the *quarter* section you were about to eat.)

Every morning there was a training class with Sr. Humiliana before they would go off to classes at the college.

"You *never* cross your legs. A lady always keeps her legs together, and feet, side by side, flat upon the floor. Posture is very important. Never lean against walls; they stand without your help. A Sister walks and speaks with dignity. We are always an example to others. Control the volume of your voice; be subdued at all times."

In fact, the girls had heard Humiliana's dictum so often that they had composed their own maxim: "Girls, subdue it. If you can't do it, glue it."

Voices were always asked to be softened, and the girls had to be reminded daily. They were not used to the soft-spoken tones expected of them, but they took their correction in good spirit. They knew Sr. Humiliana wanted only to help.

The postulants used a Courtesy and Manner handbook for reference and topics of discussion. Sr. Humiliana taught, "Our beloved father, St. Francis, once said, 'Courtesy is a sister of charity'". She would teach the girls that they could never be too courteous to one another. A lack of courtesy brought on more dissension than almost anything, she would explain.

The postulants especially enjoyed learning community history and specific community customs. They were, at times, amusing and insightful.

"We were originally a German foundation of Sisters. Many of our early vocations came from Holland and Germany. The Sisters of St. Francis of Albany, New York was established by a German bishop migrating from New York City with other Dutch and German Catholics. Blessed Paul Holdfelder may one day be canonized. We must pray for this to happen."

Sr. Humiliana passed out novena prayer cards. From then on, classes were always started with a prayer for this intention. She had a particular devotion to Blessed Paul. Her grandfather had known the man when he was a little boy and delivered chicken eggs to the rectory where Blessed Paul served as priest and pastor.

Today Sr. Humiliana had a special announcement to make. She explained that previously, groups received "rank" by signing the registration book on entrance day. The first to enter was the first to sign the book, thus receiving the rank of number one, and so on. The first to arrive would be the "oldest" in rank; the last to arrive would be the "youngest". This year, it would be different. Six weeks had passed before rank was "assigned".

Sr. Humiliana announced that Ginny would now officially be ranked as "oldest". Ginny was delighted. She had performed as the temporary or "acting number one" group member; but Susan, another natural leader, had also vied for the position. Helen was disappointed, as some of the others may have been.

Rank was now read aloud, number one to number twenty-five.

Kathleen was "the youngest" and was referred to as "the baby" of their group. Neither the youngest in age nor the last to arrive on Entrance Day, Kathleen was officially ranked in community as number twenty-five for the class of 1963 and would hold this position until she either left community or died. Sr. Humiliana said the decisions were based upon the past six weeks of observing the postulants, but made no further explanation. She added that Mother Victoria had approved of the ranking and that it was quite official.

With time, other nicknames emerged. Caroline was referred to as "Carol Barrel" because she was the roundest of the lot. Postulants called Angie "Supermouth" (sometimes shortened to "Super") because of her insatiable appetite and Italian conviviality at table. Betsy played a bass fiddle and was thus dubbed, "B.B." for Betsy Bass. Barbara, who was 26, was the oldest in years. Because of this, the group called her "Grandma" and the nickname stuck for years.

The girls often teased each other, which, at times, concerned Sr. Humiliana. She feared they might hurt each other in jest. They probably did, but this didn't stop them.

Now it *was* official: Ginny was the oldest. It felt good because the girl was probably more ambitious than nuns are supposed to be. She wanted to be number one, whatever that meant. Helen, second in rank, liked calling Ginny "Numero Zero" or simply "Zero". With Ginny as "Zero" Helen became the coveted "number one". Though it was only a joke, Ginny never liked being called "Zero". Ginny took her rank seriously and had written her parents that she had already "earned the rank of corporal." Military rank was the only image she could associate with this convent ranking.

Sr. Humiliana, who meticulously read all incoming and outgoing mail, intercepted the letter and called Ginny into her office for a conference.

"Dear, convent rank is not akin to military rank. We have no officers here. The position of "oldest" or "number one" simply means you have the responsibility of setting a good example for the others. You are to answer the door or phone in my absence and be of service to your group. We have no corporals or sergeants," Humiliana explained.

Still, Ginny took pride in being asked to lead and enjoyed the diversified tasks required of her, such as putting out candy treats during recreation or delivering messages for Sr. Humiliana.

In another of Humiliana's now routine training sessions, she told the girls not to be alarmed if they saw sisters in chapel with outstretched arms. This, too, was a community custom.

St. Francis of Assisi was known to pray with his hands held high into the air, stretched out as were Christ's arms upon the cross. After a while, arms became heavy, but a devoted and prayerful imitator of Christ and Francis would pray as long as she could in this position. This had long been a popular and secret community tradition among the sisters. It was also used as a penance, as the postulants were to learn in time.

"Girls, you may also see a novice kissing the floor after her prayer. This is an act of submissive respect to Almighty God." When Sr. Humiliana explained such behavior, it always seemed reasonable and even inspiring. These young impressionable souls longed for sisterhood all the more.

. . . .

8

While recreating outside during an upstate New York Indian summer day, Linda and Caroline heard cries of alarm coming from the motherhouse grounds, adjacent to the courtyard and novitiate. A man, flailing and running toward the cellar doorway was shouting, "Charlie, Charlie! Patsy is covered with dirt! I can't reach him! Charlie, come quick! It's caving in!"

The plight of Patsy became obvious to Linda and Caroline but neither knew how to help. Linda commanded Caroline, "Run in. Call an ambulance. Tell Sister! Run Caroline, run!" Caroline may have been something of a butterball but, in this instance, her legs carried her with remarkable speed.

Linda ran to the man buried beneath the pile of dirt, still trickling from mounds surrounding the hole. She shouted to Patsy, "Help is almost here. Someone is coming! It will be okay, Patsy." As much as Linda wanted to jump into the ditch and scrape away the dirt that covered him, she realized she might cause a worse landslide.

She began to pray aloud. Linda prayed the "Our Father," pleading with God the Father to rescue the older gentleman employed by the sisters for maintenance work. Dozens of time during the day, Linda prayed a "Hail Mary" to the Mother of Jesus, but in times of dramatic trouble, the "Our Father" came to mind. Years later, she would consider saving the really important occasions for the "Father" chauvinistic, but today, with this threat of imminent death before her, she prayed openly and with truest conviction.

She assured the man once more, "Charlie is coming! It will be okay!" Finally, Charlie and the others did arrive. Charlie leapt into the hole, risking his own life, and dug for a hand and then a head. By now, the ambulance, Sr. Humiliana, and others began to arrive. Linda was called away from the scene.

The workers successfully freed the man from his dirt constraint and placed him upon the stretcher. There were cuts on his head and shoulders caused by the digging of shovels. His tear-and-blood-stained-face passed the group of postulants and novices who had collected nearby. Charlie was quite the convent hero that day, and Linda gave thanks Someone was listening.

Well into October, Angie found the courage to approach Sr. Humiliana for permission to wear the contacts her mother and father had bought her several years earlier. When Angie applied to the convent, a letter informed her to buy glasses, as sisters did not wear contacts. Wire rims (or, as the postulants called them, "nunners") were the approved eyewear for the nuns.

Angie's mother believed that glasses improved no one's appearance and would recite, "Boys don't make passes at girls with eyeglasses." Even though the contacts were expensive, Angie soon learned they arrested the chronic astigmatism that seriously deteriorated her vision. Angie missed wearing her contacts and decided now would be a good time to ask.

It was. Angie was delighted with Humiliana's decision and shared the good news with Brigit, now one of Angie's favorite companions. One afternoon, while taking a break from their studies, Angie was cleaning her contacts in the community washroom. Brigit was curious and asked, "What does it feel like to wear those things? Do they hurt?"

"Not at all. In fact, when I don't wear them, I feel like part of my eye is missing. I've gotten quite used to them."

"What do they look like?" Brigit asked as she came closer to see.

Angie put the brown round piece of plastic into Brigit's hand for a keener examination.

"It's brown," she observed.

"It's easier to find when I drop it. I could have gotten clear, but I figure the brown would match my eye color." Angie's eyes were large and brown, teasingly described by some of the girls as "cow eyes". "They're made of hard plastic, but it's not too difficult to break them. I knelt on one once searching for it on the floor," Angie continued.

"Could I try it on?"

"I don't see why not, but it won't help you see because the prescription is for me." Angie cleaned and rinsed the contact, then added a wetting solution. "The liquid helps it stay on the eyeball." Angie carefully inserted the contact into Brigit's blue eye, not thinking for a moment how stupid a thing this was to do.

"Now, it may hurt a little." Angie recalled her first experience when Dr. Katko placed them upon her eyes. As the doctor directed Angie, Angie now told Brigit, "Look at the floor first. Slowly raise your eyes to the sink. Don't look up yet; your eye must adjust."

"It does hurt," Brigit confessed. "Can you take it out?"

Angie hadn't thought about how to get it out. She had only removed the plastic disc from her *own* eye. How could she get it out of Brigit's?

"Try to open your eyelid, so I can pull this corner of your eye back tightly. It's supposed to just pop out. It does for me, anyway."

Angie began to realize how foolish they had been. She prayed this was going to work. Angie could possibly damage Brigit's eye if she were careless. What if the contact slipped under the eyelid or on top of the eyeball, as occasionally it did move off center where it routinely rested. What if? What if? She secretly panicked at the thought of hurting her friend but did not want to alarm Brigit.

Finally, after several attempts at squeezing Brigit's eyelid to the right and pulling her skin toward her ear, the plastic popped forward into Angie's hand.

Only now could Angie admit her fear. "Brige, do you know how dangerous and downright dumb that was for us? I'm really lucky I could get it out. I've heard of people going to the hospital where they have little plungers to suck them out!"

They were both relieved and agreed not to breath a word to anyone of this silly adventure. Still, it did make them feel closer as friends to think they shared a secret.

Ginny came into the washroom to announce that Sr. Humiliana wanted everyone in the postulate. Once all twenty-five had been gathered, Sister explained there had been a death in community. A young nurse had complained of a headache and, that very evening, died of an aneurism. There had been no warning and the woman was only forty. It shocked the Franciscan community, as death was usually predictable and usually for the very old.

All of the postulants lined up in rank, as was custom, and then were led to the motherhouse parlor. Here, the deceased were waked for viewing and the visitation of community, family, or friends. Many of the girls were to witness their first corpse and, for most of them, their first dead nun.

This was another impressionable time for the girls. They were silent and followed the example of the nuns ahead of them, kneeling in pairs before the coffin for a moment of silent prayer, blessing themselves, and turning toward the hall where they assumed their rank and file once more.

Linda had been to only two funerals, those of her grandmothers. But here was a woman dressed in one of those big black dresses with the large, grotto-like veil surrounding her face. Linda was reminded of a nun doll her mother had bought at the Convent High Christmas bazaar. But this was a real person before her. It was a peculiar sight, a dead nun.

Even nuns die.

· · · · · · · ·

9

The postulants clearly understood they were not to socialize in any manner with the college girls of Regina Catholic College. On the top floor of the motherhouse there was a college dormitory that overlooked the courtyard between the motherhouse and novitiate. By now the postulants were more of a unit, a group bonding with each other and exploring each other's character.

For their afternoon recreation the postulants decided to bring their guitars, bass, and tambourines out to the courtyard. They sang "If I had a Hammer", "I Will Follow Him", "Can't Help Falling in Love", and others. The college girls watched from their rooms above. The talent of the "Blackbirds," as the college students called this unique brand of women, was very entertaining, and the girls above continued to gather to listen to the concert below.

"Awesome! You guys are great! You should be making records with that sound!" one of the watchers shouted.

"We think so too. But we can't afford an agent!" Sandra quipped back.

"I'll quit college and be your agent," another Regina girl responded.

After several more songs, Helen called up to the girls, "Is that a radio I hear? We haven't heard that song for *ages*. Turn it up, will you?"

When they did, the postulants broke into some very contemporary dance steps. Now it was becoming more than a show. It was a demonstration to the college girls that they weren't so different in spite of black dresses, oxfords, and veils.

The onlookers clapped rhythm and the postulants fed upon the approving attention of their college counterparts. All seemed in good, simple fun until Sr. Humiliana appeared at the laundry door. With a waving gesture of the hand, she called to them, "Girls, please come here a moment."

The postulants filed into the laundry and followed their mistress to the classroom. Something was obviously wrong, but no one could guess what provoked Sister's solemn manner.

"Sister Helena, as you know, is the president of Regina Catholic College. She has just called to inform me of what has been transpiring in the courtyard and that the postulants of our community were behaving in a most unedifying manner."

Like the morning sun, it dawned upon the girls that having a boisterous bit of pleasure before the college girls was not exactly "protocol".

"You know I have asked you not to have anything to do with the college girls. They are here to study, not to be your friends or to influence you. Of course, you may greet them in a friendly manner when passing; but obedience is a way of life for us. If you prefer not to be obedient, perhaps you should pack your trunks and return home. The doors are not locked from the inside. You are free to go at all times. It is far more difficult to enter our convent than to return to the world you have left behind."

The girls felt ashamed of their behavior. This was the first group correction the "silver" band of postulants experienced. (The twenty five girls had been considered a particular sign of blessing to the one hundred and twenty-five year old community, and some referred to them as the "silver" group because of their number. The postulants took pride in both their large number and the fuss made over them.) Today, they keenly felt the disappointment they caused Sr. Humiliana, who exemplified kindness and edification at all times. Several of the girls lowered their eyes in a gesture of contrition.

Ginny was the first to speak. She stood. "Sister, we really didn't realize our conduct would embarrass the motherhouse sisters. We didn't intend to be so thoughtless. It just sort of happened."

"We're really sorry, Sister," Betsy added. The nodding of heads supported their spokesmen.

"Yes, I believe you are, but in the future, I hope I will *not* need to remind you that the college *is* separate from the postulancy. You all carry a full load of college classes and unavoidably must interact with the college girls; but to associate with them will only cause you to assume their lifestyles and not that of your religious calling. You have chosen to live a life far different from theirs."

There was a heavy silence throughout the room, and the postulants found Sister's message most effective. College girls were taboo, and that was definite.

Every weekday evening, after dishes and before night prayer, postulants went over to the college to clean blackboards, clap erasers, and empty wastebaskets. Several classrooms were assigned to each postulant. Judith, a postulant from Convent High in Albany, was busy doing her charge when a college girl entered the classroom. She was an attractive girl, obviously Italian. Joni Peroni introduced herself and asked Judith her name.

"I'm Judith McCabe, but I'm sorry. We aren't supposed to talk with the college girls."

"Yeah, I know. That's what they all say every time we try to get to know one of you guys. Are you girls being punished or something?" Joni asked in reference to the board-washing.

"No, that's silly. This is our charge. We're in training to be nuns and we have certain responsibilities. We also have rules, one of which is not to be speaking with you." Judith wanted to be polite, but the longer Joni persisted in having conversation the more anxious Judith became.

"Well, what about us college girls? Maybe we need to know you guys better. Maybe we need friends, too."

"Then be friends for each other," Judith answered. "There are more of you than there are of us. If you are going to stay here, I'm going to have to leave."

"Okay! Okay! But remember the name. It's Joni Peroni and I don't give up easily." Joni picked up a piece of chalk and sketched a daisy upon the newly cleaned blackboard, then left.

"Actually," Judith thought, "the flower's cute; I'll leave it."

Halloween was just around the corner and the upstate autumn foliage was spectacular. Sandra was especially delighted with all the color. "It just isn't like home in Hawaii. It's all so colorful here. Usually our trees are green unless they have flowers. What I'm really looking forward to is snow. I've never seen snow!"

Sandra and some of the others were walking over to geography class. Janie, the postulant from Syracuse, spoke, "Sandra, snow in Syracuse can get so high we can't see the first floor of houses. You cannot believe how much it can snow in New York. I'm not looking forward to it."

"Do you think nuns do Halloween?" Helen interrupted.

Arriving early to class, the girls noticed the classroom lights had not been turned on. They looked for the switches. When Ginny found them, Sandra quoted, "And then there was light."

The girls laughed and took their seats, waiting for their teacher, Sr. Venard, and the college girls. Often the college students would arrive one minute before class.

"What if Sr. Venard doesn't come? She's always here before now."

"Well, I'm told the college girls wait for ten minutes and then leave," Linda shared.

"I suggest we wait until you-know-what freezes over before we try that," added Betsy. Betsy was an older postulant from New Jersey and spoke more directly, more coarsely than the others. She was short and stocky. The first thing you noticed about her was her nose. It was Durante-sized.

"Don't worry, B.B. It would be more likely to have an earthquake than to see a nun miss teaching her class. I spent my life in Catholic schools and can't ever remember having a substitute, except for the lay teachers," Ginny commented.

"We're supposed to have films today. Maybe Venard couldn't get a projector." As she spoke the nun entered with two college girls pushing a cart with a loaded projector.

"I'm sorry to be late, girls." By now most of the class was present. "It will take only a few moments to get our film started."

Sister Venard enjoyed teaching geography. In fact, during the 1950's she had co-authored a geography book for children in Catholic and Christian grade schools. The book was no longer in print, as it quickly became outdated.

During today's film of distant cultures and people, Sandra nearly leapt from her desk with delight. "It's Fiji! I'm sure that's Fiji!" On the screen appeared a close-up of a dark-skinned native pulling in a fishing net. Theresa, another postulant from Convent High, whispered aloud, "Do you know him, Sandra?"

"Him? Fiji is an *island*, Terry, not a person. It's not all that far from Pago Pago, Samoa, where I was born."

"I thought you were from Hawaii."

"I am, but I was born in Samoa and just before high school my family moved to Hawaii."

"Oh, I see. Samoa's like a suburb."

"Terry, you *really* need this geography class!"

Terry teased back, "Wasn't me who tried to take a cab from New York City to Albany." The girls who could hear their whisperings smiled to think they both had scored that time.

· · · · · · · ·

10

There were a lot of meals scheduled in postulancy. The main meals were called breakfast, dinner, and supper. Mid-day meals between breakfast and dinner and between dinner and supper were called "lunch". Lunch usually consisted of a cup of milk (years later it would be coffee) served with leftover toast, rolls, and peanut butter and jelly.

When the girls came back from class that day, they looked forward to supper. As they entered the refectory they all took notice of a large painted sign taped to the wall: BEWARE! THE GREAT PUMPKIN IS COMING! They also noticed liver was being served.

Liver was not much of a favorite in this novitiate refectory except with Linda. It was something she and her father had in common. After eating her portion and a few others, she knew she couldn't eat all that was being passed to her by comrades. The postulants knew one of the convent's unwritten laws was to take something of everything and to clean one's plate. It was *not* fashionable in this setting to leave food uneaten.

Linda slid the extra slices of beef liver into a paper napkin and then safely into her pocket. Later she would flush it down the toilet, as there were few, if any, other means of disposal.

At table everyone was required to drink coffee in the morning and hot tea for dinner and supper. Often the novitiate received leftovers from the motherhouse sisters. Even when not very appetizing, very little food was ever returned to the kitchen. Usually, all that was necessary was to pass the serving dishes in clockwise fashion around the table a second time, and dishes would be emptied! Unless, of course, it was something like liver!

One evening, after the college classrooms had been cleaned, Judith decided to speak for a group of the postulants who felt there was not enough food served at meals. Sr. Humiliana was embarrassed by what seemed an accusation. Other members of the "silver band" were equally embarrassed because they didn't know anything of this formalized complaint. However, it was observed by all that food thereafter came in larger, more generous portions. Even so, every bit was eaten.

Most of the postulants had forgotten about Halloween, except for Helen who loved the holiday only slightly less than Christmas. The girls had given no thought to costumes or trick or treating. The day's schedule was as routine as any other, and the sign in the refectory warning of the GREAT PUMPKIN'S imminent arrival did not provoke much speculation.

Sr. Humiliana declared it was a good evening for a walk and directed the girls to take a partner and walk in pairs. The autumn air was just crisp enough to be delightful and the girls eagerly anticipated a walk in the spectacular autumn setting. They prepared by getting their black sweaters from their assigned cubby boxes. The cubby was much like a locker, only smaller and not locked. They were located in the postulate, and were used to store books and personal items.

Angie and Brigit teamed up and shared stories of childhood and family history as they walked among the crunching leaves. They also spoke of other things as they fell in step behind the others.

"I think I finally understand what all this is about," Angie said, as if receiving an insight.

"Angie," Brigit complained, "You're starting in the middle of a paragraph again. What are you talking about? You finally understand what?"

"The convent."

"You understand what it's all about?"

"Yes, I finally understand what they want of us."

Curious, Brigit awaited an explanation.

"We're here to become perfect."

"Impossible." Brigit would not agree. "Perfect is for God, not people."

"Yes, but remember Jesus said for us to be perfect, even as our Heavenly Father is perfect."

"But, I can't be. I don't even want to be. I'd be happy just to be good. How can we be perfect?"

"Brigit, I don't expect I can. We're just here to *strive* for perfection. That's what they're really after. They want us to *try* to be perfect."

"Maybe you're right, but I just don't see it that way. They have these rules to help us, but nothing could make us perfect."

After the group had walked several blocks they were led back to the courtyard and into the laundry door entrance. No one was suspicious, but this entrance seemed an unusual choice.

The postulants were about to discover the GREAT PUMPKIN had indeed arrived! The laundry was dark but the girls could see ghosts and goblins everywhere. Novices were covered with sheets, and some had their habits embellished with brooms and make-up to look like witches. These witches blindfolded the postulants one by one and led them into a darker, more foreboding hall.

"Here are the eyeballs. I plucked them from the dead buried in the graveyard," confessed one "witch" as Ginny's hand was plunged into a bag of peeled grapes.

"My brains spilled upon the road one night when I was killed in a car accident," said another novice as Angie's hand was placed in a pan of spaghetti.

More gruesome stories followed and there were shrieks of laughter and silliness everywhere. The postulants were delighted to see that these mysterious and more experienced religious people had a sense of humor. After the excitement of the haunted house, the lights were turned on. Polka dancing, seasonal refreshments, and decorations made the Halloween party even more delightful. It was not often that postulants and novices were allowed to have fun or even spend time together. Tonight was a memorable exception, and several of the postulants took the opportunity to be with the novices they most admired, most respected, or were most interested in knowing. Postulants thought these women, who had entered only one year before them, were so much more experienced, more wise, and certainly more holy.

· · · · · · · ·

11

In early November there was a bazaar held at Convent High School to benefit the cafeteria improvement fund. Much to everyone's surprise, Sr. Humiliana gave each of the postulants a dollar to spend. They were free to explore the bazaar on their own. Any money not spent was to be given back to Sister upon their return.

It was a wonderful opportunity for some of the Albany girls to see their families or have a brief reunion with their friends. The girls, each with their dollar in hand, scattered into twenty five different directions, to explore the booths. Phone calls, tasty treats, and other simple amusements beckoned the girls and no one wasted a minute. Each planned to spend every cent of her booty, except for Karen who planned to return as much of her dollar as possible, believing Sr. Humiliana might be impressed with her frugality. Karen always wanted to impress. She wanted approval very much. There was something deeply peculiar about Karen. By now several of the postulants recognized her troubled disposition.

The evening was a huge success for everyone. Ginny had ten cents left and decided to spend it at the fishing pond. After all, the money would benefit Convent High. Ginny never expected to land anything more than a trinket. There were two tugs from below. The fish had taken bait. Ginny wondered what goodie might be clipped to her fishing pole.

"Looks like I'm about to land a bargain," Ginny played along. This game was definitely for children, but Ginny was determined to spend the last of her fortune. The time for her to report back to the novitiate was approaching. "Oh my! Look at this!" Up came a plastic beetle. "I can *really* use this! Thanks ya'll!" Ginny stretched a bit to see if she could see the workers behind the sheet barrier. Up came a little nun about the size of Sr. Geraldine. She wasn't even five feet tall.

"You are obviously one of our postulants, but are you Virginia Crow from Pau Pau, West Virginia?" the pint-sized nun inquired.

Ginny was startled, "Yes, Sister, I am." She searched her memory to recognize the woman. Her tiny stature was a clue, and Ginny wondered loud, "Are you . . . Sr. Phoebe?"

"Yes!"

"I don't believe this! How could you possibly have recognized me? I haven't seen you since first grade!"

"Virginia, I have been waiting for you to join us for years."

Virginia was stunned by the discovery of Sr. Phoebe and stunned again by her comment. "Sister, could you leave the pond for a few moments? Could we visit?"

"Of course."

They found some of chairs nearby and sat down to talk.

"Sister, what do you mean, you have been *waiting* for me? That sounds almost like a Twilight Zone thing. How could you have known I would come to the convent? You taught me in first grade! I couldn't possibly have thought about it in first grade!"

"Virginia, there was just something about you. Don't you remember you wrote to me for several years?"

"Yes, and you were always so faithful about answering me. But we lost track of each other *years* ago."

"Even in the first grade I thought you might come to religious life! There was something so determined, so caring, so animated about you. Then I heard you had moved to Maryland and went to high school with the Sisters of St. Joseph. I assumed you would have chosen their order."

Actually, Ginny had seriously considered the Josephite community, but she wasn't as fond of their habit. She had several favorite nuns in high school but had been so steeped in Franciscan tradition during her elementary school years that she felt more attracted to the Franciscan charism.

"I still can't believe you are saying this to me."

"Virginia, I heard there was a girl by the name of Crow coming to community from Silver Spring and I thought it must be you. Meeting you here is quite a co-incidence. I teach first grade in Cold Springs now. I came up only to help with the bazaar for the weekend. How did you recognize me?"

"Well, Sister. Please don't think I mean anything disrespectful, but it was your size. I remember loving you in first grade because you were the only adult I could look in the eye. I thought you did it on purpose—be our size, I mean. All the other adults were so high up, but you were different. You were like one of us." They laughed.

"You are not the only former student to tell me that!" The pair continued their visit for the next ten minutes, but Ginny explained that she needed to return to the novitiate. It was such fun to talk and it eased Ginny's disappointment that she could neither call nor visit family or friends this evening as so many of the other girls had done. It would always be a mystery to Ginny how Sr. Phoebe could have seen a future nun in a first grader. Maybe she was just saying those things to be polite. She hugged the former teacher and said good-bye. They both felt excited about this surprise reunion after so many years.

Walking home, Ginny noticed Susan standing by a boy in the parking lot. Not thinking much of it, she called out to her, "Susan, we have to be back in five minutes. Better cut it short."

"Thanks, Ginny," Susan called back.

Just ahead were Helen and Brigit, savoring their last few minutes of freedom as they slowly meandered across the parking lot.

"Hey, wait for me, you two!" Ginny cried as she hurried to catch up.

"Did you notice where Susan was all evening?" Helen asked Ginny.

"No, where?"

"Sitting in the grotto, near the parking lot."

"You mean with that boy?"

Helen nodded.

"Does Humiliana know?"

"I don't think so. Some of us have been keeping an eye out for them. They even had their arms around each other for a while."

"Well, it isn't easy to say good-bye to a boyfriend, or family, or anyone, I guess," Ginny observed. "Some of us do it more easily than others. I just hope she doesn't get in trouble. Nuns around here seem not to miss much."

Once inside, and after checking in with Sr. Humiliana who was patiently awaiting the safe return of her twenty-five chickadees, the girls stopped into chapel for a private night prayer before going upstairs. More and more, postulants would choose to stretch their arms into the air for the duration of six Our Father's, six Hail Mary's, and six Glory Be's. They would then kiss the floor and silently retire to their cells. Slowly they were beginning to imitate the example of the novices.

By now postulants had learned to run the massive dishwasher, set tables, and help in the laundry. More and more they were helping the novices who did most of the domestic work.

Dishes were not to be stacked at table until after Sr. Geraldine rang the bell for silence. Anticipating the bell was another unwritten law and would result in a frown from the head of the table where Sr. Humiliana presided.

The industrial dishwasher was no place for slowpokes. It was a fast and furious pace with table settings for over two hundred people a day, three times a day. After meals everything had to be cleaned and prepared for the next meal. Motherhouse sisters, infirmary sisters, and the novitiate all had their own procedures.

Tables had to be reset in rank: Mother's table first and then the settings for her council members. This table was always given the best of everything. A cracked dish or a forgotten spoon or cup was cause for correction. Once mother's table was set, the others were done from oldest to youngest by profession.

Learning to fold sheets, starch veils, and iron chapel wash took weeks of training, but eventually the postulants would learn the exacting and methodical procedures that next year would become their responsibility as canonical novices.

November 13th was Sr. Humiliana's feast day. The postulants had planned to surprise her by singing a song before the start of her morning class. As Sister entered, the girls stood and sang to the tune of a Rice Krispies jingle, "Good morning, good morning. The best to you each morning! With a 'How are you and what is new?' Good morning just to you!"

Humiliana was very much taken aback. "What a delightful surprise! Thank you! I'm very well, and how are you?"

The girls were pleased to have surprised her. They felt particularly awakened by the zippy melody. After everyone was seated, Sister began the prayer for the canonization for Blessed Paul and then the usual prayer to the Holy Spirit.

"I have some important things to tell you this morning." The girls listened attentively to Sr. Humiliana. "It's a rather lengthy agenda."

"You will need to decide upon a group patron before the end of the week. Every group for almost the past ten years has placed itself under the protective care of a patron saint. You may also choose God the Father, the Son, or the Holy Spirit.

The canonical novices chose Blessed Paul Holdfelder and the constitutional novices are the "Holy Spirit" group. Several have chosen titles of Our Lady. You may choose any patron you like.

After you've had time to think about it, discuss it and pray over it, you can let me know what you'd like your group to be called. You are still twenty-five strong and it is amazing all of you are still with us. Last year, one of the girls left us the day after she entered! She said she joined on a dare."

The girls smiled at the idea. Sister continued.

"I understand some of you are keeping journals and diaries. I'm sorry. This is not permitted, and if you are doing this, you need to destroy them or give them to me as soon as possible. Also, I need to remind you that you may not socialize with novices or nurture friendships with them. They mean well, but because of their inexperience, they may easily lead you the wrong way."

Sister Humiliana may have been referring to Helen and Sr. Dorothy who worked in the laundry together and were often seen obviously enjoying each other's company. Postulants and novices knew it was an infraction of the rule, but they looked the other way.

"Each day you are responsible for saying your own stations of the cross privately in chapel. If you are late for community prayer or absent because of a college class or some other commitment, you must make up your prayers that same day before you retire." The girls felt uneasy over this particular reminder because many of them rushed through stations and often found reasons to justify not making up missed prayer. The postulant schedule was often demanding; most of the girls never experienced such structure before. It was fast-paced but also uniquely challenging.

"I have some good news for myself," Humiliana continued. "It has been voted upon by council to officially change my title from postulant mistress to postulant directress. I never liked that word because of the connotation it implies nowadays. I'm *not* your mistress." The postulants smiled. "Sr. Geraldine is no longer the novice mistress, but the novice directress."

"Also, I will need to know which of you are interested in nursing. Some of you will be asked to help in the infirmary after supper for about an hour. This experience will introduce you to some of the tasks involved in nursing care."

Ginny knew this was what she wanted. In truth, her innermost desire was to be a doctor, but she would have to be patient. There were no medical doctors in *this* community, but such a practice did exist in other religious communities. Ginny was young and willing to be patient. The thought of studying medicine was compelling. Ginny, Susan, Veronica, Barbara, and Kathleen all volunteered to help in the infirmary.

"Next week is Thanksgiving. During college recess we are scheduled to make a weekend retreat at Mt. Alvernia Retreat Center on Lake George." The Albany girls were familiar with the place and responded with enthusiasm. "I'm sure you will all enjoy the experience. For some of you, it may be your first retreat." Nodding heads confirmed Sister's suggestion. "The girls from Convent High make their senior year retreat there each year." Again there were more comments of affirmation as to its picturesque beauty.

"Father Jude will not be here for confessions this week, but he said if you need to see him, he is available in the college if you want to make an appointment."

Father Jude was a short and hyperactive man who seemed to need to move some part of his body at all times. He never seemed to hold still. Fr. Jude proved to be a good confessor for the postulants, who were still new to religious life. He was younger and more "with it" than his senior counterpart, Fr. Duffy.

The first time Fr. Jude heard the confessions of postulants, about two weeks after entrance, he gave them all the same penance: Pray the Magnificat. This separated the Catholic school products from the public school products as the public school products didn't have a clue as to what Father was asking.

Class was now over and the girls were dismissed to prepare for their various courses at Regina Catholic. The walk four or five flights up was not difficult, except for Karen, Caroline, and Betsy, who weighed more than the others.

As Brigit and Angie meandered behind the others, they paused at a window landing to talk. This behavior, too, was not to be encouraged. Brigit's cell on fifth floor was directly above Angie's on the fourth. The two devised a plan.

"Angie, if I need you, I'll take my mop handle and tap it on the floor three times. If you need me, hit your ceiling three times and we can meet at the stairway."

"Good idea. I like it. Come to my room for a minute, will you. I have something I want to show you." One led the other past a few opened curtains where daily dusting was in progress, girls were studying, or a few whispered conversations were now underway.

Angie opened a drawer and took out a photograph of her mother and father. "It was taken several weeks before I came to New York. I'm glad we can write to our families so often. It helps me to be able to assure them I'm happy here. I know they are worried."

Brigit respectfully admired the photograph, gave it back, and asked, "Are you still homesick, Angie?"

"I get better all the time. I really didn't expect to feel like this, but sometimes the loneliness comes. It helps to have a friend like you here."

Just then, Betsy walked by and poked her head into the half-opened curtain. "Angie, some of us were wondering why you flatten your pillow so much. It looks like you rest your head on a cardboard box."

Angie was offended by what Betsy considered a harmless question. She did not show her hurt feelings, and responded, "I just like it like that." Angie suspected the purpose of the interruption was to get Brigit's attention. Betsy liked Brigit, and it was apparent that they often sought each other's company. Abruptly as Betsy came, she left.

"I can tell you're not crazy about Betsy," Brigit said. "She's just a little more outspoken than most of us."

"Brige, I know she's your friend, but I think she's rude, crude, and socially unacceptable."

"She can be, but I like her and she is a friend." Angie could hear the defensiveness in of Brigit's voice and decided to change the subject.

"By the by, Brigit McGinnis, would you please remember to knock before you open my curtain. You almost caught me in a rather compromising position last Saturday morning while I was changing into my work dress.

"Sure, Angie. I'll ring the doorbell next time." She left smiling and headed for Betsy's cell only two curtains away.

On Friday afternoon, November 22nd, most of the girls were in class at Regina Catholic. A few were in their rooms working on school assignments. Linda was doodling in her notebook during British Literature, watching the clock as it was almost time for dismissal. A young woman entered the room and went to whisper something in Mr. Delgross's ear. His expression was one of great disbelief.

"Girls, I think we'll end class early. I've just received word that President Kennedy has been shot and killed in Dallas. You may want to go home and listen to the news."

The entire class seemed stunned by the announcement. At first, no one responded. Then one by one, postulants and college girls silently left the room. A few approached their teacher for more of an explanation but he admitted knowing nothing more than what the messenger had whispered to him.

In the postulancy, Sr. Humiliana had brought in a portable television and three or four of the girls were silently engaged in listening to news reports. Within the hour, all of the postulants were engulfed in the continuous coverage. Even the Canonical novices received permission to observe reports televised in their community room, though there were only periodic opportunities to watch.

For the next four days, the novitiate had been granted unprecedented consent to witness the televised funeral of the nation's first Catholic president. For many, John F. Kennedy was a hero, a martyr. All of these young women experienced a very private sadness as they witnessed history unfold together. Community prayers were frequently offered for the intention of Mrs. Kennedy and his children. Often there were tears, but somehow the girls didn't discuss the events of those four unique days in November. It was as if their sorrow was just too personal to express in conversation.

· · · · · · · ·

12

Morning breakfast was always eaten in silence unless it was Sunday or a special feast day. One Friday, the girls had noticed a novice kneeling on the floor at the breakfast table. They learned from Sr. Humiliana that it was a self-imposed penance for having broken grand silence. The postulants were invited by Sister to participate in this manner if they would like to, and many did.

On Friday afternoons excerpts from the community's Constitution were read aloud during most of the dinner meal.

The novice read hurriedly; perhaps she was nervous or just didn't prepare the reading ahead of time. She concluded with Article 13.

"Aspirants who are already over the age of thirty, illegitimate, or widows who have formally belonged to another religious institute are not to be admitted to the community unless the Mother General, for grave reasons and with the approval of her Council, has granted them a dispensation."

After the usual, "Do thou, O Lord, have mercy on us" and the response, "Thanks be to God", the bell was tapped, and conversation was underway once more.

The postulants were excited about Thanksgiving. After dinner they would leave for Mt. Alvernia Retreat Center. Having something special planned helped the girls not to dwell on thoughts of their families or family Thanksgivings past.

"Sister, if it snows, may we play in it? Terry said it looks like big white bugs." Sandra was fascinated with the concept of snow. She had seen it only upon distant mountains or volcano tops.

"Yes, there will be time for recreation, but mostly there will be prayer and conferences scheduled. We are all expected to help clean while there—do dishes and anything else Sr. Kunigunda needs." Sr. Kunigunda directed the retreat center. She had been the superior since the center began.

"Theresa, why would you tell Sandra snow looks like an insect?" Humiliana's eyes smiled as she sternly addressed the Convent High postulant.

"Ahhchoo!" sneezed Susan.

"Gesundheit!" Ginny responded.

"Are you German, Ginny?" Sr. Humiliana mused.

"No, Sister." Ginny did not understand the nature of Sister's question, and then she did. "I meant to say, 'God bless you,'" correcting herself.

Sr. Humiliana smiled and conversation continued but more constrained and restrained at the head table than further down where the girls were discussing the Constitutional reading for the day.

"Do you believe that? A girl can't be a nun unless she has a married mother and father." Sally sounded a bit indignant, but not too forceful, for fear of drawing too much attention to her protest.

"Doesn't seem fair to punish a kid because her parents didn't marry," Helen agreed.

"I wonder if that stuff still goes on," Kathleen added.

"What stuff? Illegitimate kids?" asked Helen.

"No, Silly. Keeping aspirants out of the convent because they are one," she explained.

"Are aspirants the same as postulants?" Angie inquired. Public school girls often needed clarifications.

"Yes," offered Helen. "Kathleen, I haven't the slightest idea if they do or don't. What I want to know is why are the kids called 'illegitimate'. They didn't do anything wrong."

"Well, they didn't ask for my parents' marriage license when I entered. Did they ask you?" Kathleen directed her question to Sally, who had raised the issue.

"No, but if they did, I would have told them it was none of their business."

"Sure, and you wouldn't be here today either."

"Maybe that's so, but I'm telling you, the longer I stay, the weirder this place gets."

"Funny, I would think you'd be at home with anything 'weird'", Betsy interrupted, always listening and willing to comment upon any topic of interest, even when not invited.

"Betsy, why don't you put that bass viol of yours some place where the sun doesn't shine!" Sally's suggestion was noticeably out of character, but like so many of the girls she did not appreciate or understand Betsy's sense of humor. Betsy often showed a total insensitivity to the feelings of others. Betsy didn't care how people interpreted what she said. She spoke her mind, no matter what. That was unusual among the twenty-five.

"If I did, Sally, you'd miss the talent I have. Admit it, you're just jealous."

"I think not."

The bell rang and dishes were stacked once more. After dinner, Linda was excused for an appointment at the college. She was to speak with Sr. Imelda concerning the psychological tests the postulants had taken.

"I'm glad you could come, Linda. This won't take us very long, I'm sure. How is your postulancy coming along?" Sr. Imelda was very gentle and assuring. Linda took a seat across from her large, impressive desk.

"I like it very much, Sister. I didn't know becoming a nun could be so much fun, actually. I like it all—the college, my group, and especially Sr. Humiliana. I think I'm very happy."

"Well, dear, your psychological test results seem to indicate you might have been upset about something. Maybe a little depression, or homesickness?"

"I'm not sure, Sister."

"It wasn't anything alarming. I asked Sr. Humiliana if I could see how you were adjusting and she agreed."

"Well, Sister. At first, I missed my family a lot. Maybe that was my problem. I have this friend Richard who lives in the duplex above ours, and I think maybe I'm missing being around him. He has a job cleaning tables at Sienna College. He studies there."

"Is he a boyfriend?" Sister asked.

"Not exactly. He's more like a boy who is my friend. He's actually my best friend."

"Do you notice yourself doing anything unusual in the convent like rearranging things or feeling very tired?" Sister Imelda's questioning sounded a little like her exam.

"No, Sister. In fact, we haven't all that much *to* rearrange. We aren't allowed to change furniture around, or to move it, unless to clean." Then Linda remembered something!

"Sr. Humiliana suggested we put out our clean underwear and stockings for the next day before we retire. I thought it was a good idea, but I've actually never been so organized."

"You mean like always putting your shoes always in the same place, and so on?"

"Exactly."

"Well, Linda, that's a good sign. We all do that sort of thing in community. Is there anything else you'd like to share?"

Linda hesitated. She wasn't sure if she should bring this up, but decided to. "I have nightmares, Sister. I wake up in the middle of the night and think there's something evil lurking outside my curtain. Isn't that silly? I had nightmares at home too, but they seem more frequent here."

"I see."

"Well, actually, I've always liked sci-fi and all those weird monsters—vampires, Frankenstein, werewolves, mummies, the blob, and all that. My brother Larry and I both loved watching horror films."

"Well then, Linda, don't you think maybe some of these bad dreams might be your mind playing the movies back for you at night when your mind is free to unwind and relax?"

Linda liked Sr. Imelda's suggestion. It made sense. "You know, Sister, that sounds very possible." Linda had a warm feeling towards her interviewer. Their conversation continued a short while longer and then Sr. Imelda suggested she come back again and visit sometime.

"I'd love to, Sister. Maybe in a few weeks?"

"Just check with Sr. Humiliana. She knows how to be in touch with me. God bless you, dear."

"Thank you, Sister."

. . . .

13

Mt. Alvernia Retreat Center is a spacious retreat center for women of the diocese of Albany. It enjoys an impressive heritage. It was once a summer home for the Theodore Roosevelt family and then was sold to a millionaire, Joseph Entenmann, who made a fortune selling Dutch pastries.

Mr. Entenmann bequeathed his large estate to his only daughter, who had entered the Franciscan Sisters of Albany.

At first it was used as an extension of the motherhouse complex, housing the Mother General, her staff, and other administrative offices. Later, upon the request of the Bishop, it became the first and only retreat center for women in the diocese and was placed under the direction of the good sisters. The house was named for the sacred place where St. Francis of Assisi loved to pray and where he received the stigmata, the wounds of Jesus's crucifixion. St. Francis bore these marks for the final two years of his life.

Mt. Alvernia, located on the shore of Lake George, rests among the scenic splendor of other large mansions. It is near a nineteenth century hamlet nestled along the south shore of Lake George. Cottages, likewise, dot the historic shorelines. The combination of water, sky, flora, and low mountains gives the Retreat Center a distinctive natural beauty.

There was an excitement in the air as the girls arrived at Mt. Alvernia. Parents of some of the local girls were given permission to help transport the St. Jude group (the girls had chosen St. Jude as their group patron, "saint of the impossible") to their first official experience in retreating. Suitcases were unloaded and the retreat would soon be underway.

The first hour was spent exploring the four levels of architectural and natural grandeur. The first-time visitors were in awe of the entrance staircase, spacious living rooms, and the breathtaking panoramic view from the balcony which faced a lake covering a cold blue-green lake. The boathouse and bathhouse were also investigated. Assigned rooms were settled into and all looked forward to opening conference in chapel at 7:00 P.M. sharp.

The retreat master was Fr. Danforth, a pastor from an Albany parish. His sense of humor kept the postulants entertained as they feverishly took notes on his reflections of religious life. The man appeared genuine and sincere, and most of the girls were attentive while gleaning something from his efforts.

"You are not taking on an ordinary lifestyle. No, God is calling you to look for holiness above all else. Living the vows of chastity, poverty, and obedience is not something all are called to do. After all, someone has to get married, or where would we get our nuns and priests?" A few laughs were politely elicited from his captive audience.

"Now, it's all in how you ask. For example, when I was in novitiate, I asked if I could smoke while I was praying outside in the meditation garden and got a `no'. *Then* I learned to ask if I could pray during my smoking break and got a `yes'.

"However, my dear postulants, if they say to plant the head of cabbage upside down in the garden, then plant it upside down! Don't ask questions. Just do it. Blind obedience is not blind. It is trusting the judgement of your superiors who have God-given authority to know what is best for you."

"Don't be discouraged. We all pass through moments of doubt. If you are not sure you are doing the right thing, then ask the Blessed Mother for counsel. She is your mother and will never turn her children in need away from a hearing."

"Don't expect to get everything you ask for. Sometimes God's answer is `no', and you need to find your happiness in accepting God's will for you."

After the opening conference, there was benediction. Incense filled the little chapel. Night prayers were said privately, and individuals drifted off to their rooms for spiritual reading or to prepare an early retirement.

Angie remained in chapel and sat in the dark watching a few candles flicker and wondering if this was right for her. "Do I really want to be a nun?" "Yes, you know you do," her inner voice replied. "But, am I good enough? Am I worthy to be a nun?"

There were doubts. "Why are you losing your confidence, Angie? What's happening to you? Father said to ask the Blessed Mother for help. She is everyone's mother."

Even in the dark Angie could see the statue of Our Lady of Grace. Angie got up from her bench and knelt at the altar rail. She looked up and saw the open hands of the statue before her. Angie had just finished reading the story of St. Catherine Laboure. She learned how the visionary received a miraculous medal from the Blessed Mother during an 1830 apparition in Paris, France. The Mother of God had opened her hands for light to fall upon the image of the earth below and explained to St. Catherine that the light was a symbol of grace given to all on earth who asked for help. St. Catherine was directed by the Lady to have a medal made with her portrayed image and to tell others, "Wear it around your neck with confidence in me." This was the story of the Miraculous Medal.

Angie decided to open her own hands extending them in a gesture of acceptance. She prayed for the grace she would need to be a nun for the greater honor and glory of God. And she prayed for God to take from Angie's own hands the offering of each day, the gift of her own life.

Angie prayed in this position for almost fifteen minutes before going upstairs to her room. Before she left chapel, she had a great sense of peace and felt very much loved. Whenever Angie would leave chapel, she would whisper inwardly to the Eucharistic presence of Christ, "Come with me."

She walked up the stairs, opened her cell-room door, and noticed a little badge lying upon her pillow. It lay next to her crucifix. This, too, was a custom of the sisters: to place the crucifix upon the bed pillow each morning, as did St. Theresa of Lisieux.

Sr. Humiliana had told the girls a story about St. Theresa taking the crucifix from the wall each morning, placing it upon her pillow, and saying, "You have kept vigil over me all night. Now you rest and I shall serve your love to those about me."

Angie expected to see the crucifix, but not the little blue badge. On one side was an image of Mary and, on the other, the words, "My Mother, My Confidence. 300 days indulgence."

Angie's eyes began to moisten. She had asked the Mother of God for confidence, and here upon her pillow, she found a prayer to give her exactly that. But who could have done this? Who placed it there?

Weeks later she learned that Barbara had left the medallion. It had been only a simple gesture, and Barbara could not claim any thing special or insightful about it. She did not mention it to Angie until much later.

For years, Angie would carry or wear the round-framed image. When it became shabby, she kept it safely tucked in her Bible. The four short words of prayer would be said throughout her lifetime, particularly when she felt a lack of confidence or self-worth. She asked Our Lady to be *her* confidence when she felt she had none of her own. This was a profound and very personal religious experience for the eighteen-year-old. Angie was convinced that, though Barbara had placed the religious object in her room that night, Our Lady herself had directed her to do so. Having opened her hands to grace, Angie received an answer to her prayer.

By the second day of unaccustomed silence, the youngsters began to show signs of wear. Except for Mass, community prayer, and conference, there was no talking. Of course, not everyone complied with the rule, but most at least tried. The only other experience they had with a day of silence was the first Sunday of each month. On this day, retreat and recollection was expected at the motherhouse. The girls were scheduled to adore an hour; that is, to kneel or sit before the Exposition of the Blessed Sacrament in prayerful silence. They were also expected to keep a spirit of silence all day, be present for an afternoon conference with Fr. Duffy, and attend benediction at the end of day. Invariably, carrots, radishes, and celery were served on retreat Sundays, much to the chagrin of those seated in silence around the table. The sound of crunching vegetables kept many from thinking about anything else.

So, the postulants *did* know about retreats and *did* have some experience of keeping silence before Mt. Alvernia. But that was for one day at a time. At Mt. Alvernia, the expectation was for almost three whole days of silence. It wasn't so easy a task for girls who came from active, talkative, and busy lives.

Unfortunately, this evening at supper, carrots, celery, and radishes were served. Sandra could not suppress her amusement at the crunching sound which echoed about the dining room. Giggles were contagiously spreading throughout the tables. Sr. Humiliana realized she must take action. She stood and walked over to the table where most of the girls on the verge of uncontrollable silliness were sitting. She just stood there.

Everyone, awaiting some sort of admonition, continued to eat. They did not dare to look up for fear of meeting Sister's disapproving blue eyes. Somehow, not saying anything had been the remedy. Just standing there was sufficient. Almost miraculously the postulants regained composure, and Sister returned to her place at table. Retreats are interesting experiences for young and old, and at times, they are meaningful; but it can be a lot of work to exercise self-control and silence an active mind.

. . . .

14

In early December everyone realized that the day after Christmas was to be the postulants' first official visiting day. Even some of the New Jersey parents would be driving to Albany for the occasion. The girls from further away were asked to mingle with the local families and enjoy the holiday visitors as much as possible. A collect phone call home would be the "Christmas gift" for those postulants too far from home to see family or friends.

The girls were all busy making plans to write a song for Sister Humiliana and prepare a Christmas play to entertain the novices. The group had divided into songwriters, playwrights, actresses, and stagehands. Ginny, being the oldest in rank, organized the group, and Marylou, the undisputed leader of music, led the songwriters. Marylou played guitar by ear, had a very sweet voice, and lots of creative ideas. Brigit, Judith, Betsy, and Marsha were her committee.

Angie was selected to create a play with dialogue. She decided to base her play on the story of *The Littlest Angel*, a personal Christmas favorite. A harmony of purpose developed among the postulants.

Later in the evening, during recreation, while the girls carried on "secret conversations" of their plans for Christmas, Ginny and several other girls returned from their volunteer work in the infirmary. Ginny was disappointed when she found out how much fun she had missed. Sr. Humiliana had given the girls permission to play some favorite records, including "Peppermint Twist". By now, the music had been put away. Some of the girls had retired to their rooms to prepare for semester exams.

"I would love to have been here for that! I think the twist is the greatest thing ever invented!" Ginny exclaimed.

"I'm sure the back doctors think so too," added Sr. Humiliana.

"You should have seen Carol Barrel out there. What a riot! Can she ever dance!"

"It was a riot!" said Linda.

"Actually, it appears to be good exercise for those with extra weight," Humiliana remarked in Betsy's direction. Sister was not so stuffy that she wouldn't tease, as long as she thought it would not offend, and Betsy seemed impervious to criticism. (Perhaps that's why she felt so comfortable giving it.)

"Well, I don't think I would have had the energy for twisting. I'm not sorry I missed the dance or whatever," Sue offered.

"Is it hard work up there?" Linda asked, referring to the infirmary routines. Linda considered Sue a natural leader and a hard worker. The two often enjoyed conversation and walks together. The group of twenty-five was large, and with so many responsibilities, there wasn't much opportunity or time to get to know others all that well. Recreation now consisted of only a half hour in the evening, and it was the only time in the day when they were all together. Several nights a week the infirmary helpers were late, but they rarely missed the group's entire recreation as they did that particular evening.

Sue answered Linda's question. "No, the work's not hard. There is just lots of it. We had two nuns to bathe, and one of them decided to go back to chapel. When we finally found her, we were almost twenty minutes behind schedule. She was sitting up in front where it was dark. The first time I checked there, I just didn't see her."

All of the postulants enjoyed occasional visits to the infirmary arranged by Sr. Humiliana. Postulants were not free to go on their own, but when they did go, it was always an impressionable visit.

"Is everything ready?" Sister asked Sue.

"Yes, Sister," she answered.

Linda assumed their conversation was still about the infirmary and decided it was time for her to excuse herself. Exams loomed before her. The logic course was to become her downfall. Mrs. Agonito was a terrific lady and teacher, but truthfully, Linda didn't have a clue as to what "logic" was, and why Plato would be so concerned about shadows. What did P have to do with Q?

"Good night, everyone," Linda said, excusing herself as she headed for a short night prayer in chapel.

"Good-bye, Linda," Sue replied.

The next morning, as Sr. Humiliana was about to begin class, several girls had already noticed that Susan was not at her assigned desk. Some assumed she was having another bout with the flu, as she had had several weeks ago.

After prayer Sister began by announcing, "Susan will not be with us today because she has decided to return home." All eyes focused upon Sr. Humiliana. There were many looks of surprise and disbelief. "Every girl has this choice to stay or leave, and no one should be judged unkindly for their choice to leave us." Thoughts of concern filled the minds of those who had learned to respect and enjoy Susan as a friend. Others thought of that magic number—"twenty-five". This was a jubilee year for the community; God had bestowed the "silver set" of twenty-five wonderful vocations upon them. What now? They were only twenty-four. Two dozen? From "silver" to "eggs"? It seemed a let-down.

Shocked, as many of the postulants may have been, they realized it was only a matter of time before the first of them would leave. It was inevitable.

"I don't want this announcement to affect your exams this week. Susan's decision to leave has to be respected. She wants to thank you for your friendship and asked me to give you her love."

No one discussed Susan's departure, unless perhaps in very private circles. Sr. Humiliana would never mention Susan's name again before the group. Linda felt hurt that Sue had not mentioned a word before going. Last night, when Sue said "good-by" instead of "good night", Linda noticed the choice of words but did not read any significance into it. How could she be gone? How could she not have explained her decision to leave? Linda was surprised by her feelings of disappointment. She felt . . . cheated.

Linda considered asking Ginny, who worked closely with Sue in the infirmary, if she knew anything. She then decided Sue should have the privacy she wanted. Linda would not inquire about or mention Susan's leaving again until late spring.

The group's image of itself was never quite the same after the first girl left. There would always be some shocking aftermath, some degree of surprise, to learn of subsequent departures.

· · · · · · · ·

15

Christmas meant a lot of cleaning. Actually, the novices were the ones busied in every nook and cranny of the novitiate, the motherhouse, the motherhouse chapel, dining rooms, kitchen, and corridors. Christmas was the time for stripping, washing, waxing, and buffing the linoleum and wood floors.

Choir practice required extra hours and Sr. Helena demanded masterful performance. She had a pianist to assist her. She was a mysterious assistant who was never seen anywhere but before the piano or church organ. At the drop of Sr. Helena's hand, a pitch or introduction would sound. It was as if Helena turned her assistant on with a switch.

For Christmas, all of the novitiate was expected to participate in the preparation of carols and hymns. Schola, the selected few, were chosen to perform solo parts during midnight Mass.

Helena was gruff and exacting. She waved her arms so madly while directing that singers close by were on guard. Sheets of music occasionally were knocked from a novice's hand or accidently struck by Sister's wild flailing. Helena may have been overly dramatic, but she was also accomplished in the quality of music produced under her direction.

Still, novices and postulants feared Sr. Helena. They knew every mistake would be followed by public humiliation, berating, and embarrassing remarks. If a note somehow soured, Sister would glare with intent to kill; if a choir member squeaked boards while moving in her choir loft, she would be scolded. Laughter was permitted only when Helena made the joke. Ginny always wondered what could make a nun appear to be so miserable. She thought it strange that Helena seemed to take a great deal of pleasure in the humiliation of another, as if this were her avocation or "second calling".

Angie was disappointed that her voice had not been chosen for the elite schola choir, especially since she had been a vocalist in her high school operettas. On the other hand, she was grateful she did not have the extra practice sessions with Sr. Helena.

The first Christmas Eve in the convent the postulants went to bed without evening recreation. They were to sleep for several hours and then get up in time for midnight Mass. The choir lined up in the cloister outside of chapel. Most were unsure what their first Christmas would be like, even with procession rehearsals and all. As the experience unfolded, it proved to be touching and memorable.

Kathleen had the privilege of placing the ceramic infant into the manger because she was the youngest in rank. Traditionally the "baby" did this each Christmas.

For some reason, Ginny's stomach decided to spend a good deal of the evening Mass growling. Ginny hoped the gurgling would go undetected by Sr. Helena, but several disapproving glances assured her otherwise. The digestive track accompaniment was not unnoticed, nor was it appreciated.

After Mass the girls returned to the refectory for hot chocolate and sweet bread. It was particularly special being allowed to break grand silence. Postulants would have special permission to speak to the novices on Christmas Day, and they looked forward to this. By now, it was apparent that Sr. Dorothy and Helen were becoming best friends, but no one spoke openly of it. The postulants also looked forward to sharing their Christmas skit, and visiting with family and friends the day after Christmas.

On Christmas morning everyone was delighted with a festive breakfast. The postulants did not expect to be taken to the classroom but, once there, they were greatly surprised to see their assigned desks stacked with mail and gifts.

Sr. Humiliana had withheld, for several weeks, many Christmas cards and packages from the unsuspecting recipients. This added a great deal to the celebration of Christmas. For the next hour the girls shared excerpts of mail and opened gifts together.

Angie opened candy-grams from her Ohio pals, Diane and Sue. She was deeply moved by the loving messages from home. Everyone bubbled with excitement at the evidence of affection before them. Sr. Humiliana collected all the edible gifts. They would be used for community recreation. No one questioned this practice; by now they understood that all gifts became community property. Another "unwritten law".

The rest of Christmas Day was every bit as eventful. The Littlest Angel production was a smashing success. The novices and visiting sisters were delighted. It was apparent that the St. Jude group had commendable talent.

The group would never disband before being dismissed by Sr. Geraldine's "Pax et Bonum". This was a Franciscan custom, a Latin phrase wishing another "peace and goodness." Ginny could tell that Sr. Geraldine was looking to close the novitiate gathering and decided now was the time for her announcement.

"Sisters, it is my great honor at this time to speak on behalf of our postulancy, two dozen strong," she began.

"Get on with it," Betsy whispered from the right, thinking Ginny long-winded and discursive. Ginny ignored the comment.

"Sr. Humiliana, it is difficult for us to find something to give you for Christmas. We decided to compose a song and dedicate it to you." Sister looked pleased; all present were eager to hear more.

"We have known few people with the patience, gentleness, and humility you exemplify each day. We could not be more fortunate, or more blessed, to have such a wonderful example before us. We love you, Mum, I mean, Sr. Humiliana."

"Oh, my God," whispered Betsy, "How could you be so stupid?"

For a moment there was total silence. Ginny immediately recognized the faux-pas; she had spoken Sister's nickname, Mumliana. "Mum" was because she was "like a mother" to them. There was no disrespect intended, and Sr. Humiliana knew Ginny well enough to understand. Sister smiled, a sign for the others to laugh and to tease Ginny. Ginny continued, a bit more flustered.

"Well, you know our community greeting of "Pax et Bonum". You have taught us to greet another with wishes of peace and goodness. You are "pax et bonum" for us, and so we composed this song for you this Christmas, 1963."

The postulants arranged themselves and sang a lovely melody:

> Pax et Bonum, dwell within these walls:
> Peace and Goodness, endless love for all.
> We strive to reach the Lord our God,
> And live St. Francis' rule.
> In him, may we learn, to do our Father's will.

It was a short tune, but the harmony and melody were so well arranged that the sweetness of its sound brought tears to Sr. Humiliana. No one clapped, though the novices wanted to express their pleasure. The song sounded like a prayer, a hymn. It did not seem appropriate to clap. The silent response spoke well of their gift. "Pax et Bonum" became the new way of dismissing novitiate programs or special gatherings.

In years to come, "Pax et Bonum" would be a community favorite. Few ever knew it was written for Sr. Humiliana as a Christmas gift. It was just another popular tune among the sisters.

The following day was for family and friends. It proved to be just as joyous as Christmas Day had been. There were guitars, refreshments, and circles of family visitors in every parlor. Again, postulants from out of state, or far from home were enthusiastically adopted by local families. New Jersey visitors brought "tek-a-boost", cola with no carbonation, which was a local favorite. There were boxes of fruit and candy treats everywhere! Long distance phone calls that evening added to the spirit of joy among the group.

Angie spoke with her mother, assuring her everything was fine. It was difficult when her father asked, "Are you coming home, Angie? Haven't you had enough of it?" Angie did not want to hurt her father. It was difficult not to have his "blessing" in this pursuit. She teased back, "Dad, I know Sandusky will never be the same without me, but I'll be home sometime this year, I think. Fear not, you'll *never* be rid of me!" But secretly, Angie realized the phone call made her miss home all the more. It was as wonderful as it had been difficult.

All in all, the girls' holiday experiences were joyful and memorable.

. . . .

16

In January, Brigit brought a copy of *The Little Prince* for Angie to read. When she arrived at the doorway, Brigit opened the curtain and began to explain the purpose of her visit, but instead was greeted by a half-clothed resident.

"Oh, Anj! I'm so sorry!" Both girls seemed equally embarrassed. Modesty was to be expected at all times. In fact, girls were never to be seen in nightgowns without their bathrobes and headcloths. Angie was mortified but couldn't do anything except admonish her friend.

"Serves you right, you clod. I told you to knock before you opened my curtain." Angie grabbed the first thing she could find to cover her chest. "I'll be with you in a minute." Soon, Brigit was invited in.

"Gee, Angie. I really am sorry. I guess I've finally learned to knock!"

"Don't worry about it. What do you have there?"

"It's a book I've been wanting to loan you."

"Oh, really? I like the size of it," referring to the easy reader.

"It's one of my favorite stories. It says a lot about friendship. You see, Angie, sometimes, I think you are taming me."

Angie had no idea what Brigit meant about being tamed, but she didn't have a chance to ask because suddenly there was shouting and a ruckus coming from the other end of the hall. Angie and Brigit both rushed down to Marsha's room.

"I can't take it. I just can't take it another day!" Marylou was yelling at Marsha. She was obviously distressed.

"What is it with you guys?" asked Brigit as they came upon the opened curtain.

Marsha welcomed some assistance. "Marylou wants to leave," Marsha explained. "She wants to leave *now*."

"Sister Humiliana is gone for the afternoon, Marylou. Can't you wait and talk with her when she gets back?" suggested Angie. Brigit excused herself, thinking maybe she should find Ginny, the oldest.

"I can't wait! I'm suffocating in this place! I just can't take it!" Marylou shouted.

Angie sat behind Marylou in chapel and noticed how unpleasant her feet smelled. Until now, she didn't think anything of her body odor and greasy hair. They were probably signs of stress.

"Look, Marylou, what difference will a few hours make?" Angie tried to rationalize and calm Marsha's talented friend.

"That's what I've been trying to tell her," Marsha added.

Just then, Marylou grabbed her guitar. She must have come to Marsha's room with it. She pushed past Angie, still in the doorway, and ran frantically down the corridor.

"Stop her, Betsy!" Angie shouted, when Betsy, too, stepped out of her room to see about the loud voices.

"Is something wrong with her?" Betsy asked. But it was too late. Marylou stepped on the elevator and was gone.

Angie decided to follow on the stairs. She pursued Marylou who had run outdoors, guitar still in hand, with no sweater or jacket. It was a freezing January day. Snow was blowing into a blizzard of sorts. Angie had paused only long enough to tell Ginny to get Sr. Geraldine and explain that Marylou was freaking out and to get some help.

Angie thought it best to follow Marylou, and so she stepped out into the cold winter day. Marsha followed. Convent High was dismissing school and college students were also walking about. It looked a peculiar sight to see Marylou, then Angie, then Marsha, all running from the novitiate without coats. It must have looked like a "busting out" to passerbys. Angie could not be concerned with appearances just now.

Several blocks away, Angie lost sight of Marylou. Where could she have gone? It was so cold. Angie began to worry about leaving the novitiate without permission. Marsha had given up the chase not even a block from the convent.

As she began her return trip, Angie recognized Marylou in a phone booth across the street. She approached her.

"Who are you talking to, Marylou?" Angie asked.

"My mom."

"Good. Could I say something to her?" There was a pause.

"Yeah. Okay. Mom, Angie wants to say something. She must have followed me." There was another pause. Marylou gave the phone to Angie.

"Mrs. Adams? This is Angela Masucci, and I really don't understand what is happening, but Marylou wants to leave the convent. I'm sure that won't be a problem, but could you ask her to come back to the novitiate for just a little while? Something can be done, but it should be done some other way than just running out here in the snow."

By now, a car driven by a novice, with Sr. Geraldine in the back seat, pulled up to the curb. Sr. Geraldine lowered the window and spoke firmly.

"Angela, please get in the front seat."

Angela excused herself from Marylou's mother explaining, "Sr. Geraldine is here. I'm sure someone will be calling you soon." Angela hung up the phone.

"Marylou. You. In the back seat." Both girls responded almost immediately to Geraldine's directive. The drive back to the novitiate was accomplished in complete silence. Upon arriving, Sr. Geraldine spoke.

"Angela, you may return to the postulate. I'll take care of Marylou now." Sr. Geraldine sounded rather matter-of-fact. Angie obeyed and found Betsy, Marsha, Brigit, Ginny, and some others waiting for an explanation. Angela had none, just a report of what had happened at the phone booth.

By evening, Marylou was gone. Her trunk was packed and her parents came for her. There were no good-byes, and no one spoke any further of the winter day runaway. It just became another mystery for them to wonder about. All the convent seemed a mystery to these young, impressionable women.

The air of mystery stirred their imaginings. They shared rumors of dead nuns buried in the dark recesses of the motherhouse basement. Other postulants joked that the underground tunnels connecting the college, novitiate, Convent High and the motherhouse were for quick, undetected escapes. They were all silly imaginings of young women in a world surrounded by unspoken secrets and strange, new experiences.

. . . .

17

In early February, Linda felt a need to talk with Sr. Imelda again. She asked for and received the necessary permission from Sr. Humiliana.

"Welcome, Linda! I'm glad to see you again. It has been a long time since our last visit." Even though Linda would frequently see Sr. Imelda in motherhouse corridors, the refectory, or other places about the convent, they would never engage in any dialogue. "Pax et bonum" was the only acceptable exchange.

Sister Imelda opened her office door and greeted Linda warmly with a soothing voice. Both took a position in chairs near Sister's formidable desk.

"It's nice to see you too, Sister. I'm sorry I couldn't get back before this, but we carry a full load of courses at Regina, and it seems as if we spend every available minute on school work."

"Think nothing of it. I hope you understand why I have not been in touch with you and why I don't converse when we meet at the motherhouse."

"I think I do, Sister," Linda answered, but she really did not understand. Sr. Imelda was both community psychologist and vicar to the Mother General, Mother Victoria. Linda was puzzled by Sr. Imelda's cool behavior when they met in passing, acting as would a distant, uncaring stranger. Yet, here, in the office, she seemed so different. The inconsistency was probably the result of rules.

"You see, Linda, in my position, I must be very concerned with good example. Here in my office, we have both privacy and permission to speak. I could not be comfortable speaking with you any other way. By now you must be fully aware of the regulations forbidding professed sisters any contact with members of the novitiate."

"Yes, Sister, I am. We are to greet others with "Pax et bonum", then step to the side, allowing them to pass first."

The postulants had been directed to avoid all contact with the "professed", with novices, college girls, and all others. Some of the girls complied with the regulations; others chose to stretch the rule. Linda was one who tried to conform to the expectations whether she understood them or not.

"Sister, I've asked to see you because I think I may need your help."

"What can I do for you, Linda?"

"I'm not sure if I should get invested in June with the other postulants."

"Why do you say that?" Imelda sensed Linda's concern.

"I don't think I can do it for the wrong reason," she continued.

"Well, then, what was the reason you came to us?" Sister gently prodded.

"Sister, you know how the first Sunday of each month is retreat Sunday, and how they pass around those monthly practices?" Linda was referring to the custom of passing a jar of papers around the breakfast table. Each paper had "a patron for the month, a virtue to practice, and a prayer to say for some specific intention." For example: "January 25th, the Conversion of St. Paul. Practice humility. Say two Our Fathers each day for the Sisters of our infirmary."

"Well, several months ago, I received the virtue, "purity of intention". I didn't know what it meant. I asked Sr. Humiliana and she told me it meant that it is important to do things for the right reasons."

"Yes, go on," Sister encouraged.

"I want to be honest about this, Sister. I think I want to be a nun for the wrong reason."

"Why are you saying this?"

"Because I feel guilty. That may be why I'm here."

"Guilty about what?"

"When I was in high school, my grandmother died because I forgot to give my mother a message. Maa, that's what we called our grandmother. Well, she called home one day, then later she had a heart attack."

"Linda, that doesn't make any sense. What did the phone call have to do with the heart attack? How could you possibly feel responsible?"

"Well, she called and said she wanted to talk to my mother or father. I told her they were both out and didn't expect them back for at least another hour. She said to have them call as soon as they returned. It was important."

"Yes, and then what?"

"Sister," Linda fought back tears and felt heat all over her body. "I forgot to leave a message for my parents because some of my friends stopped by just then and asked me out to the A & W Root Beer Drive In. We always would "hang out" there." Linda had to stop her story and received a much appreciated tissue from Sr. Imelda.

"When I got home that evening, my brother Larry told me Maa had died. I couldn't believe it, Sister. I had talked with her only a few hours before. I asked Larry, 'How did it happen?'. He said it was a heart attack."

"Mom had decided on her own to give Maa a call when she and dad got home. They were worried when Maa didn't answer the phone and decided to drive over. It was only about ten minutes away. They found her dead on the floor, not far from the phone."

"Oh, Sister! Why didn't I remember to leave a message for my parents? How could I just go off with my friends and not leave a note? I didn't even ask her if there was something I could do, or even what was wrong! How could I have been so stupid and selfish?" Linda blew her nose and looked to Sr. Imelda for answers.

"How old was your grandmother, Linda?"

"Eighty-six."

"And you don't think maybe it was time for Maa to give up the trials of this world?"

"Sister, it is true that eighty-six might be up in years, but you don't understand. If I had left a message, or even asked Maa what was important, Maa would be alive this very day."

"Linda, you don't understand. When death comes, it comes. Even if your parents were home when she called, they may not have prevented her death. She could have called the hospital, a neighbor, anyone. It was not your fault. You must not blame yourself for what you could not control."

"My parents assured me of the very things you are saying, but I can't stop myself from feeling responsible. I'm afraid I'm here out of guilt, that I'm running away from myself. Maybe by becoming a nun, I can make up in some way for what I've done."

"Those are some very tall questions, Linda, and only you know how pure your intentions are, but I will say that I don't think anyone comes to the convent with perfectly pure intentions. We all want to gain something or get away from something by coming here. It would be nice if we all became religious women for purely unselfish thoughts of serving God, but I don't think I've met a single priest or nun who can say they have."

Linda was feeling better, just by admitting her fears aloud. She needed someone to tell her she was not a bad person, that she was all right. Actually, she wanted to become a nun for many reasons, most of them honorable, but she needed to confront this monster fear of guilt within her. Having admitted this to Sr. Imelda, she recognized the truth, and it felt good.

"Thank you for your help, Sister. I guess I'd better be going, but I do feel so much better about this."

"You'll be fine. God bless you, dear."

Linda left the office with a tear stained face but felt good about the conference. Down the hall she passed Joni Peroni who often tried to make conversation with her. Linda explained several times that college girls and postulants were a forbidden combination. Just not allowed. Joni was persistent, and was not about to let Linda pass, looking as she did.

"Linda, have you been crying?" Joni asked while approaching.

"Joni, please don't ask. You're going to get me in trouble. Just let it go."

Joni let few things go, once interested. She became more insistent and suggested, "Let me buy you a Coke in the lounge. You look like you need to talk with someone."

Linda did appreciate Joni's offer, both for a drink and a few words together, but she knew if they went into the lounge, they might be seen. Instead, she countered, "Let's talk in here a few minutes. I can't be long." Linda opened the door to an empty classroom.

"Joni, I have nothing against you. I think you are a perfectly wonderful person. I was quite happy to see the girls have elected you class president. You are always so upbeat, and no matter how many times I tell you to go away, you just won't. Don't you realize that if Sr. Humiliana, or Helena, or who knows who else sees us talking, I could be asked to leave?"

"Linda, I do understand. Believe me, I've stayed away a lot more than you realize. I don't want you to have problems because of me, but couldn't you get permission to visit with me? I've seen some of the other girls do that."

"I get the impression many of the postulants you see talking with college girls don't have permission, and those that do, do so under the pretense that the college girl is asking about how to enter the convent or something."

"So, tell Humiliana I want to be a nun."

Linda laughed. "No one would believe it, Joni. You're engaged."

"Yes, but I'm thinking of giving his ring back."

"Are you serious? You'd enter a convent?" Linda was amused. She could see Joni's defiance of authority, her outspoken ways in class, and her unwieldy self-confidence. Linda was warmed by Joni's attention and refreshing ways. She liked Joni very much, but she also liked the thought of becoming a nun someday. Joni must not run interference.

"Who knows, maybe I will. Then I'll become your superior and give you permission to talk to me every day. So, why the tears? Are they getting to you?"

"Joni, we will visit sometime. I'll get permission. Be patient. As for my problems, I can't share them. I'll be okay. In fact, I just came from Sr. Imelda. I think she helped me considerably. You just have to stay away from me. If you want to be my friend, you have to honor these rules."

Joni was no fool. She was an honor student and didn't want any trouble with the sisters. Some of them were quite formidable and could cause trouble for her. She agreed to stop approaching Linda, but only if she would agree to ask permission for a visit. Linda agreed, and Joni, in a gesture more bold than any she had made before, gave Linda a hug and left the classroom without anyone noticing. Linda waited a few moments and then followed.

In the next few months Anita and Nancy both left the St. Jude group behind. One had remarked how the bells were driving her crazy. Responding to every ring for food, recreation, and rising made her feel like one of Pavlov's dogs. Neither girl was given an opportunity to say good-bye, as they were directed to tell no one.

Signs of spring began to appear. Even Sandra, who had the most enthusiastic love for the white, crystal flakes, was happy to see winter begin its melt into spring.

Early spring did afford four postulants an unusual opportunity. They were chosen to teach religion at St. Cecilia's Sunday School for retarded children every Sunday afternoon. The lay parishioners usually drove the postulants. One time while being dropped off, Brigit quite accidently, closed the car door on Georgette's thumb.

"Wait a minute, Mr. Foster! Stop! My hand!" Luckily Mr. Foster noticed the pounding and shouts. He stopped the car before he hardly left the curb. After releasing the thumb, it began to swell and turn black. Members of St. Cecilia's packed the bruised thumb in ice to reduce the swelling. It helped. Upon Georgette's return to the novitiate, Sr. Humiliana recommended a hot bath and two aspirin.

"A hot bath for a damaged thumb?" thought Georgette. "Well, I'll try it." Actually, it did help, and Georgette *did* feel better. Though the bump on her thumb would last for years, the discomfort passed within a few days.

The girls enjoyed teaching religion class on Sunday afternoons. Those selected were good students and didn't need the extra time for study. It was a fun way to break up the monotonous routine of typically uneventful Sunday afternoons.

One exception to the quiet Sundays was the day the water pipes broke in the Convent High cafeteria. There were three inches of water everywhere, and even though Sunday was supposed to be "a day of rest", four hours of serious mopping and hauling water kept most of the novitiate very busy! Strange how misfortune could bring out such a cooperative spirit in this group of unique individuals!

One Sunday, Sr. Humiliana surprised the postulants by announcing an invitation to the home of a wealthy couple related to one of the postulants, who owned a very large house and an indoor swimming pool. They served the girls sloppy joes and French fries, items rarely, if ever, on novitiate menus.

Theresa's Aunt Catherine and Uncle Tom had mentioned to Sr. Humiliana that they would love to have the girls come and swim. Theresa's Aunt and Uncle were childless and doted upon their niece whenever possible. They were very proud that their attractive relative had attended the exclusive Convent High and now decided to enter religious life. The visit to their lovely home was a wonderful treat for the remaining twenty-one young women. It was their first chance to swim since entrance day.

The girls were not used to changing their clothes in front of each other since modesty was expected at all times in the novitiate. Most of the girls chose to wait in line for the bathrooms, while others, a little more venturesome, opted to change in groups of two or three in bedrooms.

The girls spent a hilarious afternoon splashing, diving, and being silly. The familiar experiences helped the girls feel that convent life may not be so different from what they knew before.

Sandra accidently stepped into deeper water than she intended and was panic-stricken. Angie grew up near Lake Erie, and was a strong and experienced swimmer. She went directly to Sandra and pulled her to the side of the pool. It was hardly a dramatic rescue, but Sandra reacted with tears of gratitude. Once Sandra was calmed, the teasing began, and the party atmosphere resumed.

Later on, Sandra confided to Theresa that her sister had drowned in Hawaii. She preferred that Theresa not mention this to Sr. Humiliana or to anyone else. It was a sadness she was not able to discuss. Sandra explained the afternoon incident to Theresa, but only because Theresa probed.

"Sandra, why were you so scared in the water? You wouldn't even come in the deep half, and you were hysterical after you stepped into water just over your shoulders. You weren't in any danger, but you were so scared! Can't you swim?"

"Yes, Terry. I can swim. I'm not what you would call a good swimmer, but I can swim. It's just that when my sister drowned, I developed this whole new thing about water. I'm so afraid of it. The ocean currents in Hawaii are sometimes so strong and unpredictable. One day, my sister and I were at the beach together with friends, and she went in the water. I didn't think anything of it, but Theresa, they never found her. They *never* found her! We could not even bury her body."

"Sandra, this pool is not an ocean. You wouldn't have drowned. We were all there. You were safe. But, then, I guess if I had lost a sister, maybe I'd feel the same way. I wish you'd tell Humiliana. I think she could help." Theresa hugged her friend. Sandra was grateful, but inside, she was still trembling from her remaining, uncontrollable fear.

· · · · · · · ·

18

Spring cleaning meant window cleaning. When Brigit stopped to visit Angie for a few moments, Angie was cheerfully cleaning her one and only bedroom window.

"What are you using, Anj?" Brigit asked.

"A little detergent in water."

"No, I mean, to dry it with?"

"Oh." How did she ever notice *that*, thought Angie. "It's underwear."

"Underwear?" Brigit said it just loud enough to draw the attention of Sr. Humiliana, who was just stepping off the elevator. Sister decided to investigate.

"Mum's here," Brigit whispered to Angie before Sister was in range of hearing.

"What are you two up to?" Sr. Humiliana asked upon reaching the opened curtain. It was discouraged for two postulants to be in one cell together. Conversations were preferably held in the postulate and in public.

"Spring cleaning," confessed Angie. "I just wanted to get this window done."

"She's using her underwear to dry it, Sister." Brigit wasted no time in telling.

"It's clean underwear, Sister." Angie was obviously embarrassed. "I couldn't find a drying rag." Angie glanced at Brigit with a look that could kill as Sr. Humiliana examined the window.

"Look, dear, the best way is to take a sheet of old newspaper and dry away these streaks. Wait a minute." She turned and walked toward her bedroom at the end of the hall.

"I'll kill you, Brigit McGinnis," Angie said the first available moment she could express her sentiments.

"But, Anj, if you did, who would drive you crazy? You know you love me. I can't wait to tell," Brigit teased all the more as she turned to dash toward the stairway.

"Walk, Brigit!" directed Sr. Humiliana as she returned to Angie's cell, newsprint in hand. It was a satisfying to hear Brigit being corrected for rushing. Sister Humiliana had often preached, "There is no need for a sister to run, if she is well-organized, well-scheduled, and well-planned." It was just plain unbecoming for a "religious" to be hurried.

Sister took a page of the newspaper and crumpled it loosely. "This is how you do it, Angela. Then you dry the window or wet surface as if the paper were a rag. Just rub. Actually, paper and rags are often made of some of the same raw materials. Look, it leaves a shine as well." Sister demonstrated.

Angie was amazed at how it removed the streaks. This really worked.

"The only drawback is, see what it does to your hands?" Sister showed Angie where the newsprint ink had blackened her fingers.

"Thank you, Sister. That's really a great idea."

"Good. I'm glad you approve. Now you can put away the underwear. I think I'll remind the girls in class tomorrow about this," she reflected. "They'll be washing windows, too," Sister remarked as she left.

Humiliana returned only minutes later to Angela's cell. "The reason I came up here in the first place was to tell you something important. There is going to be a vocation congress in Hoboken, New Jersey on the first of May. I'd like you to give a presentation about religious life. Georgette will drive us, and I'm asking some of the girls to help you prepare your speech. Are you comfortable with this?"

Angie was quite surprised. Wouldn't this be an honor given to Ginny, the oldest? "Sister, I'll be happy to, but why me? I don't know a whole lot about the convent. I still feel like a student."

"You *are* a student, Angela, but a very good one. Your college speech instructor tells me you are what she refers to as "a natural".

"Well, Sister. I have been on stage before, and I do enjoy it. I had speech in high school. Maybe some of the others didn't. That might make me look a little more experienced." Inwardly, Angela was excited at the prospect of public speaking. "How long is the talk?" she asked.

"Only ten or fifteen minutes. I'd rather you not discuss this with anyone until I've told the others."

"Of course, Sister. I'm more than happy to do it." Her speech would be months in the planning.

Sandra was downstairs in the parlor buffing the floor and somehow the large machine got away from her. It crashed into a life-sized statue of the Sacred Heart of Jesus.

"Oh, my God. I'm done for! They'll have my head right next to His broken foot." Talking aloud to herself was one of Sandra's most amusing idiosyncracies. Upon occasion certain members of the group would interrupt conversations Sandra was having with herself.

Ginny's room was next to Sandra's. She often heard Sandra through the curtains separating them. One day, Ginny thought there was someone in the cell with Sandra. She heard, "Look at you! Just sitting at my desk! No one wants you? Well, neither do I. Why can't you open yourselves and jump into my brain as I sleep?"

Ginny got up from her chair to peek past Sandra's curtain, only to discover she was talking to the stack of books on her desk. She also had overheard Sandra scolding her drawers for being a mess or telling her bed to make itself. Sandra had a wonderful sense of humor. The group especially liked it when she would make up words, such as "oogalated." This meant, according to Sandra, having something sticky or gooey all over your hands. The postulants would often use her invented words. Sandra was very much liked and respected by her peers.

Sandra inspected the damage to the statue and decided only the left foot had been amputated. Some glue or bonding material should do the trick. Sandra went up to the postulate to ask if anyone had glue. Judith offered some from her cubby and Sandra took it downstairs mumbling something to the effect that "his dancing days are over". She patched the statue so well that Jesus had only the slightest hairline fracture, and no one ever noticed. The only one Sandra ever told was Theresa, and she had been sworn to secrecy.

· · · · · · · ·

19

Spring is a beautiful season in Albany. First the crocuses emerge, then the daffodils and tulips. There is a sense of re-birth, of new life and hope everywhere. There were walks in the courtyard as well as outside the convent walls. Easter, soon to come, would bring the excitement of another visiting day for the postulants.

With the advent of Easter holidays just around the corner, Sr. Humiliana felt it was a good time to discuss more topics of importance during the postulant "training class".

She introduced the Breviary, a book of prayer used by the sisters in community every day. Mostly it was psalms, recited together mornings and evenings. Sister explained that it was a most serious responsibility for religious and priests to pray the "office" daily. She spoke of a priest friend who had been so busy meeting the needs of his parish that one night, on the way home from a wake, he stopped to read his prayers by the light of his headlights.

The postulants could see this Breviary was serious business. They were all attentive to Sister's directions—appropriate responses, when to sit or stand, and how to pray in chorus fashion.

Linda had observed nuns and priests walking with this large book in hand but really didn't know much about the hours of prime, terce, lauds, sext, none, or vespers. Nicholette had a look of sheer joy to think she would be schooled in the ritual of saying the office. Most of the girls were excited because this was just another step closer to what they had come for. Ginny and Theresa shared a similar reaction. One mutual glance said it all: "More prayers?"

"Girls, Mother Victoria will be stopping by during recreation this evening. She wants to meet you personally and I'm sure you will enjoy the visit. Mother was in my group when I entered community. Even though she's Mother General, I consider her a very dear friend as well. Please be yourselves, but be your best selves." The girls knew this was Sister's diplomatic way of suggesting they be on their best behavior.

Sister continued her announcements and lessons. "The topic of suffering is often discussed during Lent. I don't think anyone can explain the lessons of suffering any better than we can explain the mystery of life. Suffering is just something we must do in order to grow, just as your bones and muscles must grow and stretch, sometimes causing us pain. So must our spiritual growth require, at times, some discomfort. We should be grateful for our pain. It is a sign of growing and a need for change. We should thank God, in good times and in bad, for health and sickness." Sister would often speak of simple lessons, hoping to inspire or encourage the girls to deepen their spiritual lives.

"Speaking of growth, I think some of you may have heard that our community has purchased 150 acres of farmland about thirty miles from here, in a rural section of Watervaliet. This was done several years ago, but only now are we drawing plans to develop the land. We hope to build a new motherhouse, novitiate, home for elderly Sisters, and even a school for the mentally handicapped. These are ambitious plans. The growth of community may be a painful one for many of us, but it is wise to plan for our futures. I will put some literature on the table in the postulate for you to read." The girls were interested.

"I also need to tell you that I have asked Angie to give a talk in New Jersey at a vocation congress. She will tell high school girls what the postulancy is like." The girls glanced toward Angie. Most thought it a good choice. "Georgette will be our driver, and we'll be gone the first weekend in May."

Georgette flashed a brace-filled smile to the girls who now glanced her way. "Brigit, Helen, Betsy, and Ginny will help Angie put together some ideas for her speech."

Sister Humiliana continued, "During the first week of June you will be making an eight day retreat here in the novitiate. Mass will be held in our chapel, not the motherhouse. You will be excused from your duties in the laundry, infirmary, and kitchen, but you will continue to help with the dishes, in silence, if at all possible. Your retreat master is a priest you've never met. He's from the Syracuse diocese. His name is Fr. Pius Puff."

Janie raised her hand to speak. "Sister, he does a lot of high school retreats in Syracuse. I hear he's really well-liked. The kids called him 'Holy Smoke' . . . Pius Puff, get it?" Some of the girls understood the pun; others didn't.

Sr. Humiliana was not going to dwell on Janie's comment, but even she had to smile. "Janie, I think it's better if we call him Fr. Pius." She winked.

"Your habits are coming along nicely, but they must be finished before you begin your investing retreat." Betsy looked worried, as did some of the others.

"I will show you how to tie your cords and how to pin the veils shortly. You will be asked to submit three choices for your new religious name, but you'll not know what name you receive until investing. Remember, with a new name must come a new life, a new person, a new beginning." Sister spoke with conviction.

"For the next few months, I ask that you periodically stop by my office and beg for the habit. This is a Franciscan tradition. Francis was a beggar, a poor and humble man who asked for what he needed. The same will be expected of you."

The girls were intent upon understanding this new way of life, but some were confused by this new idea of begging for the habit. Had they not been sewing it together to wear investing day? Why beg for it?

"You will come to me, kneel down, and say: 'For the love of God, I beg to receive the habit of penance and to wear it humbly as a Franciscan Sister of Albany.' Repeat it after me." And the girls did.

It was becoming clear to them that postulancy was a vestibule to the novitiate, and that novices would become professed sisters. As novices, they would have a habit and a religious name. Then, with the taking of vows, they would become professed and have full membership with community.

Sister continued to explain. "If you practice begging for the habit now, it will be easier for you at Chapter. This is when you go before the Mother General and her Council to beg entrance into the novitiate." Slowly the process expected of them was becoming more clear.

NUN OF THIS AND NUN OF THAT, BOOK ONE

"Has our investing date been set, Sister?" Ginny asked.

"June 8th. You may tell your parents when you write them. They may need to plan ahead because your families are invited. If they come from out-of-town they will be invited to stay overnight in one of the college dorms. I shall be giving you each six invitations to mail."

Today's class had been particularly exciting. So much to look forward to! This naturally lifted the girls' spirits. Easter felt as if it were happening in hearts as well as upon the calendar.

Mother Victoria did come to visit that evening as expected. Mother proved to be delightful company. She was pleasant, encouraging, and conversed comfortably with the fledglings. She shared that when she first saw novices kissing the floor many, many years ago, she thought they were doing penance by hitting their foreheads on the floor, and likewise she banged her head until the postulant mistress commented upon the bruise. The postulants were nearly hysterical with laughter, and so recreation passed entirely too quickly for all of them.

That night, when Linda turned in her sleep, she knocked her elbow against the wall and an "electric shock" ran through her arm, numbing her fingers. She kept an ungracious comment from passing her lips and thought about Sr. Humiliana's lesson that day, about suffering. Instead of complaining, she spoke aloud, "Thanks, God." Her arm hurt, but she felt good that she was taking these things to heart.

· · · · · · · ·

20

For a while now, Angie wanted to talk privately with Father Jude concerning her friendship with Brigit as well as something else that had been bothering her. The appointment was easily arranged.

"Father, I'm a little uncomfortable with this," Angie began.

"Angie, you can tell a priest anything. We've heard it all," Fr. Jude wanted to be encouraging.

"Father, I'm afraid I'm becoming too close to one of the girls in my group." Angie was direct.

"Whom, may I ask?"

"Brigit."

"What makes you think you have a problem, Angela?" he asked, lighting his cherry-tobacco-filled pipe.

"It's the way I feel when I'm around her. At Christmas, I remember giving her a hug when we exchanged some very small gifts and I just felt something. Like—I didn't want to let go."

"And so you're afraid of an inordinate love?"

"A what?"

"Inordinate love. That's a love that may lead to a more intimate relationship."

"Well, I guess that's it. I know I love Brig, but I'm also afraid to love her. Does that make sense?"

"Of course it does. But, Angela, you can't be afraid to love your friends. Just understand how you feel. Do you think you could talk with Brigit about this?"

"I never thought to go to her. I'm not sure I could."

"I wish you would try. You need to see what she has to say about how *you* feel. Maybe you are fearful needlessly. Sounds as if you should relax and trust yourself and trust Brigit, too."

Angie was feeling much freer. It sounded like good advice, but it would be a good while before she'd go to Brigit. Besides, she was with Betsy most of the time. As long as Father didn't think it was a problem, she felt all she needed was time. She wasn't in any hurry to make a fool of herself.

There was another issue on her mind. Again Angie was blunt and direct.

"Father, why aren't there women priests?"

Father Jude raised his eyebrow, puffed his pipe, and explained that God designed women for the purpose of motherhood. Women were biologically prepared in every way for giving birth, in the same way men were designed for priesthood. A man is more aptly prepared and suited to protect and to provide for the spiritual well-being of women.

Fr. Jude's explanation was not exactly clear, nor did Angie understand what he was saying, but she trusted Fr. Jude's judgement. He was older, wiser, and more experienced. Father was the spiritual director for novitiate. She did not question further. If Father said so, it must be right.

As she stood to leave after their meeting, Fr. Jude put his hand upon her shoulder, assuring her she was a bright and compassionate young woman. "The sisters need your natural ability to lead, Angela. Just keep in mind who it is you are to follow." Angie knew to whom Father was referring.

The morning of April 29th, Linda was celebrating her 18th birthday. Age-wise, she was the youngest member of St. Jude's Group. At morning table, she noticed four postulants kneeling and found out later that Sr. Humiliana had caught them studying together after 10:00 in the storage room, using flashlights to read their notes. Dutifully, Brigit, Betsy, Helena and Sandra were kneeling to eat their cereal.

Linda examined the birthday card at her place, signed by the postulants, the vigil candle, and the array of holy cards given to her from the others. Linda thought it a nice custom to decorate birthday settings with holy cards. They were the most common exchange for postulants and often traded for a more favorite saint or prayer card.

Linda had permission to receive a phone call from her family that day. She asked about Richard. In his letters he had informed Linda of his decision to enter a religious order of Marion Brothers in Monroe, New York. It did not come as a big surprise. His experience with the Franciscan priests and brothers at Sienna College was an obvious influence. Linda missed her friend as much as she missed her family, but she felt convinced she was here to do some wonderful things with her life.

Angie wanted to ask Brigit about another idea she had for her New Jersey speech. She was nearly packed and ready to leave for

the trip but decided to run upstairs to see if Brigit was in her
room. First she tapped three times on the ceiling with her mop
handle and waited for Brigit's response. There wasn't any. Angie
thought she might be visiting someone or in the postulate. She
walked toward the stairs and, as she passed Betsy's room, she heard
Brigit's voice speaking softly.

Angie tapped and then opened the curtain, which never
assured any real privacy. Brigit was lying on Betsy's bed,
stomach down, and Betsy was sitting next to her. They were
obviously startled by the interruption and both sprung to their
feet.

During mid-year, one-piece postulant dresses had been changed
to a more contemporary look of black skirt, black jacket, and white
blouse. As Brigit stood, her unbuttoned skirt slid, and she nervously
tucked in her blouse and buttoned the skirt.

"Betsy was giving me a back rub. Things have been so intense
around here lately, I asked her to."

Angie thought the scene seemed "a little cozy". On the other
hand, and even though she felt insecure about Betsy and Brigit
being together so much, she would never suspect their friendship
was anything but friendship. Still, she felt awkward and mentioned
she just wanted to say good-bye. They wished her luck and she
returned to her room to finish packing.

The day after Angie, Georgette, and Sister Humiliana had left
for the vocation congress, Sr. Geraldine informed the girls that Sr.
Bernadette would be visiting from the infirmary. Sister would be
transported in a wheelchair. She had been confined to bed for five
years with multiple sclerosis and had never had an opportunity to
tour the relatively new novitiate building. Several novices and a
nurse would escort Sr. Bernadette and see to her comfort. Ginny
was particularly excited about the visit.

Several days earlier, Judith requested and received permission
from Sr. Humiliana for Joni Peroni to visit for an hour in the
classroom. This visit would coincide with Sr. Bernadette's visit to
novitiate.

Veronica, who also volunteered in the infirmary, approached Ginny when she learned Judith would be visiting a college girl instead of receiving Sr. Bernadette. She was disturbed by this and told Ginny.

"She can visit with college girls any Sunday afternoon. Why is she doing it when Sr. Bernadette will be our guest? It certainly doesn't seem very-community minded to me. That woman has MS, she's given her life to serve in community, and all Judith wants is to see her girlfriend."

"Veronica, I understand what you're saying, but you and I know Sister Bernadette differently from the others. We're in the infirmary a lot. Judith doesn't know Sister."

"It doesn't matter if she knows Bernadette or not. This is like history or something to have this great lady finally get to see a building she has not been able to see for three years."

"Everyone else will be here. We've planned a song or two. It'll be just fine."

Still, Veronica was angered and decided to do something about it. Joni arrived and Judith took her to the classroom. A moment later, Veronica knocked on the classroom door.

"Judith, may I see you for a moment?"

Judith complied, and followed Veronica into the privacy of the stairwell. There she confronted Judith.

"Judith, every one of us is going to be there for Sr. Bernadette. Why can't you tell Joni you'll see her some other Sunday?"

Judith was not sure what to make of what was becoming a scene. She tried to explain to Veronica, who was obviously unhappy about the situation.

"Veronica, this is the first time Joni and I have had together that I didn't have to feel like it was criminal behavior. I'm sorry Sr. Bernadette is visiting the same day, but I'm not about to ask Joni to leave."

"That nun has practically lived in bed for the past five years and rarely ever leaves her room. She has this one chance to visit the novitiate, and you prefer a college girl. Where is your loyalty to community?"

"Veronica, I have as much loyalty as anyone, but I'm not going to let you tell me how I may spend my Sunday afternoon."

Judith could tell Veronica was about to boil over. Veronica lifted her fist as if to threaten a punch, but Judith would not be intimidated. Instead, she excused herself and left the infuriated postulant alone in the stairway. Upon returning to Joni, she saw Sr. Bernadette and her entourage entering the door. "Welcome, Sister! Everyone is looking forward to your visit, but will you excuse me? I have company this afternoon."

Sr. Bernadette was a gracious lady and assured Judith it would be fine. "Just have a good visit, dear. Life if too brief not to enjoy as much of it as possible. I can always see you upstairs." Sr. Bernadette smiled and extended her hand, which was about the only part of her that could obey a direct thought.

When Judith entered the classroom, she would not mention the conflicting schedules nor the frightening incident with Veronica in the hall. It was a private matter, and the postulants were already being taught that what happens among them should remain among them. Lay people couldn't understand. Actually, in this case, neither could Judith.

· · · · · · · ·

21

Georgette and Angie were enjoying the excitement of travel. Neither had ever been to Hoboken or New Jersey before. Sr. Humiliana rode shotgun in the front seat, and Angie kept conversation lively from the back.

"Sister, are we almost there?"

"Yes, dear. We'll be staying at St. Williams's Convent smack in the middle of the miracle mile."

"Miracle mile?" Angie repeated.

"Hoboken is densely populated and the city covers only one

square mile. People say it is a miracle that so many people can occupy such a limited space. We serve Italians and Puerto Ricans here, but the large population, high rises, and poverty makes mission life unique. It takes a special kind of "religious" to be at home here. I've often heard the Sisters who have lived here say it is a wonderful city in which to serve. Georgette, turn down this street, our convent will be on the left."

Garbage cans lined both sides of the street. "It must be garbage collection day," observed Angie.

"I believe they collect garbage every day in the miracle mile, sometimes even twice a day," Sister added.

"Gosh, it must be crowded. I guess a million people make a lot of garbage." Angie was fascinated by the open windows with curtains hanging out, and by the people watching the streets from above.

The sisters greeted the Albany travelers with a delicious supper and enjoyed an update of community news. Angie practiced her speech for the sisters, and then the sisters had night prayer and retired. The convent was actually a row of two houses joined together. A small back porch had been enclosed and served as a chapel. Space was very limited. Georgette and Angie were to sleep on a couch with a hide-a-way bed. Actually, once the couch was opened, it was the room that seemed to hide-a-way. There was barely enough room to stand. Angie, the last to bed, had to crawl around Georgette, because Georgette had chosen the side of the bed next to the doorway.

Once she was under the covers and lights were off, Angie lay in bed thinking about her speech to be given the next day in South Orange, wherever that was. Finally, she drifted off to sleep, but not soundly. Midnight garbage collection with cans banging outside their window, sharing a pull-out couch with a two-inch mattress, and Georgette hogging most of the blanket. All contributed to a rather restless night before Angie's "big day" at Seton Hall.

And a big day it was! Much more so than Angie ever imagined. Seton Hall University's auditorium must have held 4,000 girls.

They kept pouring in, bus load after bus load. Balconies filled and the only available floor space was in the aisles. Angie was impressed by the crowd, but she had prepared her speech meticulously and felt confidently prepared.

The entrance procession walked down the center of the huge room, and Angie walked next to Sr. Humiliana. Georgette and some of the sisters had taken seats to the side.

The procession filed onto the stage, including a bishop, two monsignors, ten or twelve priests, and about twenty religious women sporting an array of different habits. Angie became even more animated as the impressionable young women in the audience curiously watched her approach the stage, as if she were some distinguished dignitary. She smiled to think she was about to tell these people about religious life, when she herself, a public school product, felt she knew next to nothing about convent life. She was a neophyte. "They must not have wanted experts," she thought, "to have asked me."

After preliminary opening exercises, the series of talks began. Angie listened and knew she would be introduced very soon. Turning to Sr. Humiliana, she asked, "Sister, do you think I could have a glass of water?" Panic appeared in Sister's eyes and Angie knew her joke was not timely. "I'm only kidding, Sister. I don't need any water, I just wanted to kid you." Sister Humiliana breathed a sigh and forced a polite smile. Poor Sister was practically a nervous wreck, and Angie knew she must be reassuring. She heard herself being introduced. Angie patted Sister's hand, then walked to the microphone.

Before her was an expansive sea of faces. Angie was quite prepared to greet her audience. "Most Reverend Bishop, Honored Monsignors, Good Fathers, Sisters and girls: Pax et Bonum. That is our community greeting. It is my way of wishing you peace and joy. My name is Angela Marie Masucci, but my friends call me Angie. I'm from Sandusky, Ohio, and I have been asked by members of my community to share some thoughts on religious life as I have known and experienced it to be."

"Last September, I went to Albany, New York, to become a postulant in the Third Order of St. Francis, Sisters of Albany. What is a postulant? It is the first step into religious community life. It is a nine-month trial period when you try the convent and the convent tries you. Next month I will begin the next phase of my training. I will be a canonical novice, bound by more restrictive rules and regulations. It will be a time for me to consider if being a nun is truly my vocation."

"What is a vocation? A religious vocation is being called by God to be a sister, brother, missionary, or priest. Everyone has a vocation, a calling. Each of you is called by God to serve His holy will, and only those who seek and find the will of God will have the harmony of life that leads to happiness."

"You must each ask yourself what is it you really want to become. Then ask as honestly what you believe God is asking of you. Maybe you would choose to be a teacher, a nurse, a mother, or a secretary. Last September, I decided that my vocation was to the sisterhood."

"Perhaps you may think I went to a Catholic school, like yourselves. Well, the Spirit of God does not reside in Catholic schools alone, because I felt the hand of God drawing me to religious life as a public school student. It was during CCD instruction that I felt a greater interest in becoming a nun."

"Being a public school product, I felt fairly ignorant about Catholic traditions and convent living. I didn't know what to expect, and I had thoughts of my new life requiring me to give up so much I had come to enjoy and appreciate, such as my parents, my friends, television, and use of the family car. But it didn't take me long to realize that entering the convent was not a giving up, or a giving in; it was a giving."

"Yes, I've had my share of homesickness, of missing familiar ways. That is only natural, but because I have left my family and friends, I can now more clearly see how people have so many needs and I want to be a part of many lives, to help them if I can."

"Would you be interested to know our postulants' routines? Our days are filled with scheduled prayer, recreation, study, and work. We all attend Regina Catholic College in Albany and have a liberal arts program of English, history, democracy, religion, and music. We are being educated to become teachers and nurses." "Some of us teach religion in a program for the retarded of our diocese while others are trained for nursing in our community infirmary. For recreation, we enjoy roller and ice skating, swimming, television, and singing together. We have access to a gym once a week for basketball and other indoor games. It's a changing convent in a changing church in a changing world."

"You might also be interested to know that we had our families visit at both Christmas and Easter. We will see them again in June when we are invested in our habits, and given our religious names. We write home nearly every other week, and will be able to go home for a whole week once our canonical year is completed. Sisters, in the past, had to wait years before they had these kinds of privileges, but our community feels that keeping in touch with families is a better plan."

"We try to live in a spirit of peace and goodness. We strive to imitate the poverty, simplicity, and joy of St. Francis . . . to be an example of Christ for others. You, too, are called to be a holy people. Do you love the person next to you?" At that, the girls seemed to stir and comment to each other. There was a bit of laughter. Angie was not prepared for an audience reaction. She waited until it had passed.

"Jesus has taught us to love our neighbor."

She paused again. "I'd like to leave you with a closing thought. I am very grateful to God for the calling I have. More than anything, I want to share in the same vocation as St. Therese of Lisieux when she proclaimed, 'My vocation is love'. And that, little sisters, should be your calling as well. Wherever you are, wherever you go, whatever you do, don't be afraid to ask God to help you do exactly that. Ask and you shall receive, seek and you will find, knock and it will be opened unto you. Thank you, and Pax et Bonum."

Angie enjoyed the delivery of her speech. She felt good about it and she knew she had done her best. There was enormous applause. As she turned to take her seat, she stepped directly into a table, nearly falling into it. That made the audience laugh and clap all the more. Angie picked up on the audience response and turned to them with a curtsy, which made them roar with enthusiasm.

Later on, as the girls, their teachers, sisters, and others filed past the Albany Franciscan display for hand-outs and literature, many congratulated Angie on a speech well done.

"Tell my boss you liked it," she would say, nodding toward Sr. Humiliana. And they did.

The next day Georgette, Angie, and Sr. Humiliana enjoyed a ride on the tube over to New York City for a tour of the Empire State Building and downtown Manhattan. Several sisters from the local convent acted as guides.

Upon returning to the postulate, Georgette and Angie shared their weekend adventures. Angie spoke of a bed partner who snored and hogged the covers: Georgette described a speech that nearly brought the house down.

The girls were soon back to routine jobs such as washing dishes. Ginny stopped in the linen closet to get a few rags to help dry the dishwasher aluminum sideboards. She noticed the trusty little sign above the cabinet had fallen. She picked it up, replaced it, and read aloud. "Godliness is next to cleanliness." "Humph," she thought, "they should make it say cleanliness is next to Godliness." One thing about the convent was that it was clean. It was almost unnatural to be so clean. Ginny understood the need for hospitals to be antiseptic, but she felt the convent was a home of sorts and should be a little less sterile.

As she hurried back to help finish dishes, she reflected upon the canonical novice, Sr. Alicia, complaining aloud, "I don't mind cleaning, but I hate cleaning when it's already clean!" Alicia would often speak her mind to the postulants, who enjoyed hearing the tidbits she freely expressed.

Ginny rubbed the counters dry with alacrity, as Sr. Geraldine so often suggested. Sister Aquinas was an older woman, perhaps in her seventies, but she insisted on posting herself at dishwasher for every meal. Sister helped in the novitiate. Even though she had severe cataracts and trouble seeing, she would inspect the drain boards with her hands to see if there was anything sticky or lumpy left behind.

Ginny thought she was finished with drying. "Will it pass inspection?" she asked Sister Aquinas.

"Shiny as a Black man's gold tooth," she responded.

Ginny could not imagine where she ever heard such an expression. Sister Aquinas seemed always to come up with some outlandish saying. She was a character, but the girls loved her.

One day Linda sat in Sr. Humiliana's office talking about her friendship with Richard. Sister was curious that he was such a faithful writer of letters. Linda explained his decision to enter a religious order seemed a natural one. "He cares genuinely for people." At the same time, she was a little uncomfortable with the conversation and unexpectantly found herself asking about Susan, the first postulant to leave before Christmas.

"Sister, by the way, do you ever hear how Susan is doing?"

"She's fine, Linda. It was a baby boy and they are both in best of health. I understand she is going to get married rather than give the baby up."

Linda was not sure her ears were working. She did not want to react with a response that might give away her stunned surprise. She spoke matter-of-factly.

"Thank you, Sister. I was so sorry to see her leave. We all enjoyed her so much."

"Yes, I felt the same way." Sister agreed, and Linda excused herself.

As she left Sr. Humiliana's office, Linda tried to understand what she just heard. Sue was pregnant when she left? It made sense now. The morning sickness, vomiting, and missing Mass, and the one night she heard Susan crying with Sr. Humiliana in her cell. Curtains just didn't allow much privacy. Linda thought back. She believed it was homesickness or the flu, anything but pregnancy!

Linda knew Ginny would know if it were true. They had been friends in the infirmary. She decided to ask her. Ginny was just coming back from a class for 10:00 lunch.

"Gin, may I see you in the classroom for a minute?" Linda asked, with a look of concern upon her face.

"Sure, Linda. What's up?"

"Do you know why Susan left community last December?"

Ginny looked down for a moment. She wasn't sure how she felt about the question. "Yes."

"Was she . . . ?"

"Yes."

"Why didn't anyone say something? I never heard a word of it."

"Well, I just figured everyone probably knew. It was even obvious when she left. Didn't you notice how she would stand? Even at four months, she was beginning to show."

"Yes, when I think back, I can imagine she might have been pregnant. I'm just so stunned because I found out only today."

"Susan told me that just before entering, she had been out to a party with her boyfriend. They both had been drinking. They got in his van. Believe it or not, it was their first and only time. You know how they say it takes a while, a few tries. Not for Susan.

"She wanted to be a Sister and would have been a darn good one. I thought she would be a great nurse someday, too. Even before they found out, he wouldn't let go of her. He would keep on driving around the parking lot and trying to find ways of meeting her. Sue wanted to break it off but she found it just as hard as he did. By November she knew she was pregnant. She was terrified to tell anyone. I helped her as much as I could, which wasn't much. She trusted me. I've never wanted to discuss it."

"Is she okay? I mean, is she happy?"

"Well, I've heard she is, but Sister asked her not to write to any of us. We aren't allowed to make any contact, and I've thought the less said the better. I'm not sure how many really know about it. I've just let it drop."

"Well, believe it or not, Sr. Humiliana just told me, quite unintentionally! I think she thought I knew all about it. I was really stunned, but I hope I didn't let on."

"I thought the Convent High School girls knew, especially because she was one of them."

"The others might have known, but no one told me."

"I guess there isn't anything to be done. We just have to wish her the best, and get on with it."

Linda agreed. They both went for their lunch break with the others who were coming into the lunchroom. After a glass of milk and a peanut butter sandwich, Linda stopped in chapel. As she sat in the quietude, she nodded. It was all making sense now. She whispered aloud, "God, just help her to be happy with this new family of hers, wherever she is."

· · · · · · · ·

22

Investing was only two weeks away. Sr. Geraldine decided to stop by during recreation one evening for a visit. Betsy had commented, "She's probably checking out the merchandise. It won't be long before we become her novice slaves." All of the postulants were worried about leaving Sr. Humiliana's care. It became obvious to them, during the year, that novices lived very differently than postulants.

Sr. Geraldine controlled the topic of conversation as she controlled much of the novitiate. The informal conference seemed strange but certainly impressed the young women.

"Have you noticed the two boys who walk past the motherhouse every afternoon?" Geraldine asked.

"No, Sister," several responded. A few others nodded affirmatively.

"Well, did you know they are homosexuals?"

"Homosexuals?" Linda was surprised. "How can you tell, Sister?"

"Oh, you just can. They are always together and it's the way they walk. If you know about such things, you know what to watch for."

Linda, as well as many of the others, was almost shocked to hear Sr. Geraldine speak of this. Several were bothered by the comments because they seemed unfounded. The young women had no experience with homosexuality, but they were surprised to learn you could tell by looking. Sr. Geraldine knew she had captured the interest of the girls and continued.

"If you don't think those boys are peculiar, let me tell you something even stranger! One of our sisters who recently left community had only one parting comment to leave with us. She said she felt like a man! Can you imagine?" Now there were looks of even greater concern and inquiry upon the young faces.

"What a strange thing for her to say," Ginny commented.

"Why would she say such a thing?" asked Theresa.

"Was she sick or something?" Ginny prodded.

"I haven't the slightest idea, Sisters." Sr. Geraldine would often refer to the postulants as sisters. "She always did strike me as strange. Usually that sort of problem goes back a long way."

The girls merely nodded in agreement. It did not make any sense to them. The discussion had been interesting, but odd. This had been a rare informal and candid talk with their future novice directress. Again, impressions were made, and postulancy became memorable once more.

Finally, with exams behind them and Investing retreat underway, it looked as if all twenty-one of them would enter novitiate together. On the third day into retreat, Sr. Humiliana informed the girls that Patricia, a very shy and sweet girl from Pennsylvania had returned home. The girls were disturbed by her disappearance. She was well liked by the others and it was very difficult for them to find her gone with no farewell and no explanation other than that she chose to leave.

The girls surmised it must have been a case of "cold feet", something many of them could understand.

Father Pius was good with the postulants, but they also found him frightening. His personality clashed with several of the girls, and there were some confrontational comments made during his conferences.

"You can't buck the Holy Spirit, girls. If you don't belong here, it is only a matter of time before you are gone. That's why you have to be honest. It is impossible to deceive God, but we are masters at deceiving ourselves."

Father spoke bluntly, but effectively. His masses were pleasant and intimate, just the twenty postulants. He was open to many of the new changes in the Mass and encouraged the girls to plan and do some most unusual things.

A portable altar was set up so the girls could come into the sanctuary and gather around the altar. They held hands during the Our Father and sang instead of recited the prayer. He encouraged the guitars and folk songs instead of the traditional music used at the motherhouse. In some of the parishes the girls came from, they still used the Latin Mass, so they appreciated these new changes. The Mass seemed more personal, more meaningful, and more prayerful to the young women.

During one particular lecture the girls became quite upset.

"Now, if you think becoming a sister is going to make God happy, you should reconsider. You see, God is already happy and always will be happy. You can't make God happy any more than you can make God unhappy. God is eternally blissful. He doesn't need you in a convent to be pleased."

"But Father, do you mean to tell us it doesn't matter if we become nuns or not?" one of the girls protested.

"Sure it *matters*. To you, honey. Not to God."

"I can't believe that!" Helen sounded indignant. "Why were we always told as children to do things to please God, if God doesn't need us to do these things at all?"

"Father, I was always taught that my sins displeased God. That He was "hurt" by them. If our actions have no effect on God, why are we going to give up our own will, our future lives, and become invested next week if it isn't to please God?" Brigit spoke for many of the others having the same thought.

"Because, Brigit, it will please *you*. It will make you happy. We need God, God has no real need of us. But for your own happiness, you must seek to love and serve God's holy will for you. Only then will you find happiness in this world. If you choose to become a sister, you do it for yourself and you do it for others. You don't do it because you believe it is the only way to please God."

That evening the entire group went before Sr. Humiliana, very much disturbed over Father's entirely new insight. The ideas he presented were never considered before, and now the girls questioned their "calling". As usual, Sr. Humiliana was soothing and assured the group he was probably misunderstood.

"You must not worry about these ideas of his. Just think of your own desire to serve the Church," she told the girls. She also spoke privately with Father, who would not press the issue again.

This was definitely a tense time for the postulants. Plans were in place. Sponsors were designated to help invest the girls. Sponsors were professed religious in the community who helped foster or encourage a postulant's vocation. They were usually associated with the aspirant through friendship, or an acquaintance of some kind. The sponsor was to help dress the postulant in the habit of St. Francis for the first time. It was considered an honor for both the girl and professed sponsor.

Angie was delighted to have Sr. Mary Paul as sponsor. She had admired the woman since childhood. Investing was an exciting prospect. Families would come and friends could be there. Angie was saddened that her father would not be coming from Ohio, as he still wished her to return home. She understood his feelings and felt some guilt at being their only child. There were expectations of marriage and grandchildren, but Angie respected life as a religious woman, serving the needs of her Catholic faith; she thought it the most worthy choice of spending her most precious asset, her life.

. . . .

CHAPTER THREE . . .
NOVITIATE/CANONICAL YEAR

23

The bridal gowns were removed from storage once again. One by one, each postulant was taken for a fitting. Several mothers had come to help Sister Humiliana measure the girls and make any necessary alterations. Perhaps it was because Linda's mother was such an excellent seamstress and was willing to donate a good deal of time that Linda received special permission to wear her mother's wedding dress, on the condition that she donate it to the collection for future investing ceremonies.

All the investing habits were completed in time for the ceremony. Those who finished early were expected to help those less nimble with the thimble. Rehearsals for the ceremony were over and the retreat was also behind them. Now the postulants were occupied preparing the college dorms for the out-of-town guests. Everyone was busy preparing the last minute details.

Angie's father did not come, but her mother traveled from Sandusky with her two aunts. Linda's brother, sister, parents, and her friend Richard were expected. Ginny's mom and dad would be there with four of her siblings. The only postulant with no family member or friend from home would be Sandra. Still, everyone was full of anticipation, and by now Sandra had been adopted by many of the local families, especially Theresa's.

Novices visited the fourth and fifth floors that very special morning to make sure wedding gowns and veils were arranged properly and make last minute adjustments, if necessary. The postulants were then led down the back stairs, in twos, with novices leading the way. They walked through the halls decorated with banners and crepe paper and sang hymns to the Blessed Mother. "On this day, O Beautiful Mother," sang the women, "on this day, we give thee our love."

Novices led these soon-to-be-brides of Christ to the novitiate chapel. All knelt to pray. Sister Humiliana spoke from a pew behind them into the reflective silence, "This day, you give yourself to your beloved spouse. You are His, and He is yours. Give all and keep nothing for yourself. For nine months you have been preparing to love and serve your God as a Franciscan Sister of Albany, New York. Today is the day you place yourselves upon the altar of sacrifice. Today you choose to become all for the love of Christ. God will not be outdone in generosity."

Sister Humiliana then quoted a reading from the Canticle of Canticles.

> "Hark! My lover, here he comes springing across the mountains, leaping across the hills.
> My lover is like a gazelle or a young stag.
> Here he stands behind our wall, gazing through the window, peering through the lattices.
> My lover speaks; he says to me,
> 'Arise, my beloved, my beautiful one, and come!
> For the winter is past, the rains are over and gone.
> The flowers appear on the earth,
> the time of pruning the vines has come,
> and the song of the dove is heard in our land.
> The fig tree puts forth its figs,
> and the vines, in bloom, give forth fragrance.
> Arise, my beloved, my beautiful one, and come!
> O my dove in the clefts of the rock,
> in the secret recesses of the cliff,
> let me see you, let me hear your voice,
> for your voice is sweet, and you are lovely.'

NUN OF THIS AND NUN OF THAT, BOOK ONE   141

Catch us the foxes, the little foxes that damage the vine-
yards; for our vineyards are in bloom!
My love belongs to me, and I to him;
      he browses among the lilies.
Until the day breathes cool and the shadows lengthen,
      roam, my lover,
Like a gazelle or a young stag
      upon the mountains of Bether."

After the reading there was more silence and more reflection. The novices then stood and led the women toward the motherhouse chapel where the investing ceremony was to take place. They chanted the Magnificat in Latin as they proceeded through the corridors and cloister. Now, arriving at the vestibule, the white-veiled novices went to the choir loft to join the black-veiled novices, and professed. The postulants stood in rank before their family and friends. With a very impressive entrance song under the command of Sr. Helena, they walked single file into the chapel. Ginny, as "oldest," led the way. Kathleen, "the youngest," walked last. Then came altar servers, invited priests, and, finally, the Bishop. As rehearsed, the girls filed into their respective places, and the others proceeded into the sanctuary. The Mass had begun.

After the sermon, the Bishop took a seat in front of the tabernacle. This was Ginny's signal to lead the postulants, one by one, to kneel before him. The Bishop then handed Ginny the habit she prepared during postulancy. He spoke for the first time the name she would bear in religious life. Each announcement was a revelation to the girl, to the community, and to the congregation.

To Ginny he spoke, "Sister Elizabeth, take this habit of penance and wear it clothed in humility. Serve your God with full heart and a prayerful spirit." Ginny received the package of clothing into her open hands. She kissed the floor before the Bishop's throne, as she had done during rehearsal; then stood to exit into the sacristy. From there she hurried into an adjoining annex where she would change into the black serge habit.

Her sponsor, a nurse who taught at the college and often worked in the infirmary, was delighted when Ginny asked her to help her dress, for the first time, into the Franciscan garb.

First, the black underskirt, the tee shirt, then serge habit, cord, rosary, and headgear. The veil proved to be the most complicated part. A three-cornered handkerchief was used to pull back the postulant's hair from her face, then a white linen covering which slid past her face was folded, then pinned shut in the back of the head. This coronet, as it was called, concealed everything but the front of the face. Next, a celluloid band was placed on top of the postulant's head for the white starched and another white outer veil to rest upon. Three pins were carefully inserted so as not to penetrate the scalp, and finally a white celluloid bib-like collar was placed about the neck.

The room was busied with girls dressing simultaneously in designated areas. As Angie entered the room, she gleefully announced to Brigit that she had been given her parents' names, "Sister Robert Therese". Apparently, the girls were receiving their first choice from the list of three names submitted. The days when Mother Generals dispensed the names of their liking to the newly invested appeared to be another disappearing tradition.

Most of the girls had given a lot of thought and prayer to the choice of a religious name. Many were selected for a family member, others for a friend or relative, some for a favorite teacher or saint, and some just because they liked the name. There were as many reasons as there were names.

The young novices were now lined up once more to reenter the chapel sanctuary. Ginny received a blessing from the Bishop and a lit candle as he told her to be "a light onto the world". She then turned toward the people and walked to her assigned position leading the others in rank file.

Angie was followed by Linda. Families swelled with pride at the pomp and beauty of the ceremony, but Linda's sister Margaret was overwhelmed with conflicting emotions as she saw her little sister beaming with a wild, hope-infested smile and stepping from the sanctuary into the body of the chapel.

Margaret excused herself from the bench and walked towards the nearest exit. She did not approve of Linda's decision to become a nun. Margaret was, among many other things, extremely pragmatic. She was career-minded and could not grasp what appeared to be a last minute choice during Linda's senior year of high school. Linda was bright and talented. She had wonderful friends and obviously enjoyed the company of boys. Why was she doing this? Margaret even imagined Linda might marry Richard some day. They were such good friends, and it was obvious to many their friendship was more than friendly.

Linda had been given the name "Sister Mary Alice". This was the name of her grandmother, Maa. Margaret stepped into the air outside, wondering how Linda could forsake so many opportunities for a habit and a life of poverty and servitude. After a few minutes and a few tears, and with mixed feelings of pride and sentiment, Margaret returned to the ceremony just before the sharing of Eucharist.

After investing, families gathered in clusters all about the convent grounds; some in the courtyard, others in "Mother's Meditation Garden", and more in the chapel yard. There were many introductions and, often, little gifts were exchanged. There were lots of hugs. In fact, four new celluloid collars were cracked. Habits were not designed for embracing.

The novices were totally confused by the new names and everyone was given a list for introductions. It read in order, from oldest to youngest:

1. Ginny. . . . Sister Elizabeth
2. Helen. . . . Sister Mary Peter
3. Brigit. . . . Sister Charity
4. Betsy. . . . Sister Dominic
5. Marsha. . . . Sister Michael Michelle
6. Sally. . . . Sister Maryjane
7. Sandra. . . . Sister Christine Marie
8. Karen. . . . Sister Charles Marion

9. Veronica . . . Sister Francis Anne
10. Angie. . . . Sister Robert Therese
11. Linda. . . . Sister Mary Alice
12. Janie. . . . Sister John Michael
13. Judith. . . . Sister Antonette
14. Grace. . . . Sister Martha William
15. Barbara. . . . Sister Mark Lewis
16. Georgette..Sister Mary Daniel
17. Caroline . . . Sister Mary Ruth
18. Nicolette..Sister Samuel Marie
19. Theresa. . . . Sister Leonard
20. Kathleen . . . Sister Catherine Ann

It was an exciting day for everyone. Photographs were taken, and there was the air of a wedding among the crowd. Sister Mary Paul stayed with Sr. Robert Therese (Angie) most of the afternoon. It eased the disappointment that her father had not come. Roberto remained unchanged in his disappointment that his daughter would "marry the church."

That evening, when families had returned to the college dormitory or gone home, Sr. Elizabeth (Ginny) returned to the postulate to get something she left in her cubby box. Sr. Geraldine was there talking with Sr. Leonard (Theresa). Sister asked her to be seated and to remove her headgear. "All that hair, Sister, must be cumbersome under your veil. Perhaps we should cut it back tonight." During the postulancy, many of the girls let their hair grow. Sr. Leonard probably had the longest and thickest hair. It was extremely attractive and the girls knew Sr. Leonard took pride in its beautiful wave and auburn color.

Sr. Elizabeth apologized for the interruption and excused herself; she did not want to stay to witness the haircut. As Sr. Geraldine was preparing to snip with long shears, Elizabeth returned to the fourth floor, whispering to the others that Sr. Geraldine was cutting Sr. Leonard's (Theresa's) hair.

The girls expected this to happen. They were told that Saint Francis cut the hair of Saint Clare as a sign she had renounced the wealth and comforts of this world. In days of old, a woman grew long hair as a sign of high position in life, and it was often seen as her "crown of beauty." The postulants were told that even a homely face was easily beautified by a head of comely hair. Besides, long hair under a veil was uncomfortable and unsanitary.

What the girls did not expect was that the "cutting" would be the night of investing. The rumor had been that they would all have their hair cut in a group setting several days after investing, as other groups had experienced. Apparently, this was not accurate because, shortly after cutting Sr. Leonard's hair, Sr. Geraldine elevated to the fourth floor with shears and electric shaver in hand and began her cutting spree.

Sister Dominic (Betsy) was first. It was no secret they didn't like each other. Sr. Dominic would not give Sr. Geraldine any satisfaction during her cut. She remained stoic and silent. When Sr. Geraldine was finished shaving, there remained, perhaps, one half inch of hair. This length was standard for all she visited that evening.

After Sr. Dominic, Sister went to Sr. Elizabeth's (Ginny's) room. Sr. Elizabeth sat at her desk and held a cardboard box as Sr. Geraldine filled it with curls in contrast to the black strands sheared from Sr. Dominic. When Sr. Geraldine finished, Sr. Elizabeth observed that her curls had filled the box and she wondered how much hair might have been left upon her head.

"Is there someone else you can think of, Virginia, with lots of hair?" Sr. Geraldine asked.

Sr. Elizabeth (Ginny) was not about to suggest any name. It would seem a betrayal of those she respected. Besides, she could not reconcile a need to do this to Sr. Leonard or to anyone. It was most unpleasant, but a practiced "community custom" and not to be challenged. "No, Sister. I can't think of anyone."

"Oh, I know! Sandra! She's only next door, and she has that very bushy, thick, black texture. I'll go there next."

As Sr. Geraldine began her departure, Sr. Elizabeth felt that this was probably one of those times when you should ask for a blessing. It was a custom to ask for the superior's blessing whenever you left the novitiate, returned to the novitiate, or begged a penance. This experience seemed like a good a reason as any to ask Sr. Geraldine's blessing. Wasn't this some holy ritual that was supposed to be significant, religious or something?

Sr. Elizabeth decided to ask, "Sister, may I have your blessing?"

Sr. Geraldine turned and smiled sweetly; with a most approving tone she responded, "God bless you, Sister. Keep growing."

At that, Sr. Elizabeth wanted to react with an honest thought, "Do you mean my hair, Sister? Would you love to come back and cut it again? But then, maybe you mean for me to keep growing spiritually." Sr. Elizabeth knew better than to say a word. She simply returned Sr. Geraldine's smile.

Sr. Geraldine gave quite a few haircuts that night. She cut quickly, not at all concerned with causing a bald spot or making it uneven in places.

Sandra (Sr. Christine Marie) walked into the bathroom to dump some of her hair from her dustpan into the trash bin. Some of the girls were brushing their teeth or washing out their underwear. "That damn woman! Do you believe it? She took it *all* off? What's the matter with her? She scalped me! What is she, part Indian?" The girls were quite used to hearing Sr. Christine Marie talk to herself, but tonight they knew she was talking to them as well. No one had an answer to her questions, nor did they react much to Christine's ravings. They themselves were equally dismayed and unsettled by this introduction to novitiate.

Several of the girls did smirk and spoke aloud, continuing to break the night silence.

"I can understand they might have to cut our hair, but butchery seems excessive," Sr. Mary Alice (Linda) needed to add.

"It's called a perseverance haircut," Sr. Mary Peter (Helen) explained. "Sr. Dorothy said they do it this way so that we won't consider leaving until our hair grows back."   "I'll probably be 60 before this grows back," Sr. Christine Marie (Sandra) quipped in her usual quick-witted fashion before leaving.

All of the girls concealed their hair with a white cotton headcloth introduced to them early during postulancy. No one could see the haircut of another, as no one stepped out of their cell without a head covering, a black robe, and slippers. Girls were expected to be modestly covered at all times.

Upon her return to her cell, Sr. Elizabeth (Ginny) could hear muffled sobs coming from Sr. Leonard's (Theresa's) room. She checked to see if Sr. Geraldine was anywhere nearby, then pulled the curtain aside and stepped into the darkness.

"Theresa, are you okay?" Sr. Elizabeth asked.

Sr. Leonard was in bed, overwhelmed by her hair cutting experience in the postulate. It was difficult for her to speak between her tearful gasps for air.

"I saw you downstairs. I knew you were upset. It showed all over your face. Are you okay?"

When she could, Sr. Leonard spoke to her friend. "Gin, why did she do this? I don't understand. I can't believe it."

Sr. Elizabeth spoke gently, very much aware of the fact Sr. Leonard was far more disturbed than seemed justified. "It'll grow back. It's only hair." Sr. Elizabeth (Ginny) took several Kleenex tissues from her bathrobe pocket and gave them to Sr. Leonard, as she sat next to her on the bed. They both knew what a compromising position this would be if Sr. Geraldine were to walk in on them. Still, they agreed to take the risk.

"Theresa, I can't explain what I don't really understand. We both want to be nuns and so we do these things when they tell us to. This is how we become nuns, I guess."

"It looks so terrible!" Sniffing, Sr. Leonard continued, "She just chopped it all over and seemed so happy the whole time she was doing it. I look like I have mange."

"I know. She got me too, and Betsy and Sandra. I'm not sure how many others. Some escaped by turning out the lights, and pretending they were asleep already. She'll probably come back and finish them tomorrow. The good news is you won't have to do this tomorrow!"

"Gin, I feel so ugly. She nabbed me in the postulate because she said my hair was much too long, and a cut would make me feel so much more comfortable. She's crazy. I could hate her."

Sr. Elizabeth was frustrated that she could not find words to comfort Sr. Leonard. "We're all going through this together, Theresa. Just remember the reasons you came to community. This can only strengthen our vocations. We have to trade some of our happiness to obtain a greater good. Humiliana has said that. You'll find the strength you need to get through this." Sr. Elizabeth kissed her friend upon the forehead and tip-toed back to her own room.

Meanwhile, Sister Charity (Brigit) had come down from the fifth floor and stopped to see Angie. Both had been sheared.

"Do you believe this haircut?"

Sr. Robert Therese (Angie) replied, "I know. I couldn't even bring myself to look in the shower head to see my reflection. I was afraid of what I might see."

"Angie, she shaved my face! Do you know where that soft downy hair comes down on the sides of my face, past my ears?" "Yes."

"She *shaved* it off with an electric shaver! Is she some kind of barber? I've never shaved that hair. Never! Just watch, I'll probably grow a beard."

"Well, there's nothing we can do about it, Brig. We knew this would happen eventually."

"Yes, maybe, but I never imagined it would be like this."

"I was with Betsy before. She's hysterical. I don't think she'll sleep tonight. She just keeps calling Sr. Geraldine a god-damned son-of-a-bitch. She's madder than I've ever seen anyone. I promised I'd check in on her tonight. I'll keep her company until she's calmer."

"I hope you can help. I guess there isn't going to be a lot of sleeping tonight. I just hope that when I see my mom and aunts tomorrow they won't be able to tell what kind of a nightmare we've been through. Mom's awfully perceptive. I'll really have to put on a act for her. It's hard to pretend everything is fine when it isn't. I hope you can help Betsy."

Sr. Charity left for Sr. Dominic's room. Sr. Robert Therese expected them to spend the night together. As much as she didn't like Sr. Dominic, she empathized this time. Apparently the hair cut was traumatizing for some of them. Sr. Robert Therese didn't like it, but she didn't consider it a reason to cry all night, as some of the girls obviously did.

The next morning required an earlier rising than usual. All of the newly invested were to move to second floor before morning prayer and Mass. The other canonicals moved their things to the third floor and the constitutionals moved to the motherhouse where they would prepare for vows in August.

Three days after investing Sr. Samuel Marie (Nicolette) disappeared from the novitiate. Again, there was no explanation. Sr. Robert Therese (Angie) recalled seeing her at her desk the day before she left. She was holding her head in her hands, elbows resting upon her books, and shaking her head. "I can't believe I let them do this to me. What am I doing here?"

Sr. Robert Therese entered the cell and tried to be of some comfort, not realizing the group was soon to number nineteen.

Sr. Mary Alice (Linda) joked with the others about how she looked a lot like her younger brother Larry after Sr. Geraldine's hair styling. She had some of the girls in stitches when she reminisced about Sr. Geraldine's visit to the postulate during recreation not so long ago.

"Remember when Sr. Geraldine told us about some nun who left because she felt like a man?" They remembered. "Well, this morning when I got up and put on my boxer-type underwear, my tee shirt, and attempted to comb my butched hair cut, I wasn't sure if I should tell the mirror, 'Good morning, Larry' or 'Good Morning, Linda'." Laughter was good medicine, and the girls seemed all the more bonded after their hair-cutting initiation into sisterhood.

. . . .

24

For the next several weeks, the newly invested were busy learning the charges formerly carried out by the previous canonical novices. They were assigned kitchen duties, care of both chapels, laundry for the several hundred residents of the motherhouse complex, and other such responsibilities.

The new canonicals were embarking upon their cloister year of work and reflection. They were to examine their vocations and discern if the vowed life was something they could live. Sister Mary Peter (Helen) was given charge of the laundry, probably considered the greatest responsibility. Her good friend, Sr. Dorothy, taught Mary Peter how to run the mammoth washing machines that could handle as much as 200 pounds of soiled laundry. Mary Peter was to master the huge mangle which pressed sheets and tablecloths, and many other flat items such as headcloths, napkins, etc. The laundry was supplied with two huge dryers, dozens of ironing boards, irons, and other such equipment.

Every Sunday evening the laundry was assembled for the next morning. Collections were made about 4:00 A.M., and the novices were at work by 5:00, stopping only for 6:30 prayer, Mass, and breakfast. They would return and finish before 5:00 P.M.

There were many technical aspects to the laundry that Sr. Mary Peter needed to learn from Dorothy. They both found pleasure in the extra time required, and their friendship cemented all the more. By August Sr. Dorothy and the other canonicals were to don black veils and begin their constitutional year. They were to return to Regina Catholic College (often referred to as RCC) with full course loads and would only occasionally be expected to help with domestic work given to canonicals. Mary Peter and Dorothy both knew their time for conversation and shared visits would abruptly end with Sister Dorothy's black veil.

Sister Robert Therese (Angie) was given the charge of novitiate chapel, and Sr. Mary Alice (Linda) was to be in charge of four other novices assigned to manage the cleaning of the large motherhouse chapel. Sr. Mary Alice and her crew were all under the direction of Sr. Cyrilla who had the esteemed position of motherhouse chapel sacristan, caretaker of the sanctuary and sacristy.

The kitchen was staffed by six novices who worked on a rotating basis of three hour shifts, mornings and afternoons. They were kept busy peeling, cleaning, preparing meals, or whatever else might be asked of them. Sr. Christine Marie (Sandra) and Sr. Catherine Ann (Kathleen) both worked in the motherhouse refectory with Sr. Francis Rose, a sister who came from Italy many years ago, but still kept her thick Italian accent. Others were assigned "Mother's Department", corridors, and a variety of other tasks.

All novices were responsible for the washing and resetting of dishes three times daily. They also saw to the general cleaning of several buildings and other such needs. The newly invested continued a daily class of instruction, as they had with Sr. Humiliana. Now Sr. Geraldine presided. Sr. Humiliana was away at St. Bonaventure's University, working on her masters degree in religious studies. Sr. Humiliana was sixty-two, but it was not uncommon for even the older sisters to be attending summer school. Sr. Humiliana was considered fortunate to pursue a post graduate degree. She was *sorely* missed by the St. Jude Group.

Geraldine was much tougher than the postulants imagined. She kept the girls working hard and clamped down on any behavior she considered an excess. "Only one cup of milk per novice both during morning or afternoon lunch. No one may leave the novitiate for any reason without my blessing. No one is to miss community prayer without my explicit consent. No one is to add milk or sugar to your coffee. You must use pepper in only small amounts, as it stimulates the passions."

Sister seemed to be everywhere. She would oversee work being done in the chapels, kitchen, corridors, and in the laundry on

Mondays. Once, when Sr. Dominic (Betsy) dropped her iron, Sr. Geraldine responded as if she did it purposely. With a look of disgust Geraldine scolded, "Be more careful, Sister. Irons are expensive."

"It isn't broken, Sister," Dominic protested.

"Imagine what would happen if you fell on *your* head, as did your iron. You may not work as well tomorrow," was Sr. Geraldine's comeback.

Several of the former canonical novices complained about the new recruits and the quality of their work. In fact, there seemed to be a lot of complaints and corrections now. It was becoming a way of life for the newly invested.

The novices were to kiss the floor for making a mistake in the oral recitation of community prayer. One evening when Sister Charles Marion (Karen) read the office as, "To you O Lord, I lift up my ears" instead of "eyes" it caused a muffle of laughter and shaking of shoulders. The women struggled to maintain composure. It would not have seemed so funny if another had mispoken, but Karen's ears were unusually large, and if anyone could lift up their ears, she could. This may also have simply been a moment for some healthy "comic relief", not scheduled in their long and physically exhausting days.

One summer day, Sr. Mary Alice (Linda) was cleaning the floor under the bench in the motherhouse chapel. Lying upon her stomach to reach every crevice by hand, she noticed an old woman entering the chapel. She continued to work as the woman knelt in prayer for a few minutes. Then Sister Mary Alice noticed the beckoning of the old lady's finger. The novice stood and approached the visitor who reached for the young woman's hand. She kissed it tenderly.

"Do you speak English?" Sr. Mary Alice asked. There was a shake of the head to indicate she did not, followed by a smile which now revealed her missing teeth.

"I don't know why you have kissed my hand, but may I kiss yours?"

The woman gave a questioning look. Sr. Mary Alice proceeded to kiss the aged hand, and the woman smiled again. She then continued her rosary and Mary Alice returned to her cleaning.

Later, during supper, Sr. Mary Alice told Sr. Robert Therese (Angie) about the old woman.

"That's very typical of old stock, Linda. You don't know Italians like I do. At St. Rita's in Sandusky, it could happen every day. The old women love the young nuns! I don't know why. She was probably raised to think we're all so wonderful. It was her way of showing respect."

"Well, I've never had anything like that happen to me. I wasn't sure if I did the right thing."

"I'm sure you did."

The novices were taught to eat, pray, and breathe in rank. Sister Elizabeth (Ginny) was the "oldest" and now assumed many new responsibilities as well as longer hours in the infirmary. There were nuns to bathe, rooms to clean, bedside commodes to empty.

Everyone went to bed exhausted, and lights were usually out by 9:00. Few could manage to stay awake until the 10:00 light curfew. As postulants, the only regular television program allowed was Walt Disney on Sunday nights. Now, as canonicals, the privilege would be to watch Lawrence Welk Saturday evenings.

That was the extent of TV, but there was no time for it. About half the group could not manage the late hour and often retired before the show was over.

The cloister year demanded no coverage of news, no reading of the local papers, and no social interaction with anyone except Sr. Geraldine or the other canonicals.

Life was becoming more tense and intense for the novices. Penances were begged for anything accidently broken or anything a novice considered an infraction of the rule. Resentment toward Sr. Geraldine for her constant criticism of the girls would flare occasionally and the canonicals complained daily to each other of her seemingly unfair attacks. There was no such thing as recreation without sewing or some other constructive work being accomplished. One did not just sit and talk, as they did during postulancy. "Idle hands are tools for the devil," Geraldine frequently reminded her novices.

One day, Sr. Robert Therese (Angie) needed to get away from it all. During the day, novices were not allowed in their cells, so she decided to "hide" in the second floor shower room. Here she would write a letter to her mother and hopefully not be asked to clean or paint or sew. The door was closed and she sat in the end stall. Finally, for the first time in a long time, she was alone. She could feel the tensions leaving her body when the shower door abruptly opened and Sr. Geraldine walked in.

"Sr. Dominic (Betsy) told me you were here. Isn't this a strange place to write your letters?" she demanded.

"Yes, I guess so, Sister. I just needed to get away from all the busyness for a while," the novice attempted to explain.

"Sister, you know full well you are not to be on this floor without my permission. If you have need of privacy, then ask. You don't belong here. Go and see if Sr. Mary Peter (Helen) has need of your help in the laundry."

"Yes, Sister." She knelt before the Directress and begged a penance.

"Say a rosary for the poor souls in Purgatory before you retire, and I hope we don't find you doing this peculiar type of behavior in the future, Sister. Girls have been sent home for less than this, I assure you."

Geraldine could be very intimidating, and even though others would argue her point, Sr. Robert Therese would not.

A particularly festive experience that summer was the dedication of the flag pole at Mother's farm. Mother Victoria and her administrative offices now resided in the rural farmland of Watervaliet. The community expected to expand and build extensively upon this acreage and to relocate their motherhouse and infirmed sisters to the country setting.

A swimming pool was donated by medical doctors in Albany. The former pig sty was converted to an impressive conference center.

The barn was remodeled into a recreation center for the sisters, complete with fireplace, pool table, piano, and kitchen facilities—even beds for venturesome over-nighters.

All of the canonicals were invited to what seemed an historic gathering of government and church officials. The vision was shared by many that these hills would one day nestle the next impressive stages of community growth. No one could foresee the impact of the Second Vatican Council, the exodus of religious in the 60's and 70's, nor the depletion of young women interested in religious life. The community considered itself at the brink of new spurts of growth. Instead, it stood before a precipice of financial and vocational crises.

. . . .

25

During several weeks in mid-summer, four of the novices were selected to work in an inner city Bible School program at St. Stan's parish. Sisters Robert Therese (Angie), Charity (Brigit), Mary Alice (Linda), and John Michael (Janie) were permitted to leave their cloister status for the purpose of teaching religion to Catholics in a poor Slovak ghetto. A Slovak community of sisters originally staffed a Catholic school there, but a shortage of vocations and financial problems caused the sisters to move closer to their founding motherhouse in Pennsylvania, causing the school to close. More and more of Albany was becoming inner city while urban renewal built expansive government structures in the downtown area.

The Bible School teaching experience was one all four novices thoroughly enjoyed, and they did it well. Every day for three weeks, the four novices were driven to St. Stan's and were temporarily relieved of some of their novitiate duties to plan and execute their religious teaching.

Students would rotate among Bible classes, arts and crafts, music, and playtime. Highlighting and culminating each days' activities would be a folk Mass led by Sr. Martha William and several parishioners. The youngsters enjoyed the new style of worship and the way Father spoke directly to them. This experience was far different from the ritual Sunday liturgy.

Sister Robert Therese (Angie) found herself becoming quite attached to one of her fourth grade students. His name was Donald Calabufo. Robert Therese was an only child and had always, secretly wished for a little brother or sister. Perhaps that was why the bond took place. But Donald was just as eager to befriend the young novice. Perhaps she was a beacon compared to his deprived home life, perhaps she was a sign of hope or stability, or perhaps he just genuinely liked the nun. Whatever the reason, it was obvious he was fond of her, too. He would purposely seek her side for Mass, and often tried to skip his other scheduled activities to stay with Sr. Robert Therese for her second cycle of Bible instruction.

Sr. Robert Therese and Sr. Charity (Angie and Brigit) enjoyed planning their lessons together. They were eager to make their classes enlightening and meaningful for the youngsters.

One day, while discussing some of their ideas together in the novitiate room, Sr. Geraldine approached to impose her ideas on theirs.

Out of hearing range, Sister Robert Therese whispered to Sr. Charity, "Why doesn't she ever mind her own business?"

"What are you saying?" asked Sr. Geraldine who heard the whispers.

"I said, 'Why doesn't she mind her own business?', Sister."

Somehow, Sr. Geraldine interpreted the sentence as Sr. Robert Therese being annoyed with Sr. Charity. Sr. Charity did stretch a person's patience at times, and it was no secret the relationship between Sr. Robert Therese and Sr. Charity was becoming even more strained with an increasingly exclusive relationship Brigit seemed to be having with Sr. Dominic (Betsy).

"Sister, don't be so impatient with Sr. Charity. We need to encourage one another. Now, try to get along. We're trying to be sisters for each other here. Can you understand that, Sister?" responded Sr. Geraldine.

At first, Sr. Robert Therese (Angie) did not fathom what had just happened. Then it dawned on her. Sr. Geraldine did not realize the complaint was aimed at *her* but thought the rude comment was for Sr. Charity. That was a close call! Robert Therese did not know how she could be so bold, even for a moment, but Geraldine's misunderstanding of the situation probably saved Robert Theresa's neck—perhaps, even her religious vocation.

Later the two novices discussed what a "close call" that little scene had been. It also seemed a good time to discuss their own uncertain relationship.

"It's not that we aren't good friends, or that I don't care for you, RT, but I have many other friends I need to spend time with. You want too much of me, and I just can't reciprocate," Sr. Charity explained.

"But you have all the time in the world for Sr. Dominic. Are you are dumping me for her?" Sr. Robert Therese was blunt and angry.

"Sister, I can't explain. I just need to be free. I need to be myself. I don't have time for everyone."

Sister Robert Therese knew these were words used when you want someone to keep a distance. She would respect Sr. Charity's wishes, but it did not make it any easier to work closely with her every day, yet maintain the distance Charity expected.

Sr. Robert Therese scrubbed harder, cleaned more thoroughly, and tried to dissipate an inner pain. Friendships were difficult to balance in the novitiate. The novices were frequently warned of "particular friendship", disapprovingly referenced by the religious community as "PF". PF's were forbidden among the novices, yet they all seemed to single out one or two more intimate relationships, in spite of directives. More often than not, the novices mocked the term and would ridicule a subtle message that friendship between two women would lead to sinful interludes.

Sr. Mary Alice (Linda) teamed up with Sr. John Michael (Janie) to plan their Bible Summer School lessons. They paired off as Sr. Robert Therese and Sr. Charity had. But with Sr. Mary Alice and

Sr. John Michael there was no "hidden agenda". They were very comfortable with each other and enjoyed sharing classroom experiences and classroom planning. One day, near the end of the summer program, while discussing lesson plans, Sr. John Michael took on a serious tone.

"Linda, (many of the girls had not yet become accustomed to the name changes and frequently would refer to names used during postulancy), try not to be shocked, but I'm leaving the convent the day St. Stan's Bible School closes. Please don't tell anyone. I could be in trouble for telling you. Geraldine forbade me to say a word. She told me it would only be upsetting for the group to know."

Sr. Mary Alice was stunned. She had never detected any signs of unhappiness or even a clue that Sr. John Michael wanted to leave. "Why Sister? Where are you going? What will you do?"

"It's hard to explain. Don't be upset. I'm really feeling good about my decision. You see, I used to be in another community. I entered the Sisters of Mercy motherhouse in Syracuse several years ago. I left as a second-year novice because I just didn't feel it was right for me. I came here because I thought my problem was finding the right community. I think the problem really is that I just don't belong in the convent."

Just then, Sr. Robert Therese interrupted their conversation. She knew they must have been discussing something rather serious because of the expressions still lingering upon their faces.

"Would you like me to come back later? I feel like something important must be going on."

Sr. Mary Alice looked to Sr. John Michael. She wanted her to decide if the conversation would continue or not. Both Sr. John Michael and Sr. Mary Alice liked and trusted Sr. Robert Therese.

"Sister, I was just telling Mary Alice about my decision to leave community. I know you will keep this to yourself," and she reviewed some of the thoughts the two had already shared.

"Where will you go from here?" Sr. Robert Therese asked.

"Back to Syracuse. I might go to Syracuse U. and finish a teaching degree. I'm not sure. I'll move in with my parents for a while."

"What can I do to help? This must be so hard for you," Mary Alice commented.

"Really, Linda, you mustn't worry. I'll be fine."

"What you decide to do with your life isn't my business, but I know I'll miss you. I'm so grateful you trusted us enough to say good-bye. I've always hated the disappearing act they have around here. Were you happier in the other community?" Sr. Mary Alice prodded some more.

"Not really. They were much stricter than these Albany nuns. You can't imagine some of their crazy rules. I just don't fit in. I've tried."

"I always wondered how you kept grand silence so well. You've been a perfect postulant and novice. We all felt that we could never be like you. Maybe it's because you were older, wiser, and more experienced," added Sr. Robert Therese.

Sr. John Michael wasn't sure if she was being teased with all the flattery but decided to accept Sr. Robert Therese's statement as a compliment. "I'm sure my years with the Mercy nuns have made all the difference. Linda, Angie, I can't tell you how much I've enjoyed knowing both of you this past year. I'm just hoping you'll stay in touch somehow. There are missions in Syracuse; you might be there someday. I'd really like us to remain friends somehow."

"Janie, we will. I know they won't let us write, but someday, we'll be in touch again," Sr. Robert Therese promised for the both of them.

"You must not tell anyone what I've said. I don't know what Geraldine would do if she knew I've shared this with you."

"She'd probably send you home!" Sr. Mary Alice observed.

They all laughed, shared a few quick embraces, and returned to thoughts of teaching the next day's class.

On the final day of Bible School, Sister Robert Therese gave her favorite student, Donald, a parting gift. She seriously considered giving him her most prized religious article, a small bronze statue of Mary. Her best friends, Diane and Sue, gave it to her just before she left for New York. It was a treasure that represented friendship, love, and her strong devotion to the Mother of Jesus. At the last moment, she decided her spirit of detachment was not sufficient. Instead, she gave Donald a medal and chain she received Investing Day from her aunt. She took it from under her collar and placed it around Donald's neck.

"This is so you won't forget me, Donald. I've enjoyed you so very much. I know teachers aren't supposed to have favorites, but, Sweetie, you've been a favorite for me."

Sr. Robert Therese had waited until the closing Mass ended the program. Outside of the church, she said good-bye to the little boy who wanted to take her hand, and become like family.

Sister placed a farewell kiss upon his cheek and attempted a good-bye hug. Instead, the boy ran away. There were tears in his eyes, and Angie wanted to run after him to explain that he would be fine. She wanted to comfort him, but knew she was expected to return directly to the car that would take the Sisters back to the novitiate. She felt so empty and unresolved about Donald and imagined it was probably even more difficult for a child of his age. She rode silently in the car, glanced at Sr. John Michael (Janie), and reflected upon how so very often in life people have to separate.

· · · · · · · ·

26

Sister Geraldine was packing up some of her personal effects from her office. Sister Elizabeth (Ginny) was assigned to dust and clean.

"I'm sure I'll enjoy doing catechetical ministry. Cold Springs isn't all that far. Sister, be sure to get the corners, I don't want Sr. Anita to inherit an untidy office."

Sr. Elizabeth was surprised by Sister's comments. Geraldine had not yet announced her transfer to the group.

"I didn't realize you were leaving, Sister," Sr. Elizabeth responded.

"I thought surely Sr. Dominic had told everyone. I'm not sure how she found out, but I know she's not disappointed about my re-assignment."

"I'm sorry to see you go," Sr. Elizabeth lied.

"You'll like the new mistress. She used to teach at Convent High School. She's Sr. Mary Peter's (Helen's) sponsor."

"That should be nice for Sr. Mary Peter." Sr. Elizabeth suggested. Sr. Geraldine gave Sr. Elizabeth one of her disapproving frowns. "Maybe," Sr. Elizabeth added.

Sister Elizabeth never felt she could say a correct thing in front of Sr. Geraldine. Just the other day, trying to make light conversation, Sr. Elizabeth mentioned something to the effect that "Variety is the spice of life," not really meaning anything by it. Sr. Geraldine attacked, "That's not at all true, Sister."

"Well, I have spent nine years as novice mistress, or directress, or whatever that title is. It is time for some new blood. Don't you agree, Sister?"

Sister Elizabeth didn't know how to answer. Saying "yes" might be interpreted as an insult. Saying "no" might be interpreted as insubordinate. She preferred to keep dusting and whispered an audible, "If you think so, Sister."

There were no formal announcements of leaving or farewells. Sister was gone and the changing of the guard took place sometime one Saturday afternoon. Sr. Anita called an afternoon assembly and novices were collected from their Saturday afternoon charges into the novitiate. They sat in rank and Sister sat at the head of the tables.

"I am Sr. Anita. Until recently, I have been teaching French at Regina Catholic College as well as Convent High. I am to replace Sr. Geraldine as your novice directress, and I expect each of you to carry on with your assignments until I have found reason to change them.

"My name is Sister Anita, and I do not tolerate any variation or nicknames such as `Annie, Ann, etc.`. You will continue the customary asking of blessing and begging of penances. In ten months, the community will expect you to be prepared for the more serious steps ahead. As canonical novices, you are at a spiritual peak; and if you do not practice faith, hope, and charity now, what makes you think you will as professed sisters?"

"On Monday we will all begin a week of pleasure with the constitutional novices at Mt. Alvernia Retreat Center." The news caused immediate stirrings. A vacation? With the constitutionals? Alvernia was a veritable paradise in August. There were glances of genuine amazement exchanged around the table.

"This will be a good opportunity for us to get to know each other better. I know your names and your backgrounds, and have examined your files extensively; but I think some informal time together would be good for all of us. I need to discover for myself what this Saint Jude Group is about. Are there any questions?" No one responded. "Then, I will see you all in the refectory for supper. You may return to your afternoon charges."

Sr. Mary Alice (Linda) spoke up just before the novices stood to leave. "Sister?" She was recognized.

"Yes, Sister Mary Alice?"

"Sister, do you need help arranging transportation to Lake George? My mother or father would be happy to drive."

"Sister, that won't be necessary. Cars have been arranged and drivers assigned. Just be ready to leave after dinner dishes on Monday."

"Thank you, Sister." Sr. Mary Alice responded graciously but for some reason felt embarrassed for offering.

The group disbanded but the girls were excited by the prospect of a week long vacation. Sister Anita appeared stiff and formal, but nice. It was a welcome relief from the badgering and bickering of Sr. Geraldine's directorship. Only Sr. Mary Peter (Helen) and Sr. Charity (Brigit) had known Sr. Anita as a teacher in high school. The other Convent High graduates knew her by name, or recognized her on sight, but didn't know anything else more. Sr. Mary Peter was not sure what the consequences of having her sponsor, former teacher, and inspiration to community as novice mistress would be. (The new term of "directress" was awkward and many continued to use the former title, "mistress".) Some of the novices suspected there might be favoritism, and there was.

The first day at Mt. Alvernia was a glorious experience. Sun, water, and even their frumpy, modest bathing suits were cause for camaraderie and laughter. Suits were to be changed in the bath house, as no one would dare walk the hillside up towards the Center without anything but full habit. Nylons, undersleeves, and all!

That first exposure to sunlight in over a year resulted in disaster. Two of the novices were so burned they were admitted overnight at a local community hospital with serious sun poisoning. Almost every novice went to bed that evening looking red as lobsters. Sr. Elizabeth (Ginny) was only one of many too uncomfortable to sleep. Sr. Anita noticed her light on after ten, and knocked on the door to find out why.

"I'm sorry, Sister. I just can't sleep. I can't get comfortable. I know I'm breaking light curfew, but I can't find any relief, even with cold water. It burns everywhere."

Sister Anita responded reasonably. "Wait here," she said, and shortly returned with a soothing medication.

"Lie down," Anita commanded.

Sr. Elizabeth complied and was most grateful for some help. She wanted to be a nurse or a doctor someday, but still felt embarrassed by having to pull up her nightgown so that Sr. Anita could apply the cream to the back of her legs, her back, and shoulders. Sr. Elizabeth kept modestly covered and was surprised to find Sr. Anita appear genuinely concerned. This was certainly a change from Sr. Geraldine.

"There. Do you know anyone else that might need some of this?" Sr. Anita asked.

Elizabeth thought for a moment, and then wondered if Sr. Anita had a sense of humor. "I think Sr. Mary Peter (Helen) might have gotten scorched. You may want to check her room." After all, if they were such famous friends, maybe Mary Peter would appreciate a back rub from her sponsor.

Sister Anita was quick to catch the innuendo and smiled. "Thank you, Sister. I might look into that." The light was turned off, the door closed, and Ginny slept as if in a body caste. She had forgotten how painful a sunburn could be.

· · · · · · · ·

27

Vacationing at Mt. Alvernia did not mean a reduction in prayer schedules, daily classes with Sr. Anita, dishes, or cleaning of charges. It did, however, allow canonicals and constitutionals to speak openly with each other, and permitted a few hours each day for reading, swimming, or other such recreation.

During the warm summer days it was difficult to pray the daily rosary together. Heads often nodded off to sleep, and the leader of prayer seemed to drag out the first half of each prayer. By now the constitutions proudly sported black veils to announce their new status in community. Still they lacked the Franciscan crucifix which signified their taking of vows. Sr. Mary Peter (Helen) and Sr. Dorothy were inseparable that week. Naturally, this was noticed by Sr. Geraldine's replacement.

Other than the discomfort of sun-burned bodies, the week at Mt. Alvernia proved to be a much needed change of pace for the hard working canonicals. Many long hours of manual work were expected from the newly invested, and many felt the rigorous change in lifestyle. Having returned from the break, the novices noticed a much different disposition assumed by Sr. Anita.

Sister was not smiling much now, nor was she as cordial or pleasant as she had been at Mt. Alvernia. She was giving more difficult penances, correcting countless behaviors, and taking on the critical looks of Sr. Geraldine. The novices were not sure what this new change in "climate" meant. There was a new uneasiness among the girls as they tried to understand the different behavior.

During daily instruction Sr. Anita explained that Saint Francis knew true humility. That because he knew, in prayer, the magnificence of God, and he knew his own insignificance as a creature of God. "St. Francis knew himself to be a sinner, of no importance. St. Francis often referred to himself as a worm," she instructed the young religious.

"Sister?" Sr. Elizabeth (Ginny) raised her hand, with some hesitation. She was recognized with the Superior's nod. "Why would St. Francis compare himself to a worm? I don't think it is humility to think yourself a worm if you are a person." Instead of simply clarifying or dealing with the question, the novice directress flew into a tirade.

"It is nice to know we have an expert on humility among us, isn't it, Sisters? Perhaps that is because you are the oldest among the group and less prone to postures of pride. Novices are so bold these days, not at all as in mine."

Sr. Elizabeth did not mean her question to be an attack on St. Francis or on Sr. Anita's position as teacher. She quickly regretted having spoken her true thoughts and continued to listen, as did the others.

"I think it might be a good idea to rotate the position of `oldest' in rank. Beginning this Sunday, Sr. Mary Peter (Helen) will assume the role of `number one', and you, Sister, will take her rank as `number two' until further notice."

"Thank you, Sister," was the appropriate response given by Sr. Elizabeth. This would mean Sr. Mary Peter would assume leadership in the absence of Sr. Anita. Sr. Elizabeth felt stripped of rank and glanced at her successor, Sr. Mary Peter. The favoritism was only beginning. Officially, Sr. Anita could not change rank. It was unchanging except when altered by death or departure from community. Still, in every practical way, the authority could be transferred as simply as her words now stated.

Sr. Mary Peter would not return Sr. Elizabeth's look.

Within a week it was announced that the canonicals were to move from their second floor cells to the fourth floor of the motherhouse. The college girls and novices were to change places to insure more privacy for the motherhouse professed and to allow more needed space for college dorm enrollment. Only eighteen postulants were expected for September 8th. They could occupy the south wing of the fourth floor. A very new arrangement for the novices was that four or five would sleep in a room, separated from each other only by curtains. A front attic closet would be shared by Sr. Mary Alice (Linda) and Sr. Catherine Ann (Kathleen). There was barely room for two beds, two small dressers and a stand-up room divider.

Beds and desks were carried from one building to the other one evening. The novices worked late into the night, with most of the furniture transferred before midnight. Probably the only group member to keep grand silence scrupulously was Sr. Elizabeth (Ginny). She felt it was still her responsibility to set a good example as Sr. Humiliana had instructed almost a year ago. This one most unusual evening, the group did not hesitate to converse whenever they needed. With all the activity, Sr. Elizabeth assumed it was permissible to speak as well.

That next morning, Sr. Catherine Ann (Kathleen) was joking with Sr. Anita, as she would at times. Sr. Catherine Ann was one of Sr. Anita's "informers" and unwittingly would tell Sister what might be happening among group members. Sr. Anita manipulated Catherine Ann as she so successfully pumped several others for information she desired.

In the middle of her complaints to Sr. Anita about how heavy the headboards and dressers were (Sr. Catherine Ann had back complaints occasionally), she slipped, "Sr. Elizabeth kept on telling us to speak more softly or we'd raise the dead nuns in the cellar." Sister Anita's eyebrows raised, and Sr. Catherine Ann realized she had just betrayed someone she considered "friend".

"You mean to tell me Sister, that Sr. Elizabeth (Ginny) broke grand silence?" Sr. Anita seemed delighted for a reason to correct Sr. Elizabeth.

"But, Sister, everybody did," Sr. Catherine Ann knew there was trouble brewing now.

At that very moment, Sr. Elizabeth entered the kitchen to report for morning duty to the Sister Anastatia, the head cook.

"Sister Elizabeth," beckoned Sr. Anita.

"Yes, Sister?" approached Ginny, like a lamb to slaughter.

"I don't recall you begging a penance for having broken grand silence last evening. Nor were you kneeling at breakfast. Do you always keep your faults hidden from the others, so that they might see you as better than you really are?"

"No, Sister." Elizabeth blanched.

"I have it from a very reliable source that you were talking during grand silence last night."

"Yes, Sister. I was."

"Sister, need I remind you to kneel when you are being corrected?"

"Yes, Sister. I mean, no, Sister," and she assumed the posture immediately. The usual morning kitchen bustle continued as if the scene was nothing extraordinary. Correction of novices was so common, it was hardly noticed, except by the woman kneeling before her superior.

"Sister, do you have an excuse for this deceitful behavior of yours?"

"No, Sister. I talked because everyone else was talking, and I just assumed we had permission."

"Sister," Anita's eyes widened with fury, "you ASSUMED there was permission. You should know better than to ASSUME permission to break community rules. In the future, you will come to me personally before you speak to anyone after night prayer. Do I make myself clear, Sister?"

"Yes, Sister. May I have a penance, Sister?"

"Yes, you *may*, Sister! You will wash, wax and clean the laundry floor on Saturday, *by yourself*. I will make it clear to the others that you are not to be helped, for even a moment. Is that understood, Sister?"

"Yes, Sister. Thank you, Sister." She kissed the floor and remained kneeling until she was excused.

Later, that day Sr. Catherine Ann (Kathleen), who witnessed everything, went to her friend and explained.

"Elizabeth, I never meant for her to turn on you like that. I didn't think she'd just get you. We were all talking. I am so sorry I got you in trouble. Sr. Anita is just unpredictable. Sometimes when I say something I think is funny, she laughs. Other times, she makes a federal case."

"It's okay, Catherine. I know it isn't your fault. She just loves humiliating me. If it weren't grand silence, it would have been something else. Just do me a favor. From now on, please don't mention my name for *any* reason. Okay?"

"You forgive me?"

"Of course, I forgive you. That's life in the big city, the way the cookie crumbles, and all that. Canonical years aren't forever. They just feel like they are."

The new postulants entered on September 8th. It was a welcome relief to have Sr. Humiliana back from summer school. Even though novices were not permitted to speak with Sister without Sr. Anita's consent, it was still a comfort to see her at meals and during prayer. Sister Humiliana had no shortage of understanding looks or much appreciated smiles.

Several of the canonicals were asked to compose a reception service in chapel and were busy with necessary preparations, mostly cleaning. As the entrance day for the new group came and went, there was nostalgia and conversations of their own first impressions and "entrance day jitters".

"Did we look that green?" Sr. Charity (Brigit) whispered to Sr. Humiliana.

"Much worse, Sr. Charity. These girls are a little older than most of you. They should do very well," and she smiled as she went about her many responsibilities.

The next day was Monday, and the canonicals had been working diligently in the laundry since 5:00 A.M. They hoped to have the bulk of the heavy work finished before dinner. Veils were starched and ironed, chapel laundry was done, and so were most of the sheets. Rarely did the job get finished before late afternoon, but speed and experience was beginning to count. Discussion, if any, was done in whispers. Postulants would not be asked to help in laundry for several weeks.

"Sister Mary Daniel!" Sister Anita called out her name in a tone which made each of the novices grateful it was not their names announced.

"Yes, Sister." She put down her iron, turned it off, and approached.

"Sister, how do you expect anyone to get these underpants clean? They're terribly stained!" (*All* clothing and every item sent to laundry could be identified with name tags.) "They should have been soaked in bleach before you sent them to common wash."

By now Georgette was kneeling by the two large hoppers, (wash tubs).

"I'm sorry, Sister."

"You should be. This is not something I should have to tell an adult. Your mother should have taught you to keep underwear cleaner than this! And, your veil, Sister. It is a disgrace. Look at the gray color, the ground-in dirt. You will stand here and scrub your things until they are white. I don't care if it takes three days! Do you understand, Sister?" Anita had a way about her, about as endearing as a Marine sergeant with rabies.

"Yes, Sister. Thank you, Sister." The girl was mortified, but by now the group was numb to public humiliation. It was a way of life for the canonicals. They all felt sorry for her and knew if it wasn't Sr. Mary Daniel today, it would have been another unfortunate. Even favored daughter, Sr. Mary Peter (Helen), would take a turn now and then.

But what happened next surprised the novices. Sr. Anita turned to Sr. Aquinas. Sister was in her seventies. She worked diligently alongside the novices all day long. They all appreciated and respected the old woman who liked nothing more than keeping up with "the kids".

"Sr. Aquinas, you are not folding those napkins as I showed you. Can't you follow a few simple directives. Must I have a novice teach you how to do it right?" Sr. Anita sounded lethal.

It was one thing to demean and humiliate a novice; it seemed quite another for their superior to turn on an elderly professed who was kind enough to contribute so much help. The novices bristled, but no one dared speak up.

"I'm sorry, Sister. I will not do it incorrectly again. Thank you, Sister." Sr. Aquinas accepted the correction with no excuses, a model response. Trying to explain your behavior was a challenge to Sr. Anita. She wanted apologies only and to be obeyed. No excuses.

Sr. Aquinas was wounded by the attack. The novices knew her well. She tried so hard to be a role model for them and was surrogate grandmother for all. Perhaps it was jealousy that motivated Sr. Anita's berating remarks, perhaps the thrill of power over the old woman, perhaps hormonal imbalances. Whatever the reason, the novices were to witness the humiliation of Sr. Aquinas many times before the year ended. Such unkindness to an old woman wanting only to be of service seemed inexcusable, unpardonable behavior. Aquinas saw to the needs of many of the old and infirmed nuns. She was respectful of rank at all times, yet empathized with the continuous battering of canonicals.

"Sisters, I want your attention." Sr. Anita received it immediately. She went to the center of the room where she could be seen. "Father Jude and Fr. Duffy have both asked that you stop starching their underwear. Why would you think they need a crease in their shorts, anyway? How is it possible that God could bring so many stupid people from so many places to this one novitiate during the very same year?"

With that, Sr. Anita made a dramatic exit, leaving her underlings unsure if they were expected to laugh or cry. A few blank expressions were exchanged.

Sister Christine Marie could not remain silent, but she wasn't loud enough for everyone to hear. "I was the only stupid person

Hawaii could send this year. I guess there's a shortage." Several shoulders shrugged, and the novices returned to their ironing, folding, and sorting.

Two days later, Sr. Mary Daniel (Georgette) was gone. No words to explain. No one saw her leave. Just after evening prayer, Sister Anita announced that she had gone home.

· · · · · · · ·

28

Sr. Mary Peter (Helen) never asked that her sponsor become the novice mistress. It was an act of fate that could have fallen to anyone in the group, but because she was an obvious favorite, Mary Peter's rapport with her group became increasingly strained. Sr. Charity had been her best friend throughout Convent High School, but now there were tell-tale signs of their strong bonds weakening.

Sr. Anita had drastically curtailed the number of hours Sr. Elizabeth could work in the infirmary. She knew this was her favorite task, to learn of medicine and patient care. Sr. Francis Anne (Veronica), Sr. Mary Lewis (Barbara), and Sr. Catherine Ann (Kathleen) were assigned to pick up the slack. They all knew Sr. Elizabeth was being dealt a personal blow, but directives were obeyed and never questioned.

Sr. Elizabeth was given more kitchen duty and often was sent to clean garbage cans and bathrooms. Sr. Christine Marie (Sandra) offered her friend some comfort. As a postulant, Sr. Christine Marie was routinely the cleaner of toilets and shared that it had been her favorite charge. She said it was satisfying to make the porcelain sparkle and even gave the commodes individual nicknames. She also referred to them as her "little white friends". Sr. Christine Marie tried to lighten Sr. Elizabeth's displeasure with the magic of humor, and it worked.

Sr. Elizabeth tried not to feel a growing resentment over having lost her rank to Sr. Mary Peter. For weeks she remained silent, but now her anger flared openly.

Sr. Anita was out for the afternoon and left Sr. Mary Peter to answer the phone and door. She was to oversee the general novitiate activities. Sr. Elizabeth returned from cleaning storage closets in the basement and found a moment's refuge in the first chair inside the novice's community room.

"Sister," said Sr. Mary Peter, "before Sr. Anita left, she asked me to have you re-hem the novitiate curtains. They are frayed on the bottom from rubbing the sill. She said that if you take the hem up about an inch, they'll last longer."

"I don't believe this. Why did she ask me? There are ten other novices that like to sew and sew ten times better than I do. Why me?"

Even Sr. Mary Peter looked perplexed. "I don't know Sister, but you better get something started before she gets home."

"What is it with you two? Why do you cater to her every whim? Are you kissing her feet when we're not around?" Sr. Mary Peter looked uncomfortable over Sr. Elizabeth's (Ginny's) accusation.

"I'm only obeying her directive, Sister. Don't do the curtains."

Sr. Elizabeth knew not hemming the curtains was no option. The problem was not curtains, and they both knew it.

"Maybe I'm jealous. Maybe that's my problem, but I'm learning to dislike you, Mary Peter—a whole lot. I think even years from now I will resent having to live like this, even for a while. You play into it. You love being her lackey."

Sr. Mary Peter was silent. The truth of Sr. Elizabeth's anger was honest. Still, Sr. Mary Peter was mesmerized by her sponsor in ways even she couldn't understand. Mary Peter was young and ambitious and wanted success, position, and approval as much as any novice among them. She could not keep herself from playing the game. But one day she would look back with regret for having been a pawn in a play for power.

Sr. Robert Therese (Angie) enjoyed her charge, novitiate chapel. She took great pride in her work and offered every task as prayer. Sr. Humiliana taught the postulants to do their best work to please God, and it would become an act of love, praise, and thanksgiving. Even the postulants noticed the meticulous care Sr. Robert Therese took with every detail of chapel.

Every morning, after Mass in the motherhouse chapel, novices would disband to some early task such as setting breakfast tables, taking wheel chair bound nuns to the infirmary, etc. The postulants would return to the novitiate chapel for meditation. Ritually, Sr. Robert Therese (Angie) walked into the sacristy to get a wax taper. She then took a light from the Sanctuary lamp and lit two vigil candles on the altar. On September 17th, she lit four. Returning to her bench, she knelt in prayer. Sr. Anita called Sr. Robert Therese to her side.

"Sister, why do you have four candles burning this morning?"

"It's the feast of the Stigmata of St. Francis, Sister. I just thought it would be nice to add a little more light."

"Sister, are you paying for the candles?"

"No, Sister."

"Well, until you do, you will not assume we can afford anything more than two candles."

"Thank you, Sister. May I have a penance?"

"Yes, say three Our Fathers for the Holy Father."

"Thank you, Sister." Sr. Robert Therese returned to the sanctuary and removed the candle she had placed before St. Joseph's statue and another in front of the Blessed Mother statue. She blew them out and returned them into the sacristy. Having returned to her place in chapel, Sr. Anita summoned her once more.

"Sister, I think you have enjoyed the privilege of caring for chapel long enough. I want you to trade with Sr. Mary Peter (Helen). She will teach you to run the laundry, and Sister will take your place as sacristan."

"Yes, Sister. Thank you, Sister." Sister Robert Therese was deeply saddened over the news. Chapel had been such a consolation, particularly being so far from anyone she considered true friend or family. She had prayed often over her strained relationship with Sr. Charity (Brigit). She found the room a refuge from the tension and friction so many others experienced under the watchful eye of Sr. Anita. For three month Sr. Robert Therese had managed the chapel skillfully and had flawlessly attended to its care. She was resolved that others should benefit from the peace incurred by caring for so quiet and peaceful a place.

After breakfast everyone attended to her morning charges. Sr. Christine Marie (Sandra) and Sr. Catherine Ann (Kathleen) cheerfully headed toward the motherhouse refectory. Sr. Rose was generally quite amiable as long as work was finished on schedule. Cleaning the silver for almost two hundred settings was one of the many routine tasks scheduled weekly. Sr. Christine Marie enjoyed the refectory rituals and began to hum with pleasure a melody from home.

"My, My! Our helper is sick! Someone call a doctor! You hava mucha pain, Sister? It sounsa bada!" Sr. Rose spoke with a thick Italian accent. She had amusing ways of managing her help and getting people to do her bidding. She was a hard working woman, and the care of her charge was as much a part of her as was her accent.

"I'm not sick, Sister. I'm happy."

"Well, dear, I wanta be happy-a too, and I thinka if you save-a you groanin' til-a lata, I canna concentrate-a ona whata has ta be done-a next-ta."

Sister Christine Marie (Sandra) was not at all insulted. This was standard banter with Sr. Rose. She looked at her partner, Sr. Catherine Ann (Kathleen) who looked back. Two smiles spontaneously mushroomed.

"Too mucha attachamenta! You two always-a like-a to worka together. I thinka there's a too mucha attachamenta!"

"Oh, no, Sister! I don't even like Sr. Catherine Ann. She's very unpleasant to work with," Sr. Christine Marie teased back. Wanting to change the subject, Sr. Christine Marie asked, "Sr. Rose, who was your sponsor when you came to community? I mean, who, helped you come from Italy?"

"My sponsora? Who leda me-a from Italia? The Blesseda Muthor! Thatsa my sponsora. Nowa you justa finisha disa silverware and geta all the salta and-a-pepper shakersa backa. Hurry! Rapidamente! It'sa lata."

Both novices moved quickly, with a zest that was characteristic of canonicals. Sr. Christine Marie was graceful and moved about the refectory almost as if swaying graciously to a Hawaiian hula.

The next day was Sr. Robert Therese's (Angie's) birthday. Now that she was a novice her birthday was not to be celebrated. She had a patron saint now, St. Theresa, "the Little Flower." Her feastday was October 3rd. That's when Sr. Robert Therese was to garner a bit of attention. Nuns were to commemorate the day their patron saint died and not mark the day they themselves entered this temporal world of sin and suffering. Birthday greetings were not unacceptable, but feastday greetings were more in line with religious decorum.

Sr. Robert Therese turned nineteen today. No one remembered. Again, the young woman found reason to feel a renewed wave of homesickness. At home there was quite a fuss for birthdays. Cake, spumoni, candles. Her mother prepared homemade lasagna "to die for". Dad would always dip his finger into the cake to taste the icing before it was candled and cut. It annoyed both Angie and her mom, but Dad would always say, "I want you to miss me when I'm gone! Whenever you celebrate with birthday cake, you'll say, 'It's just not the same without Dad's fingerprint!'

Today, Sr. Robert Therese was missing her dad. During recreation, Sr. Anita called her into her office. She handed the novice a telegram.

"This came addressed to Sister Angie Masucci. I imagine that means you, Sister." Already the envelope had been opened and inspected by Sr. Anita. Sr. Robert Therese was curious, as she could not imagine why anyone would be sending her a telegram. She began to read as Sister remarked, "It's from your father."

Sr. Robert Therese decided she preferred to read it alone.

"May I take it to chapel, Sister?" She feared it might be
something personal, and already group members were stretching
from the community room to see who or what merited the first
and only telegram to novitiate.

"Yes, Sister."

"Thank you, Sister," and Sr. Robert Therese left for chapel.

She turned on a single light in front, just enough to read the
short message. "Happy Birthday, Darling. I still have hope. Love,
Dad."

Angie felt warm tears cascading down her dark cheeks. This
was the first written message she had from her father since the day
he and mom took her to the Toledo airport. There had been two
phone calls, but never a letter or card. It was his way of telling her,
"I'm letting you have what you want, but I still don't like it." She
knew exactly what her father was hoping. There was no one in
chapel, but Christ in the Eucharist. She was free to sob openly as
she buried her wet cheeks into her soft hands. Sr. Robert Therese
wanted to please her dad, but she also wanted to please her Heavenly
Father as well.

· · · · · · · ·

29

Fall was becoming winter all too rapidly. The surprise
Halloween party for the postulants was just as much a success as it
had been last year. By now, already, three of the postulants were
gone, and only fifteen remained. They called themselves the
"Kateri" group, after a Mohawk Indian being introduced in Rome
as a candidate for Beatification.

The postulants often discussed the novices. They were inspired
by the white-veiled women, as if they were mystics floating about
the convent grounds. Postulants were gullible and usually naive. It
was easy to impress the impressionable. Sr. Dominic reported "from

the grapevine" that postulants referred to their favorite novice as a "Thump-thump."

Sr. Robert Therese was typically the last to hear anything "off the vine" and mused at the term coined by the new group. "Dominic, does anyone consider me a Thump-thump?"

"I doubt it, R.T." came her reply.

Postulants were now assisting with dishes. Sr. Mary Alice (Linda) was assigned to "pots and pans" and was up to her elbows in mammoth kettles and "betsys". (That was what the Sister in charge of the kitchen called her saucepans). As Linda scrubbed deep into the bottom of the large pot, she felt a rush of inner satisfaction. She scoured for the "love of God", and the hard work felt as if it was an oblation before her Beloved. There was an immediate reward of knowing she was doing her best and found herself bursting into a smile when a postulant walked past en route to the dishwasher.

Sr. Mary Alice flashed one of her remarkably warm and affectionate looks as the postulant responded, "Pax et Bonum, Sister."

Unfortunately, Sr. Anita also witnessed the more than cordial greeting. Sr. Mary Alice meant nothing by the smile. Had a cart or a tree passed, it, too, would have been smiled upon. It was just a burst of unexplainable joy. But now, she caught the eye of Sr. Anita. She knew she was in trouble.

Fraternizing with postulants was a capital offense. Any sort of communication other than that which was supervised and authorized was contempt for the rule. Sr. Mary Alice washed her hands hastily and followed Sr. Anita into her office. She was not sure how she would explain herself. Actually, of all the postulants to smile upon, the girl before her had been the one Sr. Mary Alice least liked. That would not make any difference now.

"Sister, you understand why you are here?" began Sr. Anita.

"Yes, Sister." Sr. Mary Alice was kneeling.

"Sister, would you give me just one good reason why you would inundate that girl with one of your "Hollywood" smiles, when you fully comprehend the regulation of novitiate life?"

"Sister, I'm sorry. I didn't mean to. It was an accident."

"Sister, how *does* one *accidentally* smile?"

"I can't explain it, Sister. She was all of a sudden, in front of me. I couldn't help myself. I felt so good about scrubbing the pan, I just smiled."

"Sister, if scrubbing pans delights you, perhaps I should assign you to "pots and pans" permanently."

Sister Mary Alice was at a loss for words. She just couldn't explain herself. It was time to beg a penance. "Sister, may I have a penance?"

"Yes, Sister. You certainly may. Tomorrow, during all three meals, you are to stand. You will hold your plate in the air, and eat without conversing. If I feel you have learned a lesson, I will not expect you to eat standing for the week. Do you understand, Sister?"

"Yes, Sister. Thank you, Sister." Linda kissed the floor and was dismissed to finish her kitchen work.

Standing for meals was a new penance, at least it was new to the novices and postulants. Kneeling for breakfast was common practice; but before Sr. Mary Alice, no one had been asked to stand for meals. Standing was definitely more awkward. At least, when you knelt, the food was at shoulder level. Nor did you get as much notice. No one in the refectory missed seeing Sr. Mary Alice and her dish towering above the others. No one commented much about it either. It was a penance. Sr. Mary Alice had shared with Sister Charity and a few others what happened. It wasn't all that interesting an explanation. After all, this was normal.

· · · · · · · ·

30

During the canonical year, there was very little in the way of formal college instruction. Even Sr. Anita was nowhere near as faithful to daily class with the novices as Sr. Humiliana had been. Sometimes a whole week would pass before she would summon them for some instructive purpose. Sr. Anita attempted to teach the Palmer Method for handwriting, but after two classes she realized it would take more effort and energy than she cared to muster.

Only four "outside" teachers were assigned to teach that year. All came into the novitiate classroom, as novices rarely, if ever, frequented the college campus. Upon occasion, white veils were seen attending choir practice Sunday evening.

Sister Lucretia taught "Situation Ethics" every Monday and Wednesday afternoon for an hour. As far as anyone could tell, her course could be summarized by this analogy: "If three people in a life raft had enough food for only two, would it be morally ethical for one to sacrifice his or her life so that the other two could possibly survive?" The novices never were given the correct answer and assumed that it "probably depended on the situation."

Sister Lucretia would also discuss Scripture passages from Canticle of Canticles. She had majored in Greek and Hebrew, but at the age of 78 she proved to be the driest, dullest, yet dearest member of the Regina Catholic faculty. The novices tried hard to listen, but, usually, sitting down meant naps for most. Sister's monotone voice lulled off even the most apt of students.

Sr. Stephen was assigned to give a three week blitz course in catechetical ministry, that is, the ministry of teaching religious instruction to public school children. This course, more than any other, kept novices awake, partly because Sr. Stephen was effervescent and entertaining and partly because they enjoyed the content of her lessons.

Sr. Francis James taught another three week blitz course in speed reading. The course was well-intentioned but not well executed. Years later, the only recall they would have from their three weeks would be how to poke a hole in a magazine page and then ask a partner to witness the rapid eye movement from behind the poked hole. Novices just never thought about their eyes sweeping back and forth as they read. Rachael Timmons taught music appreciation to the novices. She was only eight years older than most of her students, but she was an accomplished harpist who played for the Albany County Symphony. She too, was an enthusiastic teacher. She was so devoted to classical music that, eventually, the novices would thrill to recognize Rimsky-Korsakov, Tchaikovsky, and others.

Actually, each teacher made some lasting impression and inevitably taught something of themselves, with at least some content from their areas of expertise. No teacher could fail completely with students so eager to learn.

One day, as Sr. Anita demonstrated a dignified walk, she explained to the novices that having your hips swing was unnecessary for women. "Socially, you are taught to swivel so that you may demonstrate a certain sensual prowess. However, if you walk tall with you shoulders back, stand with your head up, and walk with purpose and dignity, you can move just as successfully without causing attention to your behinds." The novices were amused. They practiced. Arms would still swing wildly, and others stepped as longshoremen, but eventually their posture and demeanor improved. More and more, novices imitated the mannerisms of their leader.

Sr. Mary Peter (Helen) especially began to assume tones of speech, facial expressions, and gestures similar to Sr. Anita's. They were expected to model themselves after Sr. Anita. Even though her corrections were searing and even brutal at times, she had the awe, the respect and the fear of every young, impressionable protege.

Sr. Anita had charisma. Even if you wanted to hate her, you still believed her discipline and training were for the purpose of reforming your soul, improving your character, and pleasing the Creator. To obey the will of Sr. Anita was to serve the will of God.

After "walking" lessons, Sr. Anita spoke of Sr. Mary Peter's (Helen's) father. "Sisters, some of you know Sr. Mary Peter's father has been ill. Last month he was diagnosed as having cancer in advanced stages. The family has no idea how long he will be with them, but I ask you to be prayerful and supportive of Sr. Mary Peter during this trying time." Sr. Mary Peter lowered her head and tried not to demonstrate the fear and pain she felt.

"This weekend, I will be out all afternoon on Saturday as I have given Sister permission to visit her father weekly. I have decided to support her during these visits." Many of the St. Jude Group now resented some of Sr. Mary Peter's position as "favored daughter" status, but all the novices responded favorably. They could not keep from feeling an empathy for Sr. Mary Peter, and that Sr. Anita accompany Mary Peter was also considered an appropriate act of charity.

"I know Sister would appreciate our offering of daily rosary for the well-being of her father. It would be a comfort to her family to assure them of our prayerful concern." There followed expressions of agreement and the nodding of heads.

Class was dismissed and the canonicals returned to work. An endless pile of mending was kept in the novitiate community room for those "unoccupied". Sr. Robert Therese (Angie) mustered some courage and approached Sr. Anita after the group disbanded.

"Yes, Sister?" Sr. Anita knew she had some purpose in approaching.

"Sister, I know this isn't any of my business, but may I ask you if you have word from Sr. Mary Daniel (Georgette)? I mean, how is she? Is she working?" This was a bold gesture on Sr. Robert Therese's part, but she imagined that if she went to Sister Anita privately, she might be assured of how her friend was doing.

"Sister, I had to send Sr. Mary Daniel home. She was asked to leave because of poor personal hygiene. My job is not a pleasant one, but if you would have seen the condition of her dresser and her clothing you would understand. I'm sure she's doing fine. It was nice of you to ask." Sr. Anita smiled, gathered a few items from her desk, and left.

"Thank you, Sister," Sr. Robert Therese spoke to her disappearing back. She was stunned. In amazement, she walked directly to chapel, blessed herself with water from the holy water font, and knelt in her assigned place. Her prayer was angry.

"Why did she tell me that? I don't want to know Sr. Mary Daniel was kicked out for being dirty, or whatever. I don't even want to know she was sent home!" Sr. Robert Therese was fond of Georgette and found her to be intelligent, creative, and humorous. "Why couldn't Sr. Anita just have said, `She's doing very well' and let it go at that? This convent is a strange place. More and more it was not like anything she imagined. Novices were at each other's throats, vying for rank and attention. Few seemed to take the regulations seriously, and charity was not something she had witnessed since postulancy. Things were very different then. Is *this* what the convent is all about? Power? Submissiveness? Division?" Her thoughts were disturbing.

Sr. Robert Therese sat back into her bench and reached for her spiritual reading. She was almost finished with the life of Saint Margaret Mary Alacoque, visionary of the Sacred Heart of Jesus. She remembered the passage where the nuns, who acted out of jealousy, had attacked Saint Margaret Mary one evening and left her to die in the cloister. The nun had been attempting to reach the refuge of her superior who was sick in the infirmary.

"Nuns can be so cruel to each other," Sr. Robert Therese thought. "Being sent home because you aren't clean enough to please the superior was one thing, but telling *anyone* why a novice was not worthy of religious life was quite another. Maybe it *was* better *not* to know why their numbers had fallen from 25 to 17. Maybe it was better that they did "just disappear".

. . . .

31

Sr. Robert Therese (Angie) gave her best efforts to her charge of laundry. It proved to be a huge responsibility for the eighteen year old. There was a full schedule of collecting clothes from hampers and baskets on every floor of every department throughout the motherhouse complex. As she returned from a routine collection she pushed her cart into the laundry to find Sr. Mary Peter (Helen) standing near one of the industrial sized washing machines. Sr. Dominic (Betsy) stood a few feet behind Sr. Anita. She was surprised by the welcoming committee, and upon entering the room, inquired if something were wrong.

"Sister, the washing machine repair man was just here and made it very clear to me that the difficulty we've been having has come about by someone *intentionally* lifting the lid on the power box and breaking the handle which controls the normal flow of current necessary to run the machines. And, Sister, I have reason to believe it is you who has done this, probably for attention."

Sr. Robert Therese knew there were problems with the two giant machines stopping in mid-cycle and, often, not triggering the soap dispenser cups so that it had to be done manually. Still, she assumed a blank look. This input did not register. Sr. Anita believed she would sabotage these machines for attention—*intentionally*? If there was something Sr. Robert Therese didn't want, it was Sr. Anita's attention.

"Sister, are you kidding?" It may not have been an astute reply to this wild accusation, but Sr. Robert Therese was too stunned to reply any other way.

"Sister, I don't kid. The repair man just left and he insisted the damage was intentional. You are always striving to be noticed, Sister, always seeking attention. To feed this insatiable need, you have to be singular; you deliberately tried to destroy this equipment."

Sr. Robert Therese was overwhelmed by the absurdity of this scene. She was humiliated to be accused in front of the others and responded once more. "Sister, I wouldn't break a pencil if I thought it useful. I didn't break the machines. I have never opened the power box. I've never had a reason to."

"Sister, you may go to your room. When you have decided to confess this misconduct, I will be in my office. Until you do, I insist you discuss this with no one. Nor will the novices have permission to speak with you until you own up to what you've done."

Sr. Robert Therese neither knelt nor kissed the floor. She glanced with disbelief upon the two onlookers and then made eye-contact once more with her accuser. She turned and went directly to the bedroom she shared with six others. No one was there, as novices could not visit their rooms during the day unless given specific permission to do so.

She felt stir crazy with so many laundry chores needing to be done. She lost herself in a book until after supper. No one came with a meal, and Sr. Robert Therese felt it was time to try reasoning with Sr. Anita again. Only recently she had this nightmare of working in the novitiate chapel sacristy when Sr. Anita come in and attacked her, kicking her head as she lay upon the floor, helpless and defenseless. This was probably an unconscious acting out of her inner fear for the woman controlling her life. This new and twisted episode with Sr. Anita was truly psychologically damaging. Why would she accuse Sr. Robert Therese of insane behavior? Is this just another trial to see if her vocation was genuine?

Sr. Robert Therese found herself knocking upon Sr. Anita's door. It was ajar. "Come in, Sister. I have been expecting you. I'm glad you have finally decided to be truthful."

Sr. Robert Therese knelt in front of the officious looking desk where Sr. Anita remained seated.

"Sister, I wish I did have something to confess," she began. "Before God, I never have opened that power box. I'm not even sure I knew it was there."

"And you expect me to believe that?"

"Sister, I can't help whether you believe me or not. I'm not a liar. I've come to ask permission to speak with Sr. Humiliana. I know she will believe me."

"Sister, you discuss your problems in community with me or with the priest I so designate and no one else. Have we accomplished nothing with your confinement?"

"Sister." Sr. Robert Therese was determined not to show the extent of her intimidation. She relied upon human self-respect to find the courage she needed. "I have sworn to you that I could not and have not intentionally broken your washing machines. For the rest of your life you may think I'm lying, but I refuse to confess to something I have not done."

This must have been a turning point for Sr. Anita because she did not pursue the accusation. Instead, she changed the focus of conversation to the many open sores surrounding Sr. Robert Therese's fingernails. Almost every finger had split skin surrounding the sides of her nails. "What has happened to your fingers, Sister?"

Sr. Robert Therese was relieved to hear the subject change. It was a good sign. "Sister, I think it is from having my hands in water so often. Maybe it's also from the colder weather." (Though this had never happened even during the coldest of Ohio winters.) "Sr. Aquinas said it happens to her sometimes. She said hand cream might help but I haven't any, and I haven't had time to ask her for some."

"I have something we could try. This antiseptic should help." Anita called the novice to her private adjoining lavatory and took some hydrogen peroxide from the shelf. "This may sting a little but it might also help to heal some of those cuts."

Sr. Anita poured the painful antiseptic upon her fingers and looked upon her face expecting some grimace of pain. There was none. It did burn, but Sr. Robert Therese hardly noticed. She felt defeated and could not muster the energy to express discomfort. The hydrogen peroxide bubbled and fizzed the bacteria away and then Sr. Anita gave her a paper towel to pat-dry her hands.

"Thank you, Sister," said Robert Therese.

"Sister. I now officially close this case of the broken washing machines. We will not speak of it again. You may go."

. . . .

32

Sr. Elizabeth (Ginny) was vacuuming the sanctuary rug in the motherhouse chapel. Sister Cyrilla approached to ask her to turn off the machine. She did. "I need some help putting the flowers on the side altars. I can't carry them by myself. The Thanksgiving Day sprays are too large for me to lift alone. Come with me, Sister."

They both walked into the sacristy where Sister had arranged two large vases of mums and other fall flowers from the Chapel garden. The flowers were expertly situated and worthy of their place of honor.

"They are lovely, Sister," spoke the novice as she whiffed deeply from the freshly cut bouquet.

"Sister, you don't smell flowers to be placed upon the altar. The fragrance is God's delight."

Sister Elizabeth, like so many times before, was not sure about this novel idea. Don't sniff the flowers if you are using them in chapel? Every day there was something new.

"Thank you, Sister. I'm sorry. I didn't know."

"Well, now you do, Sister. Please place these on either side of the Crucifix. The small ones go on the side altars." She nodded toward two smaller vases on a side table to the left. Sr. Cyrilla was a hard worker, about sixty, and was considered eccentric. Few if any of the others really knew her, but they spoke of her as peculiar, yet harmless.

"Yes, Sister. Is there anything else you'd like me to do after I finish the carpet?"

"No, but make sure you check the water fonts before you leave."

"Yes, Sister." Ginny thought the novices will laugh to hear the latest Cyrilla episode: "Don't smell the flowers?" As if in doing so, you kept their fragrance from God? Sr. Elizabeth also learned it was not appropriate for flowers from a funeral to be displayed in her chapel—no "second-hand flowers" in this sanctuary!

Returning to the novitiate community room, Sr. Robert Therese noticed Sr. Charity cutting off name tags from the personal belongings of a deceased sister. Anything usable was appreciated by the novices who often appreciated a work habit, coronets with fewer patches, or a newer cord.

"Whatcha' doin', Charity?" Sr. Robert Therese amiably inquired.

"Trying to finish this before Sr. Anita asks for them. She gave them to me this morning, so I know she wants them before yesterday."

"Did you know Sr. Matilda?"

"Everyone who went to Convent High knew Sister. She was one of the best. Sr. Mary Alice is pretty shook up about it. Sr. Matilda was her sponsor."

"Is Sister Anita giving Mary Alice some of her things?"

"Who knows. I guess she'll give them to whomever is most in need. All I do is cut the tags off."

"What's this?" Sr. Elizabeth picked up a rope like object.

"That's a discipline."

"A what?"

"A discipline. It is a wax-coated cord used for beating yourself."

"Charity, are you nuts? You're not serious."

"Sure I am. Nuns use it for flagellation."

"Flagellation?"

"Yes, silly, you know, whipping."

"You mean to tell me nuns beat each other with this thing?"

"No, pea brain. They beat themselves. It's penance. I don't know a whole lot about it but they use it during lent or something."

"Well, they won't make me beat myself with a whip. I can't believe they do that."

"If you don't believe me, Sister, ask Sr. Anita." She continued to snip off name tags, even one from the discipline.

At that, Sr. Dominic walked in. "Robert Therese, aren't you scheduled to lead rosary in the infirmary this afternoon?"

"Oh my gosh, yes! I forgot!"

"Well, they're asking for you up there. Better hurry. They're already sitting in the hall waiting for you to start. You're lucky I had to take some wash up."

"Thank you." Sr. Robert Therese hurried, as novices are expected to energize, but never take on the appearance of being rushed.

In her haste, she accidently genuflected as she passed Sr. Anita's office. She intended the genuflection for chapel directly across the hall. This was a community custom to genuflect whenever passing chapel, only Robert Therese faced the wrong direction.

It was unusual for her not to be noticed doing something as stupid as genuflecting towards Sr. Anita's office. In novitiate, some of the novices felt as if they were continuously ridiculed for the slightest impropriety. Yet, strangely enough, others were not attacked, belittled, or harassed all that much. Years from now, they each spoke from different perspectives of novitiate training. Everyone's experience was somewhat unique, yet somewhat in common. Some of the novices would continue to live in community nearly unscathed by their years of formation; others were changed permanently.

Sr. Robert Therese was fortunate to have arrived in time. She would not have to beg a penance. After a slow and reverent recitation of the rosary, Sister Elizabeth approached the novice.

"Anita wants you. She sent me up to get you."

"Am I in trouble?" Sr. Robert Therese asked.

"I hope not, Sister," she answered. Sr. Robert Therese left the infirmary promptly, but Sr. Elizabeth used the opportunity to visit her friend, Sr. Bernadette, who was confined to bed.

"Where *have* you been, Sr. Elizabeth?" Sister greeted the novice with a delighted smile. "We hardly ever see you anymore!"

"I know, Sister. I can't explain very well. Sr. Anita doesn't think I have the makings of a nurse." Sister was very candid with her middle-aged, paralyzed friend. "I think she hates seeing me work up here because she knows how much I love doing it. If she gets her way, I'll not study medicine. She thinks I'm some garden variety incompetent. I don't think she likes me very much."

"But Sister, she doesn't know you like we do. You make a wonderful nurse! I don't know anyone who finds greater pleasure in helping us with our many aches and pains." Sr. Bernadette always had kind words for Elizabeth. "Next time you visit, Sister, could you plan some time for reading to me? I'm enjoying one of the best biographies I have ever read of St. Francis. It is so inspiring!"

"I promise, Sister. I'll even ask Sr. Anita for some time with you."

"Don't get yourself in trouble now."

"I won't Sister. She might say `no', but she might say `yes'."

"You know, dear, what the world needs most is another Saint Francis! Someone who can lift our spirits and give us cause for joy. Don't you think, Sister?"

"Yes, Sister." Sr. Elizabeth was an idealist and, for a fleeting moment, imagined herself as that message of good news. Sr. Elizabeth glanced at her watch and knew it was time to leave for dishing out in kitchen. Sr. Bernadette noticed.

"Before you leave, Sister, would you do me a little favor?"

"Of course, Sister."

"Would you take the bed pan from me?"

Sr. Elizabeth was humbled by the simple needs of the infirmary sisters. Each seemed to be special in her own way, so caring and vulnerable. Elizabeth ached to work longer hours in the infirmary, but she feared asking for more time would only cause her to lose the weekly four hours she now enjoyed.

It was better to wait. Instinctively, Sr. Elizabeth knew Sr. Anita did not believe she had the makings of a nurse. She also sensed Sr.

Anita's questioning her calling to be a nun. What Sr. Anita *didn't* know was that being raised with eight brothers and sisters gives one resilience in adversity. Sr. Elizabeth knew she could "take a lickin' and keep on tickin'." She was stubborn about the things she wanted, and she knew how to wait patiently.

. . . .

33

One early Monday morning, Sr. Mary Alice was busy ironing a starched veil. She unconsciously yawned. Sr. Anita caught her eye and glared disapprovingly. It was nearly 8:30 and the novices had been working for three hours. Morning prayer, Mass, meditation, breakfast, and dishes were already finished.

Sister Anita summoned Sr. Mary Alice with a wave of her hand. "Sr. Humiliana is in her office and wants to ask you something, Sister. Make sure someone takes over your veil before you leave." Starch could not be left unpressed once it was started.

"Yes, Sister." Sr. Mary Alice gave her project to another novice and went to find Sr. Humiliana. The door was open.

"Good morning, Sister. Sr. Anita said you wanted to ask me something."

"Yes, Linda, come in." Even Sr. Humiliana would revert to the secular names the girls had when entering. She looked a bit serious, which caused Sr. Mary Alice to become even more curious.

"I know this may sound a bit strange for me to ask, but Sr. Anita insisted that I inquire."

"Yes, Sister?"

"Have you slept with one of our postulants?"

There was silence. Sr. Mary Alice did not believe her ears. She looked directly into Sr. Humiliana's warm and compassionate eyes.

"Slept with a postulant?" Mary Alice repeated.

"Yes. Have you?"

"No, Sister. Never. I never have."

"I didn't think so."

"But, Sister, why are you asking me such a thing? I mean, have I done something to make you think . . ."

"A postulant wrote home several weeks ago that you had to stand in the refectory for sleeping with a postulant. As you know, I read their mail and when I saw this, I mentioned it to Sr. Anita. She insisted that I inquire."

"Sister, I *smiled* at a postulant. I didn't *sleep* with her! All I did was *smile*! That was *months* ago. Sister, I don't even like that postulant. I accidently *smiled* at her."

"Now, Sister. Don't get upset. It was just something we had to look into."

But Linda *was* upset. Sr. Mary Alice returned to the laundry in a state of numbness. "What an absurd accusation! What did these people really think of her? What could she be doing to foster such ideas? Just how crazy does this place get?"

Upon re-entering the laundry, Sr. Anita eagerly awaited her answer. "Well, what did you tell her?"

"I told her `no', Sister."

"All right. Finish folding these towels."

. . . .

34

Sitting next to Sr. Anita in the refectory was the most undesired of positions. Each day the novices would rotate one seat to the right, yet remain in rank. The favorite places to eat were either at Sr. Aquinas' table or far from the head of the table where Sr. Anita could not hear their conversations.

Sr. Aquinas was in her seventies and had a delightful sense of humor. When Sr. Mary Peter accidently belched at table, she begged pardon of the Sisters. Sr. Aquinas replied, "Bring it up again tomorrow and we'll vote on it." It was not exactly what you expected a senior sister to quip.

As canonicals, the group experienced new and different dimensions to Sr. Aquinas. When they were postulants, she appeared a cozy, affectionate, teddy-bear of sorts, a novitiate grandmother-type, but as novices she became an ally, a much-needed dose of sanity. One time Sr. Maryjane (Sally) broke the head off a mop while vigorously mopping the kitchen floor. Sr. Aquinas took and hid the damaged evidence just as Sr. Anita approached. She felt compassion for these young women surviving Sr. Anita's scourging in order to prove themselves worthy candidates for community. Years later, Sr. Aquinas would confess that she thought Sr. Anita may well have purged the order of future saints. It appeared as though nothing could be done.

The novices were very much impressed to hear Sr. Aquinas had earned over 168 college credits! They were just as amazed to learn she had never graduated beyond high school. This was not uncommon among the older sisters. They often had many courses and no matriculation. "Jack of all trades, master of none," she called herself.

Very few of the European community members were given much opportunity for schooling. Mostly they did domestic work in the convents. They became the cooks, the habit-makers, and the domestics. These Sisters were often considered "second class" by the professionally educated nuns. Sometimes their work was recognized and appreciated, but just as often it was not. After all, these women did not usually earn a parish salary. During the sixties there was a conscious effort to eradicate this traditional prejudice. Slowly, the old ways were giving into the new, and the caste-like barriers were breaking down even among those most ingrained and unyielding to change.

Sr. Mary Alice (Linda) had a particular affection for Sr. Aquinas and looked for opportunities to help her in any small way that she could. With permission, she read Sr. Aquinas' mail to her. Sister's vision was very poor. She had a serious stoop in her shoulders. Her head bent toward her chest and, to catch whatever light she could, Sister would twist her neck slightly toward her left shoulder.

Sr. Aquinas loved hearing the news from *The Albany Dispatch* and received stale copies from Sr. Georgine. Sr. Aquinas knew better than to ask a canonical to read news aloud. Newspapers were out of the question for canonicals. Anything they needed to know about the outside world was provided by Sr. Anita.

Several times Sr. Mary Alice was invited by Sr. Aquinas to her bedroom. It was an unbelievable stack of fruits, candy treats, letters, money, and paraphernalia of every kind. Sister always kept her door locked and insisted she knew where everything was. Piles of boxes upon her bed indicated she either moved them every night or slept in a fetal position on top of the blankets. The more critical novices referred to Aquinas as a "pack rat", but Sr. Mary Alice excused the behavior. If you had been taught never to throw anything away, couldn't see very well, and your entire kingdom amounted to a cell 12 feet by 10 feet, you had a right to live like this. Besides, Sr. Mary Alice loved the older woman and love blinded her to the older sister's eccentricities.

However, not so for Sr. Anita who often criticized the old lady: "She doesn't belong at dishwasher. She gets in the way. Sr. Aquinas can't seem to keep her collar clean or her shoes polished. Someday she's going to get her hand caught in the mangle. She shouldn't be working with novices; the demands are too much for an old woman."

Once, Sr. Anita gave Sr. Dominic and Sr. Catherine Ann a master key and told them to shovel out Aquinas' bedroom. "Bring the money to me, throw out the food, clean the bed, and throw away everything you consider trash."

That may have been the cruelest cut of all. For several months Sister moped in a depressed state over this invasion of privacy and the disposal of her many personal treasures. Sister tried valiantly to demonstrate a spirit of detachment for the novices to witness, but most of them, instead, commiserated. How old must one be in community to enjoy some respect from this much younger superior?

One cold day, as the novices enjoyed recreation in the laundry room, Sr. Mary Neumann, an invited professed sister from the college, was teaching folk dancing to the canonicals. It was a fun and light-hearted exercise for the young women. Sister Anita entered the room with Sr. Antonette (Judith) in such a way that the others could sense something amiss.

"Sisters, Sr. Antonette has decided to return to her family and friends. She asked me if she could say good-bye to you before leaving."

No one reacted at first. It was not registering. It sounded as if Sr. Anita was telling them their group member, Sr. Antonette, was leaving. Finally, Sr. Elizabeth (Ginny) spoke up.

"We'll miss you, Sister."

"Write if you get a chance," asked Sr. Charity (Brigit).

"Sure. I'll miss you guys, too." Sr. Antonette was obviously uncomfortable, as was the whole group. No one was really prepared for this kind of announcement. "I asked Sister if I could say good-bye because you know how we hate to wake up and find another one of us gone into some black hole."

The group giggled. "Well, lets get to the huggin'" suggested Charity, and each of them quickly embraced a fond farewell.

"You may continue your dancing, Sisters. I'll be back shortly," announced Sr. Anita as she and her companion went toward the elevator. The Saint Jude Group returned to their Virginia reel but not with the same gusto or silliness. These women were truly assuming a group identity and, even though they were often at odds over the most picayune of things, the loss of another group member was most disconcerting. Perhaps this was because some would genuinely miss Sr. Antonette, perhaps it was because they felt threatened every time someone chose life outside the convent walls, and perhaps it was because, as their numbers diminished, so did their security. Self-confidence was not a canonical's forte.

The next day was December 8th. The canonical novices found home-made holy cards at their individual place settings in the refectory. Printed on the front it read: "The richest man in the world is the one capable of giving himself" and on the other side, "Congratulations upon the completion of your first six months of your canonical year. Love and prayers, your little sisters." The postulants had struck a thoughtful blow. Thirteen months ago, the St. Jude Group numbered twenty-five. Now they were sixteen.

One very beautiful mid-December afternoon, the canonical novices had been invited by Mother Victoria to the farm. Everyone bundled warmly and Sr. Christine Marie (Sandra) especially became excited over the prospect of a day in the snow.

Mother had two snowmobiles. They had been donated by some wealthy benefactors and were stored in the barn. The novices were excited to take turns pulling a toboggan full of passengers over hill and dale. It was great fun!

Sr. Leonard (Therese) was an experienced driver and delighted in showing it. She disconnected the toboggan and Sr. Anita directed her novice to take her for a ride as she sat in back of this fearless driver. The novices all watched. The pair gained speed as they entered a wide open space but then charged into a snowdrift. It was fascinating to watch the forty-year-old superior embrace this spirit of adventure.

Sr. Leonard expected to sail over or at least plow gracefully through the drift. She did not expect what happened, nor did Sr. Anita and her curious spectators. Travelling at least twenty miles per hour, the snowmobile tipped to the left upon impact and both riders were thrown into the air. They landed in most unladylike positions and it was great fun to see "their lord and master" quite compromised. The novices laughed until it hurt. Neither was injured, but Sr. Leonard took on a new stature in the group as the only one to throw Sr. Anita bodily into oblivion. They were amazed to discover Sister could fall off a snowmobile. She appeared indestructible until that moment. She falls! What a delightful thought it was to many of them. Sr. Mary Peter (Helen) was the first to assist. Sr. Anita laughed along with the novices. She also could think it funny.

Mother Victoria's home was a remodelled farm house, complete with a cozy, glassed-in sitting room and fireplace. Some novices came in to warm their feet after ice-skating on the frozen pond. Others continued to explore the out-of-doors.

Sr. Mary Alice (Linda) and Sr. Catherine Ann (Kathleen) hiked into the winter wonderland. They walked to the top of a hill which offered the finest vista in the countryside of Watervaliet. It was a spectacular view. At the summit, they realized the hour was late. If they didn't hurry, they would be late for supper. Sr. Mary Alice was a more sturdy athlete and managed the descent more easily than Sr. Catherine Ann who called for her assistance.

Two things kept Sr. Mary Alice from slowing her pace: fear that if they walked into the house at the same time there would be speculation from Sister Anita that they were developing a particular friendship, and, secondly, an inner fear that being late would bring about Sister's displeasure. As much as she wanted to slacken her pace and enjoy Catherine Ann's company, Mary Alice could only call back, "Hurry up, Sister! They'll be sending a search party out after us if it gets any darker!"

Once inside, Mary Alice felt relieved. Shortly afterward Sr. Catherine Ann arrived, winded and disappointed in her roommate's abandonment. "You make a great friend, Mary Alice. except when I need you."

Sr. Mary Alice knew Sr. Catherine Ann understood. Linda seemed more interested in the food being served than thoughts of friendship. Besides, she felt forgiven. After all, they did share a friendship, not just an attic closet.

Getting over Sr. Charity's (Brigit's) rejection of friendship was still a painful struggle for Sr. Robert Therese (Angie), and Sr. Elizabeth (Ginny) seemed to offer an understanding ear. Sr. Robert Therese liked Sr. Elizabeth. Even though there wasn't much emotional between them, there was a certain comfort. This was best kept a secret, or Sr. Anita would see that they would have little opportunity to develop their mutual caring. The novices were now understanding the expectations. They were learning the game of camouflaging and wearing masks.

Christmas approached with the usual tension of cleaning, some decorating, and a certain amount of nostalgia for last Christmas. This year, only cards and letters were to be exchanged with families, but no visiting day was planned until Spring. The plan was to spend visiting day at Mother's farm, something everyone looked forward to. Many of the novices from out-of-state expected family members. Spring could not come soon enough.

The day before Christmas, Sister Martha William (Grace) left community, but it came as no surprise. Her face had broken out over a month ago and she developed a serious case of hives all over her body. Apparently, it was a case of nerves; there was too much tension and adversity among the novices to remain. She lost almost twenty pounds, more from stress than diet or heavy work.

The girls felt saddened to see such a good-natured and fun-loving person leave their ranks, but they respected Grace's decision. It was arranged that she would take a bus back to Hoboken and have her trunk sent later. Sr. Anita had been "on her case" a lot and encouraged her to go home and re-think her choice to enter religious life.

Sr. Martha William was in no condition to keep fighting for a vocation she didn't even understand. With a very informal farewell, Sr. Martha William went off to remove her habit and returned in secular dress for the drive to the bus station. The one most disheartened by the news of her leaving was Sr. Aquinas, who just shook her head and went off to pray.

. . . .

35

The motherhouse bell rang at 6:00 every morning. Morning prayer and meditation began at 6:30, Mass was at 7:00, and breakfast followed. Woe to the novice who failed to ring that bell exactly at 6:00 A.M.! Even a five minute delay caused serious disruption to the sisters' morning ritual. In addition, the unfortunate novice had to beg a penance from Sr. Anita.

Sr. Robert Therese (Angie) sprang from bed to kiss the floor as a sign of her obedient and immediate response to the bell. The novices were taught that to hesitate or dawdle after the command of a bell showed a lack of respect. The bell was God calling the sisters to task. The novices were taught to respond quickly.

Sr. Robert Therese's constitution never responded well to kissing the floor so soon after awakening. Often after rising to her feet, she became light-headed and nauseated. This morning she sat on her bed for only a moment, then began to dress quickly. Her corner of the bedroom was near a window where snow had drifted onto the sill. It was cold for most of the novices. Certain rooms provided more heat than others.

Sr. Robert Therese knew from experience that if she dressed quickly, she generally felt warmer. Paper was used to keep out much of the winter wind but it was not as effective a deterrent to snow. Next year, as constitutional novices, they would not be sleeping in dormitories. Instead, each would have a private cell *with a door.* They all looked forward to that.

Sr. Robert Therese recited prayers with each stage of dressing. She kissed her serge habit before putting it over her head. She kissed each article of clothing and prayed for purity, fidelity, perseverance, courage, and humility as she put on her collar, cord, rosary, and veil. The process usually took about fifteen minutes if you had a clean veil pinned the night before, a clean cord tied, and everything else quite in order.

It was Robert Therese who suggested they go to bed in habits; that way, they would be warmer at night and not have to make such an effort in the morning. She had a unique concern because she needed to get over to the laundry to turn on the washing machines before Mass. Some laughed at the suggestion, but others commented, "I always thought you just hung up nuns in a closet during the night and took them out in the morning." The young sisters often commented about the habit. "I could never figure out how they wrapped up their heads . . . how can they hear with their ears covered like that . . . or how could they chew and talk?" The novices now had insights they had lacked as seculars.

During the canonical year, morning meditation was usually in the novitiate chapel. In years to come, the college girls would take complete control of the novitiate building. For now, the students occupied only the four floors with bedrooms. Novices and postulants still had access to the refectory, chapel, postulate, novitiate community room, classroom, storage rooms, and parlors.

"Not to us, O Lord, not to us," the leader of prayer began. "But to Thy name, give glory," responded the others. Morning prayer and office (recitation of the psalms) were recited in chorus fashion, alternating sides according to the antiphonarian's lead. All knelt, stood, and sat at designated times.

Once again, all activity ceased as meditation began. They sat in silence. Sr. Robert Therese (Angie) watched the heads bob up and down as some would doze off. There were sounds of deep sighs, an occasional snore, and silenced yawns along with the waving, drifting, and nodding of heads.

Sr. Robert Therese tried desperately to stay awake. Sisters were often known to fall asleep during meditation, and some napped even while standing during the office! On these cold winter mornings, it seemed almost impossible to fight the urge for a few more moments of rest.

Just as Sr. Robert Therese's head fell to her chin, Sr. Anita noticed the sleeping culprit. Sr. Robert Therese was commanded to kneel in the center aisle for the remainder of meditation. Sister Anita's very approach was enough to scare up enough adrenalin for Sr. Robert Therese to remain wide awake for the next six months. Very few of the novices found the morning meditation easy or pleasant. It was just something you did because it was expected.

Sr. Christine Marie (Sandra) had a knack of articulating the thoughts shared by so many of the others. In the midst of the novices she questioned the practice of this early meditation, "Does God need my prayer so much that it has to come from my half-numbed brain and unconscious body?"

Sr. Leonard (Theresa) concurred, "God deserves a medal if he can find *my* soul *that* early in the morning. I haven't a clue what's happening."

One day, Sr. Dominic (Betsy) wanted the key to the laundry. She asked Sr. Robert Therese (Angie) for the loan of it. Now that the college girls were living in the novitiate building, many of the rooms had to be kept locked, including the laundry room.

"I don't have it, Sister. I think Sr. Mary Peter borrowed it earlier."

Sr. Dominic soon returned to the novitiate community room to say Sr. Mary Peter did not have it. She was annoyed by the goose chase and asked once more. Again, Sr. Robert Therese explained that she did not have it. It was understood among the novices that Sr. Robert Therese and Sr. Dominic did not like each other. Part of the problem may have been Sr. Charity (Brigit), but the greater part was that these two differed so in character.

Sr. Dominic decided to look for herself and lifted Sr. Robert Therese's collar to inspect underneath. Usually pins, keys, and even watches were kept under the large white bib for easy access.

Sr. Robert Therese was infuriated by the abrupt and uninvited invasion of privacy. She reacted immediately by shoving the shorter, round woman back into the sewing tables. The disruption caught the immediate attention of the other girls. It looked as if there would be a fist fight. Instead, Sr. Dominic just smiled and said, "My, we are touchy today, aren't we?"

"Sister, I told you twice as clearly and as plainly as I could that I do *not* have the laundry key."

Sister Dominic left the room only to discover Sr. Mary Peter had loaned it to Sr. Kathleen but had forgotten. There were no apologies, nor were any expected. The winter hibernation seemed to exacerbate the tensions of communal living.

It was amusing, but only in retrospect, that the controlling personalities of their novice directress and their choir directress caused and maintained a war of words throughout the canonical experience. Sr. Anita and Sr. Helena used the novices as ping pong balls to carry their insulting messages back and forth. It was so obvious that they both wanted to control. The novices feared being shot for bearing the message and tried to remain neutral at all times. Often, they could not reconcile the example they witnessed and the lessons they were taught.

Sr. Anita was always indoctrinating. "You aren't here to question the authority God has given to lawful superiors! You are here to learn how to live obedience. You will never be of any use to God if you cannot follow the orders given to you. What if the Son of God had not been obedient to the Father? There would be no redemption. You must obey, always. Your superiors are instruments for the implementation of God's holy will. Question this, and you may well frustrate your own salvation."

Sr. Anita was a very powerful person. Her words were direct and often were permanently imprinted upon the young recruits. They loved her and hated her. Unquestionably, they feared her. Those who trusted her were used to inform upon the others. Sr. Anita prided herself a psychologist, even thought she had been a French major in college. She played, effectively and deliberately, with the formative and impressionable minds under her jurisdiction.

One late afternoon, while helping dish out supper in the kitchen, the sister cook needed five more minutes to dish out food and put it into the hot portable warming ovens. The five o'clock bell for prayer rang and everyone knew what was expected of novices.

Sisters Elizabeth and Charity glanced at each other. They both realized that if they did not help with the dishing out, supper would not be ready to serve on time.

"Go ahead, Charity. I'm going to stay and help Sister."

"If you are, I will too. We can just hope for the best."

The much older cook Sister looked relieved to hear they would stay a few minutes longer. She very much needed the help.

The novices found themselves at a kind of crossroad. The choice to answer the bell immediately or complete an act of charity was before them. They chose the act of kindness. When the project was finished, they left directly for chapel.

As they glanced in, they noticed Sr. Anita. They had hoped she would not be there.

"Oh, well, here we go," whispered Sr. Elizabeth.

They blessed themselves with holy water and prayed a quick petition for protection. They knelt together before Sr. Anita, as was the custom, to explain their lateness.

"We stayed a few minutes longer to help Sr. Anastatia dish out. She needed our help just a bit longer." Sr. Elizabeth spoke for the both of them.

"You both agreed to stay, even after you heard the bell call you to chapel?" Sister Anita wanted this clarified.

"Yes, Sister," Charity nodded.

"Then you both may recite the rosary in front of chapel with your arms extended. Ask God to teach you that obedience is its own reward and staying to help Sister was not a decision *you* had the right to make. You should have asked me."

"Thank you, Sister." They whispered in unison and bent to kiss the floor. They took their office books to the front of chapel. When office was finished, the rosary began. They raised their arms before postulants and novices for the next fifteen minutes. It was as humiliating as it was uncomfortable. No one thought much about it except the two at the railing. The others were only grateful it was not their arms in the air. By now, the postulants had become quite accustomed to witnessing the public penance of novices.

Sr. Mary Peter's (Helen's) father was now in the hospital and expected to live for only a few more days. Sister had been granted permission to stay at home with her mother during this time. When available, Sr. Anita would come to be of comfort to the family. The novices were asked to make time for a holy hour of prayer each evening, asking God to provide the necessary strength and courage for Mary Peter and her family.

After his death, all of the novices dressed in their best habits, black gloves, and cloaks to attend an evening wake in nearby

Schenectady. They also attended the funeral Mass. The canonicals acted as guest choir. Although somewhat impaired by the loss of several talented vocalists and musicians, the St. Jude Group still could sing remarkably well. They spontaneously harmonized and accurately held pitch without accompaniment.

There was no quarrel with the goodness and quality of Sr. Mary Peter's parents, but there was a quarrel with political favoritism, blatantly obvious to members of the group. Sr. Anita loved Sr. Mary Peter affectionately. It was mutual, but most of the group agreed Sr. Mary Peter could not be held accountable. Even Sr. Elizabeth saw no constructive purpose in fighting a battle already lost. For all practical purposes, rank had been altered and she became more interested in getting through her canonical training rather than showing Sr. Mary Peter how she played into Sr. Anita's power games.

Yes, Sr. Mary Peter was scolded and verbally admonished like so many of the others, but it was fundamentally different for Sr. Mary Peter. She *knew* Sr. Anita berated her out of love and caring. She *knew* she possessed the esteem and affection of the one correcting and admonishing. No other novice believed Anita cared when she punished or ridiculed. Many of the girls took her words to heart when they wounded and inflicted pain, supposedly for the purpose of refining their inferior selves and preparing them for the vowed life ahead.

Sr. Charles Marion (Karen) had lost fifty pounds since her entrance into community, forty of them since investing. There was a noticeable difference in the way she now carried herself. She imitated Sr. Anita in countless mannerisms.

As a postulant, she appeared quite fat and ugly, but as a woman wrapped in serge, her appearance was much improved. Sr. Charles Marion had very plain features, and had inherited her mother's crooked nose and small chin. Her eyes her definitely her finest feature. They were large with long black lashes.

Charles Marion avoided the dynamics and interaction of community life during the canonical year and, for the most part,

avoided all but minimal contact with Sr. Anita. It was obvious to
most of the group that Sr. Charles Marion was a loner in need of
friendship. Any attention seemed appreciated. She just didn't know
how to relate very well. She was present, but she was invisible, too.

Charles Marion appeared to carry large chips upon her
shoulders. She had an attitude that kept most of the others at a
distance. Only the most charitable even bothered to be polite. She
developed a devotion to the Sacred Heart of Jesus that, instead of
impressing her peers, seemed to alienate them all the more. She
would spend hours sketching the image of Christ's Sacred Heart,
surrounded by thorns, pierced, and bloody. No one criticized
Charles Marion openly, but most considered her odd. One
afternoon Sr. Anita sat in her office having another attack of a the
colitis that plagued her. Sr. Charles Marion inquired to see if she
could be of any help and Sister declined her sympathetic gesture.

"Sister, there is something I'd like you to do. Please write a
note and pin it to the chapel door. Mother Josepha has apparently
taken a turn for the worse and I have just received a phone call
asking the novices to pray for her."

"Yes, Sister. I'll be glad to."

"Thank you, Sister."

"You're welcome, Sister."

Mother Josepha had been the former Mother General. She
commanded the community before Mother Victoria, during the
mid-forties and fifties. She led the community from near abject
poverty to a comfortable lifestyle. Now that she was dying, little
was said in her favor, nor was there much criticism. Several of her
most loyal friends who had risen to power during her leadership
spoke of her as a saint. There seemed, however, no true consensus
of her character.

Mother Josepha was a nurse who insisted upon routine health
check-ups and stringent health standards in the community
hospitals as well as the local convents. She improved the sisters'
nutrition and promoted exercise as a formidable method to improve
health, but only in the confines of convent privacy. Now her death

was imminent and the community prayerfully awaited the announcement as expected. It came the evening of March 1st.

The canonical novices were to serve as an honor guard. Three bishops were presiding and Sr. Helena had imported talent from as far away as Buffalo for the funeral Mass.

As last minute preparations were completed, Sr. Helena, overseeing the entire affair, asked Sr. Elizabeth if she was completely sure of her role. She was to lead the honor guard into a double file formation, allowing the casket to be taken through the center of the front aisle and out the left exit to the awaiting hearse.

"Yes, Sister. I know when to get up and lead the others into position," Sr. Elizabeth assured her.

"Now, Sister. There may be several thousand people attending. I want this done correctly. After the casket has been taken out of chapel, you turn to the right and file back into your benches. Do you understand?"

"Yes, Sister," she responded once more.

"Do *all* of you understand what to do?" Sr. Helena questioned them.

Collectively they answered, "Yes, Sister."

Some of the novices would reflect: "Life could be worse. What if we had Sr. Helena for a novice mistress? She appeared hard and cold. At least Sr. Anita gave the impression of being human occasionally— not often, but often enough to keep the novices in tow."

As everyone expected, the funeral service was a monumental send off. Trumpets and violins. Latin and English. A mix of old and new, all exquisitely performed. A "Helena Production" was always an extravaganza. In fact, several years earlier, Sr. Helena had created a convent choir that received national attention, cut a best selling record, and raised thousands of dollars performing live concerts . . . some in New York City. Eventually, the choir had to disband as it burdened the mission sisters who were "unchosen" and often left to carry double duty.

Just as Mother Josepha's body was escorted through the white-veiled honor guard, the choir sounded forth, "May the Angels lead you into paradise. . . ." When it was time for Sr. Elizabeth to lead her group back into their benches, for some unknown reason, Sr. Mary Peter, second in line, decided to walk down the center aisle, hands folded. The others now had to make a choice. They must either exit the chapel following Sr. Mary Peter or follow Sr. Elizabeth into the benches. Both sisters, with heads bowed and hands folded, piously did what they thought was right.

The group followed Sr. Mary Peter down the center aisle and out of chapel. Sr. Elizabeth reassessed her position, now that the entire group was exiting. To stand and join them was admitting her mistake before the entire community which over-filled the body of the church, but to stay kneeling alone still made her look out of place. She decided to remain kneeling and pray for humility as she tried to assume a complacent countenance, as if this were planned. Later, only Sr. Anita cared to comment in the midst of a half dozen novices.

"Didn't you feel out of place way up there in front all by yourself, Sister?" Sr. Anita asked Sr. Elizabeth.

"Yes, Sister, but I did only what Sr. Helena told us to do."

"She's right, Sister." Sr. Christine Marie decided to speak up on behalf of number one. "We were all supposed to go back to the benches, but Sr. Mary Peter led us down the aisle and out of chapel."

Even Sr. Charles Marion, "Sr. Mary Non-involvement", spoke up on behalf of Sr. Elizabeth. "Sister Elizabeth was the only one doing what we were told. I guess we were too eager to get out of there. We all just followed Sr. Mary Peter."

Sr. Elizabeth was grateful to hear someone speak on her behalf. This was not a common phenomena among novices, and it felt good not to be accused of stupidity for a change.

"Well, common sense should have told you to turn around and follow the rest of the group, Sister!" Sr. Anita responded.

"Yes, Sister. I guess I just wasn't thinking quickly."

"Bright light," were Sr. Anita's parting words as she turned toward her office.

Sr. Elizabeth turned to Sr. Christine Marie and Sr. Charles Marion to thank them for speaking up. Sr. Christine Marie was known to speak up when she felt it necessary, but Elizabeth was nearly stunned to hear Sr. Charles Marion say anything that challenged Sr. Anita.

"Well, it's true, Elizabeth. So often you try to do the right thing around here and end up looking like the idiot because sometimes you're the *only* one doing the right thing. I'm glad I told her. Don't give up, Elizabeth. You're a good nun, Charlie Brown."

For that moment, Sr. Charles Marion came through for Sr. Elizabeth. Encouragement was all so rare, and today it was greatly appreciated. In fact, that brief conversation would never be forgotten. Even if Sr. Charles Marion never did another nice thing for Elizabeth, what she did today was something well worth remembering.

. . . .

36

Sr. Mary Alice (Linda) was busy getting the lunch room set up in the motherhouse. It was a little kitchenette where the professed sisters could enjoy a cup of coffee and a snack during the mid-morning or mid-afternoon hours. As she unloaded the coffee urn from her metal cart, several professed sisters entered the room discussing the pros and cons of putting funeral flowers on the altar in their motherhouse chapel.

"I consider it insulting to God that we would use flowers from a funeral parlor to decorate His sanctuary!"

"But, Sister, do you realize how expensive those sprays are? They cost a fortune and in the winter there is nothing Cyrilla can get from the garden. Soon she will be able to use the pussy willows."

"I guess you are right about that. Cyrilla does a remarkable job with what she has. There aren't many chapels north of Virginia with Christmas poinsettias still blooming in March. How do you think she does that?"

"I used to think they were fake until I went up and touched them. Plastic flowers I can't abide."

Sr. Mary Alice was eager to leave the room as soon as possible. After things were in place, she smiled and "pax et bonumed" the sisters. She was eager to leave. She remembered the time she offered to carry a professed sister's suitcase and Sr. Anita found out. She got in trouble for having volunteered the help.

Mary Alice did everything possible to avoid eye contact with the professed, fearing it might lead to conversation, and that could only lead to trouble. She returned to the kitchen and began peeling potatoes. There were fifty pounds in need of peeling that day and a kitchen sister was already there beginning the task. Sr. Anna was a hard worker and usually kept kitchen conversation general and safe. She repeatedly told the novices, and anyone else who would listen, about a miracle she received as a young woman.

Working in a factory, her long hair was caught in a machine and it pulled nearly three-fourths of her scalp off before the machine could be stopped. Loosing an outer ear and her hair was the most permanent damage caused, along with scars resulting from dozens of skin grafts.

"And Sister, as I lay on the floor with all this blood all over me, I prayed to good St. Anne, the mother of Mary, and she spoke to me just like I'm speaking to you right now. Only soft and with motherly love she told me, "Darling, don't be afraid! I am with you and I promise you will be all right. Trust me. She said, `trust me' and I did. I lay there praying a rosary when the ambulance came and took me away. Isn't that wonderful, Sister?"

"It sure is, Sister. That's a wonderful story." Sr. Mary Alice answered.

"It's not just a story, Sister. You know, it really happened."

"I believe you, Sister!" This was at least the fourth time Sr. Mary Alice had heard the story of St. Anne's rescue. Whether it really happened or not was of no consequence to the novice. What mattered is that Sr. Anna believed it happened. Besides, Sr. Anna seemed the pious type, so maybe it did happen. She prayed fifteen to twenty rosaries a day and spent her hours either praying in chapel or spreading devotion to the grandmother of Jesus. Anna did become somewhat annoying by suggesting they pray a rosary while peeling the vegetables. For Sr. Mary Alice, the one rosary prayed in chapel each day with novitiate was more than sufficient.

Just then, Sr. Anita walked through the kitchen and stopped to examine the peelings.

"Sister, whoever taught you to peel potatoes?"

"I don't know, Sister. Maybe my mother."

"Will you look at those peelings?"

Sr. Mary Alice stared hard at the mound of potato peelings piled in the sink before her. She couldn't find anything since she wasn't sure what she was looking for.

"Don't you see it, Sister?"

"No, Sister," she responded as respectfully as she could.

"Look at this!" Sr. Anita lifted a fragment of the potato skin to Sr. Mary Alice's face. "Do you see how much potato is still on that skin, Sister?"

"Yes, Sister."

"Well, then, do something about it! We cannot afford to have you peel away all this potato every time you work in kitchen!"

"Yes, Sister. Thank you, Sister." Sr. Mary Alice continued to peel, only now more carefully, so as not to catch more than just the outer peel with her peeler. Once Sr. Anita had made her point, she continued on to the motherhouse refectory.

. . . .

37

Spring was a welcome relief to most of Albany, but especially to the novices who had no other world other than the inner chambers of their novitiate and the outside courtyard.

The pleasant weather prompted Sr. Anita to take everyone for a walk—outside of the convent walls! About a mile and a half down Main Boulevard was Our Lady of Angels Cemetery and, in one section, the remains of the original members of the Albany Franciscan community.

As the fifteen white-veiled novices gathered around, Sister stopped at intermittent headstones to say a few words about this or that sister. It was a delightful way to spend the afternoon and everyone soaked up the sunny warmth and bursting greenery.

"This sister was a *real* gem. She worked hard in community and always gave an edifying example. She was a cousin to Archbishop Fulton J. Sheen, but never bragged of it. Sister was a deep thinker. We were certainly blessed to have had her."

The novices were impressed by the mention of Bishop Sheen.

"Oh, and Sister Clara! What a character she was, a sister cook. Once she threw a knife at another sister who merely criticized her cooking. Wasn't all there really, but in those days domestic help didn't have to be!"

"Sister, are those stories true about nuns eating rancid food in the old-time novitiate and nuns beating themselves with a whip to do penance?" Sr. Robert Therese (Angie) thought it was a good time to ask.

"Well, Sister, sometimes that was all the food we had to eat. I have to admit there may have been a few cases of food poisoning, but it was never intentional. You were just grateful for whatever you had."

"Oh, and look here . . . Sr. Borgia. Do you know she broke her arm as a novice and wouldn't break grand silence to tell anyone until the next day? Now *that's* obedience to the rule!"

"What about the discipline, Sister? You know, that thing sisters used to beat themselves with." Sr. Robert Therese would not let her question go unanswered.

"Well, actually, Sister, we still use the discipline in community. Formerly, we had the custom of slapping our legs or our backs as we prayed certain psalms every Wednesday and Friday evening.

Many of us slept in dormitories with only curtains between us and you could hear these whipping cracks all about. Actually, we were fortunate. Other communities used chains or metal disciplines. Ours are usually leather and don't hurt as much. Today, most sisters do it only when they feel a personal need, or will do it more as a symbolic gesture as they pray.

Sr. Robert Therese listened with disbelief. "Will I be asked to beat myself?" she wondered.

"You know, Sister, St. Francis of Assisi rolled in the snow and in briars with his naked body to control the passions of 'Brother Ass' as he would refer to himself. Discipline is something we all need."

"But, Sister, to beat yourself? Isn't trying to live a good life discipline enough?" Angie protested. Only a few of the novices remained in the circle while others used the opportunity to pair off and walk about in close proximity.

"Sister, you are very young and very inexperienced. You haven't the least idea how difficult life can be. You know nothing of hair shirts, of hermits, of ascetics. No one will expect you to use a discipline. It is strictly up to each individual sister, so fear not. It really isn't as terrible as you make it sound."

The group and their leader now started for home. Soon it would be time for the novices to report for their 4:15 charges.

That same evening Sr. Mary Alice (Linda) noticed that Sr. Catherine Ann (Kathleen), her roommate was in a melancholy mood. Something obviously was bothering her and Sr. Mary Alice was not comfortable going to bed without seeing if she could help. They had been partners during the day's walk and Sr. Mary Alice sensed a quiet pensiveness about her friend. Though not in the custom of breaking grand silence, she decided to knock on the room divider and enter Sr. Catherine Ann's half of the attic bedroom.

"Catherine Ann, I know something has been bothering you today. You seem worried or something. Do you want to talk about it?"

"It's really nothing Mary Alice. Really."

"Sure. So is outer space nothing. Listen, kid, I know you pretty well and I can tell something is heavy on your mind. I wish you could trust me. Maybe I can help."

"It's silly."

"Okay. It's silly. What else can you tell me about it?"

"I don't think I'm good enough."

"For what?"

"To be a nun."

"You, too? I've had that problem since I was a postulant. You'll get over it. I've had this hang up over humility since I learned the word. I mean, at first I thought being humble meant like being a real dip, ya' know? Like telling yourself that you're no good. Then I came across something Saint Teresa of Avila once said about humility. Listen to this, Catherine Ann. She said, 'Humility is truth'."

"I don't get it."

"Well, it means you are what you are before God, nothing more and nothing less!"

"And what *am* I before God?"

"Well, that takes time. I mean we have to live a lot before we realize what we really are. But not to worry! Because, whatever we are, it can't be too bad. I think it must be something pretty good or why would God have bothered with all of creation if it wasn't meant to work out for the best? Would you offer the life of your only begotten son for a loser of a human race?"

"You don't understand, Sister."

"I know I don't. Understand what?"

"What would you think if I told you I wasn't exactly a spotless bride."

"I'd say, 'Who is?'"

"Is there some rule that nuns have to be virgins?"

"Not that I know of." Sr. Mary Alice was getting a clearer picture now of what may have been on Sr. Catherine Ann's mind. She wanted to continue the sharing. They were both careful to whisper very softly.

"Married women have been nuns and they even had kids sometimes! Like St. Monica or St. Louise. And there was some lady in England that arranged to go to a convent and her husband went to be a priest after their kids grew up. I think they are trying to get her canonized, so I don't think nuns have to be virgins."

"But what if you're not married."

"Well, you know what happened to Susan, don't you?"

"Yes."

"Do you think less of her because of what she did?"

"No."

"Well, I don't think anyone else does either, unless they just aren't human, and if they aren't human, who cares what they think? Listen kid, God *can't* be very picky. Just look at this group of ours and try to tell me God only selects the finest members of the human race for religious life. There's not one person in this convent who is as charitable and loving as my own mother. I don't think nuns are the cream of the crop, if you know what I mean. They just want us to think we are so we'll try to live up to it. I can't buy a lot of the things they sell here."

"How do you know all of this?"

"Kidneys, Catherine Ann, kidneys," and she tapped the side of her head. "The past is behind you; don't carry it everywhere if it's going to be a dredge. *No one* is perfect. One of my best friends just got married, and she was three months pregnant. Same thing happened to my cousin. If I weren't here, who knows? Maybe I would be far worse."

Sr. Catherine Ann was beginning to cry. She reached for her handkerchief. Sr. Mary Alice was truly at a loss. She had said just about every encouraging thought she had.

"Sister, thank you for trusting me with your fear and whatever else it is that's bothering you. Would you let me say one more thing before we go to bed?"

"Yes."

"Come here." She took Catherine Ann by the arm and led her to the window where a few last remaining rays evidenced a glorious setting.

"See that sun going down over there?"

"Yes?"

"Well, God was real smart to give us a new one tomorrow. He wanted to remind us each new day is a new beginning."

Sr. Catherine Ann could not hold back the tears. She sobbed even more than before and rested her head on Mary Alice's shoulder. Sr. Mary Alice knew there was much more to *this* story, but she had probed enough for now. She wanted only to reassure her friend that whatever the problem was, it had a solution. "Tomorrow will be much better, Catherine Ann. Trust me. Just don't you dare go home and leave me here wondering what happened to you!"

"I'm not going home, Mary Alice. I just needed somebody tonight. I'm glad you care. Thanks."

"You're welcome, kid. And when I need a pep talk, be sure to say some of the stuff I said tonight. It was pretty good for just a novice; don't you think?"

"Yes, I do." They exchanged a simple but meaningful embrace and parted for their opposite sides of the room divider. They were in bed when Sr. Catherine Ann whispered once more, "Are you going to kneel for breakfast, Sister?"

"Nah. But don't you *dare* tell Sr. Anita I broke silence or you're dead meat when she's finished with me."

Sr. Catherine Ann smiled and remembered. "Not a word, 'Ster. Not a word."

"Sleep with the angels, kid."

. . . .

38

The following day, Sr. Anita began her instruction by announcing several forthcoming events.

"Sisters, after Easter, you will be spending four days vacation at Mt. Alvernia." Spontaneous clapping erupted. Faces glowed with excitement and all eagerly anticipated a break in the rigors of their manual labor.

"The postulants will be joining us." No one clapped this time. Much as they may have wanted to, they refrained. Even with natural barriers between the two groups, there were mutual feelings emerging among certain individuals. Naturally, there would be some attractions. Perhaps, with fewer barriers, there may have been less need for them. But no one questioned community policy. They obeyed, or they were asked to leave. It always amazed Sr. Elizabeth to witness so many who did not necessarily obey, but neither did they "pay the piper". The convent was proving to be a place of incongruity.

"You will be given permission to associate with the postulants, but let prudence be your guide," she continued. "The first week of May, our community will be sponsoring a Vocational Congress at Convent High School and you will be asked to assist. They will need help decorating, setting up, and whatever else we are asked to do. The reason I'm telling you now is because we are responsible for planning the liturgy, giving hospitality to visiting novices from other communities, and preparing a program of entertainment. We need to form committees and begin work as soon as possible."

"The postulants will be invested on the feast of St. Anthony, June 13th. You will be permitted to go home after their ceremony for five consecutive days beginning the 15th of June. Those sisters in need of a day's travel will be permitted to leave on the 14th."

Sr. Dominic asked what they all wanted to know. "Sister, do you know when we will receive our black veils?" "You sound too eaga', Sista'." Anita smiled a wry sort of grin. "I will continue to be your novice directress until *I* decide you are ready to wear black veils. Sister Mary Edgar is in no hurry to have you. Of course, during your home visits, you will be expected to wear black veils."

With Easter came spring, and with spring, renewed hope. Canonical life was not over yet, but there was a light at the end of the tunnel. Fifteen novices remained. Five of the anniversary band left as postulants, and five as canonicals. This initiation period was expected to be a time for weeding out, they were told. It was better to go home now than to make a commitment and not be faithful to it. Vows were only a year and a half away. Even though they were only temporary (for three years), the novices were told to think in terms of life.

Finally, there were changes made in the assignment of charges. For almost a month, Sr. Mary Alice (Linda) had the unenviable responsibility of laundry. There were still problems with the washing machines getting started. One in particular would turn off mid-cycle. Sr. Mary Alice disliked reporting such problems because it annoyed Sr. Anita so. She would often pray to St. Joseph before starting the machines. He was the patron saint of labor and certainly would have compassion for those who feared the consequences of management. Besides, Mary Alice didn't want to be another "Sr. Robert Therese-break-the-machine-on-purpose-for-attention-victim".

One afternoon, Sr. Aquinas and Sr. Mary Alice were folding the usual daily lot of towels, underwear, etc., and Sr. Aquinas put the underclothing into each respective basket: postulant, canonical, constitutional.

"Sister, we have to fold everything before it leaves the laundry room. Sr. Anita told me she wants even underwear folded before it's sent up."

"Sister," Sr. Aquinas responded, "that's not at all necessary. They can fold their own underwear. I'll do the tee shirts, but they can do the rest."

"I agree, Sister. It doesn't take them but a few moments to do their own, but Sr. Anita said . . ."

"Don't worry about it, Sister. She'll never know. Just do what I say."

"Yes, Sister."

At that very precise moment, Sr. Anita walked into the laundry room. She walked directly toward the two workers.

"How is everything going?" Sr. Anita inquired.

"Fine, Sister." Sr. Mary Alice replied, hoping Anita wouldn't look into the three baskets before them. Her hope was in vain.

"Sister, didn't I tell you to fold *everything* you put into these baskets, including the underwear?" She picked out a garment and dropped it in front of the novice.

"Yes, Sister. You did." Caught again. Sr. Anita never missed a beat, and she always seemed to be holding all the best cards. It was hard not to believe God could be anywhere but on her side.

"And you prefer to ignore my explicit instructions, Sister?"

Sr. Mary Alice didn't know what to say. She wanted to defend her decision to disobey, but knew better. She hoped Sr. Aquinas would speak up and free her from this humiliating vise, but by the same token, she understood Sister's silence and why she continued to busy herself folding the towels.

"I'm sorry, Sister." She knelt to beg penance.

"You all have the same idea around here: hurry and finish. Doesn't anyone take pride in their work anymore? Sister, I want *everything* folded before that basket is returned *everyday*. Do you understand this time, Sister? Or do you expect me to follow you everywhere to see if you are doing what you are supposed to be doing?"

"No, Sister, I mean yes, Sister. I mean, yes I understand, and no, you don't have to follow me around," the novice stammered.

"And one more thing, Sister, no one is to turn that mangle on without my permission. It costs too much to operate every day. I want it used only on Mondays and Fridays unless I tell you otherwise. Is that clear enough for you, Sister, or would you like me to put it in writing?"

"I understand, Sister. Thank you, Sister." Sr. Mary Alice knew the last part of that speech was for Sr. Aquinas' benefit. Sometimes Sister turned the mangle on whenever she pleased and wasted a lot of energy for just a few items. Not intending to waste time, Sr. Aquinas often used idle moments to finish up a few left-overs that might have been saved a few days.

Sr. Anita made her typical Loretta Young exit as the two continued to fold.

After a few moments of silence, Sr. Aquinas spoke first, "I'm sorry, Sister."

"It's okay, Sister. I agree with you. I don't see why they can't fold their own underwear, but we have no choice." They continued folding. Eventually the wash was completed. Sr. Mary Alice really did understand why Sr. Aquinas had remained silent. She felt sorry for this old professed nun who had to live the life of a novice again. Besides, Mary Alice loved her.

· · · · · · · ·

39

Finally Lent was over and Easter meant Mt. Alvernia with the postulants. There wasn't much to do for the outing, just pack a suitcase and make sure a few of the last minute things were checked or finished. The constitutionals were going to cover the canonical duties while the postulants and canonicals covered the beach. The postulants had chosen Kateri Tekawitha as their group patron. Their postulancy had suffered a mortality rate similar to that of the "St. Jude" group. During the past year, they had lost four postulants and none of them were eager to leave Sr. Humiliana's care for the madness of Sr. Anita's.

At Mt. Alvernia there was music and warmth. It was, actually, unseasonably warm and light-hearted conversation which flowed abundantly between the groups and throughout the grounds. Sr. Elizabeth even brought her guitar along. She wasn't much of a player. She was self-taught but eagerly picked up method and technique from anyone who would help her.

When she was a junior in high school, Sr. Elizabeth had asked for a guitar. Her parents refused because her older siblings had all failed to practice instruments they had asked for. Besides, by now, there were too many mouths to feed and a guitar was out of the question.

For Christmas of her senior year, she again asked for a guitar. Her parents decided she needed a coat. But Sr. Elizabeth believed she could fit in her older sister's hand-me-down for another year. After all, she would be in the convent by next winter and a coat would be useless. But a guitar! She could play it forever!

The coat came for Christmas but, after a great deal of disappointment, she persuaded her parents to return it for a $30.00 guitar. She considered it among her most prized possessions, but she wasn't what you would call a "guitarist." She was more of a "wanna-be-guitarist." Her group teased and finally convinced her to give it up. She brought it along but only to strum or pick a melody or two in private.

After using the bathroom on the second floor of the historic retreat center building, Sr. Elizabeth hastily washed her hands and hurried downstairs to the living room where Sr. Anita and Sr. Humiliana were giving an informal mixed group class instruction.

After about fifteen minutes, a water leak appeared on the ceiling and spilled down the side walls until it was noticed by of one of the postulants. After some investigation, it was discovered that the bathroom upstairs, just above the living room, had several inches of water covering the floor and seeping into the hall and stairway carpet.

"Who was up there last?" Sr. Anita asked the postulants and novices. Elizabeth was mortified to admit she probably was. Even though no real issue was ever made of the fact she was the "oldest", the postulants still saw Elizabeth as someone to be looked up to. Here, she was the focus of attention for failing to notice a backed-up toilet and causing a water-stained ceiling. Sr. Kunigunda, the retreat center administrator, explained they had been having trouble with this particular toilet, and no one should feel responsible. A sign was put up until the plumber came. Meanwhile, the novice couldn't help but feel humiliated. Elizabeth was on the verge of accepting humiliation as a state of life one could adapt to and live forever.

The warm sunny afternoons invited many of the girls to lie in the sun; however, the canonicals were far more careful about how long they would tan. They remembered, all too well, the burns from last summer. A few even ventured to swim in the cold lake.

Sr. Robert Therese (Angie) endured the cold water longer than anyone. She was a strong swimmer and had learned at an early age, growing up only one block from Lake Erie.

"Aren't you freezing in there?" Sr. Christine Marie (Sandra) called from a pier of stone blocks.

"No. It feels terrific," she called back. After a while, Sr. Robert Therese decided to lie in the sun with the others. When she got out, Sr. Christine Marie touched her skin.

"RT, you feel like an ice cube! How could you stand it so long?"

"That's strange, Christine, I don't feel cold."

"Is this stone pier hot?" Sr. Christine Marie asked as Robert Therese lay down in the sun.

"No, not especially, maybe a little warm."

"Sister, it *is* hot! Have you lost your sense of feeling?"

Sr. Robert Therese thought for a moment. It seemed like a ridiculous question, but on the other hand, more and more, Sr. Robert Therese did feel as if she were loosing touch with sensation. Her canonical year had been so numbing that she now behaved more like an extreme introvert. She was not the same outgoing, confident postulant who spoke to over 4,000 people only a year ago. She felt deadened inside. Where was the Angie she had been?

Robert Therese was not the only one to suffer personality change. Sr. Mary Peter, Sr. Elizabeth, Sr. Mary Alice, Sr. Charity, and others seemed noticeably altered.

At first, the changes seems imperceivable, but now with most of their canonical year behind them, they were becoming aware of their differences.

Their forthcoming home visits would make these changes far more evident. The fun-loving high school girls who came to community in September of 1963 had transformed into trained, disciplined, and religiously formal women prepared to enter their second year of novitiate as constitutional novices.

Sr. Anita was a teacher all right—perhaps one of the most influential in the community. Sr. Robert Therese would remember her as one of the two most powerful teachers in her life: her mother in Ohio was the example of everything she wanted to imitate, and Anita was the epitome of everything she never wanted to become.

Years later, the entire group would remember Sr. Humiliana as a patient, saintly, religious woman who a gave good example as naturally as she smiled. No member of the St. Jude group would recall Sr. Anita in similar ways. Unfortunately, the community allowed her to rule for eight more years, impacting and damaging many young hopeful women coming to community. But no one is all bad. Sr. Anita was probably well-intentioned and sincere before God in these matters of formation, but the few who lived to persevere in community would, more often than not, remember her as a crazy despot with enormously abusive authority.

. . . .

40

May brought the Convent High School Vocational Congress, and with it came postulants and novices from many different communities. Rooms were prepared for the weekend visitors and preparations for the congress were planned with impeccable precision. Name tags, schedules, programs, etc. were all in order. All day Saturday and most of Sunday there would be ongoing workshops, information booths, and entertainment for Catholic high school girls throughout the tri-city area of Albany, Troy, and Schenectady. The purpose was to solicit young women to enter religious life.

Sr. Robert Therese (Angie) was incredulous that three *canonical* novices had driven, by themselves, from a Rochester, New York community to attend and work at the Convent High Vocation Congress. Sr. Stephanie, the vocation directress for the Franciscan Sisters of Albany, coordinated the inter-community affair and it seemed a tremendous success from the very onset.

The novices had never seen this much excitement. The Rochester group arrived Friday afternoon and Sr. Robert Therese was designated to be their hostess. Other members of the St. Jude group were assigned similar responsibilities. Sr. Robert Therese introduced herself and took the visitors on a tour of the motherhouse complex, including Regina Catholic College, Convent High School, the infirmary, and the novitiate. After orientation, she sat with them at supper, sharing stories of their canonical experience.

"I *cannot* believe you drove all the way from Rochester without a superior! We aren't even allowed to walk outside of these walls without ours! How is it possible?" Robert Therese could not contain her disbelief a moment longer.

"Well, it seems as if your people are a lot more conservative than our nuns." Sr. Irene suggested, "Everyone in our community wears a modified habit and you gals are still wrapped up in serge and starch."

"How many are there in your group?"

"We call it a band, not a group. 34."

"Are you losing a lot? We've lost ten already."

"We were 46 at entrance, but we lost a bunch during postulancy." Sr. Irene was very honest and Robert Therese appreciated her frankness.

After supper, last minute details were attended to in the Convent High gymnasium where thirty different communities had exhibits with hand-out literature ready for the onslaught of buses arriving Saturday morning. Even though attendance was not mandatory for the high school girls, attending the program meant a future day off during exam week in late June. Most girls considered it an attractive offer though few had any intention of entering a convent.

The more Sr. Robert Therese worked with Sr. Irene, the more she felt a special something between them. It was not her imagination. Sr. Robert Therese was surprised at the emotional attraction to the Rochester novice, because she had felt such an emotional void lately. The last person she had cared anything for was Sr. Charity (Brigit). It had taken months to feel free of that attachment, but it helped that Sr. Dominic (Betsy) consumed most of Charity's time. If she wasn't with Dominic, she was with Mary Peter (Helen). Sr. Robert Therese resented Charity's rejection, but chalked it up to experience.

Sometimes a friendship was not meant to be. Robert Therese was convinced only mutual caring could be viable.

But now, the Ohio novice was feeling uniquely alive again, as if Sr. Irene had awakened her from indifference. The change in Robert Therese was quickly apparent and Sr. Anita wasted no time in noticing. By Saturday afternoon, Sr. Robert Therese had been quarantined to her bedroom and forbidden to visit the congress again. Anita detected a small rip in Robert Therese's patched coronet, which set her off.

"How could you have been over at Convent High looking like that! Don't you think a hundred other nuns saw that tear, Sister? Have you no pride in your appearance? I can't believe you would appear in public with anything but your best coronet. I hate to think that so many may be judging our entire community because of your ragged decorum, Sister. I think it best you retire to your room for the duration of the congress. You may join us for community prayer and meals." Sr. Anita took a book from the spiritual reading shelf, *Keys to the Third Floor*, and placed it into Sr. Robert Therese's hands. "Here, take this and read it. I want a summary in writing as soon as you are finished."

Sr. Dominic turned to Sr. Catherine Ann and whispered, "I think our social butterfly just got her wings clipped." Sr. Robert Therese left for her room knowing full well this was not due to a ripped coronet.

During Sunday morning breakfast, Sr. Robert Therese had the opportunity to explain to Sr. Irene why she had not returned to the congress. Sr. Irene missed her and both were disappointed.

"Sister, we are having lunch in the Convent High cafeteria and will then be heading back to Rochester. I doubt if we'll see each other again. Can you write to me?" Irene asked.

"I doubt it, Sister. We usually are permitted to write letters only to our families. I'm sure Sr. Anita won't allow it." (She did not want to admit she would be too afraid to ask for permission.)

"May I write you?"

"Sure, I think so. I hope so. Try to, at least, okay?"

Their good-bye was a difficult parting. They had known each other briefly but these simple, inconspicuous moments proved to be a seedling for a lifetime of friendship.

That same afternoon brought an extraordinarily delightful surprise to Sr. Elizabeth. She discovered Patricia Falbo in the Convent High gymnasium. They had been biology partners at Regina Catholic as freshman.

"Patricia!"

"Ginny!"

"How are you?" There was an immediate embrace.

"What do I call you? Sister Elizabeth or Ginny?"

"Just `Sister'. Is that okay with you?"

"Of course—Sister!"

"Where are you? What are you doing? It's so good to see you!" Sr. Elizabeth was obviously excited.

"I'm studying at Syracuse U. and I love it." Patricia had graduated from R.C.C., a junior college, and had transferred her A.A. to Syracuse U. "I often run into some of your community in Syracuse and when I would ask about you, they'd always say, `She's doing just fine.'"

"So, why didn't you write and ask me yourself?"

"I did, Sister. I wrote you a number of letters, but Sr. Anita wrote and told me to stop writing. She said the things I shared were not appropriate for a young religious."

Sr. Elizabeth felt shell-shocked for a moment.

"What kind of things were you writing?"

"Oh, I don't know. The usual stuff. I wrote about my family, but I also shared about a boy I've been dating—and some of the parties I've been to. She didn't think I should be telling you about such things, I guess."

Sr. Elizabeth remained incredulous. She knew all incoming and outgoing letters were read, but this was her first experience with Anita telling a friend *not* to write. The realization dropped like a ton of bricks. At first she felt hurt, but soon her feelings turned to anger. This was so unfair! Elizabeth was terribly fond of Patricia. Didn't she have a right to know Patricia was happy, that she was well? How could Sr. Anita meddle with this friendship? There was nothing but wholesome caring between the two. Who was Sr. Anita that she could play God, deciding who could be Elizabeth's friend, and who could not. Patricia explained that their meeting was no accident.

"I came here today just to see you. I was spending the weekend with my aunt and she told me that the canonicals were helping with the vocation congress. I was sure I could find you!"

After a blissful hour of catching up, Sr. Elizabeth excused herself to work the stage curtains for a skit and song the novices were performing. Sr. Elizabeth asked Patricia to stay for the performance, and she did. This concluded the weekend activities. Unfortunately, that was the last visit Sr. Elizabeth enjoyed with her college biology partner. Somehow, they never were able to get in touch again, thanks mostly to the efforts of Sr. Anita.

The next few weeks were active and fully scheduled for the canonicals. They all had visions of June, black veils, and a new superior!

Sister Leonard (Theresa) had a doctor's appointment one afternoon, and for some reason, the only available car had a standard transmission. Sr. Anita soon discovered no one was able to drive a stick shift. Many of the older sisters did not know how to drive at all because permission to learn came from the mother general during the reign of Mother Josepha. Several women came to community knowing how to drive, but that did not mean they were given permission to do so. Twenty years ago, most convents didn't even own a car. The sisters would ask the lay people of the parish for rides to the doctor, shopping, or to the train station for longer journeys. Buses and walking suited most of their transportation needs until the late 1950's when driving became a privilege for a chosen few and cars were made available in local parishes.

Locating a stick shift driver for Sr. Leonard was proving most difficult. In frustration, she snagged Sr. Elizabeth, who happened to be walking the halls with a mop in each hand.

"Sister, can you drive a car that has to have the gears changed?"

"Do you mean a stick shift, Sister?"

"Whatever. Can you drive that sort of car?"

"Yes, Sister. My dad taught me on a stick."

"Well, go and ask Sr. Mary Peter for her driver's veil and get your license. You're going to drive Sr. Leonard to the doctor."

"Right now, Sister?"

"No, Sister. Five minutes ago. Now hurry!"

Putting the mops away without a thorough cleaning felt most uncomfortable, but Sr. Elizabeth knew Sr. Anita meant *now*, and not after cleaning the mops. She hurried up to change into a veil that did not block peripheral vision, as did the traditional grotto-like veil the sisters wore. The "drivers' veil" rested upon the head band and wrapped next to the coronet, where it was pinned on either side, just behind the ears.

As Sr. Elizabeth drove out of the parking lot, Sr. Anita watched with sheer relief. Sr. Elizabeth never felt more proud or more accomplished than she did right now. Finally, she had done something right. She knew how to drive a standard shift automobile, and Anita's precious Mary Peter didn't.

Upon returning to the motherhouse, Sr. Elizabeth felt a need to ask Sr. Anita why she had forbidden Patricia Falbo to write. She was experiencing a flash of self-confidence, and ever since the vocation congress, she had felt a gnawing desire to confront this woman. Scared as she may have been, Sr. Elizabeth, nevertheless, decided she had the right to ask.

"Sister?"

"Yes, Sister. Come in." Sr. Anita looked up from her desk as Sr. Elizabeth and Sr. Leonard came in for their blessing.

"We're home, Sister. May we have your blessing?"

"God bless you, Sisters. Did you get there on time?"

"Yes, Sister. Sr. Leonard knew just where to go and how to get there."

"Fine. Did you leave the car in the side lot?"

"Yes, Sister."

"Very well. You may both be excused. I'll discuss your appointment later, Sr. Leonard."

"Yes, Sister. Thank you, Sister." Sr. Leonard turned to leave, but Elizabeth remained at the door.

"Sister, may I have two minutes of your time?" Sr. Elizabeth respectfully requested.

"Yes, Sister. You may be seated."

"Sister, I'm not sure how to begin, but I have been needing to say something."

"What is it, Sister?"

"Sister, during my postulancy, I became friends with my biology partner at Regina. Her name was Patricia Falbo. Several weeks ago, I saw her at the vocation congress. She told me that you wrote and forbade her to write to me. Is that true, Sister?"

"Yes, it is, Sister. Now what, exactly, is the problem?"

"Well, I guess I want to ask why. I would very much like to hear from her."

"You impudent thing! You dare to question what I know is best for you?" Sr. Anita's voice raised half an octave and Sr. Elizabeth instantly regretted her attempt to reason with this woman.

"Sister, I am your novice directress! If you have not learned to trust my judgment, you have learned nothing! Without confidence in my ability to direct your spiritual life, of what consequence can this formation year be for you as a religious? I refuse to be questioned! If you do not like the policies by which you are expected to live in community, I think you seriously need to consider returning to your family. I will not be subject to your scrutiny!" She glared at the novice. "You are dismissed, Sister."

Sister Elizabeth wanted to shout back, "Why do you hate me so much? Why do you think me so totally stupid, so utterly incompetent?" She wanted to cry out, "You tell us to have no friendship but that of God's, yet you flaunt your friend, Sister Prisca, before us nearly every weekend and speak of her as if she were God's only gift to community! Not to mention your blatant and unfair favoritism for Sr. Mary Peter! You speak out of both sides of your mouth, yet tolerate no flaw within anyone of us! You destroy us and we say, `Thank you, Sister!'"

All of Sr. Elizabeth's thoughts remained unspoken. She knew freedom was only a month or so away. There would be no wisdom in fighting for rights or honesty now.

"I'm sorry, Sister." She knelt. "May I have a penance, Sister?"

"Yes, you may spend one hour on your knees before the Blessed Sacrament begging God for a contrite spirit."

"Thank you, Sister." Sr. Elizabeth went off to return the driver's veil to Sr. Mary Peter and then to see that the mops were properly washed out and put away.

That evening, Sr. Anita called her novices together to tell them they would be having a chapter of faults. Some of the novices had heard of this custom. It was quite common in the past, but less prevalent since the Second Vatican Council. Sisters were expected to reflect upon their most grievous faults and confess them before the other members of their local community. They then were to ask the forgiveness of God and the forgiveness of their sisters. Finally, the superior would assign a group penance.

"Not that we do much of this now, but I do hope you take this as a wonderful opportunity to look honestly upon yourselves. Faults lead to sinfulness, and even though you go to confession weekly, chapter of faults is a good way to examine your conscience and prepare more thoroughly for confession. You each have a responsibility to community and to confess your faults in order to receive the pardon of others. We will go to chapel now and I will help you understand the nature of this experience. You will see how it helps you grow in your spiritual lives."

This was not an option. The novices looked at each other. No one was comfortable with Sister's latest "community custom." But fifteen individuals were straining to finish this period of their formation so dutifully, they filed into chapel and knelt in silence.

From behind, Sister led a prayer to the Holy Spirit and then read an excerpt from one of her favorite spiritual reading books, *Listen, Sister.* There were a few moments of silence.

"At this time, Sisters, you may confess your faults before God and in the presence of each other. This will be done in the order of rank beginning with the youngest.

Sr. Catherine Ann was not at all happy about being first. She searched her soul until she finally remembered something. "Sisters, I beg forgiveness for not always taking my bedspread entirely off my bed every night." Sr. Anita would undoubtedly see her later about that. All of them knew better than to disobey an explicit directive. Most thought Sr. Catherine Ann either very brave or very stupid to have admitted such a fault.

"Sisters, I confess my fault before you. I skim through my prayers when I have to make them up privately. I ask you to forgive me for failing in my prayer life." Sr. Leonard sounded so contrite that it seemed almost laughable. The novices remained silent and continued to listen.

"Sisters, I don't change my bed sheet every week. Usually I do it every other week. I beg your forgiveness." Sr. Mary Ruth got her idea from what Sr. Leonard had said. She couldn't think of anything else with such short notice. She hoped it would be acceptable.

"Sisters, I beg your forgiveness because I sometimes talk with the constitutionals when I take up their laundry basket, and I was looking out the window for almost ten minutes this afternoon," confessed Sr. Mark Lewis.

"Sisters, I find myself angry with some of you and want to tell you about it, but I'm afraid to make things worse, and so I keep it inside. I ask your forgiveness and God's," said Sr. Mary Alice quite softly.

Sister Robert Therese asked forgiveness for taking two cookies off the motherhouse dessert tray when she was setting up the refectory for supper.

Sr. Francis Anne must have thought this a general confession because she went on for about three minutes. No one laughed, but they wanted to. They could not see a purpose in this. They felt uncomfortable for each other, but if this is what you had to do to become a nun, then so be it.

Sr. Charles Marion confessed she had an argument with Sr. Charity today and that she was sorry for having been rather uncooperative in laundry today.

Sr. Christine Marie said she was sorry that she talked to herself occasionally. That was no revelation to anyone, not even Sr. Anita.

"Sisters, I'm sorry for swinging my arms when I walk. I have been corrected continuously, but I still have this habit of doing it. Please forgive me," admitted Sr. Maryjane.

Sr. Michael Michelle confessed she had lost her rubbers. It seemed a good time to let Sr. Anita know. Now when she goes to beg a penance, the scene might not be quite as disturbing.

Sr. Dominic admitted that she could not think of any faults, but that she would try to lose some weight as a constitutional.

"Sisters, I confess my slowness when I work. I don't always know the fastest or easiest way to get the job done, and I rebel when others tell me what they think I'm doing wrong." They knew this about Sr. Charity, too. Still, everyone liked Charity. She was genuine and meant well. Sr. Robert Therese still wanted her friendship, but had grown more accustomed to the idea that Sr. Charity could not return it. Sr. Charity seemed lost in Sr. Dominic, and perhaps it was all for the best.

Sr. Mary Peter confessed that she seemed to break dishes more often than the others and Sr. Elizabeth apologized for her arrogant disposition toward authority, particularly for being rude to her superior this afternoon.

There was silence once more. No one knew what would happen next. The whole process had taken only half an hour. It was nerve-wracking, yet many of the girls remained on the verge of giggling. It was certainly an awkward experience, this "chapter of faults" thing.

"Sisters, for your penance, you will each pray six Our Father's, six Hail Mary's, and six Glory Be's with outstretched arms. You may then retire. God bless you, Sisters."

. . . .

41

Rehearsing for Investing Day included the usual unpleasant tension under the direction of Sr. Helena. It seemed as if nearly every session was marred by someone being castigated, asked to sing on key, or ridiculed for one reason or another.

Sr. Helena interrupted a four-part harmony with the wave of her arm. She demanded, "Don't any of you have a commitment to this song? You sing as if you drool out some message. This is for Investing, Sisters! Can't you prepare something other than drool! Don't even do it for them. Do it for the love of God. Now, which of you would dare to drool for the love of God? Sing, Sisters! Sing!"

The choir began and again they were interrupted.

"Sisters, you think you have it *so* hard! That life is oppressive and that countless demands are made of you. As you feel your self-pity, think also of me and the courtroom I am about to enter. How many of you would choose to be in *my* shoes?"

"Many of you may know that I killed a young man on a motorcycle in Vermont three years ago. (Actually, none of them knew.) I'm going to have to face the charges brought before me this summer. The least you could do is sing better than this and offer your efforts on my behalf." She was not about to stop her raving tirade. She wanted them all to know the story.

"He drove out of a side road. I couldn't see him. The prosecutor wants to hold the community financially responsible because I didn't wear a driver's veil that day. So when you feel your self-pity, Sisters, imagine how I must feel to face this young man's family!

You haven't the slightest idea how difficult life can be! Now, sing with some gusto! Some commitment!

Something, Sisters! Something other than dribble coming from your mouths!"

Sr. Helena was forceful. When it came to music, she could extract nearly any sound she wanted. Her soft tones spoke tenderly, her forte became majestic, her melodies, impeccable: Her talent was undisputed. But she was equally as ruthless and cruel unless you were among her loyal few. She feared no one. Her persuasive powers were respected, but her methods were questionable. No one considered Sr. Helena a soft touch. She was a doer, at any price. She commanded respect. Had she been more considerate, more than a few may have cared in return.

. . . .

42

Father's Day came early in June that year and the girls were busy making homemade cards for their dads. Sr. Robert Therese had the misfortune to be working at the table with Sr. Charles Marion. She had a knack for putting on a sour grape attitude about almost anything.

"I better get this card in the mail today or it'll get to Ohio late," Sr. Robert Therese commented aloud.

"At least you have a father to write to," returned Sr. Charles Marion. Everyone knew her father had died of blood poisoning when she was a small child. In those days, there were no tetanus shots. By the time they knew what the problem was, it was too late to save his life.

Sr. Robert Therese felt cheated by this cheap shot. Why should she be made to feel guilty because her father *was* alive? On the other hand, Robert Therese felt she understood Charles Marion a little better than the others. She appeared to be a deeply unhappy person in desperate search of someone to care. Sadly, in this group of people, no one really did. Charles Marion's attitude was negative, criticizing, and reeked of self-pity. It appeared to be what the others called a "martyr complex". Even though Sr. Robert Therese was far more tolerant than the other novices, it did not mean she could muster the energy to be a friend. She could only manage compassionate acceptance. She would not dignify Sr. Charles Marion's cutting response with a reply.

Instead she continued to reflect upon an early morning incident that was causing some guilt feelings of her own.

Sr. Robert Therese had taken an old nun from the infirmary for a wheelchair ride in the parking lot. It was a warm and pleasant Sunday morning. Robert Therese was stunned to see a driver pulling into the parking lot with the same habit and headgear that her Rochester friend, Sr. Irene, had worn. She immediately considered that they might know Irene, but she also knew that approaching the sisters was forbidden. This was a cloister year, one of no interaction with anyone, and especially not visitors. She wanted to do the correct thing, to smile and continue pushing the infirmary sister. This was not a moment of ambiguity. Sr. Robert Therese clearly understood right from wrong.

"Good morning, Sisters! I recognize your habits and veils as being from Rochester."

They were quick to respond warmly, "Yes, we are, Sister! We've come to deliver some materials to your motherhouse superior."

"I know a novice in your community. Her name is Sr. Irene. Do you know her?"

The driver spoke this time. "I do. She's a wonderful young Sister."

"Sister, will you give her my best. Just tell her that an Albany Franciscan novice sends her love. She'll know who I am."

"Sure, Sister. I'll be glad to."

Sr. Robert Therese's heart was somewhere in her throat. She mustn't get caught. She continued the morning walk about the grounds with her elderly charge and later returned her to the infirmary.

This incident was heavy on her mind. She had broken a rule and wanted to beg a penance, but pride kept her from going to Sr. Anita. Maybe that's why she would not react harshly to Sr. Charles Marion's insensitive remark. Recognizing her own lack of perfection made her more willing to forgive Sr. Charles Marion.

Several days later, cleaning schedules increased and pressures were on to prepare for the Investing of postulants. They were making their Investing retreat, which left more of the responsibilities to canonicals. Sr. Robert Therese (Angie) and Sr. Elizabeth (Ginny) were both trying to figure out why the floor buffer would not start. They needed to shine the waxed corridors. Sr. Mary Alice (Linda) was passing through with a load of wash and the three white veils met at the intersection of kitchen, motherhouse, and novitiate hallways. It was an opportunity to pause a few moments and dare to engage in brief conversation. Just then, from around the corner loomed Sr. Anita into their midst. All three shuddered and assumed a business-like posture.

"Perhaps Sr. Dominic can look at it for you. She's pretty mechanical," Sr. Mary Alice suggested.

"It worked this morning. I used it to buff the black rubber hall on third floor," Sr. Robert Therese replied.

"And what's this? Conversing in hallways? You people don't belong in this intersection and you know it!" Sr. Anita wore a particularly stern grimace. Perhaps she was not feeling well. They all knew her colitis gave her great discomfort at times.

"Sister, the buffer won't start." Sr. Robert Therese dared an explanation.

"What did you do to it, Sister?"

"I don't think I've done anything to it, Sister. It was working this morning."

"Then obviously you have done something to it. And what are you doing with a cart of soiled laundry?" She now focused upon Sr. Mary Alice. "That should have been collected hours ago!"

"Sister, I thought I'd begin a second collection schedule because so many people seem to drop things into the baskets after breakfast. Two trips are easier to manage when I'm collecting alone."

"You mean to tell me that you changed the collection schedules for laundry without consulting me?"

"I'm sorry, Sister." She wasn't about to defend herself.

"Sisters, I have tried so hard to teach you! As you come to the end of your canonical year, I seriously believe you should be starting it over. Sr. Mary Alice, the first complaint I'll hear of you on mission will be from your pastor! He will be furious to hear you have planned programs for his parish and *he's* the last to know!" Sr. Mary Alice kept her eyes downcast, but then Sr. Anita turned to the others. Her tirade was only beginning.

"And you, Sr. Robert Therese, I can just see you falling in love with the mother of one of your students at your first PTA meeting!" There was still another before her. "And you, Sr. Elizabeth, I really can't imagine you ever becoming a nurse, let alone this doctor dream you have. You just haven't the brains for it!" She was totally exasperated as she spoke. "Get busy and get out of this hall." She left, as she came: in her attack mode.

Her words sounded prophetic and all three stood motionless. They exchanged glances. Sr. Mary Alice was not sure if she would return the dirty clothes to the baskets from where they came or continue on to the laundry. She slowly moved toward the elevator trying to decide. Sr. Robert Therese said she would go look for Sr. Dominic to see if she could start the buffer. Sr. Elizabeth decided to mop the next hall until Sr. Robert Therese returned with Sr. Dominic.

· · · · · · · ·

43

It was another Sunday afternoon, and preparations for Investing were in good order. The postulants were on retreat and things were fairly peaceful. Sr. Anita called Sr. Elizabeth into her office and told her to tell the novices they could have some time for a walk outside.

"You know the limits," Sr. Anita continued, and she drew a shape in the air with her finger.

Sr. Elizabeth assumed this finger gesture meant outside of the walls and included places they had ventured to during the year. She left the office and announced to the others, "Sister said we can go for a walk this afternoon."

"Where to?" Sr. Mary Peter inquired.

"Sr. Anita said, `You know the limits', so I guess that means anywhere we've been before."

The novices were delighted! They broke into small groups and began their outing. Both friends and factions joined together for their outing.

Sr. Mary Alice (Linda), Sr. Catherine Ann (Kathleen), and Sr. Elizabeth (Ginny) decided to walk toward Assumption School, while others headed toward the community cemetery. The groups went in four or five different directions.

Their white veils always brought attention from passers-by. The long serge habit brought notice except to those in the neighborhood who had seen the sisters come and go over the years. The threesome walked with excited thoughts of home visits just after Investing.

"You know, the group really has me scared about flying into D.C."

"Elizabeth, they're only teasing you!" protested Sr. Mary Alice.

"I know. But I've never flown before. I have this ticket with Mohawk Airlines and they're saying Mohawk passengers are given parachutes. That they carve holes in the belly of their planes so that we can put our legs through and run real fast so it can lift off."

Sr. Mary Alice and Sr. Catherine Ann both laughed out loud.

"Now you know *that* isn't true." Mary Alice returned.

"Of course I know. They mock it because it's an economy airline. I just hope it's safe."

"It's as safe as any other airline."

"The teasing just isn't funny, but they won't stop."

"Ignore them, Sister!"

"That's like asking me to ignore Sr. Anita."

"Why do you take her so seriously?" Sr. Catherine Ann asked.

"I really don't know *how* to take her. She scares me. I mean, she's like the voice of God or something."

"That's the difference between us," continued Sr. Catherine Ann. "I see Sr. Anita as a plain ol' person who just happens to be in charge of us this year. I admit I love her, but she's only human. Not a vampire or anything." Both Sr. Mary Alice and Sr. Elizabeth knew Sr. Catherine Ann had a much better rapport with Sr. Anita, but it was never cause for suspicion.

"Well, she walloped Sr. Mary Alice and me the other day!"

"What do you mean?" Sr. Catherine Ann asked.

"She told me I was brainless and would never be a nurse. Sr. Mary Alice is going to rule pastors."

"Well, the brainless part might be correct, but Sister, I'm sure you'll be a doctor someday. Just not in this life."

"I get this creepy feeling she has a crystal ball or something."

"We all think like that some days. Let's face it, she's a tough ol' bird, but then so are you." Sr. Catherine Ann was teasing Sr. Elizabeth about her family name, Crow. Often the novices would. "Caw, caw. Get it?"

"Very funny." Sr. Elizabeth replied. Sr. Mary Alice couldn't keep from laughing.

As they continued their walk in the delightful sun enjoying the fresh hint of summer, they decided it was time to turn back.

Upon returning, Sr. Mary Peter greeted the trio with, "You guys are about to be killed."

"What did we do?" asked Sr. Mary Alice.

"We were supposed to walk around the walls, no where else. I had to go chase the group that headed for the cemetery. No one knew which direction you three took."

"We walked up to Assumption Church and back," explained Sr. Elizabeth.

"Well, she's looking for you. She's not happy."

They walked into the novitiate community room and headed for the office to get Sister's blessing upon their return. Sister Anita spoke softly.

"Where were you, Sisters?"

"We walked up to Assumption Church," Sr. Elizabeth answered.

"Sister Elizabeth, didn't I specifically tell you around the walls only?"

"Sister, I must have misunderstood. When you said, 'You know the limits', I assumed it was where we have been before."

"Sister, I *drew* a circle around the walls with my finger in the air. Don't you remember?"

"Yes, but I didn't know that the circle meant around the wall."

"Sister, I can just imagine you explaining to your head nurse, 'I didn't think you meant three pills, I gave the patient only one'. The writing is on the wall, Sister. You just can't read!"

The novices knelt. They knew it was a safer posture to assume when being corrected.

"Why would you walk to Assumption? Do you know how dangerous that neighborhood is? Weren't the three of you afraid?"

"No, Sister." Sr. Catherine Ann spoke this time. The place was obviously poor and run down. "The people seemed very friendly. We never thought of being scared."

Sr. Anita must have known she wasn't going to get very far with this. She decided to back off. Maybe it was the fact that Sr. Catherine Ann had been a part of it that she cast forth a little mercy upon the threesome. "Well, you should have been scared. It is not a safe place to walk. You may wash up for your 4:15 charges. Sr. Elizabeth, next time, I will assume nothing. Expect me to spell it out for you one letter at a time. You are dismissed."

As they left, all breathed a sigh of relief. This could have been another disaster. Instead, they were free to return to their work.

Meanwhile, Sr. Robert Therese was standing just outside the office as they passed. She still felt this gnawing guilt over having sent a message to Sr. Irene by way of the visiting nuns in the parking lot. She wanted to confess her disobedience and to beg penance, but her fear of humiliation kept her from stepping forward.

The next day, at dinner table, after the spiritual reading was completed and the bell gave novices permission to talk, Sr. Anita began the meal by addressing Sr. Robert Therese who was seated to her left. "Did you enjoy your visit in the parking lot, Sr. Robert Therese?"

The question hit her right between the eyes. Surrounding novices took notice of Sr. Anita's inquiry. They all knew this was forbidden behavior. They listened intently for Sr. Robert Therese's response.

Sr. Robert Therese was having difficulty mustering an answer. Her thoughts raced, "How could Sr. Anita have found out? Who could have told? Was it that old nun I took for a ride?" The canonical was speechless. Sr. Anita was not.

"You know, the one where you sent messages to the Rochester novice?" Anita continued.

"Yes, Sister, I know the one you mean," she admitted.

Sr. Dominic sat directly across from Sr. Robert Therese. She was certainly enjoying this. Because of Sr. Charity, there was always a competition between the New Jersey and Ohio novices. Besides, Sr. Robert Therese had acquired a reputation for scrupulous obedience. The sending of messages and illicit conversations intrigued her stocky foe.

It came as a disappointment to Sr. Dominic when Sr. Anita, just as suddenly, ended the discussion. "We'll talk more of this after lunch, Sister. In my office."

Sr. Robert Therese could not eat much that meal. She dreaded the conference ahead, and she felt so guilty. If only she had confessed as she intended a dozen times. It was too late now. She had obviously been turned in by someone. She knew that being caught meant personal disaster.

During their meeting, Sr. Robert Therese explained her behavior as best as she could. Needless to say, her actions were

inexcusable and her penance was not to wear her cord and rosary
for two days except for Mass in the motherhouse.

This look gave her habit a muumuu effect and it was obvious
to everyone she had been given a penance for rule infraction. She
expected worse, but these last few days before home visit, the group
noticed Sr. Anita easing up a bit.

Finally Investing had come and gone and the novices prepared
for their first lengthy visit with their families in almost two years.
Five days at home was a glorious thought! They gathered together
for Sr. Anita's last minute directives.

"Sisters, some of you will be leaving for home tomorrow. You
may put on your black veils. I have decided that, technically, your
canonical year will end today. However, Sr. Mary Edgar and I have
agreed that you will continue to be under my direction for two
weeks following your return from home visits. You will then engage
in schedules more suited to your black-veiled status. Are there any
questions?"

There were none. There was only silence. The novices didn't
know what to expect, but they didn't expect the changing of the
veils to be so simple. Pin black veils for tomorrow instead of white.
Their canonical year was over without ceremony, and with no pomp
or circumstance.

As their starched veils were re-pinned that evening, emotions
ran the gamut from ecstacy to sheer terror. What will come with
this new novice directress? What will *her* expectations be? What
new challenges lie ahead? Some even felt a sadness as the white veil
was undone. Many had become so used to Sr. Anita's manipula-
tive, mind controlling ways that they felt willing and able to continue their submissive lives. Others would have liked nothing more
than *never* to see this woman again. No matter how they felt, she
wasn't about to leave them alone. Upon their minds, she had imprinted her indelible damage.

· · · · · · · ·

44

Sr. Robert Therese was not sure how she managed to give her parents the wrong date for her homecoming, but no one was there to meet her when she arrived at the Toledo airport. She made a collect call and was lucky to find her dad at home. Mrs. Masucci was getting her hair done, expecting her daughter the following day. Sr. Robert Therese finally discovered the reason for the mix up. She had given the correct time, but the wrong day.

It was an exciting reunion for everyone. Each evening before 6:00, Mr. Masucci returned his daughter to nearby St. Rita's convent. The novices had to return to the motherhouse each night or sleep at the nearest local convent. Only Sr. Christine Marie could not join her family. Hawaii was too long a trip. Sr. Leonard and she were close friends and Christine Marie went home with her. It was not the custom for sisters to stay in their families' homes unless it was impossible to locate a convent within driving distance. This was to assure the continuation of convent practices while vacationing. A strict prayer schedule and participation in the local community life were considered essential. Besides, there was a concern that if religious women associated informally with family and friends, they might consider a return to their former lifestyles, or even assume some of their prior, secular behaviors.

One day, upon Sr. Robert Therese's return to St. Rita's, the local superior gave her a letter addressed to her in Sandusky and mailed from Rochester, New York. Robert Therese knew that it was from Sr. Irene. Her first impulse was to tear open the envelope and allow her heart to feast upon the message it contained. She hesitated. She knew Sr. Anita would not approve, nor had she opened her own mail for almost two years now. As much as she wanted to read this letter, she feared even more the displeasure of Sr. Anita. Sister Robert Therese would carry the letter back to Albany and present it, as expected, to her novice mistress.

During the day, Robert Therese would delight in reunion with family and her best friends, Diane and Sue. Diane was married by now. She and her high school sweetheart tied the knot before he left for Vietnam. Sue had graduated from a school of cosmetology. She was dating a policeman but was not eager to marry. They had hours and hours of catching up to do.

Sr. Robert Therese especially enjoyed eating her mother's delicious Italian dishes, and the days were filled with talking marathons. She could tell her father still drank for courage as he drove her back to the convent each evening with the smell of alcohol upon his breath. He seemed to pretend she was Angie, his daughter, not some young woman wrapped in mystery. Still, he was curious.

One day he asked, "How do you get your head wrapped up in all that?"

"Here, Dad, let me show you."

"Nah. Don't take it apart. They don't make you sleep in that outfit, do they?"

"No, Dad."

Roberto had apparently mellowed these past few years. He was gradually accepting his daughter's desire to be an Albany Franciscan. He still preferred otherwise. He hated seeing his little girl choose a life he neither understood nor respected. Nevertheless, there was a growing sparkle of pride in his eyes as he looked upon his daughter, straight and tall, soft-spoken, and eager to change the world.

"You really want this life, don't you, honey?"

"With all my heart, Dad. I think I'll be a wonderful nun."

She would never mention her canonical training or describe the rigorous schedule and self-discipline expected of her. She wanted to protect her father. Besides, he would surely drag her from the community if she even hinted what this past year was like.

As usual, on the last evening, Mr. Masucci took his daughter back to the convent. He would not see her tomorrow. He would be at work while Angie's mother drove her to the airport. Sr. Robert Therese and her father embraced as he walked her to the back door of the convent. She waved and called to him as he drove away, "I'll be back for Christmas, Dad! See you then!" Even if he was an alcoholic, he was a loving father. Sr. Robert Therese knew he was a wonderful man, but she was troubled to realize that drinking controlled so much of his life.

. . . .

45

Sr. Elizabeth dreaded the flight home, though she eagerly anticipated being with her family. The plane ride proved uneventful, but the novice could not help feeling uncomfortable. She sat next to a businessman in a gray suit. She couldn't keep herself from grasping the rosary she wore, and silently, she prayed it three times before landing at Dulles Airport.

Sr. Elizabeth had found the excitement and bustle of her home visit more draining than she imagined. It was wonderful to be home again. Neighbors rang out shouts of welcome from a distance and high school friends were eager to see what Ginny would look like, transformed by convent life. Would she be that same crazy, fun-loving teenager that left Silver Spring nearly two years ago? Many were surprised to discover a very proper and lady-like demeanor. She was definitely different.

Sr. Elizabeth tried not to feel like a guest in her parent's home, but she felt strangely disconnected, even while love and concern enveloped her. She looked about the familiar house with a critical eye, noticing it was not as clean as the convent had been. The stove, the cap on the ketchup bottle, the carpeting, even the furniture looked in need of help. Everyone spoke too loudly, and her many brothers and sisters moved so quickly. It was a far cry from the cloister environs. Sr. Elizabeth believed her home and family, and even her friends, had changed so much, when in fact it was she who had changed.

As the days progressed, Sr. Elizabeth actually looked forward to her trip back to Albany. She could not understand her feelings and her disappointment.

· · · · · · · ·

46

Sr. Mary Alice left the motherhouse a day after the long-distance travelers. Girls within an hour of home left after community Mass on the 15th of June. They were expected to return each evening before 6:00 P.M. Sr. Mary Alice's whole family arrived to get her— her mom and dad, her sister Margaret, Margaret's husband Mike, and her brother Larry. This was not the first time Sr. Mary Alice had met Mike, but it was the first time she had seen him since he and her sister stopped by the novitiate for a few minutes after their wedding. Sr. Mary Alice had asked Sr. Anita for permission to attend their wedding, but she was told, "Not during your canonical year."

They all drove to the nearby Perkins Pancake House off Central Avenue and chatted eagerly about each others' lives. Margaret shared her social work stories. They were countless and always fascinating to her younger sister.

Margaret counselled runaway teenagers and worked for the local county agency, even though she had earned a B.A. in English from Sienna. "We had a girl in yesterday. She ran away from home for two days. Only a 7th grader. Goes to Catholic School. She and her girl friend slept in the boy friend's garage. She admitted that she's using drugs. No father, and her mother drinks. She told me her mom got so drunk and angry that she threw a knife at her daughter and barely missed."

Sr. Mary Alice was appalled. She could not imagine youngsters in such serious trouble. "Seventh grade? What can anyone do for her?"

"There won't be any easy or quick solution. We'll place the girl in a detention home for a while, and then maybe the courts will put her in a foster home. I doubt if her mother will get her back. At least, not as long as she's drinking and acting violent. It's still too early to know what or how much help we can find her."

"How tragic," Sr. Mary Alice mused softly.

"It's so hard for those kids out there, Linda. I see too much of it. Abusive parents, drugs messing up any chance for normalcy. You name it: In social work, we see it. It's not a pretty picture."

Linda had often thought to follow in her sister's footsteps: to be a social worker, to help the poor, to be there for others. She also believed that by being a good teacher, she might temper some of that ignorance that spawns the illnesses within society. She had chosen a religious order of teachers and nurses. There were no social workers among them, as such. Mary Alice would teach.

Her brother Larry worked as a apprentice for an electrician. His real interest was solar energy. Larry, too, shared enthusiastic stories about his job.

Their father was teaching school that summer, but Mrs. Pettigrew was free to help Sr. Mary Alice in her many plans for the next few days. They shopped together, ate out, and ate in. It was an exciting change from the convent routines.

Richard Vercillo, her close childhood chum, planned an afternoon with Sr. Mary Alice. Richard was in his second year of seminary training but was able to borrow a car and drive up to Albany for the day. He looked forward to time with his friend. Richard proudly sported his black robe and collar as the two of them sat at a picnic table overlooking the Hudson River. The setting was picturesque.

"Are you happy, Linda?"

"I think so, Richard. You can't imagine what this past year has been like. Are they strict in your community?"

"We have rules, but I can't say the guys take things very seriously. Actually, it hasn't been too bad at all. We study a lot. I enjoy our trips into New York City for Broadway shows and Radio City."

"I can't believe you guys do such things. We weren't even allowed to walk around the block without permission. Are we working in the same Church?"

"Sure we are! It's just that the Church doesn't expect men to live the way they want women to live. Once the novitiate is behind you, things will be better. This is something you endure for something much better to come."

Sr. Mary Alice never breathed a word of novitiate training to her family, but she shared freely with Richard. As always, his insights were comforting. "Linda, we obviously have more freedom. Our novice master isn't any barrel of fun, but your Sr. Anita sounds like some nun-from-hell horror flick. This Sr. Mary Edgar seems like she'll be a good change. Just hang in there." He took her hand into his and she felt strangely free. Richard understood.

"Rich, I want to change the world somehow. I want to be a beautiful nun so that people will look at me and say 'Your God must be so good!' I want to be another reason why people praise and thank the Creator. I want to be good for my students and give people a message of hope."

"Linda, you *are* good for people. You're good for me. I want these same dreams. I hope you'll always be there for me."

"Silly Richard. We're best friends and you know it. Just remember me when they put you in charge of the order and I'm asked to run a soup kitchen!" They laughed and continued to reminisce about their youth and years of friendship. This was unquestionably the highlight of her trip back home. She loved Richard and probably always would.

At her final evening meal at home, all the family came together: Sr. Mary Alice's mom and dad, her sister, brother-in-law, and brother. They decided a formal prayer of grace before dinner was appropriate and asked Linda to lead. Instead of saying the traditional family grace, she prayed spontaneously from the heart.

"Lord God, thank you for this meal given through your mercy and providence. We are glad to share it with each other and ask you to bless us with continued happiness and good health. Amen."

She began and ended her prayer with the sign of the cross.

Mary Alice glanced up to catch her brother-in-law's skeptical gesture. He had rolled his eyeballs as if to say, "She's gone holy-roller on us." Simple as her original prayer had been, Sr. Mary Alice, often timid but even more shy now, had dared to venture forth with her own prayerful thoughts. It had taken some serious courage. She had felt a need to speak from the heart. Mike's disapproving look devastated Mary Alice, crushing the confidence she had mustered to expose the innermost gratitude she felt at being back home. No one else had noticed the disapproving look. Before the final dish had been passed, Sr. Mary Alice excused herself from table. She could no longer keep back the tears.

Margaret decided to follow her sister into the upstairs bathroom.

"What's wrong, Linda?" Margaret asked. Sr. Mary Alice could not explain. She didn't want to cause any argument between Margaret and her husband, but she needed to satisfy Margaret's concern.

"I'm just so glad to be home. It's been so long since I've had time with any of you. I guess it's just too much excitement."

Margaret was extremely perceptive and knew there was more to this than being happy. Still, it was not a good time to probe. Supper was hot and everyone at table was worried.

"Well, come on! Let's get out there and enjoy what little time we do have. Linda, you know, in terms of miles, you are actually closer to Mom and Dad than Mike and I are. You won't be in novitiate forever. There will be many more years to enjoy ourselves! Now, let's get downstairs before we end up taking you back to the convent hungry. You don't send out for pizza much, I expect." Margaret was trying to lighten the mood.

"Yeah, you're right. Let's eat. We don't send out for pizza. At least, we haven't yet." Mary Alice dried her face with the large white cotton handkerchief she carried in her underskirt beneath her habit.

"One thing, Linda, before we go back there. Why does it look as if you've shaved your temples? Did they cut your hair off under that thing?"

Sr. Mary Alice was not about to get into her hair-cutting stories with Margaret. Not yet, anyway. Margaret had not been fond of Mary Alice's choice of life with nuns over college opportunities, Richard, and her own dream to be a social worker. She answered the question as forthrightly as she thought she could, "Of course not, Margaret. I do shave my temples though. Hair hangs out if I don't. It's almost as long as yours." Sr. Mary Alice considered this only a white lie.

They returned to table and everyone continued with dinner. They were genuinely happy to have Linda home, if only for a few days.

. . . .

47

It was not long before the St. Jude Group met, once more, before Sr. Anita in the novitiate community room. For the first time, she addressed the young women in their black veils.

"I hope you all enjoyed your time at home. Sr. Christine Marie has next summer to look forward to . . . three weeks in Hawaii after vows should help make up for the fact you couldn't get home this year. Did you enjoy your visit with Sr. Leonard's family?"

"Very much so, Sister. Sr. Leonard and I enjoyed several exciting day trips together. Her family could not have been more hospitable. I had a great time."

"Actually, I recall my first home visit as a rude awakening. I hope you weren't disappointed. Sometimes we anticipate too much and are disappointed. People change, and maybe things aren't quite the way you remembered them. Well, as you know, our time together is coming to an end. There is something I have not yet shared with you, but believe I should." She opened a box in front of her and removed a tan colored discipline. "No one will be expected to use this, but I consider it my responsibility to see that you receive one."

The discipline was made of thick braided cord dipped into wax and tied to create a handle-like end and five or six flagella. No one spoke as she gave each of the fifteen novices their own personal whip.

"You may wish to assume the custom of the discipline privately, but I am not instructing you to do so. Are there any questions?"

The young women remained silent.

"Very well, then. You are dismissed, Sisters. Welcome home."

As the group dispersed, Sr. Robert Therese approached Sr. Anita with her unopened letter from Rochester.

"Sister, may I have a few moments of your time?" she requested.

"Yes, Sister. Come into my office."

Sr. Anita took her seat and gestured for Sr. Robert Therese to sit in the chair in front of her desk.

"Sister, while I was home in Sandusky, it came to St. Rita's convent and the superior gave it to me."

"Yes, Sister?"

"Well, Sister, I began to open the letter, and then I thought you would prefer I bring it back to you." Sr. Robert Therese extended the envelope toward Sr. Anita. She took it, opened it, and read the letter.

"It's another one from that Rochester novice, Sr. Irene. The one you met at the vocation congress."

"Another one?"

"Yes, Sister. She has been writing ever since. I have been throwing her letters away. I knew that if you would break rules to send her messages from the parking lot then she could not possibly be good for your vocation. Anyone who leads you into disobedience cannot be a wise choice for friendship."

Sr. Robert Therese was stunned to think Sr. Anita would make these decisions for her, but she found a moment's courage. "Sister, may I have the letter?"

"I really don't care, Sister. Take it. Apparently someone gave her your Ohio convent address. She's quite persistent. Sister, I forbid you *ever* to write to her, see her, or pursue this relationship. She cannot be well-intentioned. Do you understand me, Sister?"

"Yes, Sister. Thank you, Sister." Sr. Robert Therese excused herself and headed for chapel to read the letter. She loved hearing from Irene and tucked the letter gently into her underskirt pocket. It had a return address and a phone number.

She prayed and realized she would not respond, as Sr. Anita had directed. Painful and disappointing as her decision was, she also believed Sr. Anita knew things beyond a novice's understanding. She knelt before the tabernacle and softly spoke the names of Jesus, Mary, and Joseph. Then she whispered the words: "faith", "hope", "charity" several times. She said the words over and over again, trying to mend the frustrations within her.

Sr. Robert Therese felt shame for the anger and animosity she carried for Sr. Anita. Only a few more days to endure! She feared this tower of intimidation, but decided, with discipline in hand, that there would come a day when she would confront this woman. She would ask her "Why?" "Why the accusations, the humiliations, the cruelty?" She thought, "Even if I have to wait *ten* years to find the courage to confront this mean-spirited woman, I promise *someday*, I will."

. . . .

CHAPTER FOUR...
NOVITIATE/
CONSTITUTIONAL YEAR

48

Sr. Mary Edgar was a large woman in her fifties. She was the college registrar for Regina Catholic. Sister had served many years teaching in the Hawaiian missions and had a reputation for being a very tough superior in her younger days. Now she was showing some signs of slowing her pace and mellowing with age. Her reputation was one of being reasonable and the novices anticipated a good year ahead. Some feared the intense schedule of study planned for the new group of constitutionals.

Sr. Elizabeth delivered some mail to Sr. Mary Edgar's office and Sr. Mary Edgar invited the novice to sit and visit for a while. Sr. Elizabeth felt comfortable and had no reason to fear this pleasant woman.

"Tell me, Sister. Why did Sr. Anita appear to single you out so often this past year?'

"Sister?"

"I know this past year was extremely difficult for many of the novices, but it seemed to me that she had some personal grievance toward you. What did you do?"

Sr. Elizabeth was surprised by the comments and the question. She had no idea anyone could see into the canonical world. She was grateful that Sr. Mary Edgar seemed to care.

"Sister, I honestly can't explain what happened this past year. I tried very hard to please her, but I honestly think she didn't believe I had a religious calling to community. I also believe she thinks I'm too incompetent to study nursing. She did everything she could to keep me from the infirmary. She knew I loved being there." Sr. Elizabeth stopped there. She was uncertain about adding her other theory concerning rank. If she got rid of Elizabeth, Sr. Mary Peter, her protege, would become the "oldest", number one.

"I'm going to see that you have more time in the infirmary, but not enough to run interference with your heavy class schedule. I don't agree with Sr. Anita. I think you will make an excellent nurse. I also believe you and the others will be much happier this year." Mary Edgar's eyes smiled whenever she smiled. Sr. Elizabeth felt a new sense of hope, a new beginning.

Among the first things to happen was that Sr. Elizabeth's status as "oldest" among the St. Jude group was re-established. She was asked by Sr. Mary Edgar to lead group meetings and to organize and plan various affairs. Her full load of classes proved to be challenging. Consequently, she could not manage as much time in the infirmary as she would have liked, but she had the option to go and help whenever she could.

Sr. Mary Alice was totally engrossed in a biography of Saint Catherine Laboure. Spiritual reading was required every day and proved to be a marvelous opportunity to learn of saints, church history, and the teachings of popular church theologians. Constitutional novices were always walking about with edifying books.

Saint Catherine Laboure came from a large family in France. Her mother died when she was very young and Catherine was expected to help cook and clean on the farm. Even at a very tender age, she walked over a mile to daily Mass before she prepared breakfast for her family and hired hands.

Sr. Mary Alice was developing a deep and reverent devotion to the Mother of Jesus. As a youngster, Sr. Mary Alice's grandmother, Maa, had taught her "The Hail Mary," Mary Alice's first prayer.

She had grown up with a special love for the Blessed Mother, but this book nurtured her natural inclinations all the more..

Deprived of her natural mother as a child, St. Catherine Laboure turned lovingly to devotion to Mary. In her twenties she finally obtained permission from her father to enter a convent founded by St. Vincent de Paul and St. Louise de Marillac. As a novice, Sr. Catherine Laboure received apparitions of Our Lady. Once, she even rested her arms upon the lap of the Blessed Mother in a convent chapel located on Rue de Bac in Paris. This was the only historically recorded "physical contact" of a visionary and Marian apparition. The more Sr. Mary Alice read of this life, the more enthusiastic she became. She was on the verge of becoming a zealot, according to the other novices who were forced to listen to her recounting of the book.

"Our Lady gave Catherine the task of having a medal cast in the image of the Blessed Mother standing on the world with her hands extending rays of grace to all who have asked her intercession. She wants us to pray, 'O Mary, conceived without sin, pray for us who have recourse to thee'. The back side of this medal has two hearts, one with a crown of thorns and one with a sword piercing through. There is a cross, the letter M, and twelve surrounding stars creating an oval-shaped frame."

"You really are into that story, aren't you?" Sr. Mary Peter remarked as she helped to wipe down the wet counters at dishwasher. Constitutionals would still occasionally help with dishes.

"I guess I am. But, you know, Sister, I don't think many Catholics even know the story of the Miraculous Medal. They wear it more for jewelry than for what it was intended. This priest, Fr. Aladel, wouldn't believe St. Catherine when she told him in confession of the apparitions. Finally, the Blessed Mother gave her some message that made him a true believer. He didn't doubt her after that, and he got the bishop to have the medals made. The Lady promised anyone who wears this image around his or her neck with confidence in her would receive an abundance of God's grace."

"What are these medals? I don't think I've ever heard of them."

"People nicknamed them "miraculous medals" because since 1830 they have been credited with countless miracles."

"So, did the medals make St. Catherine famous?" Sr. Mary Alice was thrilled that Sr. Mary Peter would ask.

"Not a bit. She kept it a secret for forty years that she had been the visionary to receive the medal. Even when Fr. Aladel died, he took her secret to the grave."

"Well, then how do *you* know she was the one to get this medal from the Blessed Mother if everyone kept it secret?"

"Well, just before she died, she told her superior because the other job the Blessed Mother gave her was to have a statue made of Mary holding the world."

"And her superior believed her, just like that?"

"Well, mostly because of the credible life she had lived, I think. She worked with old people and always exercised the patience and charity of a saint. When she died, they buried her. A hundred years later, they exhumed her body and found it incorrupt."

"Incorrupt?"

"Yeah, like not decayed."

The drain boards were finished and the floor mopped. Sr. Mary Alice followed Sr. Mary Peter to the hopper room where she could wash out the mop. Sr. Mary Alice wanted to finish the story.

"Mary Peter, her eyes were as blue as the day she died. No one can explain it. The wooden statue she had carved stands just above her glass coffin. Wouldn't it be neat to go see it someday?"

"I'm sure. It will also be neat if I'm not late for my English Lit class." Sr. Mary Peter had to hurry off, and Sr. Mary Alice walked over to the motherhouse chapel for a short visit. She knelt in silence and prayed. This is what it must feel like to teach people about the saints and to share her devotion to Mary, Mother of God. It was a wonderful feeling, though she felt a tad patronized while sharing the story with Sr. Mary Peter.

· · · · · · · ·

49

Constitutionals were also called black-veiled novices or senior novices. The difference between canonical and constitutional novitiate was tantamount to night and day. Life was dramatically different. Sr. Mary Edgar made few demands, none of which seemed irrational. She expected the fifteen to be personally responsible for their studies, prayer, charge, and meal schedules. They were still expected to help with laundry, dishes, and cleaning, but not as much as last year. All matriculated toward a junior college liberal arts degree at Regina Catholic, except for Sr. Mark Lewis who worked routinely in the infirmary. She was a licensed practical nurse.

Sr. Mary Peter spent a good deal of time visiting Sr. Anita. The group speculated she was keeping the canonical novice directress well-informed as to what was happening on the third floor of the west wing of the motherhouse. Here the black-veiled novices lived in private bedrooms, each with a wooden door!

Sr. Gregoria also lived in this part of the house. She had been born in Germany and served as housekeeper most of her life. Since an emotional breakdown on one of her mission assignments, she had become a permanent fixture at the motherhouse. She was an extremely gifted seamstress and produced most all of the nun-dolls crafted in the Albany area. She could create the most clever items sold at fund-raising activities sponsored by Convent High or Regina Catholic College.

Unquestionably, Sr. Gregoria did a lot of good for the community with her talents for crafts, but she was so touchy and odd at times that most preferred to humor the old nun. The novices listened politely for as long as they could, but excused themselves the first moment they were able. The professed sisters were seldom as tolerant. Gregoria complained and gossiped most of the time. She was ultra-sensitive and perhaps that is why she preferred her cell to be some distance from the others.

One afternoon as Sr. Christine Marie (Sandra) returned from class she walked into the main hall of third floor to discover Sr. Gregoria sprawled on the floor in front of her room. Fearing the worst, Sr. Christine imagined heart failure. She called out for Sr. Mark Lewis (Barbara), an LPN and the oldest, chronologically, of the St. Jude group.

Sr. Mark Lewis had been resting in her bedroom and came running into the hall without veil or shoes. The shout of panic brought several of the others into the hall as well.

"What is it?" Sr. Mark Lewis called as she rushed to kneel beside the elderly woman. "What happened?"

Before the nurse could check any vital signs, Sr. Gregoria burst into laughter and sat up before them. "I really had you guessing, didn't I?"

Sr. Christine Marie felt adrenaline still pumping as she questioned the older woman. "You mean, this is a joke?"

"Sure! I'm healthy as a horse. I just wanted to see if anyone around here cared!" She continued her laughter as if delighted to see that some apparently did.

Sr. Christine Marie looked at Sr. Mark Lewis. Their eyes exchanged a similar message. The others returned to their rooms and Sr. Gregoria sprang to her feet. "I really had you fooled, didn't I!"

"Yes, Sister. You did." Rather than try to explain the story of Peter and the Wolf to the eccentric woman, Sr. Christine Marie preferred going to her bedroom. She thought, "She's too old and too far gone to understand our dismay." Besides, it was not the place of a novice to speak boldly, not even to the likes of Sr. Gregoria.

One Sunday morning in early August, the constitutionals were resetting the breakfast tables. It was the custom to reset the tables after each meal, as refectories were used only as an eating place. Sr. Mary Edgar had been called to the phone in the hallway. Shortly afterward, she sent for Sr. Robert Therese who was busy inspecting each table. The head table, where Mother and her council sat in rank order, was always set first. It was always double checked before leaving the refectory.

"Sr. Mary Edgar wants you in the hall, RT," Sr. Charity announced.

Sr. Mary Edgar stood holding the phone. She spoke gently, "Sister, this is your mother on the phone. Your father has been in a car accident and it's rather serious. Be strong for her now."

"Yes, Sister." The news had not yet registered. As Sr. Robert Therese listened to her mother's voice she knew she must remain assuring.

"Sr. Mary Edgar said you may come home, Angie," added her mother.

"She did? Okay, Mom. Try not to think the worst. Maybe he'll be all right. As soon as I know details of my arrival, I'll call you. I love you, Mom."

Sr. Charity was not far away. She stood with Sr. Mary Edgar who directed the novice to pack for the trip. She would make the plane arrangements.

About ninety minutes later, Sr. Robert Therese called home and gave her Aunt Helen all of the details. Again, she made an effort to give some words of encouragement. Sr. Charity stood by her friend with silent, supportive prayers.

Sr. Mary Edgar and Sr. Charity drove the novice to the airport.

"Don't worry about when you must return. There are still several weeks before RCC begins fall semester. Do what you have to, Sister, and call me when you know something." Sr. Mary Edgar could not have been more understanding. Sr. Robert Therese wanted to cry but held back, fearing tears would be a sign of weakness. She embraced her friend and then her superior. She left to board the plane.

Her mother met her at the Toledo airport. Again, she preferred to suppress her own fears and to be supportive of her mother.

"Your father had been out drinking. He was celebrating our wedding anniversary. He asked me if I wanted to go with him. You know I lost interest in his bars years ago. I cannot believe how drinking changed him. I wanted no part of it."

"What do the doctors say?"

"They won't tell me much. We can see him for five minutes every hour. He's unconscious. He's in intensive care: They tell me it's very serious."

"When did it happen, Mom?"

"About three this morning. He came out of the bar to cross the street and this driver just didn't see him. The car threw your dad thirty feet into the air. The driver was drunk. He was just coming back from some party. He's a lawyer."

By now they had arrived at St. Vincent Hospital in Sandusky, a Catholic hospital staffed by the Precious Blood Sisters of Tiffin, Ohio. Sr. Robert Therese had been born there, as had both her mom and dad. Mrs. Masucci had worked there ten years as a nurse's aide to help compensate for her husband's drinking and gambling habits.

The two entered the intensive care unit. Her mother whispered, "Here he is, Darling."

Sr. Robert Therese looked upon the ashen face of her father and was speechless. She knelt beside his hospital bed and prayed for help. After a few moments, her mother helped her daughter to stand. She explained, "You may try talking to him. The doctor thinks he might be able to hear. He just hasn't been able to respond in any way."

Angie still felt as if she couldn't speak. Finally, she tried. "Dad? Dad? It's me, Angie."

There was no response. Sr. Robert Therese had never seen anything like this. She felt strange, as if she was not really there. She stood at his bedside for a while as her mother wiped her dad's forehead with a wet cool washcloth. Her mother spoke soothing words and kissed him upon the cheek. The nurse approached and explained it was time to leave.

For the next two days, there was nothing to do but wait. Her father had been a construction worker most of his life and had a very strong and healthy body. The doctors felt Roberto managed to hold on because of his athletic youth and good physical condition.

Downstairs, in the waiting room, Sr. Robert Therese received a long distance call from Sr. Mary Paul. It was a welcome and needed voice of concern.

"Sister, I wish I could be there with you in Ohio, but it's just impossible."

"I understand, Sister. It's such a distance. I don't expect anyone could be here. We're holding on."

"My thoughts and prayers are with you. You need to pray with your dad. Pray out loud. Touch him and tell him that you love him. Try not to be afraid."

Sr. Robert Therese accepted these words as if from God. She felt so inadequate standing near his bedside, not knowing what to say, not even sure of what she felt. She was helpless. Sr. Mary Paul had told her to pray aloud and so she did. Taking her father's hand into hers, she began. "Dad, it's me, Angie. I'm here with you, Dad. Pray with me. God will hear our prayer." The novice began to pray the Our Father as she had never prayed it before. It felt as if all those around her prayed with her. As she uttered the final words, her father's hand squeezed Angie's. It happened again and then again.

Sr. Robert Therese looked to his nurse for an explanation. She suggested, "Sister, I think it's a spasm. He hasn't responded to anything we've done." In the eyes of a medical caretaker it may have appeared to be a spasm, but in the heart of the young woman, it was a sign that he shared their prayer.

Mrs. Masucci could not bring herself to leave the hospital and had, for the past two nights, slept in the waiting room. Sr. Robert Therese was given a guest bed in the convent of the hospital, though she spent very few hours resting there. She preferred to stay with her mother. It was Sr. Virginia who insisted that Sr. Robert Therese rest in the privacy of the convent, a third floor wing of St. Vincent's. Sr. Virginia had also encouraged Mrs. Masucci to go home and sleep. In the cafeteria, meals were free for the novice, as they were for all visiting priests and sisters. Everyone was hospitable and caring, yet the days of waiting were long and difficult.

Sr. Virginia was a nurse. It was the custom for off-duty nuns to stay with a family in times of critical care. Sr. Robert Therese had never met the nun before but was surprised to sense the huge comfort of her supportive presence. Mrs. Masucci's mother and sister came and stayed for hours. Diane came too. Sue was working, but called frequently. Sr. Virginia was a remarkable comfort to everyone.

Sr. Robert Therese reflected, "I don't even know this person. She doesn't even wear a habit, just that tan suit. Still, she is such a help to us. It means so much to have her near. I wonder if I might bring that magic to people when they are in need of a sister." Angie did not know why she felt the way she did. She only knew she felt braver and more hope-filled when Sr. Virginia had time to be with them in the waiting room.

That night, her mother had been persuaded to go home to sleep. Sr. Robert Therese would slept in the hospital convent. She took her first shower in three days and fell off to sleep as soon as she pulled up the cover. Three hours later, the phone rang loudly.

"Sister, your father's condition has worsened. Your mother has been called. Will you come down to ICU?"

"Yes, I'll be there as quickly as I can dress." Her mother and aunt arrived shortly thereafter.

"The doctor wants to talk with us, Angie," her mother said.

They waited another five minutes. Sr. Robert Therese decided she should put on her contacts. She could see better with them on and so she excused herself for just a moment.

"I'm so sorry about your father, Sister," offered a nurse who had been on duty. Sr. Robert Therese understood her words of compassion as the usual supportive statements she had received from the hospital staff.

"Thank you. You have all been so good to us. I'm sure my father will be all right." The nurse gave a startled look and Sr. Robert Therese continued on to the lavatory to put in her contacts.

A few moments later she joined her mother. Just then the doctor joined them to explain, "I'm sorry. He has died. Would you like to come with me?" He led the group into the room where they held each other and wept. Sr. Robert Therese lapsed into a numbness that kept the reality of death some distance away. It was not yet real to her. She comforted her grandmother, her mother, and aunt. She must be strong, for them.

Later in the day, she realized that the nurse who had approached to offer a word of comfort must have known her father had died. The nurse had looked startled because she could not understand Angie's response that her father would be fine. "Oh dear," she thought, "that poor woman probably thought I flipped out or something! That would explain her startled look."

All Sr. Robert Therese ever recalled of the funeral was that, when the veterans shot rifles into the air she leapt an inch off the ground. She was not prepared for the gun salute. She just could not believe her father was gone.

The Albany motherhouse sent a carload of nuns to Sandusky for the funeral. At first, Sr. Robert Therese hoped it would be Sr. Charity and other members of her group, but instead, it was a car full of strangers. These were nuns who had, at one time, been missioned at St. Rita's and were glad for the opportunity to visit parishioners and friends in the area.

In the procession from the funeral parlor to the cemetery, the nuns rode ahead of the hearse. Sr. Robert Therese thought of her Methodist father, who was not so fond of the nuns leading his only daughter into the convent. Now nuns were leading him to his final resting place. This was irony.

Upon returning to Albany, Sr. Robert Therese was greeted with words of encouragement and sympathy.

"Here's your wallet, Sister." Sr. Robert Therese returned it to Sr. Mary Edgar. The novice directress had been in such a state when taking Sr. Robert Therese to the airport that she accidently gave her wallet to the novice just before she boarded the Ohio-bound plane.

"It's good to have you home with us, Sister. If there is anything I can do for you, you must tell me."

"Thank you, Sister. You've done so much just by making sure I could be with Mom. She needed me. She's going to continue to need me."

"I'm sure you should call her frequently for a while. That might be of some help to her."

"Yes, Sister. I think it would help us both."

Later that day, Sr. Robert Therese stopped over to the novitiate building to visit the chapel. In the hallway, she met Sr. Anita.

"Oh, Sister. I'm sorry to hear your father died. Come here for a minute; I have something for you." Sr. Anita returned to her office to get an envelope off her desk. "I wanted to mail this but didn't get the chance."

Sr. Robert Therese opened the sympathy card signed at the bottom, "Sr. M. Anita."

"Thank you, Sister."

"You're welcome, Sister." Sr. Anita continued on her way and Sr. Robert Therese went into chapel.

As she knelt to pray, her thoughts were anything but peaceful. "Sr. Mary Peter's father dies and the whole novitiate goes into mourning . . . cards, rosaries, visits, prayers, on and on . . . my dad dies and she can't take two minutes to address a sympathy card."

· · · · · · · ·

50

Being a senior novice was a peaceful experience for most of the St. Jude group. There are hundreds of different religious communities throughout the United States and their various stages of training and formation are as unique as the communities themselves. Some were established for the purpose of serving the poor; others to nurse the sick, care for the elderly, or promote the faith. Most wore distinctive garb until the mandate of the Second Vatican Council ordered the religious to simplify their habits.

In 1964 the Franciscan Sisters of Albany still had their traditional look, including five yards of serge pleated fourteen times in both front and back. In the August heat, sisters walked more slowly to keep perspiration at a minimum. Hot weather typically drenched several layers of underclothing.

People would often ask the sisters, "Aren't you hot in that?" Answers ranged from, "Heat is relative; it's mind over matter; I begged for a habit of penance, and I got one" to "It's not as bad it looks," or "Didn't you ever notice in warmer countries people are all wrapped up?"

Few sisters would openly complain. Heavier-set sisters tended to suffer more during the heat of summer. In winter, sisters usually wore a woolen cloak. The many layers of material and undergarments proved to be helpful insulation from the cold. In general, the young sisters were taught that the habit is a holy sacramental, not to be modified or criticized. A good sister should never complain of her discomfort.

Late one September night, Sr. Elizabeth awoke from sharp pain in her abdomen. She could not recognize this piercing discomfort, nor could she relieve it. After an hour or so, she decided to wake Sr. Mary Edgar and ask for aspirin or some form of pain killer. It was 2:00 A.M.

"Sister, I'm really sorry to wake you, but I have this sharp pain in my abdomen. I thought it might go away after a while, but it seems to be getting worse. May I have some aspirin or something?"

"Sister, I think you should go over to the infirmary and ask them for something. Let them make sure you're all right. Let me know what they say."

"Yes, Sister."

Sr. Elizabeth walked to the infirmary in her robe and night clothes. Sr. Patrick was on duty. This was Sr. Elizabeth's least favorite nurse, but she reported her discomfort just the same.

After several questions were answered, Sr. Patrick had the novice lie down. She proceeded to insert a rectal thermometer. Sr. Elizabeth felt uncomfortable and embarrassed. "Why didn't she just use the oral thermometer?" she thought. Still, she remained compliant.

"Sister, your temperature is slightly above normal. I'll tell Sr. Mary Edgar what I think and get back to you."

"Thank you, Sister."

The decision to drive Sr. Elizabeth to the hospital for further examination came as a surprise. All she expected were several aspirin and now she found herself riding to the emergency room with Sr. Patrick, with a habit over her nightgown. Sr. Patrick explained Sr. Mary Edgar's decision on the way.

"Sr. Mary Edgar told me that as a child she often babysat for her little sister. Once she complained of stomach pain, but Sr. Mary Edgar did not consider it a problem. She came to find out her sister's appendix had nearly ruptured. Ever since, she says, she tends to over react to this sort of thing. I don't think it's anything too serious. But she said to come."

In the emergency room, Sr. Elizabeth experienced her first complete rectal and vaginal examination. Meanwhile, blood and urine were analyzed. Her first exposure to genital scrutiny left the young novice with feelings of violation and embarrassment. Sr. Elizabeth found her vulnerability a valuable learning experience. She would understand, in later years, how unpleasant such exams could be for her patients. The sharp pains had now subsided, and Sr. Elizabeth was seriously regretting not having waited longer before waking her superior.

Within several hours she was home. Blood in the urine, and a high white cell count indicated the problem may have been a kidney stone.

That morning, Elizabeth slept through morning prayer and Mass but was up for breakfast. Sr. Mary Edgar was surprised to see her dressed for class.

"I thought you'd want to stay in bed this morning, Sister. I didn't expect you'd be going to class," said Sr. Mary Edgar.

"I prefer not to miss school, Sister. It's so easy to fall behind."

"Well, it's good seeing that you feel better."

"I really do. The doctor wants to check me in a few days. They'd like to take an x-ray, I think."

"Fine. You arrange the appointment, and let me know."

The following week, Sr. Elizabeth returned for x-rays and a general check-up.

As she walked from the dressing room to the x-ray table, she wore only a hospital gown and her three-cornered head cloth. It was obvious to the technician that she was a nun. He said he was surprised that anyone so young could enter the convent.

"You must be all of fifteen."

"Nineteen." Sr. Elizabeth did not appreciate the insinuation that she was too young for sisterhood. Besides, young people who look younger than their age are often sensitive about it.

"Well, you're too pretty to be a nun, if you ask me."

Sr. Elizabeth was not sure how to respond. She decided to keep it simple.

"Thank you, I think."

Apparently, the problem had been a kidney stone that either dissolved or passed. She would never forget the intense pain such a little thing could cause. As a nurse-hopeful, there were many lessons to be learned in all of this. And if she ever did become a doctor, she would try not to say insensitive things. She would be understanding. Being in pain and subject to physical inspection were most unpleasant. Sr. Elizabeth was resolved to remember this kidney stone experience. It would make her a much better person and care giver.

. . . .

51

Autumn is usually spectacular in upstate New York and this October was no exception. One class the St. Jude group had in common was Sr. Christian's biology class. Sister was a dark-skinned, rotund Hawaiian and a marvelous teacher. She was organized, precise, and inspiring. The slowest learners were successful under Sr. Christian's tutelage. She had a remarkable gift for encouraging and reinforcing positive outcomes.

This particular class included no college girls. One day, Sr. Christian announced it was time for some "field experience." The novices were not sure what this expression meant.

"Young scientists should have a smattering of all the sciences. Confining our studies to labs and lectures is not sufficient. I have arranged with Sr. Mary Edgar that this Sunday, after Mass, we will visit a wildlife refuge just outside of Troy. There we can more effectively examine local geological formations, fauna, and flora."

"Sister, what are fauna and flora? Geological formation, I understand, but I don't recognize the other words." Sr. Michael Michelle asked forthrightly and the novices smiled. They preferred to let on that they knew the terms, though most did not. Asking questions revealed one's ignorance, and most of them, with few exceptions, didn't want to reveal any more ignorance than absolutely necessary!

"Sister, that means we will study animal and plant life."

"Will we need our notebooks, Sister?" Sr. Robert Therese asked.

"No, sister, I will provide all the necessary materials."

The news of a field trip caused great anticipation among the girls.

When the day of their outing came, three cars pulled out of the motherhouse parking lot. They eventually arrived at a cabin surrounded by woods, and near a lake and stream. It was a most delightful trip, but the real delight was yet to be. Upon entering the cabin, they discovered several of the college sisters had prepared a picnic barbecue for the novices. The cabin belonged to Sr. Christian's priest friend, Fr. Conrad.

Several priests dropped by to visit the party. Fr. Conrad brought several of his friends. One priest, a gifted guitarist and singer, spent most of his energy getting to know Sr. Elizabeth. She was flattered and impressed by the man not much older than she, who was obviously interested in her.

The loan of the cabin meant an opportunity for guitar music, singing, walks in the woods, great barbecue, and simple recreation. Not an ounce of study during this field experience! It proved great medicine for these serious-minded college students. Their day at the cabin was not unlike the day spent at Mother Victoria's farm during their canonical year . . . when Sr. Anita bounced wildly into the air and landed in a huge drift of snow. It was just like Sr. Christian to arrange a surprise such as this. She understood the pressures of school and the need to *be* and not just *be* busy. The day away was much-needed rest and relaxation for all the group.

Schoolwork was demanding, but often the novices turned to each other for help. Studying together proved a valuable resource for many of the girls. For example, Sr. Robert Therese often coached Sr. Leonard before history exams, and was equally fortunate to find Sr. Charles Marion an eager, competent math tutor. School was always on their minds. The college girls did not appreciate having the novices in class. Too often, they changed the shape of grading curves. The college girls, more often than not, had more in their lives than school. The novices did not.

One weekend, Sr. Mary Ruth asked Sr. Robert Therese for a haircut.

"I don't cut hair, Sister. I'm afraid I might do some damage. It's not that I mind doing it, I just don't think I know how to do it."

Sr. Mary Ruth insisted it would be all right. "So what if you cut it a little lop-sided? What difference would it make under my veil? Please?"

Sr. Robert Therese yielded. They would meet later in her cell. "How long do you want it, Mary Ruth?"

"Short."

"Well, how short?"

"Just short."

"Okay." Sr. Robert Therese confirmed. "It will be short."

As the two chatted away about school or what they imagined mission life might be like, Sr. Robert Therese trimmed and trimmed some more. For some reason, novices did not share stories of their families much. It was a topic usually avoided in those days. Finally, Sr. Robert Therese considered the job done and offered Sr. Mary Ruth a mirror.

"Oh, my God, Robert, you took it *all* off!"

"Mary Ruth, I thought you wanted it short."

"Short. Not gone. Who taught you how to cut hair . . . Sr. Geraldine?"

Sr. Robert Therese felt terrible. She had tried to warn her friend that she was not an experienced hairdresser. Sr. Mary Ruth realized she was over-reacting. She caught herself.

"Oh, it'll grow back. It always does. Don't worry about it, Robert Therese, it's only hair." Sr. Mary Ruth covered her head with a head cloth and left with a few words of thanks.

Several days later Sr. Charles Marion entered the lunchroom for a cup of coffee. Sr. Robert Therese was already there having a snack. Novices did not sit at table (in case an older, professed sister might want the chair), nor look out the windows (for fear someone might interpret the stare as a longing to be on the outside), nor lean against the walls (considered inappropriate posture for a religious). But the lunchroom was a great place to hear community talk. Sr. Charles Marion got a certain look on her face whenever she was dying to share some gossip. Sr. Robert Therese recognized she was eager to share something now.

"RT, did you hear what happened to Sr. Mary Ruth?"

"No, what?"

"You won't believe this story."

"Sister, tell me! Is she all right?" Sr. Charles Marion played this game of pull-it-from-me, when in fact, she was dying to tell all she knew.

"This morning, Sr. Mary Ruth was painting her bedroom and fell off her ladder."

"Was she hurt?"

"Only her pride."

"What does that mean?"

"Well, actually she hit her head and had to get two or three stitches. They took her to the emergency room. She had to sit in the hallway in this wheel chair with full habit and no headgear! She said she wanted to die because she didn't have a head cloth with her. When Mother Victoria happened to pass by she didn't even recognize Mary Ruth. She had this incredible haircut that made her look like a man in a habit."

Sr. Robert Therese choked on her coffee. "Guess what, Charles."

"What?"

"I gave her that haircut and I have a feeling I'm going to hear about this for the rest of my life."

Sr. Mary Ruth took the embarrassment in stride, but referred to the haircut and stitches tale whenever she wanted to tease her friend or spur a bit of laughter.

Prayer schedules for constitutionals were not much different from those for canonicals. One change was that they now had an opportunity to attend the college Mass daily as well as the morning community Mass. Sr. James taught French at the college and played her guitar at the 11:00 folk Mass. Everyone was singing something written by Ray Repp in those days. The older sisters did not approve of guitars, tambourines, and such at Mass. Change and the acceptance of change came slowly and painfully to the Franciscan community. The majestic organ music was preferred by most over the age of thirty. Younger sisters quickly adapted to the new liturgy. The novices felt they benefitted more from their prayers at the later Mass. They were more awake and enjoyed the songs Sr. James taught.

A survey of the sisters might confirm that most of them would not win any beauty contests. This was very true of Sr. James. She had a huge nose, high cheek bones, and a long thin chin. Her body frame and gestures seemed masculine, but when it came to leading song during Mass, she excelled in both talent and enthusiasm. "Beauty is as beauty does" is an old saying that holds true of many, particularly nuns. They may not always come in the prettiest of packages, but their exercise of charity and service to others made them downright beautiful to the people and children they helped.

In addition to the second Mass, Sr. Robert Therese found time to meditate for an hour each afternoon. In an area known as "Mother's garden" which was once the private space of the reverend mothers, Sr. Robert Therese and other members of community could now walk freely. As a postulant, Sr. Robert Therese had discovered a statue of St. Francis that resembled her own, now recently deceased, father.

During her constitutional year, her habit of daily meditation became obvious and made some of the girls uncomfortable. A few believed it to be excessively pious behavior; others thought it a waste of time. A few even considered the Ohio buckeye something of a mystic. Even as a child, Sr. Robert Therese had often walked the shores of Lake Erie alone to think. She loved solitude and the spontaneous prayer that often came when she would hold still for a while. Her inner prayer life was a rich and satisfying gift others could not always understand. It was not unusual for her to find time for three rosaries a day. She had many reasons to pray. The young sister's tendency to seek quietude for reflection was unique in the group. This was sometimes considered, by the others, to be "singular" behavior—acting differently and causing one to be noticed. Sr. Anita often accused the novice of being "singular." The novices were expected to conform, to blend. Individual behavior was suspect. It was just not the convent way.

· · · · · · · ·

52

Sr. Humiliana had been sick for several days with what appeared to be a flu virus. Sr. Elizabeth was assigned to take her meals and to her and check to see if she needed anything.

In the laundry, Sr. Elizabeth noticed that Sr. Humiliana's flannel pajamas were worn thin in the knees and the elastic band was stretched into uselessness. The sisters had permission to wear pajamas instead of night gowns for only the past few years. The black bath robe was also regulation. Sisters, particularly those on mission, were pushing for change. They resisted the required white sheets, solid-color bed spreads, and plain decor. Permission to wear pajamas was a major concession.

Sr. Elizabeth never was fond of sewing, but she thought she would repair the pajamas as a nice surprise. After considerable effort, she managed two patches over the knees and successfully replaced the elastic.

As she knocked on Humiliana's door, she felt like a child with a "big treat for mommy". Sister answered.

"What is it, Elizabeth?"

"Sister, I know you aren't feeling all that well and I decided you needed a get-well surprise."

"A surprise?"

"Yes, Sister." With that, she brought the flannel pj's from behind her back. "I have mended them, Sister."

"Oh, Sister! You shouldn't have."

"I really wanted to do something for you."

"No, I mean you *shouldn't* have! I've been looking forward to making rags of these. I've worn them threadbare so that I might buy something new. Now it looks as if I'll be wearing them for another year or two."

"Gee, Sister, I'm sorry. I guess I should have asked you first. I didn't know you wanted to get rid of them." Elizabeth's apology was genuinely remorseful.

"Sister, I know you meant well, but if I need any mending, I'll be sure to ask."

"Yes, Sister."

"God bless you for thinking of me, just the same. I don't mean to sound ungrateful." Sr. Humiliana knew she had burst Sr. Elizabeth's bubble.

"I understand, Sister. You know, I'm not very handy at sewing. The repairs won't last as long as you imagine." Sr. Humiliana smiled.

"I'll see you at supper, Sr. Elizabeth. You are bringing my tray, aren't you?"

"Yes, Sister. Is there anything else I can get you?"

"No, dear. I just need the rest. I'll be fine soon."

Sr. Elizabeth left the doorway, feeling a bit disappointed that her surprise surprised them both. She realized Sr. Humiliana could see the good intentions. That was her practice for the month, "purity of intention". She wanted to do good things for the right reasons. Good deeds were far more meaningful if spurred by the right intentions.

That same afternoon, as community rosary was nearly finished, Sr. Elizabeth excused herself and headed for the kitchen. She had to fix the sick-tray for Sr. Humiliana. Completing the tray, she decided to walk through the annex hall where there would be little or no traffic. She was surprised to see the motherhouse door closed. As she reached to open it another sister pushed it open from the other side. The tray and all of its contents flew into the air and into the novice. The professed sister begged pardon and insisted on helping to clean up the mess, but Sr. Elizabeth insisted she could take care of it.

"I have time to get this, Sister. Really, I can do it. I know you are in a hurry to get somewhere. I'll be fine."

The sister seemed grateful and continued on. Sr. Elizabeth returned to the kitchen.

"What happened to Sr. Humiliana's supper? Why are you wearing it?" asked Sr. Anastatia.

"Sister, I walked into a door. It was closed and as I went to open the motherhouse door, another sister burst through and pushed the tray into me. Everything spilled."

"Well, Sr. Anna will help you prepare another. Be more careful, Sister."

"Yes, Sister." The supper bell rang and Sr. Elizabeth realized she now would be late to table. Still, the unfortunate accident was not nearly the crisis it might have been if she were still a canonical.

Sr. Elizabeth thanked Sr. Anna for her help and decided to take a different route this time. She hurried down the corridor only to have her large Franciscan sleeve catch on a doorknob. She continued forward, but her right arm did not, causing the tray to sprawl before her.

"I do not believe it!" she cried out loud.

"How could I be so stupid as to let this happen again," she thought. Several sisters stopped to help her pick up the food and dishes. Returning to the kitchen would not be amusing to Sr. Anastatia, nor would she be as understanding as before. Sr. Elizabeth was correct.

"Sister," Sr. Anastatia offered, "would you like me to deliver Sister's tray?"

"No, Sister. It couldn't happen again. I'll be more careful."

"We don't have food to be throwing about, Sister! Perhaps you need an assistant."

"I can do this, Sister. I guess I'm just trying too hard."

This was insight. Novices often try "too hard" to do things well. All too often things were broken and accidents befell their sincere efforts. Countless penances for breakage were begged in many novitiates. Even during the sixties, sisters on many of the missions also begged penance from superiors when they accidently caused property damage.

Elizabeth's third attempt was successful.

"I thought perhaps you had forgotten me. Why are you so late?" Sr. Humiliana politely inquired.

"Sister, I had two accidents. The second time, I brought it on myself. I was worried about being late and my sleeve caught a doorknob. I'm sorry, Sister."

"There's no problem, Sister. You had better hurry to your own supper. Sr. Mary Edgar will be worried."

"Yes, Sister. Thank you."

Sr. Elizabeth returned to the refectory. She first approached the superior of the motherhouse and begged pardon upon her knees for being late to supper. Then she went to Sr. Mary Edgar who had already heard of the accidents.

"Just get something before it's all cold, Sister. Try not to have an accident at table," she said with a wink.

"What an exasperating day," thought Sr. Elizabeth. "Some days just aren't worth the effort."

. . . .

53

Winter break had come to Regina Catholic College and most of the girls were home, except for the foreign students. The constitutionals were scheduled to take a two week "blitz" course in art. Sr. Raymond would instruct. This still left a few days after Christmas for the novices to visit their families. Everyone felt sorry for Sr. Christine Marie who could not visit Hawaii, but volunteers eagerly invited her to come home with them.

The "blitz" course was a fast three credits in art and easily arranged by a community with a junior college and a nun-instructor. The required hours of class were relaxing and therapeutic. Sr. Raymond believed in "live and let live". She stressed the positive aspects of creative talent and encouraged the St. Jude group to enjoy the process. Sr. Raymond was considered a "maverick" in community, as were many of the artistic, creative types.

The time passed quickly. Sr. Helena's chorus preparation for the Christmas season was not accomplished as easily. There was the usual amount of ridicule and insult. There was more pressure than pleasure preparing for the holidays, but the thought of family visits kept spirits high. Everyone returned to the motherhouse refreshed and revived by the brief change of routine. The visits meant a great deal to the families as well.

Winters in upstate New York wore the patience of the housebound. Missions in Syracuse, Oswego, and Buffalo reported far worse storms and amounts of the white stuff that year. Cabin fever, as some called it, was a familiar experience.

To this day, the novices aren't sure what caused the outburst, but Robert Therese remembered it well. She had fallen asleep at her desk when loud shouts awoke her. She opened her door to watch Sr. Francis Ann fly past in a whirl of black to her room several doors down. The door slammed with a mighty blow! She wasn't sure what she could do to help, but decided to see.

Just then, Sr. Dominic, a large round mass of serge, darted with remarkable speed toward Sr. Francis Ann's cell. She pounded with impressive strength upon the door. Sr. Robert Therese decided to intervene. She moved in front of the novice's door.

"Get out of my way, Robert Therese, before I hurt you as well!" Dominic threatened.

"Sister, calm down. You're out of control. What did she do?"

"None of your damn business. I don't want to hurt you, but I'm telling you: Move!" The nun was furious.

Sr. Robert Therese felt a protective adrenalin flow. She wasn't terribly fond of Sr. Dominic, but neither she did not want to see Francis Ann hurt. Only a small latch kept the two foes at bay. Sr. Robert Therese was afraid to step aside for fear Sr. Dominic might rip the lesser physically matched opponent to shreds. Nor did she want a battle of fisticuffs with charging, angry woman. She tried to calm Dominic.

"Sister, please back off for a few minutes and think about this. It can be settled in a better way. What good will fighting do?"

"I'm warning you for the last time, Robert Therese, if you don't step aside, you're the first to go down! Open that door, you coward!" she yelled to Sr. Francis Ann.

"Never!" the voice shouted from inside. "Stay out! Go away, Lardo!"

By now, a crowd of curious onlookers had gathered. Sr. Mary Edgar was gone for the afternoon. No one was exactly sure what would happen next. Surely, they didn't expect what was about to unfold.

From around the corner stormed Sr. Anita. Approaching the scene, she commanded, "Kneel!" No one hesitated.

"What is this shouting? I demand an explanation."

No one wanted to speak, but Sr. Robert Therese took the initiative. "Sr. Dominic and Sr. Francis Ann are having an argument."

"Argument? It sounds more like a war! I could hear shouting and banging from two halls away! Where's Sr. Francis Ann?"

"In the bedroom, Sister," explained Sr. Robert Therese.

Sr. Anita tried the door. It was locked. She then commanded the novice to unlock and open it. There was silence and no response. She repeated her directive. The group waited in suspense. Finally came the rattling of the latch and slowly the door opened.

"The rest of you assume your responsibilities. Sr. Robert Therese, are you a part of this?"

"Not really, Sister. I was just trying to keep them apart."

"Then go to your room. Sr. Dominic, Sr. Francis Ann, follow me."

Never had two people looked more like they were heading for the dog house. Sr. Mary Peter had gone off to get Sr. Anita when the shouting first began. She knew Sr. Mary Edgar was out for the afternoon and that no one else could calm this in-house winter storm.

Sr. Anita led them directly to her office in the next building. They followed in complete silence. When they arrived the two were asked to be seated. This was definitely different from what might have happened during their canonical year. Sr. Anita spoke calmly and professionally.

"Sr. Mary Edgar would be rather disturbed over this behavior of yours. Do you not agree, Sisters?"

They looked down and then glanced toward each other. "Yes, Sister." They spoke in unison.

"I would hope there is a very good reason for such an outburst as this, but I sincerely doubt you are able to justify your conduct." The two remained silent. "Sr. Dominic, I will allow you to speak first, and then Sr. Francis Ann will have her opportunity to explain.

Sr. Dominic mumbled something under her breath.

"Sister, speak up. Did you say something about a nose?"

"She ridiculed my nose, Sister. She said it was where I keep my brains. I could loose ten pounds if I only blew it."

"Is this true, Sr. Francis Ann? You said such a thing?"

Sr. Francis Ann bore a guilty look as she spoke, "Only because she told me I was fat, Sister. She has no room to talk. She outweighs me, Sister. I didn't appreciate her comment."

"I think it apparent that both of you could benefit from some more exercise or a healthier food plan, but I still do not understand what provoked your remarks. There is a reason, isn't there?"

Again, the room was silent.

"Sisters, something *must have* precipitated the crude insults. As far as I can see, you both have demonstrated juvenile and unjustifiably violent behavior. Is that the report I am to give your superior? This will not look good upon either of your records of conduct."

It was obvious that neither sister wanted to explain, but finally Sr. Francis Ann decided it might be better to tell the story as it happened.

"Sr. Dominic wanted to borrow a text book I was using in the community room. I didn't like the way she asked for it. She told me to let her have the book, and I was using it. Instead of explaining, I told her to get lost. I felt she was rude, so I gave her some of the same."

"Is this true, Sr. Dominic? The insults and the chase and the whole nonsense was because of a book?"

Sr. Dominic did not want to admit that so much grief had mushroomed from her simple, but rude request. "Sister, I just told her to let me see it for a few minutes. I had to look up something. I planned to give it right back. She just over-reacted."

"*I over-reacted?*" Sr. Francis Ann's tone of voice sounded as if she wanted to continue the argument. "Sisters, this is the dead of winter. We have all been indoors too long. There is no good excuse for what either of you have said and done. I cannot justify your behavior, and I don't believe you have given me a single good reason to excuse your conduct even for a moment. I would like you to

MARY HILAIRE TAVENNER, PH. D.

recognize that name-calling, pounding on doors, and carrying on in such a manner as you have is anything *but* lady-like, adult, or religious behavior."

She continued. "I believe I now know what happened and I will advise Sr. Mary Edgar. I'm sure she will know how to help you improve your conduct. I see this as a case of 'cabin fever' that comes from living in such close proximity as we must in community. I also believe you have both exercised extremely poor judgement. I feel there is nothing more I can do. Unless you have any further comment, you are both excused. Sr. Mary Edgar will finish this when she returns."

. . . .

54

It was Sr. Mary Edgar who first mentioned that the Blessed Mother might be appearing in Garabandal, Spain. The novices were curious to hear more about these strange events. "Imagine the Eucharist mysteriously materializing upon the tongue of a visionary—and young girls in ecstasy!" Sr. Leonard responded.

"Sr. Petra knows more of this than I do," Sr. Mary Edgar returned.

"But is there any proof?" Sr. Leonard asked for the others.

"The Church refuses to say anything officially. It's much too early. Rome is very slow to decide such matters."

"Then how are we to know if the Mother of God is really appearing to these four girls? How did Sr. Petra learn of these visionaries?" Sr. Leonard was obviously fascinated.

Sr. Petra had a reputation among the sisters as being extremely pious. After communion she returned from the altar rail, with hands folded, eyes downcast, and a look of serenity upon her face. Many in community considered her affectacious but others believed her to be a suffering, saintly martyr. Sr. Mary Edgar thought she was sincere and well-meaning.

"Next month, Sister has invited a blind man by the name of Joe to visit Convent High School. He knew Padre Pio. It was Padre Pio who led Joe to the young women of Garabandal."

"Are we going?" asked Sr. Elizabeth.

"I think it would be a good idea for all of us to go."

"Who's Padre Pio, Sister?" asked Sr. Michael Michelle.

"He's the Franciscan priest with the stigmata of Christ. He has the same crucifixion wounds St. Francis bore, doesn't he Sister?" Sr. Mary Peter offered.

"Yes, exactly. Many consider him a living saint. There is so much for novices to learn! I'm not sure what to make of these Spanish visionaries, but after we've heard blind Joe share his stories, maybe we'll know more."

Joe did come to the Convent High School as planned. He spoke of his conversion from street gangster to promulgator of Padre Pio and the visionaries of Garabandal.

"When I lost my eyesight, I had to take stock of my life. I went to confession to Padre Pio who told me my sins before I spoke a word. You can't imagine how all of this has changed my life!"

The New Yorker spoke with a "tough guy" accent. He also spoke with remarkable conviction. The audience was impressed by his sincerity and watched his slide presentation with great interest. After the session, the novices had not been convinced of Garabandal, but they certainly had been inspired.

Spring returned once more to upstate New York and the St. Jude group eagerly anticipated graduation from Regina Catholic. The end of May meant graduation and mid-June meant first profession. The fifteen had lost no members this entire year. Their original number had dropped by ten, but it seemed all fifteen would be taking first vows. They were told they would receive their first obedience in August. That is, they would find out where they would be living for the following year. At that time, novices did not go on mission until they had made first vows.

Sr. Charity, Sr. Robert Therese, Sr. Mary Peter, Sr. Mary Alice, and Sr. Catherine Ann had all been honored for their outstanding grade point averages. They were inducted into Phi Beta Kappa Honor Society, but little was made of it. The other novices were not invited, nor were families. Sr. Mary Edgar permitted the novices to attend, but she considered it a night to honor the college girls more than the nuns. Academic achievement was expected of the religious; bestowing honors upon sisters, especially novices, was not.

Sr. Mary Alice loved her studies at Regina Catholic and she felt well-prepared to be a teacher. But she struggled inwardly with a personal calling to social work. She wanted to help the homeless, the battered, the abused, and the less fortunate. The community offered no work of this kind. Sr. Mary Edgar explained that the order was a teaching and nursing community. There was no other choice.

Sr. Mary Alice knelt in prayer before the statue of Mary in the novitiate chapel. Mary Alice extended her hands in the manner of Mary, "Our Lady of Grace", as she had posed upon the Miraculous Medal.

"More than anything, you know I desire to serve your most suffering of souls. I respect the work my sister Margaret does for you. I wish I could go into the streets and be there to help. But, it appears, you will have me be a teacher. A teacher, then, I will be. May this, too, serve your purpose for good." She prayed alone before the image of Mary. She was accepting of the classroom, knowing she could help the needy even there.

Sr. Robert Therese's mother flew to Albany for graduation. It was a great surprise. She was very proud to see her daughter receive the associate in arts degree. She flew back again several weeks later to be there for first profession. Sr. Robert Therese felt deeply grateful, because she was very much aware of the costs incurred by her father's hospitalization and death. There were no lawsuits for drunk driving then. No recompense. Just, "I'm sorry."

A much greater surprise was that Sr. Christine Marie's mother flew in from Hawaii for two weeks. After profession, they would return to the islands for Christine Marie's home visit. She had not been back for three years.

The visit of Christine Marie's Samoan mother was cause for celebration! They enjoyed Hawaiian dancing, foods, and festivity! No one knew how gracefully Sr. Christine Marie could hula until she and her mother entertained one evening. They shared many Hawaiian melodies and danced the Hawaiian wedding song. The approach of first profession was an exciting prospect for the girls who had come so far.

Sr. Elizabeth always enjoyed her jaunts to the infirmary. She came to write letters, give baths, and listen to patients. They waited in excitement for the approaching ceremony that would confirm the young woman as a professed sister among them. The taking of vows was a serious step.

One afternoon, while visiting Sr. Marie Bernard, Sr. Elizabeth listened to her oft repeated story.

"I was the regional superior of our Hawaiian missions many, many years ago. I made the decision to buy the fifty acres of land in Honolulu on the island of Oahu. Everyone criticized me for making that decision, Sister. Now we have the hospital there, the high school, and the orphanage. We staff several elementary schools on Oahu. All of that could not have been possible without my very unpopular decision."

"Yes, Sister, I remember your telling me. Thank God you had such foresight. You made a courageous decision, Sister."

"As courageous as the decision you are making when you ask for vows." Sr. Elizabeth smiled.

"I don't regret the good I've done for community, Sister. But I'm an old, sick woman now. I do regret that I have never been recognized for making that choice, in spite of what all the others wanted." She lay quietly for a few moments, then continued. "They were going to send me home, Sister. When I was a novice, I had this terrible cold. It was probably pneumonia. You know, in those days, if you were sickly, they sent you home."

"Yes, Sister. I know."

The frail old nun had told her the story so many times before. But, Elizabeth listened patiently.

"I prayed, Sister! I didn't want to be sent home. I wanted to be a nun! One night when I felt the worst, my aunt, God rest her soul, came to me and put her hand upon my chest. My aunt had died years before. She was a member of this very community for fifty years! Somehow, when I woke in the morning, I was completely cured. You believe me, don't you, Sister?"

"Of course, I do, Sister." At least she believed that Sr. Marie Bernard believed.

Sr. Elizabeth went to visit her friend with multiple sclerosis, Sr. Bernadette, and many of the others. Several were confined to bed for years. Others were confined to their rooms, and some were in restraints. She was a ray of sunshine to these women, so helpless and frail, so in need of care and compassion.

Practice for first profession was underway. Most of the parents who had to travel a long way skipped graduation in order to afford the time and cost of coming for this impressive, first vow ceremony. Music was conducted by no other than the "Great Helena". Everything was carefully cleaned and prepared.

"When you take your first vows, Sisters, you should have the intention of making them for life. These past three years provided an opportunity for the community to teach you about the vows of poverty, chastity, and obedience. The next three years, we will watch you practice these vows. You will be re-evaluated before you may renew for an additional two more years. After living the vowed life for five years, you may be granted permission to make your final vows." Sr. Mary Edgar had explained this process many times before, but she reviewed it again.

"You will sign a document that waives all rights to any inheritance you may receive as a vowed religious. All that you earn from your work as a Franciscan sister or receive as gifts from your families or friends will become the property of community. You may make no claim of recompense of any kind if you should leave community. Is this understood?"

"Yes, Sister," they responded. But in fact, most of them did not understand. This was like a pre-nuptial agreement, stating that if the party chose to separate from this "contract of marriage" all assets remained with community. If a sister, twenty years later, chose to leave the order, she was to take nothing for her years of work. Nothing but the interest accrued from her $100.00 dowry, which was invested since her entrance day. In twenty years, the hundred dollars might be worth one thousand.

Sr. Mary Alice felt there never was a satisfactory explanations of the vows. Instruction was usually vague and general. Poverty was meant that sisters were to share all things in common. No individual could accumulate financial or material wealth. Years ago, even underwear was shared, according to stories shared by the older nuns. There was no need for name tags on anything. If things didn't fit exactly, you made do.

Chastity was explained in many different terms. The novices knew it meant no marriage. It also meant no sexual activity and avoidance of all temptations. This included movies, books, and entertainment that might arouse the sensual appetites.

Obedience, more than the other two vows, had been spoken of every day of their canonical year . . . Do what you are told! Do not question your superior's command. Rules are there to be followed. Superiors are spiritually endowed with the grace of God and the authority to present God's holy will upon their charges.

The Saint Jude group was on the verge of professing these three vows. They were young, unsure, and naive, but filled with hope. This was their step into the unknown. It was not entirely unlike the faith one needs to marry. Only this was not a marriage of two individuals; it was a blind journey into the lives of so very many.

· · · · · · ·

Edwards Brothers Malloy
Thorofare, NJ USA
September 30, 2013